Criston unlashed himself and swung down, clinging to ratlines that were slick from the pounding rain.

With hands that were strong and callused, he worked his way to the first yardarm, hooked his arm through the ropes for stability, and looked out again. Yes, the beacon was still there—and brighter now. Surely other crewmen had noticed it! He stared, yearning for that light, knowing what it represented. He wasn't looking down at the sea. Even if he could have sounded an alarm, it was far too late.

The monster that rose from the black depths was impervious to the storm, greater than ten sea serpents. Its bullet-shaped head was as large as the *Luminara*'s prow, and when it opened its maw, Criston saw row upon row of sharp teeth, each one as long as an oar. It had a single round squidlike eye in the center of its forehead, and spines like a mane around its neck and ringing its gills. Armfuls of tentacles sprouted from each side, lined with wet suckers, each with a barb in its center. The tentacle ends were blind sea serpents, opening to show fang-filled mouths.

For a moment, Criston could not speak, could not breathe. He found his voice and bellowed with all his strength and all his soul, projecting his voice with enough power to call the attention of the sailors on deck. *"Leviathan!"*

Books by Kevin J. Anderson

TERRA INCOGNITA

The Edge of the World

THE SAGA OF SEVEN SUNS

Hidden Empire

A Forest of Stars

Horizon Storms

Scattered Suns

Of Fire and Night

Metal Swarm

The Ashes of Worlds

Veiled Alliances (graphic novel)

Kevin J. Anderson

The Edge of the World

orbit

www.orbitbooks.net

New York   London

Orbit
Hachette Book Group
237 Park Avenue, New York, NY 10017
Visit our Web site at www.HachetteBookGroup.com

First Edition: June 2009

Orbit is an imprint of Hachette Book Group. The Orbit name and logo are trademarks of Little, Brown Book Group Limited.

The characters and events in this book are fictitious. Any similarity to real persons, living or dead, is coincidental and not intended by the author.

Map by Patrick Simmons, simpaticoartstudio.com

Library of Congress Cataloging-in-Publication Data
Anderson, Kevin J.
    The edge of the world / Kevin J. Anderson.— 1st U.S. ed.
        p. cm.—(Terra incognita ; 1)
    ISBN 978-0-316-00418-3
    I. Title.
    PS3551.N37442E34 2009
    813'.54—dc22   2008051025

10   9   8   7   6   5   4   3   2   1

RRD-IN

Printed in the United States of America

To Neil Peart,

A friend for nearly twenty years, and his music has given me tremendous inspiration for much longer than that. Without those lyrics triggering a cascade of ideas, many of my stories would never have been conceived.

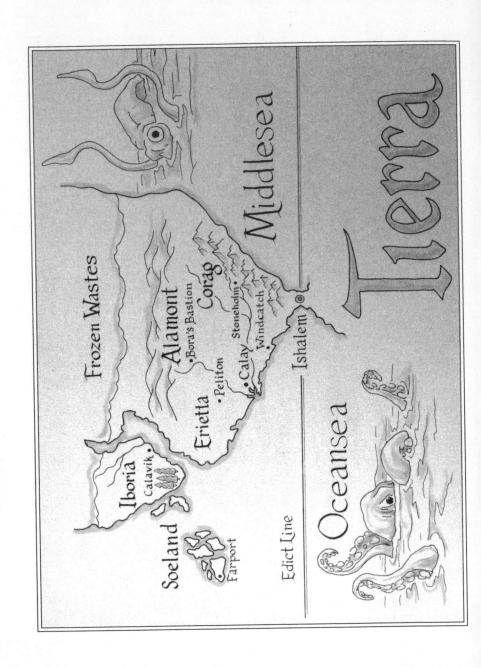

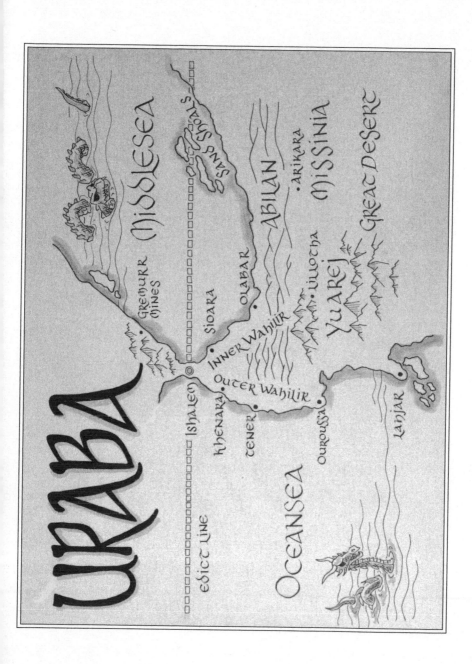

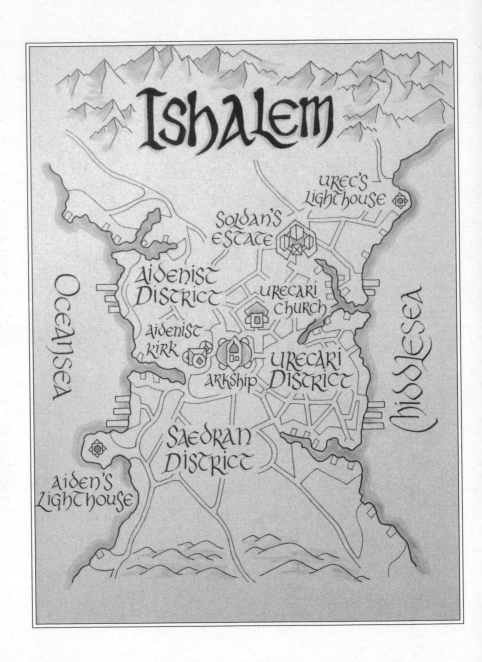

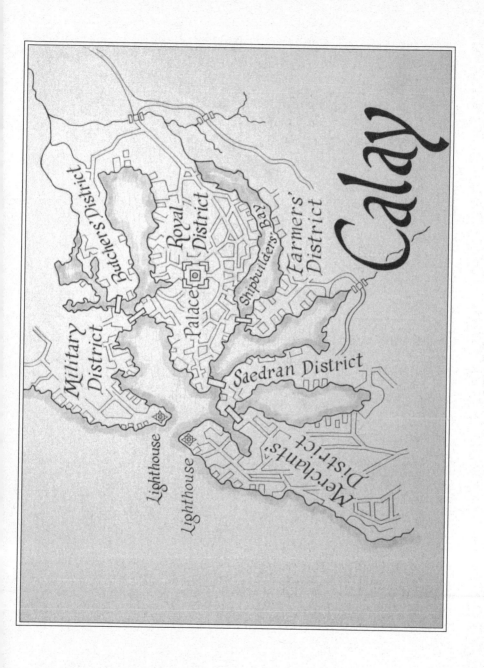

"When you reach the edge of the world, you can fly."
— The Book of Aiden

Part I

1 *Off the Coast of Uraba*

These foreign seas looked much the same as the waters of home, but Criston Vora knew the lands were different, the people were different, and their religion was contrary to everything he had been taught in the Aidenist kirk. For a twenty-year-old sailor eager to see the world, those differences could be either wondrous or frightening — he wouldn't know which until he met the people of Uraba, which he was about to do.

The *Fishhook* had made this voyage several times, and Criston's captain, Andon Shay, was confident in his abilities to negotiate another trade deal with the Uraban merchants. The young man kept his eyes open and studied the unfolding coastline as the ship sailed far, far south of everything he had known.

From his fishing village of Windcatch, he had always felt the call of the sea, wanting to see what lay beyond the horizon, yearning to explore. Though he had signed on for only a short trading voyage, at least he was seeing the other continent: *Uraba.* A place of legends and mystery.

Though connected by a narrow isthmus, the world's two main continents, Uraba and Tierra, were separated by a wide gulf of history and culture. Ages ago, at the beginning of time, when Ondun — God — had sent two of his sons in separate sailing ships to explore the world, the descendants of Aiden's crew had settled Tierra, while those from Urec's vessel colonized Uraba. Over the centuries, the followers of Aiden and the followers of Urec developed separate civilizations, religions, and traditions;

despite their differences, they were bound together by ties of trade and necessity.

On a bright sunny day with a brisk breeze, Captain Shay called for the sails to be trimmed for a gentle approach to the city of Ouroussa, where they hoped to find eager customers. The hold of the *Fishhook* contained barrels of whale oil from Soeland Reach, large spools of hemp rope from Erietta, grain from Alamont, and, in a special locked chest in the captain's cabin, beautiful metal-worked jewelry made by the skilled smiths of Corag Reach. Though the bangles and ornaments would be sold to the followers of Urec, the Corag metalworkers had subtly hidden a tiny Aidenist fishhook on each piece of jewelry.

Captain Shay would sell his cargo at prices greatly reduced from what the other Uraban merchants and middlemen could offer. With fast vessels, intrepid Tierran sailors braved the uncharted currents and sailed directly to Uraba's coastal cities, bypassing the much slower overland merchants (much to their consternation).

Near the ship's wheel, Criston paused to look at the two compasses mounted on a sheltered pedestal, a traditional magnetic compass that always pointed toward magnetic north and a magical Captain's Compass that always pointed *home*. The silver needle of the Captain's Compass came from the same piece of precious metal as an identical needle in the Tierran capital city of Calay. These twinned needles remained linked to each other by sympathetic magic, as all things in Ondun's creation were said to be linked.

Now, as the *Fishhook* closed in on Ouroussa, the crew saw a flurry of activity in the distant harbor; a ship with a bright red sail set out to meet them, sailing toward the open water. Captain Shay gestured to Criston. "Go aloft and have a look, Seaman Vora." Shay's dark hair ran to his shoulders, and instead of wearing a full bushy beard like most ship captains, he kept his neatly trimmed.

Nimble and unafraid of heights, the young man scrambled up the shroud lines to reach the lookout nest. During the voyage, Criston had enjoyed spending time high atop the main mast overlooking the waters; he had even seen several fearsome-looking sea serpents, but only at a distance.

As the Uraban ship approached, Criston noted its central painted icon on its square mainsail, the Eye of Urec. He spied additional movement in the harbor, where two fast Uraban galleys launched, their oars extended, beating across the water at a good clip. They spread apart, approaching the *Fishhook* from opposite directions.

Captain Shay called for a report, and Criston scrambled back down the lines to relate what he had seen to Captain Shay. "I couldn't see many crewmen aboard the main ship, Captain. Maybe they just want to escort us into port."

"Never needed an escort before. These aren't waters that require a pilot." Shay snapped orders to his crew, and all twenty-eight men came out on deck to stand ready. "Once they know what we're offering, they'll welcome us with open arms, but don't let your guard down." He turned back to the young sailor. "This could be a very interesting first voyage for you, Seaman."

"It's not my first voyage, sir. I've spent most of my life on boats."

"It's your first voyage with *me*, and that's what counts."

Criston's father, a fisherman, had been lost at sea, and Criston himself had served aboard many boats, working the local catch but dreaming of more ambitious voyages. Though young, Criston owned his own small boat for carrying cargo up to the Tierran capital of Calay, but the prospect of paying off the money-lenders seemed daunting. So when the *Fishhook* had passed through Windcatch on her way south and Captain Shay asked for short-term sailors to accompany him on a two-month trip to Ouroussa, offering wages higher than he could make on his own boat, Criston had jumped at the chance.

Not only would it help him pay off the debt, but it would give Criston a chance to see far-off lands. And when he returned to Windcatch with his purse full of coins, he would finally be able to marry Adrea, whom he had loved for years. Once the *Fishhook* unloaded her cargo in Ouroussa, Criston could be on his way home....

As the scarlet-sailed Uraban ship closed to within hailing distance, he spotted a man standing near the bow dressed in loose cream-colored robes, his head wrapped in a pale olba. Only five crewmen stood with the man on the foreign vessel's deck. The robed man shouted across to them in heavily accented Tierran. "I am Fillok, Ouroussa's city leader. What goods have you brought us?"

Shay lowered his voice to Criston. "Fillok...I know that name. I think he's the brother of the soldan of Outer Wahilir, an important man. Why would *he* come to meet us?" He frowned in consternation. "Men who consider themselves important sometimes do brash things, and it's rarely a good sign." The captain raised his voice and called back across the water, "We are on our way to port. I can give your harbormaster a full list."

"It is my right to inspect your cargo here and now! How do we know your boat is not filled with soldiers to attack Ouroussa?"

"Why would we do that?" Shay asked, genuinely perplexed.

If Fillok did not change course, his ship would collide with the *Fishhook* within minutes. Captain Shay eyed the two swift war galleys coming toward them from both port and starboard. "This doesn't feel right, Vora. Go up there and have another look." The young sailor slipped away and scrambled back up the ropes to the lookout nest.

Tierran traders often made great profit from selling to Uraban cities, but many vessels vanished, more than could reasonably be accounted for by storms and reefs. If Fillok were an ambitious and unprincipled man, he could have attacked those traders and seized their cargoes. No one in Tierra would know.

When Criston reached the lookout nest and peered down at the foreign ship, he was astonished to see far more than just the five Uraban sailors standing at the ropes. At least a dozen armed men crouched out of sight behind crates and sailcloth on the deck; the hatches were open, and even more Uraban men crowded below, holding bright scimitars. Criston cupped his hands around his mouth and yelled at the top of his lungs, "Captain, it's a trap! The ship is full of armed men!"

Shay shouted to his crew, "Set sails! All canvas, take the wind *now!*" Already on edge, the men jumped to untie knots, pull ropes, and drop sails abruptly into place.

Criston's warning forced Fillok into abrupt action. The Ouroussan city leader screamed something in his own language, and hidden men burst into view, lifting their swords. Shrill trumpets sounded a call to battle. Ropes with grappling hooks flew across the narrow gap between the two ships; several fell into the water, but three caught the *Fishhook*'s deck rail. Answering horns and drumbeats came from the two closing war galleys, and the rowers picked up their pace.

Shay reached down to grab a long harpoon stowed just below the starboard bow of the *Fishhook*. The Tierran men armed themselves with boat-hooks, oars, and stunning clubs. Criston clambered back down to the deck, ready to join the fight. He held a long boat-knife to defend himself, though its reach was much shorter than that of a Uraban scimitar.

Criston ran to the straining ropes that bound the ships together, just as five Urabans jumped across the gap with an eerie inhuman howl. Ducking the wide swing of a Uraban sword, he sawed at the first rope until it snapped and immediately set to work on the second one.

The *Fishhook*'s sails were fully extended now, giving her a much greater canvas area than Fillok's small Uraban ship. The ropes creaked as the Tierran vessel tried to break away. One of the Tierran sailors went down, bleeding from a deep gash in his head.

Ignoring the mayhem around him, Captain Shay cocked his arm back and let the long harpoon fly toward the other ship. Where its sharp iron tip plunged directly through Fillok's chest. The Ouroussan city leader staggered backward, grabbing the harpoon's shaft in astonishment, before he collapsed into a pool of blood on his own deck.

The Uraban attackers howled in rage upon seeing their leader killed. They piled against one another, preparing to leap across and slaughter the Tierrans. Racing in from shore, the two war galleys closed in a pincer maneuver.

Criston sawed with his knife until he severed the third grappling rope, and like a freed stallion, the *Fishhook* lunged free, separating from the Uraban ship as many of the enemy fighters leaped across. A dozen men tumbled into the deep water, and only two managed to cling to the side of the *Fishhook*, clutching nets and an anchor rope. Leaning over the rail, Criston lopped off fingers with a knife slash, and the screaming men slid into the water.

Though he was as white as a sheet, Captain Shay's voice did not waver as he shouted, "All speed—head north! Out to open sea!" The *Fishhook* began to pull away.

Only three enemy soldiers remained on the deck. Captain

Shay's crew quickly dispatched them and dumped the bodies overboard.

With Fillok killed—the brother of the local soldan!—the remaining Uraban sailors were in a frenzy aboard his ship. The drums of the approaching war galleys beat furiously, but the *Fishhook*'s sails pushed the cargo ship faster. The coastline began to dwindle in the distance, but Criston knew the uproar would not die down. "Captain, what just happened? Why did they do that? We came only to trade."

"They wanted our cargo, and now they'll want our hides as well." Shay looked sick. "Fillok's brother will go to Soldan-Shah Imir and demand blood. I suppose the blood of any Tierran will do. We have to get to King Korastine as quickly as possible." He gave the young sailor a weary smile as he turned the wheel and aligned the course with the Captain's Compass. "When we pass Windcatch, I can drop you off, Mr. Vora. But for the rest of us…" He shook his head, still frowning. "I think we just started a war."

2 *The Royal Cog, Sailing to Ishalem*

Three Months Later

The royal ship sailed southward through the night, following the Tierran coastline. She was a single-masted cog with her square sails trimmed so that she made slow headway under the stars. Because the route down to the holy city of Ishalem was so well charted, with lighthouses to mark hazardous stretches, the captain was comfortable with proceeding in the dark.

Even so, King Korastine of Tierra could not sleep, caught between hope and anxiety about the upcoming meeting with Soldan-Shah Imir. After the disastrous clash between Captain Shay's trading ship and the Uraban privateers, he could just as easily have been leading warships down to ransack Ouroussa and sink enemy ships in the harbor.

Instead of leaping headfirst into war, the Uraban leader had dispatched his best ambassador, a man named Giladen, to search for a peaceful solution. Though neither leader would admit it, both knew that Captain Shay should not have gone where he did; they also knew that Fillok should not have attacked a peaceful trading ship, and that a harpoon in the heart was exactly what he deserved. Though their respective populations were inflamed, both the king and the soldan-shah believed they had a chance to salvage the situation.

Long past midnight, Korastine stood on the raised bow platform and gazed into the misty shadows that lay ahead, imagining their destination. *Ishalem.* The sacred city built on the narrow isthmus that connected the continents...the most ancient settlement in the known world, considered holy by both the Aidenist religion and the rival Urecari religion.

Korastine wrapped weathered hands around the wooden balustrade. He was a thin man, wise-looking, barely forty. His long hair and neatly trimmed beard were light brown, salted with graying strands. He could already see what he would look like when he grew old, and times like these aged a man more swiftly.

In Ishalem, he and the soldan-shah would sign a treaty blessed by the Aidenist prester-marshall and the head sikara priestess of the Urecari church. After so many years of turmoil, they would divide the known world in half, clearly defining the two spheres of influence. That would settle the matter for all time, and at last there would be peace.

So why couldn't he sleep? Why did his stomach insist upon knotting itself with doubts? With a heavy sigh, he tried to convince himself that he was just being a fool, stung by too many disappointments, too many misplaced dreams.

The mist intensified the salt-and-seaweed smell in the air. The whispering laughter of gentle waves against the hull planks was soothing. Though there were hammocks below, most crewmen chose to sleep on the open deck. A puff of breeze luffed the sailcloth, making the masts and rigging creak.

Korastine barely heard the soft barefoot tread ascending the steps to the forecastle platform. He turned to see his beloved eleven-year-old daughter rubbing sleep from her eyes. "Are we almost to Ishalem, Father?"

"We'll be there in the morning." He reached out to hug her, and she comfortably folded herself into his arms.

Princess Anjine had straight brown hair, parted in the middle. When she was at court in Calay, she brushed her hair many times nightly, as her mother had once insisted, but on the five-day voyage, the girl didn't bother with such silliness, and the king couldn't blame her.

Though Queen Sena had been dead from pneumonia for half a year now, Korastine and his wife had often disagreed on the raising of their only child; the queen insisted that Anjine ought to be ladylike and courtly, while Korastine wanted the girl to focus more on leadership—while also being allowed some measure of her own childhood. As an uneasy compromise, the princess had learned both.

Knowing how much was at stake with the upcoming treaty, the king insisted that Anjine accompany him now. He could never forget the responsibility he had to his people and to his daughter. One day, he would leave Tierra in Anjine's care, and he did not want to give her a broken, war-torn land.

Korastine glanced around for his daughter's constant companion. "Where is Mateo?" One year older than Anjine, the young man was Korastine's ward by virtue of a heartfelt promise made when Mateo's father, a captain of the royal guard, had died in the line of duty.

"Oh, *he* has no trouble sleeping." Anjine lounged back against the rail. "Should I go splash a bucket of seawater in his face?"

"Let him sleep. We're going to have a busy day when we reach port."

As the royal cog had sailed out of Calay Harbor, Anjine and Mateo had chattered with excitement about the exotic things they were going to see. Neither had ever been to Ishalem, though they had heard plenty of stories from sailors, presters, and teachers. By the second day, however, the excitement of the voyage faded, and Mateo made it his personal mission to entertain Anjine. After the king had scolded the two children for scrambling up the mast and hanging on the rigging, Mateo devoted himself to playing strategy games with her. They hunkered down together on the deck boards, sketching out a chalk grid and making their marks. Korastine noted, proudly, that Anjine won more often than the boy did.

Queen Sena would have argued against bringing Mateo Bornan along at all, claiming that the king had gone far beyond the requirements of his promise to care for the boy. Though he did not like to think ill of the dead, stuffy Sena was no longer with them, and Korastine could raise his daughter as he pleased.

Now, wide-awake and eager as the ship sailed on, Anjine stood next to her father. Though her head barely came to his chin, he could think only of how tall, how mature his little girl was becoming. Where had the years gone? He felt a hint of tears welling in his eyes. By signing the Edict, he would leave her — and all his people — with a better, safer world.

Anjine strained to see through the fog, then pointed. "Is that Aiden's Lighthouse?"

Korastine did see a flicker, like an ember suspended in the air. "If it isn't, then we're far off course." The tall tower of sturdy rock had been erected on a jutting point of land outside of Ishalem. Its light burned constantly, not just to warn ships of the reefs that lay farther south, but to represent the light of Aiden's wisdom.

A groggy Mateo hurried across the deck, and the twelve-year-old sprang onto the forecastle platform to stand between Anjine and Korastine. So full of energy, like his father had been! The dark-haired young man would make a fine soldier someday — a high-ranking officer, if Korastine had anything to do with it.

Before long, they could see a silvery fringe of dawn on the eastern horizon. The off-watch crewmen began to awaken, and the cook stoked his stove in the galley to begin cooking breakfast. Men worked the rigging, pulling ropes to stretch the sails, now that the captain could see his heading. Ahead and to port, the shore loomed out of the shadows.

Korastine stared at the western edge of the isthmus that separated the vast Occansea from the calmer Middlesea. He remembered the first time he'd sailed down the coast at his own father's side, being trained to lead Tierra.... He had made the voyage six times now, always on matters of state, always in response to a major or minor political emergency. After this time, though...

Finally the warm sun burned off the rest of the morning fog, and the whitewashed buildings of sprawling, majestic Ishalem came into view. Ah, he remembered the amazement and wonder with which he had first viewed the holy city. Anjine would be seeing the same thing now, through the clarity and optimism of youth.

On the Aidenist side of the city, the architecture showed familiar Tierran influence, similar to what one might find in any coastal village, while in the Uraban District on the opposite side of the isthmus, the buildings looked alien, with unusual curves and angles, stuccoed rather than timbered, the roofs tiled rather than thatched.

On the highest hill in the center of Ishalem stood the ruins of the Arkship, little more than a skeletal hull with one broken mast, like a giant beached sea beast, lying far from the water. Anjine pointed as soon as she spotted it. "That's the ship! Aiden's ship."

Korastine uttered an automatic awed prayer. "Yes, the actual one."

Prester-Marshall Baine appeared on deck, wearing a long, dark brown robe trimmed with purple silk. An Aidenist fishhook pendant hung at his throat, nearly covered by his unruly red beard. King Korastine not only revered the energetic religious leader, he *respected* Baine as an intelligent, thoughtful friend. Though he was only in his mid-thirties, Baine had reached a high position of authority and responsibility, thanks to his forceful personality and his persuasive words. The prester-marshall closed his blue eyes as he bowed in silent prayer. "The holy Arkship."

"But how could such a big ship get so far from the water?" Mateo asked pragmatically, and Anjine gave him a brisk kick in the shin.

The prester-marshall chided her. "Some presters might tell you never to question, but that is tantamount to telling you not to *think*. Ondun created us to explore, to experience. There is no harm in raising questions, and Mateo has asked a good one. That conundrum has puzzled scholars for many generations."

Mateo flashed a vindicated grin at Anjine, but the prester-marshall didn't exactly answer his query. "Now would be a good time to reflect upon where our people came from. You have heard the story all your life, but when you gaze upon Ishalem, you can see in your heart that it is more than just a *story*.

"At the beginning of the world, Ondun created the continents and the seas and the skies. He made His own perfect holy land, which He called Terravitae, and Ondun filled the land with crops and orchards, forests, animals, birds, and insects. He populated it with His own people. Then He made other people and scattered them across the remaining continents. When He was finished with all His work, Ondun created three special sons — Aiden, Urec, and Joron.

"Satisfied with all that He had done, Ondun bequeathed stewardship of the world to His heirs, for He had other worlds to create, and He would soon depart. Ondun instructed Aiden, Urec, and Joron that they must keep this world intact, improve it, make it thrive. While the youngest son, Joron, remained behind to rule Terravitae, Ondun commanded that His two older sons go out in separate ships to explore His creation."

Baine related the tale to Anjine and Mateo with an earnestness that village presters could never match. Korastine smiled: No wonder the man had risen so quickly in the church hierarchy. "Before the voyage, Ondun gave Urec a special map to show him how to find the mysteries of the world, and the key to creation. To Aiden, he gave a special compass to facilitate his return to Terravitae, for its needle was charmed always to point home."

"Like a Captain's Compass," Mateo interrupted.

"The very first Captain's Compass," Anjine corrected.

"Aiden and Urec each constructed a giant Arkship, and taking their crews and families with them, sailed away from Terravitae on separate routes. But Urec was arrogant and sure of himself. He would explore the world, but considered the map an insult to his bravery, a way of cheating. Urec threw the chart overboard and chose his own course." Baine raised his bushy red eyebrows for dramatic effect. "Now, the Urecari will tell it differently, because such foolishness does not reflect well upon the man they consider their prophet! But we have the Book of Aiden to tell us the truth."

The prester-marshall looked up as the cog sailed toward the crowded maze of wharves. "We know that one of Aiden's crew members was secretly a spy for Urec, though the Urecari deny it. As soon as Aiden's ship passed well beyond sight of Terravitae, the Urecari spy damaged the sacred compass so that Aiden, too, became lost.

"After voyaging aimlessly for years, Aiden's ship came to rest here. The crew intermarried with the people of Tierra, and their descendants now populate half the world. When Urec's ship landed, he, his crew, and their children settled in Uraba to the south."

As the royal ship pulled into the harbor, Korastine saw the buildings clustered like devout worshippers kneeling before the many-spired Aidenist kirk built on the western side of the Arkship hill. The cog drifted up to a long dock festooned with pennants and garlands. Gulls greeted them with a raucous fanfare. Ishalem looked so glorious that Korastine could almost believe that their meeting was blessed by Ondun.

Anjine glanced up toward the gigantic wreck on the hill. "So how do we know that's Aiden's ship, instead of Urec's — as the Urecari say?"

"Because we *know*. Yes, we know."

3 The Soldan-Shah's Galley, on the Middlesea

A sea serpent rose up in front of the gilded ship before Soldan-Shah Imir could reach Ishalem, and the crew prepared for an attack.

The silken mainsail tilted on its yardarm to capture cross-winds as the narrow galley, a dromond, cut across the Middlesea. Imir stood at the pointed bow, where he could feel the salt spray, straining to see the low coastline of the isthmus, though he knew they were at least half a day from their destination.

The huge sea serpent rose up barely a spear's throw from the bow, startling Imir out of his thoughts. The monstrous head breached the waves on a long stalk of neck covered with shimmering blue and silver scales; seawater sheeted down from the sinuous form. A jagged line of fins coursed the neck like an aquatic mane, and the serpent's reptilian jaws parted to display curved teeth and a forked tongue. The gleaming eyes were the black of the Middlesea's greatest depths; two long horns curved from the skull, deadly enough to gore a whale. The creature flared a set of scalloped gills and emitted an ominous bellowing hoot, as though challenging the dromond's right to cross the open water. A shrill jet of steam blasted from the blowhole on the back of the beast's head, vapors that were said to be poisonous.

The galley's captain shouted orders, drums goaded the slaves to pull their oars faster, turning the ship. But this monster was a demon of the sea, created by Ondun Himself to be a sleek, fast predator on the open waters. No matter how swiftly they rowed, this ship could not outrun the serpent.

The dromond's crew gathered spears; some ran forward with shields to protect their leader. Imir glowered at the beast. Though the creature could have plucked him from the deck like a honeyed date from a serving platter, he dared not show fear in front of the crew. "I am the soldan-shah! Allow me to pass!"

The lead sikara priestess strode boldly to Imir's side. Ur-Sikara Lukai's long hair was the dark brown color of scorched wood, and her scarlet robes whipped around her slender body in the brisk wind as if she were engulfed in fabric flames. Her dark eyes could be quite beautiful when her expression softened, but her expression was not soft now. "Begone!" She raised her hand to the silvery-blue monster. "In the name of Urec, I cast you back to the depths. We are on the holy business of Ondun. *Begone!*" She leaned across the prow, both arms extended, and her voice rose to a fearsome screech. "Begone!"

The serpent regarded her curiously. Its enormous body undulated as it swam to and fro, still blocking the dromond's path, and another jet of spray came from its blowhole. The rowers had finally turned the ship so that the mainsail could catch the wind fully, but the serpent casually kept pace, emitting another strange bellowing hoot. Finally, bored with its unusual prey, the scaled monster circled the vessel once more, then submerged, its sharp dorsal fins tracing a sawblade pattern through the water as it swam off.

Ur-Sikara Lukai seemed satisfied with the demonstration of her powers. "You are fortunate to have me here, Soldan-Shah. I drove the monster away."

He regarded her wryly and kept his voice low. "I am even more fortunate that it was a silver-blue serpent, for I know those rarely attack."

Lukai was surprised by his comment, but she admitted nothing. "Sea serpents are unpredictable. It is wise to have Urec's shield."

As the galley turned toward Ishalem, Imir shuddered to imagine what might have occurred between Tierra and Uraba if he were unexpectedly killed here, like this, in the Middlesea. He had left his older son and heir, Omra, back in the capital city of Olabar to make decisions and to manage the various soldanates in his absence. Omra was an intelligent man and a good leader... but he might have been forced into action.

King Korastine would have been blamed for some treachery, and the resulting war would have been worse than if they had never tried to make peace at all.

Fillok, younger brother of the soldan of Outer Wahilir, had been arrogant and brash, and he failed to think of the consequences of his actions. He had probably considered himself brave to provoke the Tierran trading ship, and all he had received was a harpoon through his chest.

Though the soldan-shah did not sanction Fillok's foolish action, once the man had gotten himself killed, Imir was unable to ignore the provocation. But knowing that both sides benefited far more from trade than from open warfare, he refused to let himself get drawn into further conflict. Now that Ambassador Giladen had worked out terms, Imir and Korastine would put an end to the tensions.

The soldan-shah's head and cheeks were clean-shaven, his scalp oiled. Years ago Lithio, his first wife, had fretted so much over the appearance of his beard and hair that one morning Imir had shaved himself clean in hopes of silencing her. Instead, Lithio had told him he looked handsome that way. He didn't believe that she actually thought that, but Lithio had a talent for frustrating him. After she had borne the requisite son and heir, he had been happy to "allow" her to return to her native soldan-ate of Missinia, where she'd lived a quiet and comfortable life for the past twenty years.

His second wife, Asha, who divided her time between her private villa near the Olabar palace and the soldan-shah's guest residence in Ishalem, was much more adoring and attentive...but utterly obsessed with her pets. Any animal that Ondun had seen fit to place upon His world, Asha wanted to keep and adore. Imir had not seen her in months and looked forward to their reunion in Ishalem, though he did not relish the prospect of all the noise from the hounds, songbirds, cats, peacocks, and whatever other creatures she had managed to acquire in the meantime.

As the burning coppery sun settled to the horizon, Imir could see the distinct line of the isthmus like a barrier against the setting sun. As they neared the eastern curve of the sandy harbor, pelicans wheeled overhead. Fishing boats plied the waters, bringing in the day's catch; small sailing craft dipped out to deeper water, then circled back in toward the coastline. Though the day was clear and bright, the smoky torch of Urec's Lighthouse had been lit as soon as spotters saw the approach of the soldan-shah's dromond.

Even from far away, Imir could see the great hulk of the Ark-ship, Urec's ship, washed high and dry upon the tallest hill. The prime Urecari church, a lovely construction comprised of a central dome surrounded by tall, thin spires, was an unmistakable landmark on the eastern hillside below the wreck.

Ur-Sikara Lukai rejoined him, pointed to where a slow-moving passenger barge emerged from the city's main canal and proceeded toward them. "Look, Asha is coming to welcome you." Her tone dripped with disrespect.

Imir hardened his voice. "Asha means well, and you will be polite to her. That is my command."

The ur-sikara gave him a sour look, but he insisted, and she finally bowed slightly. "As the soldan-shah wishes."

Though she had her own power as the church's lead priestess, Lukai was also close friends with Villiki, the soldan-shah's third wife and mother of Imir's second son. Villiki stridently expressed her opinions of her husband's leadership and complained frequently to Lukai. He supposed he was lucky, in a way, that only one of his three wives was so obviously ambitious. Men had their wars, but women had their schemes.

Asha never harbored an unkind thought toward anyone, and it was her childlike innocence that had endeared her to him in the first place (as well as her exceptional body). Her welcome barge approached, and Imir realized he was smiling. She must have spent days festooning the barge with garlands and ribbons. Now she stood waving at him, accompanied by three small dogs that yapped constantly. But even that did not discourage the soldan-shah; he hoped Asha had prepared a private—quiet—room for the two of them...someplace without her pets. He needed a good night's sleep before the all-important Edict ceremony.

4 *Olabar*

Zarif Omra loved to study maps of the world—not out of mere intellectual curiosity, but in order to understand the resources, boundaries, and limitations of Uraba. "Tactical geography," he called it. Sitting in the palace throne room, Omra traced his finger along the lines on the chart spread out on his mahogany side table while he waited for the first supplicants to be shown in. He needed to familiarize himself with the entire continent he would one day rule. He was only twenty-four, but there had never been any doubt he would succeed the soldan-shah.

Uraba was defined by sea and sand, anchored in place by Ishalem, and divided into five soldanates. The lands north of Ishalem were much sketchier, since few details of Tierra were known to Uraban cartographers. Zarif Omra did not worry about those unfamiliar lands, however. When his father retired, Omra would have enough work simply managing his own people.

Now that Imir had sailed off to Ishalem, Omra got a taste of the work that lay in store for him. He wore a loose purple chalwar and a sleeveless tunic; he rested comfortably upon the cushions piled upon the dais, from which he would listen to supplicants. A gold earring hung from his left ear in the fashion of the Missinia soldanate, to honor his mother. While his father had gone soft and heavyset, Omra was fit and muscular, his lean face edged by a neatly trimmed black beard. His hair was long and oiled, and sometimes he let his beloved wife, Istar, plait it for him. Teasingly, he threatened to shave his head as his father had done, but Istar had convinced him how much she liked his hair. She was now pregnant with his firstborn child, and he could deny her nothing.

Istar would arrive soon to join him, since she loved to hear the people present their issues before the dais, even though Omra found her to be distracting when he most needed to show his strength. Anxious to get started, he clapped his hands to summon the first visitor.

Dressed in dyed linen garments, a young man entered—his cousin Burilo, the eldest son of Xivir, the soldan of Missinia. Burilo was the same age as Omra, but gangly and awkward, since his growth spurt had occurred much later than Omra's. The zarif welcomed him warmly. "What news have you brought from Arikara? Is my mother well?"

"Lithio is quite comfortable and happy, though she'd be happier if you visited her more often."

Omra chuckled. "Yes, whenever I can break away from my obligations here in Olabar." His mother often asked him to make the trip down to the capital of Missinia, and he suspected she did it more as a teasing way to annoy his father than because she had a heartfelt desire to see him. "To what do I owe the pleasure of this visit?"

"I bring you a joyous gift, Zarif." Burilo called his servant, who entered the throne room carrying a large square box. Burilo lifted the lid and reached in to withdraw a decapitated head that had been smeared with tar. The dead man's lips were drawn back to reveal crooked and yellowed teeth; dark tattoos showed on the skin even through the preservative coating. In disgust, Burilo tossed the head to the floor, and the tar from the head stained the polished driftwood tiles. "One less desert bandit to prey upon our villages and farms. Our soldiers killed the leader of the band."

Omra leaned forward to inspect the head. Years ago, Soldan-Shah Imir had declared a bounty on the ruthless bandit tribes who lived in the inhospitable sands of the Great Desert. The bandits emerged like a sandstorm on swift and sturdy horses to harass small Missinian villages. After stealing, raping, and pillaging, they vanished back into the dunes faster than Soldan Xivir's armies could respond. Whenever a military force pursued them into the sands, the bandits ran circles around the soldiers, picking them off until they were lost.

Omra's expression darkened. "I doubt the bandits will be deterred by their loss. They are like a demon serpent—cut off one head, and two more grow in its place."

Burilo gave a strange, cockeyed grin as he answered. "Then there will be more bandits to kill, and more bounties to earn."

Omra told his chamberlain to pay Burilo the promised reward, then directed servants to place the head in a trophy case. Two silent slaves hurried forward to clean the tar stain from the polished floor.

Beautiful Istar entered the throne room. After bowing formally before her husband, she sat on a pale green cushion below the raised dais. He reached out and took her hand. At five months, her pregnancy had begun to show, though draping Yuarej silks covered her. In private, he loved to run his palm over the swelling curve of her belly. Istar's dark hair hung in a single braid interwoven with gold ribbon. As a secret between the two of them, she had decided to wear her hair in one braid for the first child she would bear; when she gave birth a second time, it would be two braids, and so on. They often joked about how many braids her lovely head could sustain. Omra wondered if other Urabans would adopt the tradition.

"Before your next visitor, I have called for tea and almonds," she told him demurely. The treat was as much for herself as for him.

Istar was the daughter of one of the most powerful merchants in Olabar, a man whose ships ran the coast of the Middlesea to trade with Sioara and other ports of Inner Wahilir. Omra had fallen in love with Istar and married her. However, since Istar's blood wasn't noble, the zarif's choice of her as his *first* wife raised eyebrows among the extended families of the other soldans; conversely, his selection pleased the merchant families.

His half-brother Tukar also entered the throne room, finding a seat in the back where he could observe quietly. A stocky young man two years younger than Omra, Tukar rarely participated in the discussions—in fact, he usually appeared bored—but his mother Villiki insisted that he watch and learn from court politics. Villiki had great plans for him, though the young man himself showed no signs of being dissatisfied with his subordinate role.

Merchants from the soldanate of Yuarej entered next, carrying bolts of the finest silk, which they spread out to display dyed patterns of the unfurling fern, the Urecari religious symbol representing rebirth and potential. Istar delighted in the brilliant green, blue, and scarlet fabrics. "We can have garments made for Sikara Fyiri, since she made such a wonderful blessing for the baby."

Omra squeezed her hand. "It was a wonderful blessing, indeed."

With the church's main sikara accompanying the soldan-shah to Ishalem, Omra and Istar had enlisted the service of a young priestess with no obvious political agenda, though the zarif was sure she would develop one in time, as sikaras usually did. Fyiri had come for the sunset ceremony, bringing her copy of Urec's Log and ribbons of colored paper on which she would write prayers before tying them to sticks to flutter in the wind where Ondun could read them.

"We accept your offering of the silk," Omra said to the merchants. "My wife certainly approves." He ate one of the warm almonds roasted in sea salt, while Istar poured cups of sweet tea for both of them. At the back of the room, Tukar employed a piece of chalk on a square of slate, writing a note to himself.

Omra called the next visitor, knowing that this was what his father did every day. No wonder Soldan-Shah Imir had been so eager to make the voyage to Ishalem.

5 *Ishalem, Urecari District*

Prester Hannes wore dirty clothes in the Uraban style, shapeless rags draped over his shoulders to make him look like a beggar, because beggars drew very little attention. The people he encountered on this side of Ishalem automatically assumed he was a follower of Urec. Though that meant his disguise was perfect, he still resented being confused for one of the loathsome heretics.

But he had to be convincing, had to fit in. "Consider yourself a spy for God," Prester-Marshall Baine had told him more than a year earlier, before sending him to Ishalem. Fortunately, Hannes's faith in Aiden was unwavering, and Ondun Himself knew the difference between truth and lies.

Head down, he wandered the streets in the Urecari District, noting how the merchants cheated their customers, listening to the gossip and the delusions. These people went about their lives without even realizing their sins. As a prester, he was a kind and compassionate man, doing the work of Ondun, but sadly none of these Urabans could be forgiven.

Beneath the gigantic wreck of the Arkship — *Aiden's* ship, though all these people pretended it was Urec's — devout Urecari made pilgrimages up the switchbacked path to stand in the shadow of the ancient, ruined hull. Pilgrims petitioned sikaras, paying fees to climb the hill and even touch the holy wood of the enormous beached vessel. Prester Hannes had been up to the Arkship many times since arriving in Ishalem. He climbed the hill at night and slipped past the church guards, just so he could have private time with his prayers.

Now, as thin brass bells pealed in the minaret towers of the prime church, he moved along the streets, blending into the crowd of worshippers called to sunset services. The outside of the monumental heathen church bore carved stone stations, each panel depicting part of the story. Some images were correct, in order to lull the faithful: Ondun and his sons in Terravitae...Aiden and Urec sailing off in their separate vessels, leaving Holy Joron behind... Urec with his map, Aiden with his sacred compass.

Then the deception began: Urec and his ship arriving on the shores of Uraba...battles with the natives who viewed them as enemies...Urec's decision to take multiple wives for himself, a rule that all Aidenists despised...then an aged Urec planting the golden fern before wandering off to become the Traveler.

Hannes had seen these images many times, had heard the lies in the sermons given by the sikaras. He still felt the knot of anger each time he witnessed the dissemination of such blatant untruths. *Aiden* had become the Traveler, not Urec. Unable to build their own religion, the Urecari had obviously co-opted the tenets of Aidenism. And yet they were blind to their delusions. He both pitied them and reviled them for it.

With the sunset services about to begin, Hannes followed the crowd, steeling himself. "The truth of Aiden is the truth of God," he muttered, reciting a well-known prayer that Prester-Marshall Baine had taught him. "And the truth of God is the truth for all, even those who refuse to hear it." Hannes squared his shoulders and, still wearing rags, approached the church.

Outside the large stone-and-wood building, numerous banners hung down, swirled with the unfurling fern symbol. Vendors sold trinkets to visiting pilgrims; a majority of the vendors were Saedrans, "Ondun's stepchildren," who believed that their people had left Terravitae at a later time and were not descendants of either Aiden's crew or Urec's. As a people, Saedrans kept to themselves, but their craftsmen created mementos, candles, or prayer ribbons, which they sold outside the kirks and churches, catering to both great religions.

Prester Hannes didn't hate the Saedrans for their lack of belief; at least they weren't as completely *wrong* as the Urecari. *The truth of God is the truth for all.*

Taking that command to heart, Aidenist missionaries had ventured into Uraba. The Book of Aiden gave all of his followers the freedom to trade wherever they wished, to correct Urecari misconceptions wherever they encountered them. But the followers of Urec had not received the missionaries well, and many were killed for daring to speak of their religion. Hearing such stories made Prester Hannes hate them even more.

As he paused before the prime church's tall wooden doors, Hannes saw a Saedran vendor behind a small table displaying beautifully molded candles, all of which burned with tiny protected flames. The candlemaker had a balding head, long white hair, and a square-cut gray beard. "Candles! Candles for the faithful." He lifted up a dark red wax cylinder that bore the fern spiral. "Ten coppers apiece. Show your flame to Urec. Burn the light of his words in the church."

Hannes recognized the candlemaker as Direc na-Taya, a man who alternated his wares as trade dictated; today he had come to the Urecari church, and tomorrow he would be selling fish-hook candles to Aidenists. Seeing Hannes's ragged clothing, the vendor ignored him, assuming a beggar would never buy his candles.

Hannes brushed past the Saedran and entered the church. He wrinkled his nose at the smell of their pressing bodies, their oils and perfumes, even the odd stink of their cooking and spices. Inside the vast nave, banners hung from stone arches in the vaulted ceiling, each one covered with a written prayer, as if Ondun would bother to read them…but He was off creating other worlds and had neither the time nor interest to read notes from the subjects He had left behind.

The worshippers entered on a spiraling path of dark tiles inlaid on the floor, walking around the central altar. The track was designed to imitate the unfurling fern, though it forced the crowds to stand in an unnatural coil, all striving to see the sikara in the middle of the chamber. The orderly wooden benches in an Aidenist kirk made so much more sense.

The head priestess had recently arrived in Ishalem, just as Prester-Marshall Baine had come with King Korastine. Usually other sikaras led the service, but for this ceremony Ur-Sikara Lukai herself delivered the homily. As the red-gowned woman stepped up to the long wooden altar crowded with goblets, urns of fragrant oil, braziers, tall candles, and other talismans, Hannes scrutinized her.

Lukai wore necklaces of beaten gold; bangles hung from her ears and wrists. To most of the crowd, she appeared statuesque and beautiful, but his discriminating eye could see that her face was covered with thick makeup, her eyes outlined with heavy kohl. He saw past the trappings to the signs of age on her face, the faint wrinkles that could not entirely be concealed. The wearisome burden of deception and lies must have aged her prematurely.

Among the worshippers, Hannes stood silent and uncomfortable, listening as Ur-Sikara Lukai invoked chants and read passages from Urec's Log. Though Hannes pretended to listen, his mind was closed down. He recited a litany of his own prayers and quotations from Aiden to protect him from the heresy surrounding him.

As a special commemoration of her visit to Ishalem, the ur-sikara presented an ancient medallion of gold inset with chips of lapis lazuli and encircled by small topaz stones. She held it up, and the trophy gleamed in the light of the candles and braziers around the altar. Lukai was rewarded with a chorus of awed gasps. "This amulet was worn by Urec himself on his voyage. He gave it as a gift to his wife, Fashia, upon their arrival in Uraba. It belongs here, at the altar of our prime church."

With obvious reverence, the sikara placed it between two massive candles, each as thick as Hannes's thigh, then spread the heavy golden chain on a blue velvet pad in the center of the altar. "Ondun Himself gave this amulet to His son. And now we give it to the church."

Hannes narrowed his intense gaze. If Ondun had indeed created that amulet, He would not want it to remain in the hands of heretics.

Throughout the remainder of the service, Hannes wrestled with his thoughts, trying to decide what he should do. Outside once more after the service's conclusion, Hannes crouched at the mouth of an alley, leaning against the whitewashed wall of a potter's shop that had closed for the church services. Wrapped in his thoughts as well as cloaking rags, Hannes gave little consideration to the picture he must present.

A rich Urecari merchant walked past, still glowing from the service. The man paused when he saw Hannes, reached into the purse at his waist, and retrieved three *cuars*. He tossed the silver coins at Hannes. "These are for you, my brother. God has hope for all of us. Your life, too, will shine with the blessings of Urec."

Hannes muttered automatic thanks to the man and picked up the *cuars*. *With the blessings of Urec*.

As soon as the man was out of sight, he cast the coins into the alley shadows in disgust, afraid they might burn his skin.

6 Calay, Saedran District

With the thick curtains drawn and the candles lit (though it was bright daylight), Aldo na-Curic sat at a table in the main room of his family's house in Calay. He faced his nemesis, his teacher, his tester. He knew what was at stake.

Aldo, a clever young Saedran man of eighteen, had always admired the gruff, stern elder. Sen Leo na-Hadra had a deep voice, a lined face framed by a long thick mane of gray hair, and an equally thick gray beard. His pale blue eyes were fearsome, and they did not blink as he leaned closer to Aldo and mercilessly fired questions, one after another. "Name the eleven main Soeland islands, their villages, and the village leaders—in order from smallest to largest."

Aldo did so without even blinking.

"List the nineteen coastal villages from Calay to Ishalem."

"There are twenty-three coastal villages."

Sen Leo smiled. That detail had been part of the test. "Then name all twenty-three."

Aldo did so. This was too easy.

The old teacher wore dark, shapeless robes that masked his body. Aldo suspected the older man was somewhat heavyset, but he could never know for sure. Sen Leo slid a blank piece of paper forward, gave Aldo a lead stylus. "Now draw, as exactly as you can, all the stars in the Loom as seen from far Lahjar."

Aldo had expected questions like that. Taking up the stylus, he quickly made marks, needing no tools, estimating the angles and distances with an expert eye. Lahjar was the city farthest south on the outer coast of Uraba; no known settlements lay beyond, since reefs and intense heat blocked the passage of ships. Aldo had never seen the constellations from that distant corner of the world, but the details had been reported reliably by Saedran chartsmen.

Their libraries held thousands of volumes written in a coded language that required expertise to read; no outsiders could decipher their complex letters. Every Saedran home, including Aldo's, held dozens of heirloom volumes, luxury items that most Tierrans could not afford.

Finished, the young man slid the hand-drawn constellation map back to Sen Leo, who glanced at it, then brushed it aside. "Describe in detail the streets in Bora's Bastion, the capital city of Alamont Reach. Tell me in particular what the houses look like, and list the merchant stalls in order, as one would encounter them walking clockwise across the central district from the riverport."

Aldo painted the picture in his mind as vividly as if he had seen these things himself. He did as the old teacher asked. He had never been to Lahjar, nor to Alamont Reach, nor to any place other than the city of Calay, yet his answers didn't waver.

Sen Leo watched him intently; Aldo hoped for a smile of approval, but did not expect to receive one. With each question, the examination was bound to get much harder.

Among Saedrans, occasionally a child would be gifted with perfect recall, the ability to memorize details at a glance and retain them without flaw. Saedran families carefully tested their children, watching for any hint of the valuable skill. Anyone who demonstrated a particularly sharp memory was marked for special teaching, in hopes that he or she would become a chartsman. Aldo had been developing his talent for so many years that he could answer all the instructor's questions as a matter of course. After today, he *would* be a chartsman.

As navigators aboard sailing ships, Saedran chartsmen were highly prized and highly paid. The captain of any large cargo vessel desiring to take the fastest course needed a chartsman aboard; otherwise, he wouldn't dare lose sight of the coastline. Skilled chartsmen, however, could navigate theoretical courses and locate a ship's position by esoteric means. They knew how to use astrolabes, sextants, and ship's clocks to determine the precise latitude of sailing vessels. Their intricate sealed mechanical clocks allowed them to tell time with sufficient accuracy to calculate longitude. Only Saedran chartsmen understood how to do it, and they carried no documents, no books or tables; they had to have every coordinate memorized.

Though their population was small, Saedrans were crucial to Tierran society as well. Even those who did not have perfect recall served vital roles as astronomers, alchemists, cartographers, apothecaries, surgeons. They did not follow the Aidenist religion, but they were not persecuted. Even so, his people drew no attention to themselves. It would not do for other Tierrans to realize just how wealthy the Saedrans were, or how much political influence they wielded.

Sen Leo forced Aldo to keep demonstrating what he knew, asking him to recite passages verbatim from random pages of obscure volumes. Aldo sat back, closed his eyes, and spoke the words as requested. The teacher had chosen one of his favorite passages — unintentionally, Aldo was sure — a story about the Saedran origins, the continent his people had discovered and settled, which had tragically vanished beneath the waves, sinking forever to the ocean's bottom. Perhaps it was actual history, perhaps only a myth.

Finishing his recitation, Aldo looked expectantly at Sen

Leo na-Hadra. His throat was dry, his voice hoarse, and gauging by the thin line of orange sunlight that seeped between the gap in the curtains, he had been at his examination for several hours.

Sen Leo extended a cup of water, and Aldo gulped. The old man smiled. "I welcome you to the ranks of chartsmen, Aldo na-Curic. We Saedrans have one more mind and one more set of eyes to see the world."

After everything he had just spoken, Aldo found that he had no words. His mouth opened, closed, and finally settled into a relieved grin. Sen Leo strode to the door and flung it open. In the next room waited Biento and Yura, Aldo's father and mother. The old teacher held on to the doorframe, as if he were exhausted as well. "He has passed."

His mother drew a delighted gasp, and his father beamed, stepping away from the easel that held the painting on which he had been working. Aldo walked on unsteady legs into the outer room.

His younger brother, Wen, heard the news and beamed. "I'm going to be a chartsman someday, too!" Wen, though, changed his mind every other week, and showed no inclination for the long and tedious study required to memorize so much data.

His little sister, Ilna, sat at a table drawing crude sketches, imitating her father's work. "We're proud of you Aldo!"

"But he still has much to learn," Sen Leo cautioned. "He must acquire a greater breadth and depth to his knowledge, but he does have the skill—perfect recall. He is a chartsman."

Aldo straightened his back and said formally, "I pledge to do my best."

Sen Leo gathered his robes and departed, marching out into the narrow streets of Calay's Saedran District. The teacher had not brought a single book, map, or reference catalogue with him. He, too, had every one of the words, maps, and numbers memorized.

"We should celebrate!" Biento scrubbed a hand through his son's curly brown hair, an unruly mass that made him look years younger than he actually was. Right now, Aldo's flush of embarrassment at the attention made him seem even younger still.

"This celebration should be for *him*," Yura replied. Her long straight brown hair was bound in a scarf. Her face was smudged with flour, since she had been baking small round loaves of bread during Aldo's lengthy examination. "Let him go down to the Merchants' District and buy something for himself. He deserves it, and you know how he loves to watch the ships."

His father put away his paintbrushes, with one last appraisal of the commission he had nearly completed—a portrait of a minor nobleman, a vain old man whose villa was a bit too close (or so he always complained) to the smells and noises of the Butchers' District.

Since the Aidenist religion forbade artistic expression for the glory of any individual person, even Saedran painters like Biento na-Curic were not allowed to create private portraits. The presters insisted that the only proper subjects for a painter were scenes from the story of Terravitae and the voyage of Aiden. Obeying this restriction to the letter, though not the spirit, noblemen found ways to make themselves appear in the religious paintings. Biento had completed a work that showed sailors on the prow of Aiden's ship as the lookout sighted the coastline of Tierra for the first time. Most of the figures were vague and shadowy in the background, but filling much of the painting was one "crewman"—who happened to look exactly like the commissioning nobleman.

Biento made a good living for his family by doing such work.

He frequently traveled so that he could do his painting inside noble households or merchant offices, and sometimes he disappeared for days at a time, with no one knowing exactly where he was, but he always returned home looking satisfied.

Wiping his hands with a rag, Biento withdrew a small box hidden between two thick volumes in the family library and took out ten silver coins, more money than Aldo had ever held for his own use. "This is for you—treat yourself."

"I appreciate your faith in me!"

"How can we not be proud? You've brought honor to all of us—and once you start voyaging, you'll be able to pay us back tenfold in no time."

"I'll be a chartsman, too," Wen declared.

"Only if you study," his mother said. The boy did not appear to be excited by the prospect.

Aldo couldn't think beyond today as he left the house and bounded down to the merchants' quarter, imagining all the things he could buy.

Aldo walked past the goldsmiths, the gem sellers, the weavers. His nose was drawn to the confectioners' tents, where sweet treats were made with honey and cane sugar. Other vendors roasted savory skewers over low smoky fires. His mouth watered . . . but buying food seemed a waste of his money. He might be satisfied for a few hours, but then his stomach would demand more the next day. For such a momentous occasion, he wanted something permanent, something special.

A lanky man with intense brown eyes and a narrow, weathered face sat upon a splintered barrel, ignoring the bustle and chatter of the merchant stalls. He leaned forward, bony elbows on the patched knees of his breeches, spreading his hands as he told a tale with great vehemence and enthusiasm, though to only a few listeners. The man saw Aldo and called out, as his other listeners wandered away. "Boy, you should hear my story. You will find it of value."

"I'm not a boy." Aldo squared his shoulders. "I'm a Saedran chartsman. A *chartsman*." It was the first time he had said it, and the title felt very good.

The lanky man smiled. "And I am a sea captain without a ship. But I do have a tale. Listen." He beckoned Aldo closer.

Now that he was a chartsman, Aldo realized, part of his responsibility was to gather information from sailors and explorers. Even though he hadn't gone to the edge of the world himself, eyewitnesses could provide details that might not yet be known. He had heard tales about enormous sea serpents of any stripe or color, ocean witches, nettleweed that could reach up and sting a sailor so that he never woke up, stories of terrible storms and the more terrible Leviathan.

This man, who introduced himself as Yal Dolicar, spoke with passion and intensity, conveying indisputable truth. "I captained a ship bound for Ishalem with a cargo of hemp rope and cured hides from Erietta. She was a two-masted cog, twenty years old but well caulked, well rigged, her sails patched but intact—until we encountered the storm. Hellish storm! For five days the winds blew us far from the coast. We had no Saedran chartsman aboard, mind you. Hah! We could have used *you*!" He jabbed a finger at Aldo. "We were at the mercy of the waves and currents. We were lost.

"When the weather cleared, leaving the sun as bright as a gold basin and the waves as smooth as a mirror, we had come to a cluster of islands not marked on any chart! Swimming creatures circled our battered ship, sleek gray fish that could transmute themselves into human forms. They dove beneath the waves, playing with us, leading us on. And when we looked down through the water, we saw cities deep below—towers made of coral, houses and kirks built from mother-of-pearl. And mer-people swimming with lumps of gold and coral in their outstretched hands, pearls as big as your fist."

Aldo caught his breath. This sounded like the story of the sunken island continent of his people! What if this man's storm-driven ship had truly found the remnants of the lost Saedran civilization? What if those people really had found a way through alchemy or sorcery to transform their bodies into sea-dwellers who could survive even after their land sank into the depths?

"No one has seen the things I've seen," Yal Dolicar said. "The mer-people towed us back into a strong current, and we eventually drifted to land, where I was rescued…but my ship sank in another storm, and I lost most of my remaining crew." Dolicar leaned forward, grasping Aldo's wrists to show his earnestness. "I can't go back there, because I have no ship. But *you* could. You're a Saedran chartsman. Perhaps you might lead an expedition?"

He reached into his loose shirt and pulled out a rolled strip of paper. "I drew a map by estimating the course and distance the storm blew us. I sketched the outlines of the islands. I marked the location of the undersea city here." He held up the tightly rolled paper. "Would such a map be worth something to you?"

Aldo's eyes were wide, and his heart pounded with hope. He couldn't entirely believe this man's story, nor could he entirely dismiss it. "Let me see the map."

Dolicar waggled a finger. "Ah, but you've already revealed that you're a chartsman. One glimpse and you'll memorize it all; then I'd be cheated."

Aldo held his ground. "And why should I purchase something I haven't seen?"

Dolicar gave a quick laugh. "I like you, young man. Perhaps a bit of trust is warranted here. I'll show you a corner." He unrolled the paper just a little, displaying crude coastlines, the perimeter of one oblong island—territory that did not match anything he had previously committed to memory. Aldo fingered the coins in his purse. If accurate, this map was a better investment than any treat or trinket.

"I have ten silver pieces," he said. "No more."

Dolicar's brow wrinkled. "A small price to pay for access to a whole new continent. Perhaps fifteen silver pieces would be more appropriate?"

"This is not a negotiation." Aldo crossed his arms over his narrow chest, trying to sound tough. "I have ten silver pieces. That is all I will pay you." The more he thought about it, the more he was convinced that he needed to have that map. His father and Sen Leo would both be proud of him. On his first day of becoming a chartsman, he could expand the wealth of Saedran knowledge.

"Very well, I can see that you wouldn't try to cheat or lie, young man," Yal Dolicar said. "The map for your coins. And I promise you, every scrap of payment goes toward commissioning a new ship of my own."

Aldo took the map and unrolled it, staring eagerly at the drawn islands, the coastline, the estimations of distance. This information would be invaluable. He took a few steps along, wandering through the Merchants' District but engrossed in the chart. Recalling his manners, he turned to thank the sailor . . . only to find that the barrel was now empty and Yal Dolicar was gone.

Rolling up the map once more, Aldo hurried home.

7 *Ishalem*

On the morning of the Edict ceremony, Anjine dressed in her finest court gown, which had been packed in a cedar chest for the trip from Calay. When she emerged from the guest room, King Korastine stared at her with a mist of tears in his eyes. "You look like a little queen."

She laughed. "I *am* a little queen."

Anjine had wanted to rush up the hill to see the holy Arkship as soon as they arrived in Ishalem, but the king had told her to wait until it was time. All the previous afternoon, she had looked out the open windows of the royal residence, watching pilgrims march up to behold the shipwreck.

Now, when the ceremony was set to begin, bells rang out from the main kirk. On the opposite side of Ishalem a similar campanile answered from the Urecari church. King Korastine extended an arm, which his daughter took, and they emerged together from the residence to join the formal procession with an honor guard of lower-ranking presters hand-picked for the event.

Mateo Bornan was already there, very handsome and looking quite mature for a twelve-year-old in a modified royal guard uniform, just like the one his father had worn. Prester-Marshall Baine had combed back his flaming red hair and donned midnight-blue vestments adorned with the fishhook symbol. Spectators waved pennants and shouted the king's name; Anjine even heard a few calling out to her.

Though crowds lined the streets below, the Pilgrim's Path had been cleared. This meeting between the king and the soldan-shah, the prester-marshall and the ur-sikara, was a private matter between the rulers of Tierra and Uraba, under the eyes of distant but all-seeing Ondun.

Following Baine, who led the procession up the winding path, Anjine watched in awe as the rising sun silhouetted the Arkship's single broken mast and winked through gaps in the crumbling hull. The rest of the ancient vessel had weathered into dust and fragments of wood. A new rope ladder hung down the intact part of the hull to the Arkship's bow, on which a special altar had been constructed. A golden rail ran along the slanted gunwale. The hilltop and the skeletal vessel carried an aura of majesty, a corona of holiness; Anjine glanced at Mateo and saw that he felt it too.

A hush fell as Prester-Marshall Baine and King Korastine moved to where ribs and hull planks lay scattered like bleached bones. Turning back to gaze upon their followers gathered on the Aidenist side of the hill, both men raised their hands so everyone in the streets below could see them.

On the prow high above, two figures appeared in traditional Uraban garb, Soldan-Shah Imir and Ur-Sikara Lukai. Moving nimbly, like the captain of his kingdom, Korastine scaled the ladder to stand on the reinforced deck. Prester-Marshall Baine ascended behind him, carrying one beautifully illuminated document: a copy of the Edict. Ur-Sikara Lukai carried a similar one. Each document bore the same content, written in both languages.

Aboard the ancient ship, the holiest site of both the Aidenist and Urecari religions, the two political leaders and two religious leaders faced each other and spread out their documents. Anjine held her breath and listened.

King Korastine read in a booming voice: "This Edict removes

all cause for future conflict between our two lands. By drawing this line along the meridian of Ishalem, we split our world into equal halves, Tierra and Uraba, Aidenist and Urecari. All lands, known or unknown, to the north of this latitude shall fall under the purview of Tierra. All lands, known or unknown, to the south shall be encompassed by Uraba."

The sikara came forward to speak, as if she wanted to upstage the plump soldan-shah. Ur-Sikara Lukai's pronunciation of the Tierran words was rough, but understandable. "This is as Ondun wished it, the world split equally between the descendants of Urec and Aiden, while Terravitae — wherever it is — remains in the hands of Holy Joron."

Then she and Imir repeated the speeches in Uraban.

Having studied the maps of the known world, Anjine understood the consequences of this division. At first glance, the split did not seem particularly fair: The northern half of the Middlesea was above the latitude line, in Tierran territory, but the impassable mountains of Corag Reach blocked access from that direction. The only way to reach that coastline was by water, and the Urabans now controlled the Middlesea ports on the other side of the isthmus of Ishalem.

On the other hand, great portions of the map remained blank, unexplored. The islands of Soeland Reach hinted that there might be valuable lands to be found if one simply sailed farther west into the Oceansea. Urged on by Prester-Marshall Baine, Korastine had already decided to expand exploration, commissioning a special ship to sail beyond all charted territories.

Korastine spoke in the rich, resonant voice he had cultivated over a lifetime of speaking before crowds. It was paternal and sincere, and he lifted his eyes as if addressing distant Ondun rather than the gathered listeners. "This Edict is not merely a document. It is not a piece of parchment. It is not a list of words. It is my promise, as the king of Tierra, in the name of Aiden — a promise to be kept in calm seas and storms, an irrevocable vow." Korastine was a direct descendant of Aiden, and Imir traced his ancestry back to Urec. This treaty could never be broken, no matter what happened in the future.

Soldan-Shah Imir gathered his copy of the document and read the same words that Korastine had spoken, but in the Uraban language. Anjine could hear cheers and exotic musical fanfares from the Urecari side of the city.

After the terms of the Edict had been read aloud in both tongues, and the prester-marshall and the sikara each offered a prayer, Korastine took a small dagger, pricked the end of his thumb, and squeezed out a ruby drop of blood, which he pressed into the weathered wood of the Arkship's prow. "This agreement is sealed with the blood of Aiden."

He passed the dagger to Imir, who likewise cut his thumb and made a dark red smear next to Korastine's. "Sealed with the blood of Urec."

Each leader turned to his side of the hill and raised his hands to the crowds. "Let the celebrations begin!"

After the signing of the Edict, the two peoples began to accept the fact that there would be peace, but they didn't know how to rejoice together. King Korastine and Prester-Marshall Baine extended an invitation for Ur-Sikara Lukai to say a prayer with them inside the main Aidenist kirk — a prayer to *Ondun*, calling for His return, hoping that their demonstration of resolve was the final piece in the puzzle God was waiting for. No mention would be made of either Aiden or Urec.

Looking stiff and out of place, Lukai came into the kirk wearing her bold scarlet gowns. The prester-marshall and the ur-sikara stood together before the gilded fishhook in the worship area under paintings of Sapier and the sea serpent.

Though this was supposed to be a brief and private moment for the leaders of the two continents, Aidenists crowded the doors for the service. Soldan-Shah Imir was curious to see the architecture of the foreign kirk; clearly, neither he nor the ur-sikara had ever set foot inside an Aidenist house of worship.

King Korastine, with a thin scholar at his side who served as an interpreter, talked with his Uraban counterpart. "I'm glad we came to terms, Soldan-Shah. I have learned as a king that when you cannot win, you should cut your losses and compromise. The person who will not compromise in an untenable situation is a fool, not a leader."

Imir waited for the translation, then smiled and nodded. "We have finally found a way to peace."

King Korastine had already suggested building a Tierran harbor on the northeastern shore of Ishalem, which was technically above the Edict Line (although the soldan-shah seemed extremely uncomfortable at the prospect).

The two men agreed that their Edict was binding beyond any possible breach, because they had sworn in blood on the prow of the holy Arkship.

Across the city, Tierran merchants went to the eastern neighborhoods, meeting their counterparts in Uraban markets. They gazed at the Middlesea shore, which had traditionally been cut off from them. The people on both sides of Ishalem would celebrate far into the night.

When the prayers were finished inside the kirk, Ur-Sikara Lukai felt obligated to reciprocate, inviting King Korastine to the main church of Urec, so that he could walk the unfurling spiral to the altar. The services would be over well before sunset when the main worship began. The Tierran king was exhausted and drained, but triumphant about what he had accomplished for the world.

Direc na-Taya had never sold so many candles in a single day. The feasting, dancing, and singing had lasted through the heat of the afternoon and now past sunset. As the streets of Ishalem grew dark and the people were sated with food and fuzzy with drink, pilgrims became belatedly pious. They made donations to their respective churches, buying and lighting candles to shine a thousand lights up to heaven, so that if Ondun ever chose to return to the world, He could see His way back to Ishalem.

Within an hour, Urecari worshippers purchased everything the Saedran candlemaker had prepared beforehand. Now, in a crowded backstreet not far from the prime church, his small shop was filled with pots of melted beeswax and bubbling tallow; a framework dipped wicks into the wax, layering tapers, while larger molds held thick candles that hadn't hardened completely because the workshop was so stifling. Direc stoked his fires to keep the liquid bubbling, pouring molds as quickly as he could, splashing them with water so the wax would solidify.

As soon as he had another dozen candles ready, he cracked them free, used a small craftsman's trowel to whittle away the marks of the mold and to smooth the curling fern symbol. He had similar candles cooling that displayed the Aidenist fishhook, but he doubted he'd have time to run to the other side of the city and sell them. Direc na-Taya was having a very profitable day, indeed. These finished candles would fetch the unheard-of price of a *cuar* each.

Leaving his workshop behind, with vats of wax and tallow bubbling over low fires on stands precariously balanced amongst the molds, he rushed to the front of his shop and opened the slatted door to find a crowd clamoring for his candles.

"I don't have many," he cried. "Only twelve."

The customers offered handfuls of coins and shouted outrageous prices, which startled Direc. He realized that he would not be cheating them if they *offered* him that much money. He raised one candle, displayed the unfurling fern design. "Here is the first — who will bid for it?"

Someone shouted, "Two *cuars!*" Another cried, "Three!" The price finally stopped at five, and he took the money, unable to believe his good fortune. He raised the second candle, listening to another round of bids. At least by drawing out this process, his new batch would have more time to cool.

He sold the dozen candles and told the customers to wait, promising to return with more as soon as possible. "Please be patient — such work cannot be rushed. Pray or meditate while you wait."

Direc closed the door and took the time to lock his embarrassingly heavy pouch of coins in a safe cabinet next to his books before he hurried to his workshop. By now, maybe some of the tapers would be solid enough, though the thicker candles were definitely still too soft. But if he gently wrapped them, told the people to be careful, they might serve the purpose. . . .

Wiping sweat from his brow, Direc opened the door to his workshop, and an unexpected blast of furnace heat enveloped him. A wax block had melted, a brazier tipped over. Aromatic oil had splashed across the bench top, and flames had caught. He staggered back, eyebrows singed, hair smoking. He drew in a gasp, and the heat burned his lungs. He couldn't shout.

The back of his shop was crowded against many homes and vendor stalls, and the building quickly became an inferno.

The flames escaped into Ishalem.

8 *Ishalem*

The soldan-shah relaxed in his residence that evening with his beautiful wife. After enjoying a victory feast and drinking good Abilan wine, Imir lounged on cushions and stroked Asha's long hair. The caress tickled her, and she laughed like soft music. Imir felt languid and content. His wife was sweet and oh so lovely....

Caged songbirds produced a chirping cacophony without regard for whether anyone *wanted* to hear them sing. At least minstrels and court singers could be commanded to withdraw when he wanted a moment of peace.

Roaming freely throughout the Ishalem estate, more than a dozen cats had to be kept separate from the ever-present temptation of the caged birds. Asha possessed six little dogs that loved to sit upon her lap, trot from room to room behind her, bark incessantly, and chase the cats.

Then there were the four large and rambunctious hounds kept in a run outside the residence. These hunting dogs barked and bayed throughout the night, craving exercise, but Asha was no hunter; she simply liked the idea of having them. In a separate conservatory, a dozen potted mulberry trees fed Yuarej tentworms. Though Asha had silks enough, she delighted in the fluttering moths that emerged from the tentworm cocoons.

Imir's wife Villiki complained about Asha's privilege in having a separate home here in Ishalem, in addition to a private villa near the palace in Olabar. Villiki claimed he was spoiling his second wife, to the detriment of herself, his third. But it wasn't a matter of spoiling her. Imir was compelled to provide Asha's separate residences for his own protection, and his very sanity. He simply couldn't abide all the animal noise, the excremental debris, and the smells.

Now, as he relaxed with her, Imir felt pleased with the signing of the Edict. By the strict terms of the agreement, he could not prevent King Korastine from building his own shipyards and port on the eastern side of the isthmus. The soldan-shah no longer had any legitimate reason to deny them, though the uneasy Uraban merchants would not be keen to offer their cooperation. Aidenist ships on the Middlesea would fundamentally change the seafaring trade, but by the same token, Aidenist captains could no longer sail south of the Edict Line and trade with Uraban ports. Perhaps there would be some sort of balance. . . .

The street celebrations rang out even louder than the noises from Asha's animals. Tierran merchants roamed the streets on the eastern side of the city, singing boisterously, calling out to their new friends and business partners. Many new deals would be made in these heady hours as the golden possibilities occurred to former rivals.

Imir doubted he would get much sleep tonight. But because he was with a beautiful woman for the evening, he didn't want to sleep, anyway. . . .

Then, like the arrival of a sudden squall, the celebratory sounds changed outside. He detected a note of alarm amidst the music and cheering—outcries, then loud bells tolling. Next to Asha, he propped himself on an elbow, furrowed his brow.

A guard yanked aside the hanging doorway curtains without regard for ceremony or propriety. "Soldan-Shah!"

A breathless crier stood next to the guard, his robes disheveled, his face white with fear. "Soldan-Shah, the Urecari district is burning, and the prime church is in flames!"

Ignoring Asha's startled cry, Imir sprang naked from his cushions. The crier pointed toward the open balcony, where gauzy silk curtains whipped a bit more strongly than in the earlier breeze. Imir threw a sheet around himself and cinched it in a knot at his waist as he ran barefoot across the polished stone floor with Asha at his heels. They both gazed at a terrifying vista of flame rolling across the canals that wound through the Urecari District, a fire that leaped over the rooftops toward the holy shipwreck on the hill.

In the crowded Merchants' District near the prime church, fiery strands draped like spectacular gold necklaces flung in all directions. Flames licked up roofs, consuming the wood and awnings of the stalls of salt sellers, sandal makers, and leather craftsmen. Hot dry winds goaded the sparks and embers, and a veil of black smoke wafted into the air.

While Imir regarded the sight, speechless, Ur-Sikara Lukai pushed into the room past the guard, her face as angry as the spreading fires. "It was a trick, Soldan-Shah. Aidenists have set fire to our church! They mean to burn Ishalem! The Edict was simply a ploy."

Imir whirled, his fear giving way to anger. "Do you know this? Where is your proof?"

Lukai stalked onto the balcony and gestured toward the view. "The Aidenist District is not aflame—only ours!"

The courier added, his voice high and piping, "There was a brawl down by one of the wine sellers, an Aidenist merchant smashing bottles. King Korastine's soldiers joined in...and now the same area is on fire."

Imir's throat was dry. Everyone else down there would be drawing the same conclusions. Throughout the Urecari section of Ishalem, the flames continued to intensify...as did the outrage of the people.

*   *   *

Hearing the alarms and seeing the orange glow that silhouetted the majestic Arkship from the eastern side of the city, King Korastine summoned help. With the furious sirocco winds of the season, fire would race through the crowded, tinder-dry houses that were adorned with celebratory trappings and cloth banners.

Prester-Marshall Baine met the king outside the Ishalem royal residence, and the two moved into the streets at the head of a swiftly growing crowd. Roused from their beds, Anjine and Mateo hurried after them. Korastine bellowed commands to rally the people. "Get pumps to the canals! Bring buckets and washbasins! Hitch horses to wagons so they can haul barrels of water! There is no time to lose. We have to work together, or we will all be lost."

The prester-marshall used the passionate voice that had inspired thousands of followers, calling for faithful Aidenists to save their brothers under Ondun. Only if the people of Ishalem put aside their religious differences could they conquer the flames.

As the hastily gathered procession hurried across the city to the Urecari District, Korastine watched the increasing firestorm, which began to curl along the Pilgrim's Path up the hill, following the waves of dry grasses. Soon, flames would reach the sacred wreck of Aiden's Arkship.

Volunteers rushed through the narrow streets, shouldering wash buckets and half-full casks, driving carts barely balanced with heavy rainwater cisterns. But as the men and women raced toward the Urecari District, Korastine heard a rumble of ironshod hooves and defiant shouts. Horsemen wearing the blue head coverings of the Urecari guard and wide white sashes of Yuarej silk across their tunics, brandished long scimitars and charged headlong into the foremost Aidenist water bearers. They bellowed challenges in the Uraban tongue and struck down the first disbelieving people.

Korastine did not understand the shouted words, but hatred required no translation. His people screamed as weapons fell toward them in shining arcs, hacking them to pieces. The Aidenists dropped their buckets, spilled their water into the streets, and scattered in panic. "No!" he shouted. "No!"

Behind the first line of riders came other men bearing torches, which they flung onto the roofs of Aidenist buildings. Prester-Marshall Baine yelled for his followers to retreat, but they had already fled into alleys where the Urecari hunted them down.

Anjine grabbed her father's arm and pulled him back as the vengeful riders wheeled about and veered toward him. "Father, we've got to find shelter!"

Mateo balled his fists. "I wish I'd brought a sword from the residence. I'll protect you, Anjine. And you, too, Majesty." Taking action, he found the door of a sturdy warehouse and kicked it repeatedly until he knocked it open. He grabbed Korastine's sleeve. "Anjine, get inside. Majesty, hide here until the riders are past."

They all ducked into the building as the Urecari attackers passed them in a blind and senseless rampage, hurling torches to set the Aidenist Merchants' District alight. Inside the questionable shelter of the wooden building, Korastine clenched and unclenched his hands, watching in despair as the fire spread on both sides of the city.

9 *Ishalem, Urecari Main Church*

The flames were deadly, yet beautiful. The fires of faith, the test of truth. Prester Hannes saw it as purification rather than destruction. The vendor tents, craftsman shops, weaver stalls, calligraphers' shops, streaming banners, and crowded dwellings were nothing more than tinder piled up around the Urecari prime church. A bonfire for God! Perhaps, Hannes thought, Ondun needed to cleanse the world and remove the blight from His sacred city of Ishalem before He would return to His people.

Comfortably disguised in Uraban rags, Hannes hid in the alleys and watched the panic and chaos. He kept no fishhook pendant on his person, fearing that someone might see, but he always carried the symbol in his heart, along with the prayers he had memorized from the Book of Aiden.

While many of the Urecari fled down to the nearby harbor on the Middlesea shore, some people stayed and tried to fight the flames, beating desperately and ineffectually at the blaze with brooms and rags. Buckets of water sloshed onto stucco-and-wood buildings were mere thimblefuls against a conflagration. Orange fire washed up the building walls and caught on the rooftops. A basket maker's stall under a patched brown awning collapsed into blazing embers.

Shallow canals wound along many of the main streets, but this far inland, upslope toward the shipwreck hill, the water was stagnant and shallow, covered with fetid scum. These canals were mainly wide drainage gutters used for sewage and waste water and were not deep enough for the firefighters to use hand pumps.

The air was so hot Hannes could not breathe, and he covered his mouth with a dirty rag as he worked his way with determination to the prime Urecari church, heedless of his own safety.

Glancing over his shoulder, Prester Hannes watched in disgust as the Urecari fled before the blaze. Though their church was on fire, they did not stand and fight for it. How could they simply abandon their primary house of worship, leaving it to be consumed by the fire? While he had no love for the religion, the people, or their relics, he was most disturbed by their lack of *faith*. Were they not willing to give their lives to save their church?

Hannes, on the other hand, was afraid of neither pain nor death.

He circled the prime church and found a side door left ajar by some foolish acolyte who had run away. Hannes kicked it open the rest of the way, ducked his head, and rushed into the smoke-filled chamber. Fire had already climbed into the main worship center and begun to feed. The lead channels holding myriad bits of colored window glass had melted, and the jewel-like mosaics crumbled to pieces.

Inside, cloth pennants hanging from the high ceiling were wreathed in fire. One of the support timbers overhead had already burned out of its joint and collapsed in a great crash onto the spiral-path area where Urecari worshippers would wave the ribbons upon which their pleas were inscribed. With everything on fire, Hannes wondered if they still believed that Ondun could read the messages in the smoke....

Hannes stared ahead through stinging eyes and pressed forward to reach the altar in the middle of the spiral. He could think only of the amulet of Urec that the priestess had presented as the most sacred relic of the church, the amulet that Ondun Himself had supposedly given to Urec. Why had He not given it to Aiden?

Hannes would save the object from the flames and make his way back to the Aidenist kirk on the other side of the city. He would find Prester-Marshall Baine and present the most sacred object to his mentor. After spending years among them, Hannes had completed his mission here. He had learned much about the enemy.

On the wooden platform, the thick candles had melted in the heat, and he spied the amulet, surrounded by flames. On either side of the display stood ewers of sacred oil, which the sikaras used to fill their braziers. With a crack and roar behind him, another rafter tumbled into the nave, spraying flaming debris. Hannes knew he had to move quickly.

He tore part of his cloth sleeve to protect his hands and wrapped the fabric around the amulet; even so he could feel its heat burn his fingers... or perhaps it was a tingle of holiness. If Ur-Sikara Lukai's words were to be believed, Ondun Himself had touched this medallion.

Hannes took his prize, tucking the object securely into his belt. But when he turned to leave, he saw that the fire had advanced deeper into the church, catching all the structural beams on fire, melting the metal hinges on doors and windows. A heavy block broke loose from the arch above, triggering an avalanche of stones that crashed down onto the altar. The carved platform splintered and collapsed, sending the ewers of scented oil flying toward Hannes. He crouched to shield himself, but the oil dowsed his clothing, and the flames quickly caught the new fuel.

Screaming as the fire licked his skin and ignited his hair, he rolled on the floor, but the oil had covered his skin and soaked through his garments. Unable to put out the flames, he staggered back to his feet and ran blindly. He hit the stone wall hard and reeled along, beating his clothes with his hands until he reached a window that had already halfway collapsed. Unable to think, he plunged through the remaining glass, knocking the softened lead tracks free.

Outside in the alley, Hannes shoved himself away from the church, striking the walls of close-packed buildings. He didn't know where he was going, could not run from the pain. He pitched forward as the ground disappeared beneath him, and he slid down an embankment into one of the stagnant canals of brackish water. He splashed and rolled into the stinking sluggish current, desperate to extinguish the flames.

But even when the fire was out on his garments and skin, agony continued to scream through his nerve endings and his mind, never fading away.

10 *Olabar Palace*

The priestesses called it a bad moon over Olabar, hanging low in the sky with an orange cast caused by thin dust blown in from the Great Desert. *A bad moon.* From the sky, it seemed to threaten Zarif Omra like a raised fist.

He stood on the tower balcony, gazing across the many-tiered city, but not seeing it. He gripped the balustrade until his knuckles whitened, so engulfed in his thoughts and worries that he could barely breathe. His eyes burned until he remembered to blink. Still he continued to stare. Far off, he could see the deceptively calm waters of the Middlesea....

Istar had spent the day in an uneasy malaise, which had transitioned to nausea, horrific cramps, and crippling muscle spasms. While Omra was walking her up the long marble stairs to their chambers, letting her hold on to his arm, Istar had suddenly collapsed, moaning in pain. The silken skirts swirling around her legs began to seep a rich red.

Omra had shouted for doctors, demanded assistance, set the entire palace on alert. Now, as he stood outside in cold contemplation, he realized that the sikaras had not mentioned the omen of the moon until *after* Istar had been brought into her bedchamber, *after* the complications were painfully apparent. Now the sikaras pointed at the moon and nodded knowingly. What good was an omen if the priestesses could not warn him beforehand?

Omra closed his eyes against the stinging tears. He could not block the sounds from the bedchamber, the urgent whispered discussions of sikaras and midwives, the sudden sharp cries of his beloved. Istar had been on the bed for hours, but the women would not let him inside to see her.

He wrestled with impatience, terror, and anger. As the zarif of Uraba, he could have ordered them aside and pushed his way into the room, but if there was any chance the sikaras and midwives could help Istar or save the baby, Omra would do exactly what they said. He, the son of the soldan-shah and heir-apparent to all of Uraba, could do nothing but stand by and wait.

And wait.

The moon taunted him with its ruddy colors, hanging there against the midnight sky. A Saedran astronomer could have explained the phenomenon by saying that dust storms often muddied the skies, adding spectacular colors to sunsets, playing tricks with the eye. But Omra didn't care. Reasons and explanations did not matter to him.

Behind him, unmuffled by the silk hangings across the entryway, came another sharp scream, followed by a long and even more unsettling moan . . . then a silence that was infinitely worse. Hearing the approach of sandaled feet, the rustle of fabrics, he turned to face a sikara who held her news like a defensive weapon. Her elegantly coiffed hair hung in disarray, the strands dampened with sweat; her complexion was ashen.

In her arms, she carried a small object wrapped in cloth. Omra saw only the blood. "Your son has not survived, Zarif Omra. I am sorry."

He didn't know the sikara's name, didn't care. Omra stared at the crimson-splotched wrappings. The priestess hesitated, unsure, then moved the folds aside to show him the tiny head, small arms and legs, the twisted back, blotchy milk skin covered with a film of blood. His son—no larger than his hand.

It seemed unreal. Urgency flooded through him, and Omra shoved aside the priestess with her grisly offering and charged into the bedchamber. He ripped the hangings away as though they were phantoms, tearing them entirely from the hooks and casting them in a pile on the floor.

Desperate hope pulsed through him like a hot storm wind. Istar was his first wife, and this his first child, but they were both young. He and Istar would have other sons, as many babies as she liked. As the future soldan-shah, Omra needed to have many heirs. He would show Istar his love. He would nurse and watch over her until she regained her strength.

But when he saw her lying on the bed like a broken doll propped up by cushions, the sharp sword of reality ran him through. The death of the unborn infant was not the worst thing this bad moon had brought him. So much blood covered the sheets, the silks, the pillows, everywhere. The sikaras and midwives hovered over a motionless Istar like carrion birds expecting an imminent feast.

She was breathing, but just barely, her breaths thready and fast. The chief midwife looked at him, more disappointed in her own failure than stricken by genuine grief. Omra fell to his knees beside the bed and took Istar's hand. She stirred a little, eyes flickering as though she were summoning the last of her strength just to lift her eyelids.

One of the sikaras bent close. "There is nothing to be done, Zarif. The rest will be peaceful now. The pain is over. The child was just..."

Enraged, Omra pushed the red-robed woman backward and focused entirely on Istar. Sweat dotted her brow, and her face was oddly pinched. She breathed out a long sigh and just barely managed to form words. Only he could hear the voice that came from her bluish lips. "My love..."

Omra squeezed her hand and whispered to her, reassured her, lied to her. Istar didn't seem to hear. She did not open her eyes again, nor did she attempt to speak.

He remained there for more than an hour, *willing* her to hold on, until she finally passed the threshold into death. Still kneeling at Istar's side, he realized that he was alone.

11   *Saedran District, Calay*

Engrossed in the exciting new map he had purchased from Yal Dolicar, Aldo leaned against crates full of raisins from Erietta. He held the paper up to the sunlight so he could study the hand-drawn lines and mysterious landforms, coasts, islands, reefs. He absorbed everything in his perfect memory.

The information on this map would open a new window to the world and shed light on Ondun's secrets. As a chartsman, Aldo had already begun his sacred duty of illuminating the world; he could hardly wait to show the map to his father and take it to Sen Leo at the temple. With a spring in his step, he hurried home.

Aldo entered the house with a secretive smile and the rolled map tucked into his shirt. "I met a sailor at the docks," he blurted to his parents. "He's had an amazing adventure." His brother and sister came close as the young chartsman summarized what Yal Dolicar had told him; as if unveiling a great treasure, he spread the map on the wooden kitchen table, which was still dusted with flour from his mother's baking.

Biento slid the easel and canvas out of the way and set aside his paints to bend over the map. While Aldo could barely contain his excitement, his father frowned, his eyes darting over the drawn coastlines, reading the words written in an unsteady hand. The creases deepened around his mouth.

Aldo kept talking to counteract his father's unexpected reticence. "See, these islands — nobody knows about them, but with this chart, a good captain could find them again. Using them, we could step our way even farther across the oceans, expand our horizons, maybe even find the sunken continent. This could lead us to the original land of the Saedrans!"

Biento shook his head. "This map is a fake, son. You have been cheated."

Aldo had expected skepticism, but not such outright denial. "I heard the man's story. If he saw this with his own eyes —"

"You have been cheated."

His father's voice held such flat conviction that Aldo grew angry. He averted his eyes out of respect, but spoke assertively. "Sen Leo says that Saedrans should try to discover new knowledge, no matter what its source. This man was an unusual reservoir of information, and this map is unique. We should at least consider it, not just discard it outright."

"But you have let yourself be deceived." Broad shoulders slumped, Biento touched his wife's arm. "I'll take him to the temple. There is something Sen Leo has to show him."

Confused but insistent, Aldo held up the map. "But how can you *know?*"

Biento took his arm. "I will show you."

Deep in the Saedran District, the buildings crowded together and the close-knit people kept themselves apart from the Aidenist majority. The Saedran temple had a nondescript sandstone facade with engraved letters written in their private language. Outside visitors in the district wouldn't give it a second glance.

Inside the temple Aldo followed his father along a narrow hallway and down a short set of steps to a circular fellowship chamber where Saedrans attended weekly services. Now the place was empty; all the benches were bare, the floors scrubbed, and the book-laden shelves dusted for the next gathering.

Biento did not stop in the fellowship chamber, though. The far wall held a large mosaic showing the sunken land of the Saedrans. He ran his fingers along the tiles and pressed a particular garnet-colored square, which released a latch. A thin crack appeared along the line of the mosaic.

Aldo had been here countless times before, but now he was astonished. "What is this?"

"A secret only a chartsman can know. Few Saedrans have ever seen this room."

"But you aren't a chartsman."

Biento pushed the mosaic panel inward to reveal a hidden passage from which came the yellowish orange glow of oil lamps. He looked sideways at his son. "And where do you think you got the gift?"

From behind the secret door, Aldo felt a cool breeze, smelled dry air with a hint of mustiness and old papers. He followed his father down a sloping ramp. When they rounded a corner, Aldo stopped in awe.

The chamber was huge. In this hidden vault beneath the Sae-dran temple, maps covered the walls, and painted constellations sparkled across the curved dome of the ceiling. Such detailed paintings! Aldo saw the careful outlines of Tierra, the streets of Ishalem, the currents in the Oceansea, even the boundaries of the Middlesea on the other side of the isthmus. Densely writ-ten notations marked the landforms, uncertain outlines followed sketchy reports of possible islands, seasonal whirlpools, barrier reefs that had been sighted out near the horizon.

It looked nothing at all like the map Yal Dolicar had sold him.

He noticed sturdy mahogany tables piled with charts, log-books, and diaries. Compasses and protractors lay next to ink pots and paints. Staring at the dome overhead, he recognized the familiar constellations visible from Tierra, and as his gaze moved onward, he noted other star patterns, groupings he had seen only in books but never with his own eyes. One set of stars continued from another to another in a clear progression all across the painted sky.

Aldo turned slowly around, drinking in the impossibly mag-nificent work of art. He tried to take in everything at once. He marveled at the network of rivers leading from the highlands to the sea, the hills of Alamont, the plains of Erietta, the Soeland islands, the dense and cold Iborian forests, the impassible moun-tains of Corag. He felt as if the breath had been stolen from his lungs. He was looking at the *whole world.*

Belatedly, he noticed Sen Leo sitting in the room, watching him with a bemused expression on his face. The old scholar turned to Aldo's father. "Are you certain this isn't too soon for him?"

"He's a chartsman, after all," Biento said, then added, "And it was necessary. He needed to know what we already know. He's still very young and gullible." He nudged his son.

Aldo was not certain what to do or say as he sheepishly extended the fanciful map. "I ... I bought this from a sailor."

Sen Leo glanced at it for only a moment before shaking his head. "Completely inaccurate. A fantastical representation, with just enough known details to fool the unwary." He narrowed his eyes. "People like Aldo."

Holding Dolicar's fake map up to the landscape on the temple wall, Biento used a paint-stained finger to trace the outlines of real islands and the extended coast, pointing out how the two did not match. "Can you see now that this is completely fictitious? Look here, and here." He strode over to a different part of the wall. "And look, no islands exist in these waters. And where is this reef, and the two large islands here? The man who sold you this map was simply fabricating a story."

Aldo flushed. "It's so obvious." He turned his shame toward himself for being so easily fooled, but even that could not diminish the sense of wonder that surged through him now. He went closer to the walls, staring at the names of specific rock outcroppings, small patches of forest, lighthouses, villages. "But this — all this — is *known* and verified?"

"This is our Mappa Mundi," said Sen Leo, "the manifestation of the most sacred quest for all Saedrans — to discover the world, to map and record what we see. When our chartsmen return from far lands with new observations, we draw more lines on the map. Once we have succeeded in charting all of creation, Ondun will reward us by raising our sunken homeland."

"Is this the only Mappa Mundi?"

"Every Saedran temple has a secret map room." Biento looked at his son. "I am a cartographer. I don't sail off to far ports, but I have a chartsman's memory and knowledge, and I travel around the countryside to paint a perfect copy of the map in each temple. That's how we share information."

"But you said you painted commissioned portraits of nobles!"

Biento gave him a coy smile. "Oh, that merely provides a good excuse for me to travel so widely. Your mother knows the real reason."

Aldo couldn't tear his eyes from the map of the world. He saw the precise details in the Tierran continent, but noted the sketchier outlines of Uraba and the many blank areas beyond. "And we have no better information about this half of the world?"

"Parts of it, but not enough," Sen Leo said. "There are Saedrans in Uraba, but the Urecari won't allow us to interact with them. Their maps of Tierra are probably just as sketchy. With the signing of the Edict, maybe we can share information and work together at last."

12 *Ishalem, Urecari District*

Thickening smoke worked its hazy tendrils through the streets of Ishalem. The animals inside Asha's residence were disturbed, some frantic; the songbirds flapped against their cages, the hounds bayed. Most of the cats had already fled, and Asha couldn't find them, though she looked everywhere.

The soldan-shah burst back into their private quarters, his face flushed, eyes red and irritated from the smoke. Perspiration sparkled on his shaved scalp, and his voice cracked with alarm. "Asha, tell your servants to pack your things! Grab only the possessions you value most and get down to the docks—hurry! I have already sent men to prepare your ship for immediate departure to Olabar."

Asha was bewildered. "How can I possibly take everything? I'd need days to—"

"*Now.* Only what you need, only what you value the most, only what you cannot replace. You have less than an hour." Throughout their marriage, Imir had done his best to keep her happy. He denied Asha nothing and had never raised his voice to her—she'd given him no cause—but now he was brusque. "With the winds whipping up, nothing can stop this fire. Ishalem will burn to the ground."

Asha gasped. "But that's impossible! This is . . . this is *Ishalem!*"

Imir headed for the doorway. "One hour, Asha. Be on the boat, or be left behind."

"But if it all burns—"

"It *will* all burn. One hour." He marched into the corridor, and guards quickly folded around him.

Her small dogs wouldn't stop barking, and she shooed them away as she called for her handmaidens. The serving women had already recognized the danger and started throwing their own possessions into trunks and baskets. Now they flurried about gathering her silks and jewels with a grim efficiency.

From the balcony, Asha saw the fire advancing like a golden army, orange flames moving from street to street, sweeping up the side of the hill to the sacred Arkship. In the streets outside the residence, horsemen galloped, people shouted or screamed. Seeing that the Aidenist side of the city was also on fire, she was surprised that sparks could blow so far and so swiftly. Even the Saedran houses and shops had caught fire. The entire city! Imir had not exaggerated the danger, and she realized how little time they had.

"Forget the silly possessions! We must take my pets. Grab the bird cages. Put leashes on the hounds, and bring my little dogs in their baskets. Oh, how are we going to catch the cats?"

Asha turned around, desperate for help. "Get carters, find wagons — we'll make a procession down to the harbor. Our boat is waiting in the main canal."

The handmaidens were startled, their arms heaped with bright cloth, embroidered cushions, ornate golden ewers. "Go!" Asha cried. *"The pets!"* They burst into motion, though a few of them pocketed jewels and gold chains, not even bothering to be surreptitious about it. Asha didn't care, so long as they rescued the animals.

Asha joined the women, carrying two cages of shrieking birds out of the main entrance to a waiting cart. Despairingly, she called for her cats, but they did not respond. The little dogs yapped, poking their heads out of the baskets, but handmaidens nudged them back down. Well-muscled manservants struggled to lift the larger animal cages onto carts. The hounds pulled against the leather leashes, straining at their collars; one of the straps snapped, and the dog raced into the streets. Asha shouted after him, but the hound vanished into the smoke and chaos. The manservant looked at the frayed end of the leash. "Shall I catch him, my lady?"

"We cannot wait, Lady Asha," cried one of the handmaidens. Tears filled Asha's smoke-reddened eyes, and she knew the woman was right. Two wagons had already departed into the tortuous and crowded streets toward the harbor.

Nearby, the Urecari prime church was a towering bonfire, fueled by the sacred pennants and tapestries. Asha mumbled a prayer to herself for the church, for Ishalem; she couldn't believe Ondun would let this happen. How could Ishalem, the holiest city in the world, be allowed to burn to the ground? Only an hour before, she would have asserted that Imir's guards and soldiers could extinguish the flames, and that would be that. Now she doubted any man, even the soldan-shah, could save the city.

They fled the residence as the flames encroached. Making their way downhill toward the docks, they followed the choked drainage canals, until they reached a shallow-draft boat with a man aboard waving to them from the anxious crowds on the edge of the canal. "Lady Asha! Soldan-Shah Imir commanded me to wait for you. You and some of your party can ride with me!"

With her closest handmaidens, she crowded aboard while the rest of her servants took the heavily laden carts directly to her barge. She kept the voluminous birdcages with her. The manservants and two armed guards had to beat away desperate people who clawed and pushed, trying to board the small boat. Asha hated to leave them behind. "But...all these people! We should save them."

The manservants and guards were momentarily speechless; finally, one of the men gestured around to indicate their single small boat. "My lady, we cannot! Our orders are to save you."

Asha felt her heart lurch in her chest. The desperation of these poor people called to her. The people of Ishalem, faithful to Urec. They were only trying to escape the fire, having left every possession behind. But the guards were right—the boat had no room, not with her pets in their bulky cages and baskets. Two bright green parakeets squawked and fluttered against the bars. She was surprised to see that one of her cats had been caught after all, and now it yowled piteously, fur bristling.

Uneasy with the angry crowd, one of the soldan-shah's guards untied the painter, even as Asha tried to think of a solution. Before she and her handmaidens were fully settled, the boatman used a pole to shove his craft into motion, leaving the shouting crowd behind. Some of the people even cursed her!

"Wait!" Asha yanked out her birdcages. "I'll make room. We can save *somebody*." Since she and the soldan-shah had had no sons or daughters of their own, her pets had always been like her children. Now she opened the cages, shook the bars to force the squawking and frantic birds into the air, ignoring her deep sadness as they flew off into the smoky night. She knew she would never see them again. Asha tossed the cages overboard. "There, now take some children perhaps." She looked to the side of the canal, reached out her hands as they drifted past the terrified people.

But the guards ignored her. "I am sorry, my lady. We have to get you down to the docks." They refused to obey! Continuing to push the boat along the canal, the boatman picked up speed. The heavily laden craft scraped bottom from time to time, and two men had to push with poles to free them.

Barely able to breathe, she looked over the side of the boat as it drifted along the canal, forlorn. What would happen to all those people? If the whole city was going to burn, as Imir said, where would they go? She began to grasp the horror of just how many might die here this night. "No!"

Though the canal deepened as the boat drifted, the water was cluttered with debris and coated with an oily scum. Asha spied a burned man floating amongst the flotsam, his head above water, arms clinging to the side of the canal. His clothes were singed and in tatters, his face and hands covered with soot. Much of his hair was gone. And she saw he was alive.

"Wait! That man needs help!"

"We've already told you, Lady Asha. There is no time." The boatman looked up as a shower of sparks glittered above them in the night sky. "We cannot save him."

The man feebly lifted a hand, eyes closed, face drawn in agony. The cooling water of the canal must have saved him, but he would die soon unless a healer tended him.

"Stop! That is my order! We must save *someone*." The unwavering command that charged her voice sounded new and completely foreign to her servants. "We *will* take him. So many are being left behind, we can at least rescue this one."

"But, my lady," said one of her handmaidens, "if you save this one, you must save all of them, and you cannot."

"So I should just give up on everyone?" Asha straightened on her unsteady seat. "Urec would never forgive me for that—and you should pray for days to cleanse your mind of what you have just suggested!"

"I will pray that others will help them."

"He will likely die, Lady Asha," one of the guards warned. "He is badly burned, and these waters will have poisoned him."

Stubborn, she commanded the boatman to nudge the limp figure with his pole so that Asha's servants could reach him. Guards hauled the burned man over the gunwale, and Asha snapped imperiously to her horrified handmaidens, "Help them—we don't have much time!"

With clear distaste on their faces, the women clutched at the muddy black tatters that clothed the man's body. He groaned as they pulled him aboard, but he was deeply—and mercifully— unconscious. He retched, having nearly drowned in the shallow water. His skin was raw, red and black, but he breathed.

Asha thought of all the pets she had saved in the past, the animals she'd rescued—birds with broken wings, dogs with splinters in their paws, scrawny cats that had been tormented by evil boys—all of them lost causes, and yet she had healed them. "We *will* take him to the ship. We *will* tend him. I have doctors to heal his injuries."

"My lady, your physicians know how to care for animals. This man—"

"This man will survive," Asha stated bluntly.

Though the fire raged through the streets and the great church burned, she fixed her attention on this poor human being who needed her help. She could save this one man. It wasn't much, but it was a symbol of hope. Even if he healed, the pain would be terrible, the damage great, the probability of infection certain.

Nevertheless...

Picking up speed as it entered the wider canals, her boat finally reached the harbor, a scene of further chaos as every ship tried to depart at once, wide cargo barges, narrow galleys, fishing boats, small one-person pleasure craft. The soldan-shah had his own dromond loaded with soldiers and salvaged possessions.

Imir had arranged for Asha's ship to be waiting and ready for her at the dock, and she stepped onto the pier, rocking the shallow-draft boat. "Carry the pets' cages! Watch that the cat doesn't escape. He's the only one we rescued." She looked anxiously up the streets, searching for the carts loaded with her other pets. They should be arriving soon.

While her handmaidens and guards rushed to follow her instructions, Asha devoted her attentions to the poor burned man. She needed to get him aboard, bathe him in cool water, and use whatever salves her physicians had. Looking down at his grimace, his shut eyes, she could tell very little about the man, whether his burned clothes had been the rags of a beggar or the vestments of a rich merchant. Thanks to the soot and dirt, she couldn't even tell the true color of his skin or hair.

Aboard Asha's ship, her handmaidens gathered cushions in a pile so extravagant that even a dying man would have found them comfortable. They laid him out, careful of his wounds.

She leaned over the man and whispered, "You'll be all right. I will take care of you." She began to sing one of her favorite songs, soothing him with a ballad of Urec as her boat sailed away from the fires of Ishalem.

13 *Ishalem, Aidenist District*

Across the Aidenist section of the city, Urecari raiders raced at a gallop as they cast their torches at buildings, but the fire was a living being now and needed no help. Instead of fighting the conflagration, Korastine's soldiers struck down the Urecari attackers with spears, clubs, and arrows, killing hundreds.

The main Aidenist kirk was fully engulfed now. When its roof collapsed with a groan and a roar, flames belched from shattered stained-glass windows.

As guards rushed them out of Ishalem in an urgent procession to the harbor, Anjine's throat was raw, her heart heavy. They had abandoned the few things they'd brought with them from Calay. Mateo was anxious to fight the fire or kill the Urecari, but King Korastine refused to let either the young man or Anjine out of his sight. "This is not a game we play in the castle. Tonight we are witnessing what may be the beginning of the end of our world."

More and more people ran down from the streets, trying to get to the water as a refuge from the spreading flames, giving up on the city. Brisk, parched winds played across Anjine's face, swirling her light brown hair.

As soon as Prester-Marshall Baine and her father were escorted aboard the royal cog, with Anjine and Mateo following close behind, sailors struggled to raise the gangplank, pushing back any refugees who tried to crowd aboard. So many people swarmed on the docks that the boards creaked, and several people tumbled off the sides. One sailor swung a boat hook, knocking a man into the water. The shouting crowd grew louder and angrier.

With a voice already hoarse from the thick smoke in the air, Korastine ordered his men to stop. "I am their king! Take aboard as many of these people as the cog can carry. Bring their injured, their children."

A sound like a rush of relief passed through the crowd. Then their voices surged louder as they clamored for the limited spots aboard the king's ship, showing very little regard for giving priority to the wounded or the young. The panic and desperation on their faces was raw, palpable. Protectively, Mateo moved Anjine to the meager protection of the raised forecastle platform. During the chaotic few minutes while frightened, moaning people spilled aboard and packed the deck, Anjine looked at the lines of refugees searching for safety at the harbor's edge; she didn't think their numbers had diminished at all. Every one of them wanted to escape from Ishalem.

Now the king had no choice but to turn the rest away. Anjine could feel the weight in his voice as he told his men, "Detach the gangplank—we can take no further passengers." When the people on the docks refused to let go, still struggling to climb aboard, the sailors had to use axes to sever the ramp itself, letting it fall into the harbor. Crewmen slipped the knots from the pilings, used poles to push off, and the cog drifted out into the deeper water.

Already, people were streaming away from the city center into the scrubby hills or rushing along the coastal paths to flee the fire. Others climbed aboard any boat they could find. Suddenly orange flames rose along the docks as well. Many of the fishing boats that were crowded in slips began to blaze from spilled oil and thrown torches. Urecari raiders were intentionally burning the docks, cutting off any escape. Whistling and cursing, they rode off, though the wall of fire cut them off from the opposite side of Ishalem.

"They are so bloodthirsty and hateful!" Mateo seethed, watching them. "How could we ever have tried to make peace with animals like that?"

Anjine felt just as furious, although she wondered if vengeful Aidenists had done the same thing on the other side of the city, racing in to torch any Uraban boats in the Middlesea harbor.

The fire roasted the night sky with a coppery glow. On the steep and sacred hill, bright flames silhouetted the lines of the Arkship. Aiden's ancient vessel had rested there for all of history. Now it was dying in one night. Anjine could not tear her eyes away. A great gasp went up from all the rescued people aboard the royal cog as the remaining timbers of the huge Arkship collapsed in a burst of embers and flame.

"May the Compass guide us," Baine said in a low whisper.

Anjine took Mateo's hand, and he was too angry to be embarrassed about it. "We're the last ones to have seen the glory of Ishalem."

The unpredictable winds, combined with fire-borne gusts, propelled ash into the air to land all about the cog and its passengers. The world was now muffled, transformed into an eerie otherworldly landscape by the falling soot. There was no sound but the wind and the fire and the distant screams.

She realized she was weeping. She turned to the king, searching for some hint of hope and reassurance. How could she ever face such terrible events when she became queen? "We can never fix this, can we, Father?"

Korastine stared past the bow into the inferno. He kept his voice low, as if he didn't want the rest of the refugees to hear him. "No, we can never fix it." He looked haunted. Pale ash settled into the lines of his face and on his hair, making him seem a much older man. His voice was scratchy and rough. "Now there will be generations of war . . . the worst war our world has ever seen."

Part II

Two Months Later

14 *Outside of Calay Harbor*

The small boat scudded northward up the coast, dancing across the white-capped waves, a square sail straining on her single mast. The salty breeze was invigorating, full of speed rather than storms. At the tiller, smiling as the wind whipped the brown hair from his face, Criston Vora pointed out the mouth of the harbor ahead, which was mostly hidden by headlands.

"There's the entrance to Calay, Adrea. Once we're past the lighthouses and inside the harbor, then you'll see it for yourself..." He let his silence fill in the rest of the details.

Standing close to him on the rocking deck, Adrea smiled back. "You've made Calay sound as magical as Terravitae. Now I'll see if my husband is an astute observer of details, or just a teller of wild stories."

"Which would you prefer?"

"Hmm, each has its advantages. I'd like a dash of both."

Adrea's hair was a shade darker than yellow; her delicate cheekbones, pointed nose, and narrow chin gave her an ethereal presence. When Criston had first noticed the girl in Windcatch, he had thought she was a water spirit washed up on shore. Adrea had laughed when he'd called her that during their courtship, and he had loved her laugh.

Before his brief voyage to Ouroussa with Captain Shay, Criston had taken his small boat on several trips from Windcatch to Calay, delivering loads of preserved fish, processed seaweed, or kelp liquor. Each time, he'd returned home with stories about the capital city.

Coming home after the Uraban attack on the *Fishhook*, Criston had finally married Adrea, pleased with his sailor's pay and worried about the possibility of war against the Urecari. Although large-scale politics did not affect the daily life of the Windcatch villagers, Criston still needed to support his family. He had made three more trips to Calay in his cargo boat in the four months they had been married, and this time he had promised to take Adrea along.

Now that he'd made the difficult decision to sign aboard a new sailing vessel, with Adrea's blessing and encouragement, he was going to be gone from home for a long time — if Captain Shay would have him again. He wanted her with him for every possible moment.

Of course, they weren't exactly alone. Adrea's brother worked his way out of the cabin, where he'd been napping. He rubbed sleep out of his eyes and looked around in surprise. "Are we almost there?" He moved across the deck with the balance of a seasoned sailor on a rolling sea, despite his heavy limp.

"We were planning to wake you up before we sailed home," Adrea said.

Ciarlo, two years Adrea's junior, had suffered a severely broken leg when he was nine years old. The bones had never set properly, and now he walked with a pronounced limp. He dreamed of being a sailor, as did all young boys from Windcatch, but his movements were so ungainly that no fisherman wanted him aboard. They needed agile sailors to scramble up the rigging and stand balanced on narrow yardarms; one fisherman had rudely opined that he did not need another anchor aboard his boat.

Criston could understand the young man's dream. He had spent most of his life on the sea, aboard boats, learning the nuanced language of sail, current, and wind, but he longed for adventure rather than simply going out to the same waters and coming back every day. The sea had called to him most of his life, and even his unsettling encounter with the Urecari pirates had not made him want to stay home.

When he had asked Adrea to marry him, flush with his payment from the *Fishhook* voyage, she had accepted on the condition that he take her brother into his home as well. Upon learning what his sister had done, Ciarlo was extremely upset. "I don't want to be a burden to you! I can find work."

Adrea did not let him sway her resolve. "You are not a burden — you're my brother." She and Ciarlo had raised themselves with very little help from their mother; Adrea knew how to keep her family together.

Ciarlo had accompanied them on this voyage for practical reasons. If Criston did manage to secure a place in the new ship's crew, he'd have to sell his boat so that Adrea would have enough money for the year he'd be gone, and he didn't want her to make her way back south to the fishing village alone. She and her brother were perfectly comfortable traveling together.

Now Criston tied off the sail and adjusted the tiller. He had built this craft himself, staking his catch and cargo against the large debt he had incurred purchasing the materials. He had named the boat *Cindon* after his fisherman father, who had vanished in a storm at sea, his boat lost with all hands. His mother, Telha, was a sea widow, like so many others.

At the mouth of Calay Harbor stood a pair of identical lighthouses built from stone blocks and each etched with a massive figure, the northern lighthouse showing Aiden and the southern tower depicting Sapier, grandson of Aiden and the founder of the Aidenist religion. The two lighthouses showed the light of Aidenism, and the sight was quite awe-inspiring for visitors to the capital.

The sheer number of fishing boats, sloops, and cogs indicated that a populous city lay within, like a hidden treasure. He noted at least six military ships with long, sharp beaks at the bow for ramming enemy vessels. "I've never seen so many patrol boats."

Adrea shaded her eyes, scanning the waters. "After the burning of Ishalem, who knows what the Urecari will do?"

When the *Cindon* entered the sheltered bay, the water suddenly grew calmer. Calay was a perfect harbor: Like splayed fingers, inlets of deep water protruded inward, offering countless safe anchorages. Spits of land between the inlets divided the city into separate districts, making Calay a mosaic of different architectures, colors, and smells. The districts were connected by bridges, each built uniquely by the merchants, the rivermen, the farmers, the Saedrans, or the military.

In the Royal District, atop a rise overlooking the harbor, stood the stone castle of King Korastine. Covered with barracks, armories, and parade grounds, the Military District watched over the northern peninsula, while the Merchants' District comprised the southern peninsula, a place for incoming traders to unload exotic cargoes. Warehouses crowded the wharves at the waterline.

Criston was pleased to watch the expressions of Adrea and Ciarlo as they sailed into the colorful bedlam. "You underestimated the wonders by half," she said. "I never imagined the size, or the number of people, or all the buildings!"

Her brother added, "The whole population of Windcatch would vanish into one district here."

Criston did not immediately guide the *Cindon* to a public marina in the Merchants' District, where he could rent a slip, tie up the boat, and unload his cargo of salted fish. "I've got something else to show both of you first."

He passed under the bridge that linked the Saedran District

to the Royal District and entered the narrow Shipbuilders' Bay. Stripped logs floated against the shore, and up on land sawmills whined. Four different dry docks held the keels and ribs of ships under construction. Many piers extended into the water, piled with lumber, ropes, barrels of caulk and tar, and wooden derricks, blocks and tackle, cranes.

On his previous trip to Calay, Criston had learned of a great project begun by King Korastine and inspired by Prester-Marshall Baine. To launch a golden age of exploration, ship designers had crafted a new type of vessel for long voyages, with three square-rigged masts in contrast to the single masts used for sloops and fishing boats, or the two-masted cogs that were adequate for coastal trade. The new ship was named the *Luminara,* "to shine light on the dark corners of the map."

The *Luminara*'s charter was to voyage outward and return in a year, to explore the unknown and discover new lands for Tierra. Since the Edict divided the world in half, King Korastine hoped to find uncharted islands, perhaps even new continents that lay above the latitude of Ishalem. In the aftermath of the great fire, the need was even greater, the necessity for hope undiminished.

The king guaranteed high pay for all seamen aboard the *Luminara* — enough to make Criston a wealthy man when he returned to Windcatch. He had talked with Adrea, and though it pained them both to be parted so soon after being married, Adrea was a wise and practical woman; she could read his dreams as easily as he could read the currents in the sea.

"You can't pass up this opportunity," she said. "Let's consider it an investment. Ciarlo will take care of me."

"We'll take care of each other," her brother said.

"And I need you both to take care of my mother," Criston said.

He loved Adrea all the more because she could see how much

this meant to him. The *Luminara* was the first purely exploratory ship Tierra had ever launched. If this voyage proved successful and they did find rich new territories, there would be other such expeditions... but there would be only one *first* voyage. And Criston wanted to be on it so badly that his heart ached.

As his small boat passed deeper into Shipbuilders' Bay, Criston saw the breathtaking ship under construction. The *Luminara* looked like music on the water, a graceful sculpture of curved wood and soaring masts. Teams were laying the rigging and stretching the shrouds like a delicate cat's cradle of ropes, ratlines, and pulleys. Mountains of white sailcloth lay folded on the decks as sailmakers cut and stitched large rectangles of fabric, adding eyelets, threading ropes. Though the three-masted carrack was huge compared to the fishing boats Criston knew, the *Luminara* was also delicate, a ship poised to glide across the Oceansea.

"She's beautiful," Adrea breathed.

"We didn't arrive any too soon." He was amazed at how far the construction had come. "It looks like the *Luminara* will be ready to sail within a week."

15 *Calay*

Two months after the burning of Ishalem, the last of the Uraban diplomats and merchants were evicted from Calay. A wave of raucous jeers and threats came from the people crowding the wharves and docks of the city.

Feeling both angry and sad, King Korastine watched as royal guards escorted the foreigners from their holding barracks.

Some departing Uraban merchants already stood on the decks of the two ships ready to cast off. The soldan-shah's diplomats ignored Korastine's escort, ignored the hurled insults from the crowd, and walked along the wooden pier to the waiting ships. They looked happy to be leaving Calay.

"By my command and by the Grace of Aiden," Korastine announced to the Urabans, "your lives have been spared." The king stood on the docks, wearing formal robes and his crown. "Tell your soldan-shah that we can neither forgive nor forget what the Urabans have done, not the deaths of my people, not the burning of Ishalem."

The diplomats shouted a response in their own language, which no one bothered to translate. Korastine didn't care to know what they were saying; the meaning was clear enough. He had hoped for such an entirely different outcome when he and Imir had signed the Edict. But after what he had seen that night, there could be no turning back....

His ship had sailed back to the capital, while to the south the smoke remained like a giant pillar in the sky for days afterward. On the voyage, Korastine had begun to form plans to fortify his defenses. Sitting on the deck for hours, he talked with Anjine, telling her ideas as they formed in his mind. Though she was still young, he considered it imperative that she understand the difficult decisions a leader must face.

His advisers, the people, the presters, the traders, all of them made the same demands. As king, he should have been able to make the choices *he* wanted, not the choices that circumstances pushed him into. Korastine could no longer abide trade with Uraban merchants, and the five reaches of Tierra would have to look to their own mines, farms, rivers, and grazing lands in order to produce what the people needed.

Immediately upon reaching Calay, Korastine issued orders

for his guards to round up all Uraban diplomats in the Royal District. The news of the fire had not yet spread throughout the city, but from that day forward, every follower of Urec had to be considered an enemy and a potential spy.

City guards isolated indignant and confused Uraban merchants, herding them to a separate area in the Merchants' District. Korastine ordered their goods "temporarily" confiscated, their ships impounded until he could make his decision. He did not want to keep these men in Calay, but he feared he might need hostages. Soldan-Shah Imir was sure to do the same—or worse—as soon as he got back to Olabar.

The stuffy veteran leader of the Tierran military, Comdar Delnas, dispatched the available warships to turn back any vessels showing distinctive Uraban sails. Many such merchants had been sailing for weeks from ports in Outer Wahilir, working their way northward from one stop to the next, unaware of the destruction of Ishalem. When their ships were boarded and King Korastine's proclamation was read to them, the Uraban merchants expressed disbelief and outrage, sure that the Aidenists were to blame.

Their cargoes could just as easily have been taken as prizes, but the king issued orders that the men were to be sent home, unharmed, in hopes that the soldan-shah would follow the same rule. He feared, though, that any Aidenist trader who pulled into a Uraban port city would suffer a harsher fate.

In the following weeks, Korastine dispatched scouts down to Ishalem, and they reported news as grave as he had expected: The out-of-control fires had burned Ishalem virtually to the ground, eradicating the shrines, the main Aidenist kirk, the merchant districts, the royal residence. Nothing but charred fragments remained of the Arkship. The Urecari side of the city was also destroyed.

Now, on the day of the final eviction from Calay, when the

last foreigners had boarded their ships, Korastine gave orders for the exotic-looking vessels to cast off. Hooting crowds followed the drifting boats, throwing horse dung and rotten fruits at the decks. Though they were clearly furious, the departing Urabans held on to their dignity as their ships headed toward the mouth of the harbor, closely escorted by Tierran military vessels until they were out in the open sea.

Korastine had hoped to feel relief now that the decision had been made and implemented. But his heart remained heavy and unsettled.

Returning to the castle, Korastine passed through the gauntlet of courtiers, functionaries, and servants, and headed to his withdrawing room. Through long habit, he wanted some time in private after his public appearance and prior to his afternoon meetings.

For the rest of the day he would sit with representatives of the destrars, the leaders of each of the five reaches, all of whom brought their local problems and complaints — none of which could match the far greater crisis that faced their entire world. Unable to see the potential wealth that exploration could yield, the destrars complained about the increased taxes Korastine had levied to pay for constructing the *Luminara*. They also complained when he built houses for the healers and shelters for poor dockworkers. In some things, he could impose his will.

Construction of the exploratory ship had begun well before the signing of the Edict. Some might have said that after the burning of Ishalem, the terms of the Edict were no longer in force, but Korastine refused to think that way. He and Soldan-Shah Imir had sworn an oath. They had pressed their *blood* into the helm of the Arkship. Their promise was sacred before God and binding upon their souls.

Prester-Marshall Baine had preached a "new revelation" from the Book of Aiden to the hundreds who gathered for services in Calay's large Aidenist church. Holding up Aiden's command that all people should "learn and remember Ondun's glory," Baine interpreted the Law of Laws to mean that humans should engage in *discovery* rather than rote memorization.

Many presters were uneasy with this shift in focus, wanting to stay in their small village kirks and preach what had always been preached, what they themselves had memorized. But Baine's enthusiasm was infectious. "For the longest time, we believed that Aiden's arrival at Ishalem was the end of our journey. But what if this is only the beginning? What if our whole continent is merely a stopping point on the great voyage of destiny?"

With his forceful personality, he excited a sense of wonder in his listeners. He made people dream again. And he had the ear of the king....

Korastine removed his crown and set it on his writing-desk, then pulled off his heavy embroidered robe, though an army of servants would have liked to assist him with the dressing and undressing chores. His ruffled linen shirt was formal enough for the rest of the day.

His bedchamber had seemed quiet and empty since the death of Queen Sena. Now, hearing a rustle in the library alcove, he called out, "I am ready for you, Sen Leo. Advise me before the destrars come and harry me like birds fighting over a sunflower head."

The Saedran scholar emerged from the alcove, absently carrying one of Korastine's books. Though Sen Leo had thousands of volumes of his own, he was always engrossed in Korastine's books when he came to visit. The king enjoyed speaking with the

Saedran scholar both before and after difficult meetings. He was one of the wisest men Korastine knew.

"The *Luminara* is nearly ready to launch, but the destrars will resent their share of the cost until they actually see gold come back into their treasuries," the king said. "It'll be a year before the ship is due to return."

"Destrars complain—it is a fact of life," Sen Leo said with a snort. "They look at their crude maps, and because they see no islands or coastlines, they assume nothing is there, just the edge of the world."

Korastine slumped into his high-backed chair. "Don't belittle their concerns. Because of the Ishalem fire, we'll have to build up our military, construct a more powerful navy, recruit many more soldiers. Perhaps they are right that we can ill afford such an expensive discretionary venture now."

Sen Leo was alarmed. "We can ill afford to forsake it, Majesty! As you say, the ship is nearly done. Further expenditures will be minimal." He shook his head and extended a large-knuckled finger, as if scolding imaginary listeners. "Besides, their investment paid for barely half of the expedition. Without the help of my people, you would never have begun the project in the first place."

Private Saedran treasuries had secretly funded a large share of the *Luminara*. Though quiet and unobtrusive, the Saedrans had amassed huge fortunes, and Korastine was amazed at how easily Sen Leo delivered chests of gold for the project.

Now he leaned forward and met the old scholar's eyes. "Why are your people so interested in a voyage of exploration? You cannot hope to recoup your investment. You aren't a merchant."

"Ah, but we will profit in knowledge. Who can place a price on the new things we might learn?"

Korastine frowned. "Now you sound like Prester-Marshall Baine."

The scholar gave him a mysterious smile. "Where do you think Prester-Marshall Baine got the idea in the first place?"

16 *Calay Harbor*

The next morning, freshly shaved and wearing the best clothes he had brought from Windcatch, Criston made his way to Shipbuilders' Bay and the construction dock that held the *Luminara*. The spicy fragrance of fresh Iborian pine clashed with the bitter lacquer and caulking tar. Once aboard, he made his way to the stern and knocked at the door of the captain's cabin. He heard a man's voice call for him to enter.

Captain Shay sat at a small writing desk crowded with books and charts, a measuring stick, an ink pot, and several quills. The cabin walls held numerous sketches, detailed anatomical drawings of dissected fish, plump aquatic worms, unusual undersea plants. One intricately drawn picture showed a seagull's wing with its feathers splayed, each type labeled. A collection of unusual seashells lined one of the narrow shelves, tacked down with wax.

He stacked his papers and turned to look at Criston, smiling in surprise. "Ah, Mr. Vora! You've come back." Ink stains covered his fingers.

"I would like to sail aboard the *Luminara*, sir." He stood ramrod straight. "I'm glad you remember me from the *Fishhook*."

"And I'm glad to see that our little adventure didn't turn you into a landsman. We won't be seeing many Urecari pirates where we're going this time."

"That would be fine with me, sir. We'll see other interesting places."

The captain motioned for him to take a small wooden stool. "This isn't a week-long voyage, like the other one. Tell me why I should let you join my crew."

"Because I'm a good sailor and a hard worker. I understand currents, I know how to weather storms, and I can catch the faintest breath of breeze in a dead calm."

"Impressive." A smile quirked Shay's lips. "Maybe you should be the *Luminara*'s captain instead of me."

Criston wondered if he had bragged too much. "My father was a fisherman, sir. He died in a storm."

"Many fisherman die in storms, and we're bound to encounter plenty of storms ourselves, as well as things we can't even begin to imagine."

Criston nodded. "I'm ready for the storms, sir, and anxious to see what else the seas have to offer."

Shay rocked back in his chair. "Aren't you terrified of the unknown? Most people are."

"The unknown doesn't have to be frightening. There'll be wonders, too."

The captain chuckled. "I'd say that qualifies you to join the *Luminara*'s crew. And, as I recall, you were the first to spot Fillok's plot as we approached Ouroussa, so I could certainly use you. But what does your family think? You'll be gone a whole year — *if* the voyage goes as planned. Your father's dead, you say. What about your mother? I can't remember from before — are you married? Any children?"

"I have a wife, and I have a mother. They both support my decision." Leaning forward on the stool, Criston put his elbows on his knees and spoke in an earnest voice. "When I was only thirteen, my father bought his own fishing boat. He'd worked for most of his life as part of another man's crew, and he wanted to be a captain himself, to have something of his own. He went into a great deal of debt to have his own vessel, but I saw how happy it made him. He was on top of the world!" Criston glanced at the colorful shells, the naturalist drawings, the unrecognizable potted plant hanging from a hook near the latticed window of the cabin. "And one night the fishing boat vanished. It might have just been a storm, or it might have been the Leviathan.

"The loss of that boat left us nearly destitute. We had no way to pay back the loan, so I lied about my age and signed aboard other boats. I worked hard, I took care of my mother, and eventually—seven years later—I commissioned my own boat. When I told my mother what I intended to do, she didn't want me to follow in my father's footsteps. She didn't want me to be lost at sea."

"I doubt any mother does, young man."

"To save money, I did most of the work with my own hands. And now we'll sell the boat so that my wife and mother can live on the money while I'm gone. Then, when the *Luminara* returns, I'll buy an even bigger boat."

"Very ambitious."

"I can do it."

The captain opened a large logbook on his desk, dipped a quill in the inkwell, and handed it to Criston for his signature. "Welcome to my crew. We sail in six days."

While Criston went to the *Luminara,* Adrea and Ciarlo attended to business of their own. Though Calay was a strange place to them, Adrea wasn't afraid to ask questions, and she could be bold when she needed to. She talked to dockworkers; she stopped at taverns; she asked about captains who were without ships. She searched for men who might want to buy the *Cindon.*

Before departing to present himself to Captain Shay, Criston had taken a long slow walk around the deck of his boat, touching the rails, the Captain's Compass, the hatches. He ran his fingers along the sailcloth, tugged on the secure knots, as if saying good-bye. Adrea knew how much effort and love he had put into this boat, how he had spent his nights sanding the hull, pounding in caulking ropes, lacquering surfaces exposed to the weather. But sailing with the *Luminara* meant even more to him. She had no doubt in her mind that he would secure a position on the crew, and if he did he would have to sell the boat.

After Adrea and Ciarlo had made many inquiries, three men came to see the *Cindon*. One was a drunkard, and Adrea doubted he had enough money to buy a sail, much less a boat. He poked around and made insulting comments, gave a rude scowl to Ciarlo, as though to convince himself that he didn't really want a boat that he couldn't afford anyway.

The next was a gaunt older man with long hair and a full beard. He had been a sailor in his youth, but when his older brother died, he'd been forced to stay home and manage the family pottery shop. Now his own sons were old enough to do the work, and the old man still felt the call of the sea; he wanted a boat of his own, but he could not afford Adrea's terms.

The third man was a rich merchant searching for an invest-ment. She haggled enthusiastically to reach an agreement with him; then she talked him into business terms with the wistful old sailor. The sailor would be the captain, and the merchant would take a share of the profits. As part of the deal, Adrea insisted that the old sailor grant her and Ciarlo passage back to Windcatch — if Criston was accepted as part of Captain Shay's crew. She had all the details taken care of. The high selling price further eased the sting of having to surrender the boat. Her brother was quite pleased with the result.

When Criston rushed back to the *Cindon*'s slip in the marina, he was grinning, his boyish face extraordinarily handsome. Adrea kissed him before he could even tell her his news. "I knew the captain would accept you."

He wrapped his arms around her waist and pulled her close. "And how did you know? Even I wasn't sure."

"I *knew*, because you belong there."

17   *Olabar Palace*

The death of Istar so devastated Zarif Omra that he had little grief to spare when word arrived about the burning of Ishalem. The soldan-shah's galley had arrived in port, bringing the terrible news. In the streets of Olabar, the people shouted their fury at the Aidenists and flocked to the churches to hear the sikara priestesses demanding retribution.

Omra did not feel that passion, though. He could think of nothing beyond the loss of his wife.

He had declared a week of mourning in the city and spent a full day in silent vigil at his wife's side, holding conversations with her that she could not hear. Istar's body had been washed, perfumed, and wound in Yuarej silk dyed orange, her favorite color. The small half-formed baby was cradled in her arms, also wrapped in silks.

With the heat of the season, the funeral could not wait. The young sikara Fyiri—who had previously blessed the pregnancy—completed the rites, lighting the pyre that rapidly consumed Istar's lovely body. Omra was barely able to see through the tears in his eyes, but when the smoke finally cleared and nothing remained of her but ashes, he had dried his eyes and emptied his heart....

Barely settled in back at the palace, Soldan-Shah Imir called an immediate war council. He summoned representatives from the soldanates of Missinia, Yuarej, Inner and Outer Wahilir, and Abilan. Ur-Sikara Lukai spoke for the church, her words sharp and strident, for this was to be a religious war (or so she insisted). The merchant families demanded to know what was to become of them if they could no longer trade in Tierran goods.

As the heir to the soldan-shah, Omra was required to participate in the intense discussions, but his thoughts were obscured by the veil of his grief and the sharp pain of his loss. He saw the palace around him, the city of Olabar, the whole world, in a different light. Details were sharp, but the colors had faded.

The zarif dutifully sat by his father's side at the long table, saying nothing even as voices were raised, shouts layered upon shouts. He gave the appearance of listening to the debate, his expression cold, but he could not bring himself to care. When the spokesman for Outer Wahilir demanded that a large portion of the treasury be diverted to his soldanate, since a new Uraban fleet must be built there (and because the murder of city-leader Fillok by the Tierran captain had not yet been avenged), the representatives of the other soldanates nearly came to blows. Still, Omra did not rise from his seat.

His father looked at him, growing more and more disturbed. Finally, Imir rose and bellowed, "Leave! All of you. I must speak with Zarif Omra."

The delegates were shocked, and an indignant Ur-Sikara Lukai insisted on staying, but the soldan-shah shooed them all out of the room. Preoccupied with their own worries, none of them had noticed any difference in Omra's demeanor.

When they were alone, Imir resumed his seat, folded his

ringed fingers together, and spoke sternly to his son. "You are my heir. You will be the next soldan-shah. Do these matters bore you?"

For Omra, even raising his head felt like lifting a great weight. "Few matters interest me. My wife is dead."

"So get another wife. Countless women would be happy to marry you. You should have had more than one wife by now anyway — then you wouldn't be moping around so uselessly."

His father's callousness ignited a flicker of anger in Omra's chest. "I said, my wife is *dead*. My son is *dead*."

"It is a sad fact of life, my son, but women die in childbirth all the time, just as men die in battle. You can have more sons, but only if you have more wives. Remember the story of Urec and Fashia. It is your obligation."

Omra's throat was dry. Yes, it was his obligation. As the son of the soldan-shah, he had many obligations.

Although Urec's wife Fashia had accompanied him on his voyage from Terravitae, she was unable to conceive a child. Since he was the son of Ondun, Fashia insisted that Urec take other wives so that he could spread his family when they reached the new world. But Fashia did not surrender her role as his first wife.

When his exploration ship landed on a new continent and Urec tried to befriend the original Urabans, those natives did not know Ondun, and they received the newcomers with violence. They tried to murder all the people on the ship, and Urec's sailors fought back. After much killing on both sides, the surviving natives finally accepted the word of Ondun and made peace.

Because there were so many more women than men after the slaughter, Fashia suggested that *all* of Urec's surviving crewmen also be allowed to take more than one wife, provided that the women were willing and provided that the men could care for their wives. Only that way could they populate the land that Ondun had promised.

But Zarif Omra could not think of other women. His thoughts were haunted by memories of Istar whispering in his ear, Istar coming to watch him hold court during his father's absence, Istar braiding her hair. She had loved Omra not because of the power and wealth he embodied, but because of who he was. All the reasons for taking multiple wives seemed cold and political to him, having little to do with love.

And yet he would be the next soldan-shah. Obligations...

His father was actually in a jovial mood. Imir had declared a halt to further council meetings, much to the consternation of the other participants, insisting that he needed to take care of other matters first. Omra suspected that his father was glad to apply himself to a problem with a real and immediate resolution.

Though Omra could hear whispers and the rustle of clothing in the tiled corridor outside his opulent private quarters, the soldan-shah sat on a cushion in front of him, holding a private conversation with him. "I have not told you this, Omra, but your mother suffered two miscarriages as well. I commiserate with the pain of your loss. But eventually Lithio gave birth to you—and you were definitely worth waiting for."

Imir lounged back. "Your mother was my best choice when I was young, and she is still very special to me, though I haven't seen her in years. All three of my wives are special to me. Asha, who is so sweet and beautiful...Villiki, who knows so much about court politics that she could have been a soldan-shah herself. She has already spoken to me twice since I've returned, stating that because of your grief you are no longer fit to be zarif and that our son Tukar should take the role instead."

Omra made a scoffing noise. "She always speaks like that."

His father continued, as if he didn't want to lose track. "You must make similar choices, my son. Hundreds of women across Uraba would claw one another's eyes out to be your next wife."

"I don't want women who would claw one another's eyes out to have me."

"You have a point—that may not be the best criterion. But if you choose several wives, one of them may make you as happy as Istar did. I know you don't think that now, but trust me, when you've been with enough of them, most women are very much the same."

The soldan-shah clapped his hands, and the hangings stirred with a clicking rush of beads. Two silent guards ushered in a petite young woman followed by three smiling and self-satisfied-looking officials. The young woman had large brown eyes, perfect skin, and elegant dark hair. As she walked, numerous gold bangles, necklaces, anklets, and bracelets jingled. She wore a rainbow of silks, scarves, and wraps dyed the brightest colors imaginable, and her face was exquisitely painted with makeup as if she were a living work of art. She demurely averted her eyes.

Soldan-Shah Imir stood from his cushion. "I've taken the liberty of choosing someone I believe should be your next wife. When you married Istar, you ruffled a few feathers by choosing a merchant's daughter rather than a child of a noble family. This lovely child will quiet the lingering ill will and strengthen the bonds among the soldanates."

"Does she have a name?" Omra asked sourly.

"Oh, yes, of course. This is Cliaparia, only daughter of Soldan Andouk in Yuarej." Imir lowered his voice to a conspiratorial whisper. "I've owed him a favor for a long time."

Cliaparia extended her hands to her sides and slowly pirouetted so that her silken garments fluttered about her like butterfly wings.

"See—she is intelligent. She is beautiful. She is talented in music. And most of all, she wants to please you. What more could a man want?"

"Indeed," Omra said, feeling nothing. "What more could a man want?"

Taking that as acceptance, the soldan-shah clapped his hands again, and a sikara rushed in. "Good, we can marry you right now." He seemed afraid Omra would change his mind. "Later, we will announce a joyous reception. The people will be happy for some cause to celebrate after all the recent dire news."

Omra remembered everything he had been taught, the purpose behind all his training, and he saw how he had withdrawn from the world. In his mind, he could imagine Istar scolding him for allowing his sorrow to weaken Uraba. He could not do that. "As you command, Father."

The sikara held a gilded scroll containing passages from Urec's Log along with the wedding ritual. Soldan-Shah Imir stood proudly next to Omra and pulled Cliaparia closer to his son. "Let's have this over with, so we can get on with our work."

18 *In Darkness*

Even in his blackest pain-filled dreams, Hannes was surrounded by fire. He lay in delirium, wrapped in ointment-soaked bandages that felt like chains. His skin burned, his eyes burned, his lungs burned. He was lost in the depths of nightmares and memories. But he found no refuge in his past; he was trapped there, as well.

He'd been a young boy when his mother abandoned him. She hadn't particularly cared for Hannes and had despised his father, a man named Bartho, who was quick to anger but slow to consider consequences. Hannes remembered little about his mother except for her shrill voice, her tears, and how often she had struck him (usually after Bartho had beaten her). When she was no longer around, Bartho simply turned to Hannes as the next convenient target.

The man's attitude toward his son was not so much hatred as indifference. Bartho was not the type to think even two days into the future; he did not plan how he might better his situation, how he might find another wife who could raise Hannes or even bring in more food or income. Bartho lived each day and complained about each day, letting himself drift like a rudderless boat rather than trying to steer away from jagged rocks.

In their small dockside home in the Butchers' District of Calay, the wind from the tanneries brought a constant stench and the sounds of terrified livestock being slaughtered. Hannes and his father rarely had enough money for food, yet Bartho could always afford a jug of grain beer or occasionally something stronger. Fortunately, when he drank, Bartho did not become more violent, simply more lethargic. When the man finally fell asleep grumbling, Hannes could slip out of the house and make his way through the streets.

After one particularly severe beating, the boy had run away, vowing never to return. He'd done the same thing several times previously, but always came crawling back a few days later. Bartho never seemed to notice that he'd been gone. This time, though, instead of trying to beg for scraps from the food vendor stalls or earn a few coins mucking out the offal trenches at the slaughterhouse or using buckets to splash away the blood on the ground, Hannes took refuge in an Aidenist kirk.

He had always found the architecture to be graceful and beautiful, the pictures intriguing: proud Aiden on his Arkship with his crew, the first landing at Ishalem, even a painting of the mysterious old Traveler, who was Aiden in his later years wandering the world. As a dirty young boy, unlettered and quiet, Hannes sat in the back of the kirk and listened to the presters.

One compassionate young prester named Baine noticed Hannes and took him under his wing. Prester Baine taught the boy how to read by using the Scriptures, and also taught Hannes how to pray. During prayers, the boy silently cast his words out, hoping Ondun would hear him from where He had gone to create other worlds... or he prayed to the spirit of Aiden, who might still be alive, wandering as the Traveler. Prester Baine did not know what the boy prayed *for:* With his eyes screwed shut and lips moving faintly to the words that he shouted inside his head, Hannes had prayed for revenge, begging for something terrible to happen to his father.

One day his prayers were answered. A bull about to be slaughtered broke loose from its handlers and gored Bartho, ripping open his stomach. Men in the Butchers' District added gruesome details as they told and retold the story, how Bartho had stared down at his intestines spilling out of the gash, trying to hold them in place, the other animals going wild, already terrified from the smell of death around them. Bartho had tripped on his own entrails, and the animals had trampled him. According to one story, Bartho's body had been so broken and mangled that one of the disreputable butchers threw it into a rendering bin, where the man had later been made into tallow.

Certain that Ondun had performed a miracle, Hannes gave his life to the church from that day forward. He declared to Prester Baine that he wanted to be a prester and showed a strong devotion to the rituals and sacraments. He read the entire Book of Aiden, and studied the many stories of the Traveler. Then he read the Book of Aiden again. And again.

Once Hannes was formally ordained in the Aidenist church, Prester Baine took him aside. "I have a great plan for you, Hannes. This is an assignment that I would trust to few others."

"I will do my best." Hannes did not even ask for details. "I swear on my life, for the memory of Aiden and the glory of Ondun, that I will do as you ask."

Baine handed him a copy of Urec's Log, and Hannes jerked his fingers back, as if the volume contained pestilence. "Do you want me to burn this? It is blasphemy."

"It is *information*," Baine corrected. "I don't want you to burn it. I want you to *read* it. Study it."

"No!"

Baine looked angry. "Did you not just swear that you would do as I asked? Did you not vow before Ondun?"

Hannes flushed, ashamed that he had been so quick to break his oath. "Perhaps...if you explained to me why."

"Is your vow conditional upon my reasons?" Baine had often challenged him with such conundrums.

"I will obey. You have my promise." Hannes drew a ragged breath. "But will I not be damned forever if I read this?"

Now Baine smiled. "Though these may be lies, you will not be tainted, so long as you don't believe what you read. Think of it as *strategy*. Know your enemy, so that you can see weaknesses, since the enemy is too blind to see his own flaws. Learn from Urec's Log. Tell me what you find in these writings." The redheaded prester smiled, tapping the cover of the thick book. "This should strengthen your faith, not challenge it."

And Hannes did exactly as he swore to do. He learned the Uraban language. He read Urec's Log with a scornful and skeptical eye. He noted so many errors and contradictions in the passages that he found the whole book laughable. How could the ignorant fools in the Urecari church believe such nonsense? They must either be gullible or stupid.

Years later, when Baine was elected prester-marshall of the Aidenist church, he had secretly dispatched Hannes to Ishalem. Hannes at first considered this his reward, the most important posting in the church. But rather than becoming the prester assigned to the central kirk in the shadow of the holy Arkship, he was told to live among the Urecari, to disguise himself, to learn their ways, and to watch them.

"Consider yourself a spy for God," said Prester-Marshall Baine. "Your discoveries will be vital to the church of Aiden."

And Hannes did, letting himself be swallowed up in their foreign culture. He spoke their language with barely an accent. Since Ishalem had many pilgrims from all the scattered soldanates of Uraba, no one gave him a second glance....

Thrashing now in his delirious dreams, the languages combined in confusion. He dreamed of the fire in the church, and he remembered grasping the sacred amulet—what had happened to it? Like a punishment from Ondun, he felt the flames pour over him, smelled the stinking canal whose waters had provided little relief.

And now, as he thrashed, passing in and out of consciousness, he babbled hateful memorized verses from Urec's Log. As if from a great distance, he felt people tending him. He heard a woman's voice, speaking Uraban. Trying to escape his dreams, Hannes struggled toward consciousness, but he awakened only to pain.

So he released himself and plunged back into darkness.

19 *Calay, Saedran District*

Now that he had been accepted as a chartsman, Aldo was eager to see the world. He dreamed of visiting exotic places, of voyaging farther than anyone else so he could add details to the Mappa Mundi—*accurate* details, unlike the embarrassing map he had bought from Yal Dolicar.

He knew the mathematics of navigation and how to recognize the stars in every known constellation. He understood the currents in the Oceansea and the prevailing winds from the frozen seas of the far north down to the isthmus of Ishalem and all the way past far Lahjar, where the heat and reefs blocked further passage.

A chartsman could tell his captain to set a course in a seemingly nonsensical direction until the ship caught a swift current or encountered favorable winds; a chartsman could guide them safely away from reefs or shoals, maelstroms, or doldrums. Saedrans allowed none of their maps to be published or disseminated outside of their own people, and only the most foolhardy or overconfident captains would sail far from the coastline without a chartsman.

As part of Aldo's education, he had studied the numerous tales of the Traveler, descriptions of journeys made by a nearly immortal man. The Aidenists said that the Traveler was Aiden himself, who had struck out on his own to explore unknown lands after establishing himself in Tierra. For their own part, the Urabans claimed that *Urec* was the Traveler. Rumored sightings of the Traveler had continued from one generation to the next, and villagers always gave hospitality to wandering hermits, treating them kindly because any one of them might be the Traveler himself.

According to tradition, the Traveler kept notes about the places he'd been and things he'd seen, and whenever he filled a volume of writings, the old man gave it to the first person he encountered. Thousands of these logbooks had appeared in villages and Aidenist kirks across Tierra.

Looking at the documents objectively, Aldo could see that the handwriting varied wildly from volume to volume, and it seemed clear to him that most of the books were hoaxes written by tricksters — like Yal Dolicar, he supposed — but perhaps some of them were true. Regardless, the descriptions of distant lands were vivid and detailed, and might contain accurate information. Until verified, however, the data could not be permanently painted into the Saedran Mappa Mundi.

While Aldo pored over the written tales in his continuing daily studies, Sen Leo entered the temple vault and was pleased to find the young man so diligently working. "The *Luminara* is about to sail, and we have chosen our chartsman to join the expedition."

Aldo's heart leaped as a giddy yet unrealistic hope ran through his head. What if, despite his youth and inexperience, he had been selected to voyage to those lands unknown, to accompany Captain Shay and crew, far out on the Oceansea?

"Sen Nikol na-Fenda is gathering his materials even now."

Aldo was crestfallen, though he tried not to show it.

"Sen Nikol is a very knowledgeable and talented chartsman. He is also objective, and his observations will be accurate. The Mappa Mundi requires accuracy above all things. When the *Luminara* returns in a year, our mission might be complete." Sen Leo sounded like an excited boy; he had spent his entire life dreaming about the expansion of knowledge. "We may finally possess a map of the whole world."

"Someday I hope to see it with my own eyes," Aldo said.

Sen Leo pulled out several thick volumes from the temple's bookshelves, setting them down with a heavy thump on the table. "That is what we all hope—but you have more studying to do before we can turn you loose on the world." He tapped the hard leather cover of another log of the Traveler. "You must learn what we already know before you dream of discovering something new."

20 *The* Luminara

After the *Luminara* was fully rigged and loaded, Criston Vora stood on the dock in Shipbuilders' Bay, not quite ready to board. Crowds had gathered for the launch of the magnificent three-masted carrack. Criston saw King Korastine himself standing with Princess Anjine and Prester-Marshall Baine, who had blessed the ship and its historic quest.

Jerard, the bearded old ship's prester assigned to the *Luminara* had come aboard after the dawn services, bearing his holy books, sacramental vestments, and relics. Behind him came an intense man about thirty years of age, who hurried past them and up the gangplank to the deck. He had short dark brown hair and was clad in Saedran clothing; he carried several intricate and ornate navigational instruments in his arms, refusing to let a porter bear them.

Criston drank in the noises of the city, the smells of people, the play of boats in the numerous bays—but he was focused on Adrea. His fellow crewmen hurried up the boarding ramp with bundles of clothes to last them during the year-long voyage.

With his back to the ship, he held Adrea, not wanting to let go, his arms wrapped around her like anchor ropes. "I'll think of you every day. I will write letters to you."

She laughed. "How do you expect me to get your letters if you've sailed beyond the edge of the world?"

"I'll throw them overboard in bottles, and the currents will take them to you." Criston had no doubt that sympathetic magic — the strands that connected all things in Ondun's creation — would be strong enough. "Let me have a lock of your hair. If I put a strand in with each letter, it'll be drawn back where it belongs."

Adrea separated out a small bunch of her golden-brown hair, and he used his knife to cut it off, leaving a ragged, prominent missing patch. Criston lovingly twisted the strands, then tucked the lock into his pocket. "We'll be like a Captain's Compass, bound together. The currents of the sea will feel the magic and bring the bottles back to Windcatch."

"It's a pretty thought…pretty enough to believe in." She toyed with the gap in her hair. "Now every time I see myself in a looking glass, I'll be reminded that part of me is with you."

Her brother limped forward, extending his hand. "I'll take care of everybody while you're gone."

Criston ignored the younger man's hand and gave him a sturdy hug. "You'd better. Don't just sleep all the time!"

The ship's bell tolled, and the *Luminara*'s crew manned their stations. First Mate Willin shouted orders, and Captain Shay took his place at the prow, wearing full colors and fine garments, hat in hand against his chest; a broad white plume from an exotic bird waved jauntily in the breeze.

Criston refused to release Adrea. "One more kiss." He touched his lips to hers and lingered there. This kiss would have to last a year. When he finally let go, he felt his knees weaken, as though he had suddenly lost his sea legs.

"Goodbye, my love," she said.

He tried to answer her, but the words caught in his throat. He hurried up the gangplank, the last man aboard. Sailors loosed the hawsers and pulled the plank back onto the deck.

On the docks, Prester-Marshall Baine raised his hands and intoned, "May the Compass guide you." The crowd of onlookers set up a loud cheer. King Korastine lifted his hands and called, "Ondun watches us all!"

Heaving on pulleys, the men raised the yardarms to unfurl the sails, and the sheets grew taut. Slowly, the *Luminara* eased away from dockside, drifted into the main channel, and rolled out of Calay Harbor on the departing tide.

Criston stood by the rail, his eyes never leaving Adrea's as she grew smaller and smaller in the distance. The first mate clapped him on the shoulder, startling him. "We've all left someone behind, sailor. Get to work!"

Abashed, he ran toward his station, grabbing a rope and helping to pull and set a sail. He turned away from the crowded city to face the bowsprit, looking out to sea.

Once past the lighthouses at the mouth of the harbor, the *Luminara* headed due east in open water. Captain Shay set course for Soeland, the group of islands that formed the most distant reach of Tierra, where they would take on whale oil and a few last provisions. The chartsman could have headed directly into the unknown, but Soeland was like a stepping-stone, the farthest point explored by Tierrans.

Captain Shay took meticulous notes of their speed, the winds, the color of the water. Though numerous ships had plied these waters between Calay and the Soeland islands, he began the voyage by testing his own powers of observation. He dropped lines overboard tied to weighted cylinders with tallow on the ends that sank to the bottom. He recorded the depth to the bottom and the composition of the seabed — sand, clay, crushed seashells, pebbles.

He asked Criston if he might like to help with some of the naturalist activities. "Most of my sailors do not have the abundance of curiosity you do, Mr. Vora," Shay said. "Not even First Mate Willin. I think I should make use of your skills." The young man jumped at the chance.

The Saedran chartsman, on the other hand, simply watched the activities around him, keeping himself separate. Sen Nikol na-Fenda stood at the side of the vessel, gazing at the waves as though the reflected sunlight sent him secret messages. Other than his ornate navigation instruments, Sen Nikol carried no charts, no maps, no logbooks.

Criston could not figure out what fascinated the Saedran so. When Criston wasn't occupied in holystoning the deck and washing down the planks with buckets of seawater, he struck up a conversation with the man. "Shouldn't you keep track of this voyage? Why aren't you making records?"

Sen Nikol regarded Criston with heavy-lidded eyes. "I *am* keeping records. I remember every detail." Then he turned to look out at the waves again.

Over the next few days, Criston learned that until recently Sen Nikol had a fairly lucrative career guiding ships down past Ishalem to the distant coastal cities of Khenara and Tenér, but he had seen them as mere destinations, not wonders.

"Those routes are closed to us after the burning of Ishalem, so my expertise is no longer needed," Sen Nikol said. "Perhaps when the *Luminara* returns in a year, the conflict will be resolved and trade restored between Tierra and Uraba. Then I will have my old job back."

"You expect the conflict to be resolved that quickly?" From

what Criston had heard, he was sure the bloodshed would last for generations.

The Saedran shrugged, speaking as though he were explaining a simple concept to a child in school. "In the long run, the demands of commerce will outweigh the demands of religion. Both continents need the trade, so the king and the soldan-shah will find some compromise. And then the world will go back to the way it was."

Criston didn't believe it. "But you are thinking logically."

Sen Nikol shrugged. "Yes, yes I am."

Soeland Reach was called the "Thousand Islands," though Captain Shay's maps showed no more than eighteen named patches of rocky land, some of them barely large enough to support colonies of migratory birds. The hardy Soelanders were an isolated and independent people, but they were also devout Aidenists and called themselves Tierrans.

The *Luminara* wove a course through the clustered islands in a procession from one small harbor to another, so that the people in the bleak, windy fishing villages could watch, wave, and remember them. They had never seen such a vessel before. Most Soelanders had never heard of Prester-Marshall Baine's revelation and were unaware of the *Luminara*'s mission. Many of them apparently didn't know (or didn't care) about the burning of Ishalem, which seemed like a distant tragedy to them.

The Soeland destrar, Tavishel, did not think of himself as royalty. Although the man lived in a large blocky house in Farport, the capital of the innermost island, he still sailed his own large fishing boat and raised his children to hard work; he had no patience for pampering. As destrar, Tavishel did not tax his people any more than was absolutely necessary, proclaiming that their lives were already hard enough. They didn't need to freeze and sweat, he said, just so the nobles in Calay could buy luxury items.

The *Luminara* pulled close to shore at Farport and dropped anchor, since the small docks could not accommodate such a large ship. The anchor—cast in the shape of two joined Aidenist fishhooks—sank to the bottom and caught hold.

Captain Shay, Sen Nikol, Criston, and four burly sailors took one of the two ship's boats over to the docks, to haggle with a local shipper for a dozen casks of whale oil. When they agreed on a price, a flatboat was dispatched to the *Luminara,* where sailors used a block and tackle to lift the barrels up to the deck, then stored them below in the holds.

The Saedran chartsman sought out local fishermen as they repaired their nets and patched the hulls of overturned dinghies and pressed them for details about the islands, the depths of channels, the preferred routes. Criston was surprised to see that not even the chartsman knew much about the outer Soeland islands. Some of the passages, while adequate for shallow-draft fishing boats, would make a vessel the size of the *Luminara* run aground.

After returning to his cabin and weighing anchor again to set off, Captain Shay spread out his maps and charts, studied drawings of the known islands, and plotted his course to the edge of the windswept archipelago.

For the next two days, as the ship passed through safe channels, the islands became more rugged. Criston noted Sen Nikol studying the coastlines as they passed, memorizing everything he observed.

Nobody lived on the outermost islands; they were simply rookeries filled with squawking gulls, and the immense racket carried across the waves. The sheer cliffs were white and beige, streaked with ochre. Guano ships anchored close to the cliff, while islanders went ashore with shovels and pickaxes to harvest the layers of stinking fertilizer, which was transported in sluggish barges to Calay. With grim pride and not a hint of humor, Soelanders claimed their main exports were whale oil, salted fish, and the highest-quality shit in Tierra.

Though this was the last land they would see for a long while, the stench was so terrific that Captain Shay ordered the *Luminara* to steer clear, and the carrack sailed past the boats anchored near the guano-encrusted islands, leaving the filthy workers to stare at them without waving.

A day later, out on the open sea, they did encounter a whaling ship. After hailing them, Captain Shay pulled alongside the long and sturdy vessel, and the other captain came aboard, marveling at the ornate complexity of the exploration ship. Shay told the whaler's captain of their historic mission, and the other man was astonished by the audacity of the *Luminara*'s quest.

"The weather gets worse the farther out you go," the whaler captain warned. His face was weathered and windblown, with craggy eyebrows that now drew together. "You don't belong out there." He pointed to some undefined point westward. "Treacherous currents, whirlpools that will suck down even a ship like this, sea serpents—and the Leviathan. Nobody has ever sailed beyond and returned."

"We will," Captain Shay said with aloof confidence. "This is the finest ship Tierra has ever built. I've already seen most of the fearsome things the sea can throw at me."

"Suit yourself." The whaler captain shrugged. "But I warned you. I warned all of you." He climbed back aboard his ship, and the two vessels separated. The whaler headed back toward the islands, while the *Luminara,* all sails set, cruised off across the open waters, leaving the known world behind.

21 *King Korastine's Castle*

Something had to be done about Ishalem.

Anjine sat with her father, listening in on the private tower-room sessions with Prester-Marshall Baine and Sen Leo na-Hadra. King Korastine consulted his small cadre of advisers when he had difficult decisions to make. As he rested bony elbows on bony knees beneath his gray robe, Sen Leo said, "We cannot leave the city in ashes."

Baine added, "Do we let the wound fester, or do we help it heal?"

The windows had been thrown open so the fresh breeze could circulate around the room, and a pool of bright sunlight warmed the rugs covering the wooden floor. A buffet of cold beef, fresh bread, pastries, cheeses, and red apples had been spread out in a casual feast, and the men picked at the lunch as they talked. They drank mugs of fresh-pressed cider.

Korastine sliced off a chunk of beef, put it on his plate, then used the same knife to cut and core his apple, though he showed little appetite. "Are you sure the wound isn't already mortal?"

"We must make the gesture, Majesty," Baine said. He quoted from the Book of Aiden: "'It is better to fix than to break, better to stitch than to tear, better to caress than to strike, better to build than to knock down.' We should return to Ishalem, bring a reconstruction crew of carpenters, stonemasons, farmers. We cannot replace, cannot forget, but we *can* rebuild."

Anjine's father looked very tired. "Ishalem will never be the same."

"No, it will not," the prester-marshall agreed, showing some of the zeal that had so inspired his followers, "but what we propose will not only benefit the Aidenists, it will show the Urecari our good intentions. Maybe we can avert a war after all."

Since seeing Ishalem on fire, Anjine felt as though a large part of her childhood had gone up in smoke. She had always thought Tierra would be the same when she was queen as it had been for her father, and for King Kiracle before him, but in a single year she had seen her mother die, Ishalem burn, and the holy Ark-ship destroyed. Tierra and Uraba were poised to collide in a war that might not end until one continent or the other was utterly devastated. Her life was no longer certain, and her instruction in statecraft was no longer an esoteric exercise.

Prester-Marshall Baine was relaxed next to the old Sae-dran scholar. The two were obviously friends, not religious rivals; Aidenists had long ago given up trying to find converts amongst the Saedrans, and the Saedrans themselves never proselytized.

"But *how* can we rebuild Ishalem?" Sen Leo sounded quite pragmatic, as though the decision had already been made. "Ishalem has few forests. All the trees in the surrounding hills were cut down long ago. Our crew will have to bring everything with them." He ticked off a list on his fingers. "Tools, workers, materials, food. We can order a raft of logs straight from Iboria, commission bricks and rope from Erietta. With ashes, lime, and sand we can make mortar."

Though Anjine could not forget the images of the city in flames, her imagination gave her other visions: new homes built on the charred ground, pilings installed in the waters, new docks erected... and a rebuilt primary kirk to take the place of the one that had burned.

A seemingly small event could have tremendous consequences;

a pebble could start an avalanche...a spark could start a fire. Nothing was certain.

Anjine recalled the story of how Korastine himself had unexpectedly come to the throne. King Kiracle, her grandfather, had loved to ride his horses, and while visiting Erietta he had gone out on an impulsive ride, ignoring the dark thunderclouds. When Kiracle had stopped on a hilltop to survey the reach, a bolt of lightning struck him. The horse miraculously lived and bore the dead king back to the stables of the Erietta destrar. Thus, Korastine had come to the throne.

Anjine spoke up for the first time during the meeting. "Didn't Aiden write that the air smells freshest after a storm? His Arkship may be gone, but the memory is still there, the truth is still there—in Ishalem. The spot is still there."

Sen Leo chuckled. "We have indeed been through a terrible storm."

Prester-Marshall Baine said, "Your daughter will be a wise queen one day, Majesty. Perhaps reigning over many new lands, if the *Luminara*'s voyage is successful." He glanced at the intricate model mounted on a firm wooden shelf.

The perfect scale replica of the *Luminara* was held in this secure tower room—a detailed copy down to the last rigging rope and sailcloth, every piece made from counterpart materials on the ship herself so that it was connected by sympathetic magic. The wood of the model's hull had been cut from the same planks; the sails were swatches trimmed from larger sailcloth; the ropes were strands taken from the thick rigging ropes. Through careful observation of the model, Korastine's advisers would have some inkling as to what was happening to the actual ship. The model was a thing of beauty in itself.

Anjine knew all about chasing dreams. In Calay, with its mixture of cultures from the five reaches, as well as being the center of trade for exotic Uraban goods, her upbringing had been asparkle with myths and stories. Anjine had always seen them as *possibilities*. Sometimes, Mateo lured her away from her tutors and diplomatic teachers so the two of them could explore the city. "Practical learning instead of book learning," he'd told her with a grin. "A queen needs both."

Wanting to see the city as average people did, without anyone recognizing Anjine as the king's daughter, Mateo had scrounged a drab but comfortable outfit from one of the serving girls; a smudge of hearth soot on Anjine's left cheek and a yarn hat pulled down over her golden hair completed her transformation into a scamp. After Mateo picked suitable clothes for himself, the two appeared to be street urchins out running errands or causing mischief.

To amuse them, one of the washerwomen had spun tales of two lovable scamps, an orphaned boy and girl named Tycho and Tolli, who had all sorts of adventures: being shanghaied aboard Urecari ships, running afoul of pickpockets, discovering buried treasure along a riverbank, or rescuing children even less fortunate than themselves.

Whenever the two of them went out into the sunny streets of Calay, Mateo and Anjine took those names for themselves. Tycho and Tolli. It was a perfect disguise because, Anjine later realized, the washerwoman had modeled her stories after the two of them anyway.

She remembered their first secret outing so clearly. Jewelers called out their wares, offering abalone pearls of the darkest luster, web-fine golden chains said to be spun from undine hair, masculine pendants crafted of gold-plated sharks' teeth. Scruffy merchants offered pilgrims' badges from Ishalem, so that any worshipper could pretend to have made the journey to the holy city.

The disguises worked so well that most of the traders had chased them away, sure the two were thieves. Anjine sat down on a crate in an alley, wiping sweat from her brow and adjusting her yarn cap. She said with a sniff, "What *I'm* looking for won't be set out among all the other wares. If it existed, then everyone would know about it."

"Oh? What are we looking for?"

"Aiden's Compass," she said in an awed whisper.

"That was lost centuries ago!"

"It was *broken* centuries ago. But Ondun created it to guide Aiden on his voyage. Do you really think it can't be fixed?"

His brow furrowed. "If it could be fixed, wouldn't somebody have done it by now?"

"Maybe it's just been hidden away, waiting for the right time. Maybe Aiden locked it away somewhere, left it for some later generation...like us."

Though intrigued by the idea, Mateo remained skeptical. "Like Tycho and Tolli, you mean? And how do you expect to find it?"

"By *looking*, of course. You can't expect to accomplish something difficult the first time you try. We'll just have to keep sneaking out of the castle and exploring." Mateo had completely agreed with her.

Not the first time you try...

Now, bringing herself back to the discussion in the castle tower room, Anjine turned to Korastine. "You don't want to be known only as the king who reigned when the city burned, Father. If you rebuild Ishalem, you will become a legend."

The king turned away, but not before she saw unshed tears sparkling in his eyes. He said, "Tierra will throw its resources into the holy city. I will command all destrars to send workers and materials to Ishalem. And to show how important this is,

Prester-Marshall Baine, *you* will lead the construction mission. Maybe Soldan-Shah Imir will see what we are doing and help us rebuild the city to the greater glory of Ondun, rather than continuing strife between the brothers."

22   *Calay, Saedran District*

Though he had already spent months studying volumes and maps in the Saedran libraries, Aldo still waited to be assigned his first mission. Whenever Aldo expressed impatience to go off to sea, the old scholar simply sent him back to the tomes. "Before a Saedran chartsman can leave home, he must build a perfect map of the known world in his mind."

When he wasn't studying books, Aldo took it upon himself to acquire knowledge in other ways. Down in the Merchants' District he watched arriving vessels tie up to docks and unload their cargoes to a flurry of eager merchants and curiosity seekers. Aldo studied the ships' profiles and forms, the length-to-beam ratios, the varying arrangements of rigging, the square-rigged or lateen-rigged sails, or a combination of both.

He talked to sailors returning to port, whether they were captains or regular seaman, pumping them for information. He became an astute observer of human expressions, watching how the men's eyes would light up or flicker away. He learned to distinguish when they were telling the truth from when they were deceiving their listeners. He did not forget how Yal Dolicar had duped him with his fake map. When he smelled the salt air, watched the shifting tides, and saw seabirds wheeling overhead, Aldo felt the invisible currents and tides of the Oceansea.

He waited with all the patience he could muster, longing for the day when Sen Leo would send him out on an exploration of his own. Finally, one morning the old scholar came to him in the underground temple vault with rolled-up hand-drawn blueprints. "I have a mission for you."

Aldo was diligently reading the last few books he had not yet memorized in the Saedran library. His face lit up, already imagining forgotten shores and exotic seaports.

"I am sending you inland," Sen Leo said. "I have work for you in the mountains of Corag." The scholar spread his drawings on the table, moving the open books aside. Aldo could not hide his crestfallen expression, but Sen Leo gruffly kept his attention on the matter at hand. He tapped the blueprints, which showed intricate gears and graduated metal arcs, angles and dials to be calibrated and set by the stars. "These are new navigation instruments for Saedran chartsmen. The workings are complex, and the manufacture must be precise. There is little tolerance for error."

He revealed another drawing, a set of gears, springs, and spinning counterweights. "This is a sealed navigation clock, vital for determining longitude. A variation and improvement on our other models. If our designs are followed properly, the clock will be accurate enough for a chartsman to pinpoint his position, latitude and longitude."

Aldo could not make sense of the designs, but Sen Leo dropped a bag of silver pieces next to the blueprints. "Sophisticated metalworkers in Corag Reach can make these instruments with the required accuracy. If you promise not to spend this money on another silly map of imaginary lands, I entrust you with this mission to Corag Reach. See that these instruments are made precisely according to design."

Though he was disappointed that he would not be going off to sea — yet — Aldo turned his mind eastward, looking at the rivers, imagining the open lands of Tierra. For Aldo, the whole world, not just the sea, was unexplored territory. He resolved to fill his mind with sights of cliffs and crags, rather than islands and waves.

His mother helped him pack for the journey, while his younger brother and sister seemed more excited than he was. With his satchel in hand, Aldo followed his father to the shallow interior basin at the far end of the Butchers' District, into which one of the primary rivers emptied. There, upon locating a flat riverboat designed for hauling both cargo and passengers, Biento bargained with its bearlike captain, who smelled of cloves and sweat, booking passage for his son. Aldo said goodbye to his father and stepped aboard with his pack of clothes, the drawings Sen Leo had given him (rolled up and sealed inside a special locked cylinder), and carefully hidden coins to pay for the instruments.

Grinning, Aldo found a spot for himself on the wide deck. With all the space belowdecks reserved for cargo, the handful of passengers had to spend their time out in the open air or under fabric awnings. At this time of year, though, the weather was fine, and he didn't mind. When he was settled, he turned to wave farewell to his father; Biento stood on the dock, waving back.

The itinerant rivermen pledged loyalty to no particular destrar and claimed no individual reach as their own. They plied their trade up and down the rivers, always moving; their homes were their boats. The flatboat was broad and sturdy, its construction entirely different from the oceangoing vessels Aldo had studied.

A mast and sails could be set out to take advantage of a favorable breeze, or the muscular men could use long oars to row against the current. In shallow waters they could push the craft with long poles.

Every man wore a beard; all the women covered their heads with scarves that were dyed and embroidered in a riot of colors, and the women looked just as powerful as the men, bred for heavy labor.

Aldo stared at everything, drinking in details as the boat pushed off and began to make its way upstream. It did not take him long to notice that the rivermen laughed a great deal more, and over more trivial things, than Saedrans did. They broke into song for no reason whatsoever, and each riverman carried some sort of musical instrument, either a jangling tambourine, a raucous-sounding squeezebox, a shrill flute, or a fiddle. They played whenever they felt like it, whenever a tune struck them. They made no attempt to coordinate as a symphony, but the conflicting strains of music made a song all their own.

Over the next hour, Aldo watched Calay diminish into the distance, vanishing as the river curved around a line of hills. Never in his life had he been away from the great city, and now the open lands of Tierra swallowed him up.

After speaking with them, Aldo learned that the rivermen were bound by family ties. The barge captain was a man named Sazar, a leader of several interconnected clans. A bearlike dark-bearded man with a gold ring in each ear, he called himself the "destrar of the River Reach." The big captain took Aldo under his wing, chatting with him during the slow voyage.

"We don't often get a Saedran chartsman on the river. Some would say you're going the wrong way." Sazar laughed. "My clan has mapped all the rivers and streams, the tributaries, the oxbows and the mud shoals, just like you Saedrans know the way of the oceans. If you tell me all your secrets of the sea, lad, I'll tell you the secrets of Tierra's rivers."

Aldo had seen the serpentine blue lines drawn on the Mappa Mundi, so he knew that Saedrans had already charted the inland rivers. "This is the first time I have ever left Calay. What makes you think I know any secrets of the world?" As a chartsman, he had sworn to keep their proprietary knowledge from falling into the hands of any outsider.

The burly river-destrar let out a booming laugh. "Because you're a Saedran. And Saedrans know everything." He lowered his voice and leaned forward. "Except how to lie. Lad, the truth is as plain as a mud smear on your face."

Destrar Sazar had his own violin, and he stood at the bow of the barge gazing upriver. He sawed his tunes—sometimes mournful and beautiful, other times reminiscent of a tortured cat. He launched into a deep-throated song, making up words that rarely rhymed, with a tune that did not match the music he played. Sazar sang about the wealth of the people of the River Reach, about mysterious stashes of treasure that the clans stored in uncharted swamps, caches of supplies that only a river-man could find. Aldo didn't know whether to believe the tales, though, for Sazar sang with equal gusto about the beauty of their women, and so far Aldo had seen little evidence of that.

At night, the barge pulled into a calm oxbow; crewmen lit lamps around the barge, and food was served—cold smoked fish, beets, and a mush of overcooked greens. Aldo didn't care for the peculiar spices, but he ate and listened and watched.

Sitting alone under one of the awnings, he worked the intricate seal at the end of the watertight cylinder that held the blueprints. The lock was keyed to Saedran symbols and could be opened only by someone who understood the code. Aldo unrolled the drawings of the navigation devices and leaned forward to study them by the light of a lantern, intent on grasping the secret workings. This would be a very complex task for even a highly skilled metalworker, but his brow furrowed as he tried to understand the design.

Though Aldo had studied numerous Saedran treatises on mathematics and mechanics, he could not fathom the reason for half of the gears and curves and angular measuring levers. He understood the Saedran notations marked on each gauge, but they didn't *make sense* to him. He traced with his finger, imagined how the pieces fit together, which component did what.

With a start, he realized that the mechanism had many extraneous and needlessly complicated pieces—intentionally so. The added components served no purpose, except to confound anyone else who might try to copy the design. Now it all made sense: merely another way for the Saedrans to maintain their secrecy.

Aldo rolled the blueprints again and huddled under a blanket that Destrar Sazar had given him. Listening to the slow lap of the river, Aldo fell into a contented sleep.

Three days later, the riverboat made its way into the highlands, fighting through narrower channels and swifter waters. They arrived at the outskirts of Corag Reach. The barge had stopped at river villages along the way, unloading cargo, dispatching passengers, taking on new items. An hour after daybreak, the barge pulled up to a wide wooden wharf that ran along the bank. Nine people stood waiting with their packs for passage back downstream to Calay.

Aldo rubbed his eyes and stretched. He looked past the landing to the stark and towering mountains beyond, a wilderness of black and white and gray, crowded crags that looked impassable.

"This is as far as the river can take you, lad," Sazar said. With a thick finger, he pointed past the landing to a dirt path that wound through grassy meadows and up into the forbidding peaks. "From here on, you are on foot."

Thanking the riverman, Aldo shouldered his pack and stepped onto the wharf. Nobody else disembarked from the barge, so he would have no walking companions. Setting his feet upon the narrow path, he trudged away from the boat and the river.

23   *Uncharted Seas*

Once past the fringes of Soeland, the *Luminara* sailed along without seeing any sign of land. Criston, with his sharp eyes, took many shifts up in the lookout nest, gazing at the endless water in all directions, clouds scudding through the vast open sky overhead. For more than two weeks, the sea remained unbroken and unending.

Criston couldn't remember the last time he had seen a bird. This ship had voyaged much farther than any Tierran had ever sailed, and he could not imagine how much more distance they had yet to cover. Captain Shay anticipated a journey of one full year, and they had been gone from Calay barely a month.

All alone atop the mainmast, Criston had hours to let his thoughts wander, with Adrea prominent in his heart and mind. He wondered what she was doing now, whether she was thinking of him, how she and Ciarlo were managing without him. If he continued to think like that, he knew he would drive himself mad, so he concentrated on the waves, keeping watch ... until his thoughts drifted back to Adrea again.

Other times, Criston helped Captain Shay with his experiments. An amateur naturalist, the captain kept dozens of pot-

ted plants, herbs, and flowers that grew in baskets rocking back
and forth as the ship swayed in heavy seas. Every day, the captain gave orders for the men to cast nets overboard and bring up
the haul, dumping a variety of unusual fish onto the deck. Like
a child playing a game of marbles, Shay would bend over the
creatures, prodding with a toe or finger, sometimes using a stick
if the fish looked particularly fierce. He sketched any unusual
specimen in intricate detail. Some of the smaller oddities he preserved in jars; the rest of the catch he turned over to the cook, a
portly man of few words named Orico, who added any fish that
looked and smelled edible to the stewpot. He dumped buckets of
offal over the stern, and sharks began to trail the *Luminara,* looking for a free meal.

Once, when Criston helped empty the bucket of guts and
scales, the sharks suddenly scattered. A green-scaled sea serpent
rose up, it's head as large as a cargo crate, to snatch a mouthful
of chum, then dove under; its sinuous form rolled and curled in
the wake for several long minutes until it finally vanished. The
crewmen let out such a cry of alarm that Captain Shay rushed
onto the deck, disappointed to have missed the spectacle. He
insisted that Criston describe the serpent as best he could, then
asked Sen Nikol na-Fenda to add more specific detail as he took
notes for his journals.

Over the next two days, they sighted three more serpents,
each with a distinctly different appearance. One red-and-copper
specimen had spiky fins and long whiskers about its fanged mouth
like the barbs of a catfish. A blue-and-silver one had a rounded,
stubby head and a small vestigial dorsal fin, making the creature
look like a very large earthworm. The third serpent was black
with gold spots and two large frontal fins that extended to the
sides like wings as it reared out of the water. All of them had
blowholes, which they evacuated upon breaching the surface.

Though these monsters unsettled the crew, the sea serpents simply swam around the ship, more curious than ferocious. Captain Shay, intrigued, offered a gold coin to the next man who saw a new species of sea serpent....

At sunset in calm seas, Criston assisted the captain inside his cabin. "Why are you so interested in drawing sea serpents?" he asked.

"When we return, I intend to publish a book. On this voyage, we'll see more wonders than we can possibly catalogue, but I have it in my mind to develop a naturalist's guide to sea monsters. If King Korastine launches more long voyages, such a book could be of great practical use to other captains."

"I never thought about that before." Criston scratched his chin. "But I agree. I'll definitely keep my eyes open for unusual specimens."

"Mr. Vora, you are possessed of a curiosity that I admire. Oh, the rest of my crew do their work and they do it well—I am, after all, a well-respected captain." His lips quirked in a smile. "But they don't see a fundamental difference between this voyage and any other long haul, except that their pay will be significantly higher when we get home."

As he talked, the captain sketched a fierce-looking spiny fish that had startled even the cook when the net was dumped onto the deck that afternoon. "You've got a good head on your shoulders. I'm glad to have someone I can rely on. We've had smooth sailing so far, but that won't last."

"We can trust our luck, sir."

"I'd rather be pragmatic. In an emergency, I've got to know how my crew will react. You never know..." The captain put his quill aside and stoppered the bottle of ink. "Ten years ago I faced a terrible storm when I was outbound from Erietta. The winds whipped up just as the sun went down, and I watched the clouds charge in like stampeding horses. We tried to reef the sails in time, but the blast hit us. We could only hold on and wait for the skies to clear. My Saedran chartsman was thrown overboard. I lost twelve of my crew in that awful storm."

His gaze was distant. "I swear to you, Mr. Vora—in that storm, through the bursts of lightning, sheeting rain, and explosions of spray, I saw something. I *saw* something. A large bearded man in a boat like a chariot being drawn by two sea monsters. It was Holy Joron, I know it. I'll believe that to my dying day."

The captain took a breath. "By the time the storm cleared, we'd been blown so far off course we had no way of knowing where we were. In the distance I saw low clouds that must have been strange coastlines, uncharted islands...but our ship could barely limp along. We had lost many of our supplies. We headed due east, hoping we'd eventually hit the Tierran coastline.

"I brought my men home, which is what a captain should do. But I've never stopped wondering what might have been on those shores I glimpsed. Could it have been Terravitae? Were we so close to Holy Joron's land that if I had just sailed a little farther..." He shook his head.

"And that's why you wanted to captain the *Luminara*? That's why you were chosen?" Criston asked.

Captain Shay chuckled, embarrassed. "That—and for more pragmatic reasons. After our last little misadventure at Ouroussa, King Korastine wanted me to leave Tierra. I don't suppose it matters anymore, but before the signing of the Edict, he had already made up his mind to send me away...to the edge of the world if necessary."

The *Luminara*'s Aidenist priest, Prester Jerard, performed services each dawn, calling the men on deck and raising his voice in prayer as the sun rose. Other than that, the prester had very few duties. Busy with their own chores, the sailors were polite and respectful to him, but tended to avoid the religious man.

Prester Jerard was far friendlier, however, than the aloof Saedran chartsman who stared at the sea day after day. Whenever he had the opportunity, Criston sat with the soft-spoken prester. The only thing the humble and unassuming man was vain about (though Criston was sure he would deny it) was his long, flowing beard, which Jerard claimed not to have cut in more than nine years.

Jerard was earnest about his faith, unlike the village priest in Windcatch, Prester Fennan, who merely read from the scriptures and followed the service without any particular imagination or interest. Jerard, on the other hand, seemed genuinely enthusiastic about his beliefs—not fanatical, but confident.

Like all presters, Jerard wore a simple fishhook pendant at his neck. To strike up a conversation, Criston asked him about it, and the old prester happily recited the familiar story of the founding of the Aidenist church.

"Sapier was the grandson of Aiden, the founder of our church. Long after Aiden departed to become the Traveler, young Sapier wanted to build his own ship and find his way home to Terravitae, so he could tell Holy Joron what had happened to his brothers, Aiden and Urec. Sapier's ship sailed for months, far beyond any charts, and the crew grew frightened. When they began to run out of food and water, they mutinied and threw Sapier overboard, then sailed off, heading back home.

"Stranded in the water, Sapier had only a few pieces of discarded wood, a fishhook, and a line. He floated for days in the great emptiness. He prayed for Ondun's guidance, hoped for rescue, but a great sea serpent came for him. Instead of giving up, Sapier threw out the fishhook, which caught on one of the monster's scales. Stung, the sea serpent pulled Sapier along at a furious pace.

"Astonished, he arrived back at Tierra even before his treacherous shipmates did, and when the cowardly sailors told the lie that Aiden's grandson had been eaten by a giant monster, Sapier came forward to confront them. Seeing him alive, the mutineers were stricken and ashamed. Some of them threw themselves into the sea to drown, and others were driven out of Tierra.

"But during his long privation at sea, Sapier had a revelation that became the basis for the church of Aiden." Jerard held up the pendant. "Sapier said, 'This fishhook and line are like my faith that pulls me through life and secures me to the truth.' Thus the fishhook became the symbol of the church."

Criston had heard the tale many times, but he was pleased to listen again, and Jerard certainly enjoyed telling it. "You're a good teacher," Criston said.

Jerard seemed embarrassed. "I suppose the quality of my students speaks to the quality of my teaching. A long time ago, when I was just a prester in a small kirk, I taught a very skilled young man named Baine."

"You mean Prester-Marshall Baine?" Criston asked.

"Well, he wasn't prester-marshall then, merely an acolyte. But he rose quickly in the church, and now he chose me for this voyage." Jerard spread his hands as the two of them looked out to sea. "If we do find ourselves facing Holy Joron and the people of Terravitae, someone aboard had better be conversant with the Book of Aiden."

24 *Windcatch*

Over the next few months back home in Windcatch, Adrea's life settled into a new routine without her husband.

She had not imagined Criston's absence would feel like such an emptiness. She wondered if this was like what an injured fisherman experienced when he lost an arm but continued to feel ghost sensations from the missing limb. But she had promised that she would be all right without him. Adrea had made him swear not to worry about her. With the money from the sale of the *Cindon,* she could run their household for more than a year.

Now, though, everything had changed…and she couldn't even tell him the news herself.

Instead, she had to rely on her family. As she helped Criston's mother, Telha, cut up vegetables and slice strips of dried seaweed from the last year's harvest, she smiled to herself, drew a breath, and announced, "I have news, Mother Telha. Exciting news. I waited until I was sure."

Telha raised one eyebrow, as was her disconcerting habit. "News?" She continued to wash green mussels and throw them into a boiling pot of salted water, while Adrea added the vegetables. "Is it the news I've suspected for days?"

"How did you know?"

"I've seen a difference about you. I can tell."

"What news?" Ciarlo sat surrounded by ropes and cords, the tools of his trade.

"Criston and I are going to have a child."

"That's wonderful," Ciarlo said, then muttered, "But he picked a fine time to go away."

Telha drew a deep breath. "You'll have all the help you need here. Ever since my Cindon was lost at sea, I've been looking forward to grandchildren."

Ciarlo grunted as he shifted his stiff leg to a different position, then pulled a large ball of string from the basket beside his wooden chair. He made his living repairing nets for the town's fishermen. Though he could walk only with great difficulty, Ciarlo's fingers were nimble, and he knew a thousand different types of knots. His hands were always busy. Even when he had no net to work on, he used short scraps of string and thick threads, tying them together in intricate spiderweb sculptures. Virtually every home in Windcatch had one of Ciarlo's sculptures hanging from the rafters inside.

Now it appeared that the young man had another career ahead of him. Prester Fennan had taken Ciarlo on as his acolyte and made no secret of the fact that as soon as he wanted to move into the small kirk, Adrea's brother could become the town's assistant prester.

As the vegetables and herbs simmered with the mussels, fish, and pungent seaweed, Adrea added a pinch of coarse black pepper she had purchased from a spice merchant in Calay. She wanted to extend her supply for as long as possible, but she imagined that Criston would return with treasure chests of exotic spices from his extensive voyage. In a year.

Prester Fennan arrived just as Telha was removing the pot from the fire. He seemed to know exactly when dinner would be served. At first it had been a quiet joke in the family, and then they accepted his arrival at mealtime as a matter of course. Fennan generally paid for his supper by instructing Ciarlo how to read the Scriptures in the original archaic language.

At the crowded dinner table, the prester offered the blessing and Ciarlo mouthed the words, practicing the ancient tongue. For his contribution, Fennan had brought half a loaf of old bread one of the parishioners had given to him. They shared the stale bread around, dipping chunks into the soup to mop up the broth. Afterward, satisfied, Telha busied herself in the kitchen, while Ciarlo and the prester sat with the open Book of Aiden by the soft glow of a whale-oil lamp.

"We must learn the Scriptures," Fennan said. "We must be prepared. Ondun has left us here with a quest, and we dare not disappoint Him when He returns."

"But...I don't understand the quest," Ciarlo said.

"I have taught you the words. We must improve the world, by the grace of God. Ondun created this place. We are its caretakers, its artisans."

"Prester-Marshall Baine says that we've got to explore and learn," Adrea interrupted. She thought of Criston, far off beyond the horizon in uncharted seas. "That's how we improve the world and ourselves."

Prester Fennan frowned, obviously uncomfortable with the idea. "That is an ambitious interpretation, but we cannot all be explorers. Most people can improve the world just by being good, by taking care of one another, and spreading the Word of Aiden."

Some presters believed that people should use the world Ondun had given them, by planting crops, mining metals, fishing the seas, and hunting in the forests. More ambitious followers wanted to build kirks and monuments to prove to Ondun's all-seeing eyes that they remembered and appreciated Him. Adrea liked to think that Criston was doing great work by seeing every aspect of creation, for perhaps Ondun had left majestic secrets behind as a gift for the faithful.

Prester Fennan opened his worn Book, which had served the

last four presters of Windcatch. "Read with me, Ciarlo. I know it's a tale you like—the story of the Leviathan."

Adrea stood behind them, trying to be unobtrusive as she looked over their shoulders. She'd been present at all of her brother's lessons, deciphering the obscure letters of the strange old language. Adrea found to her surprise that she had more of an aptitude for the studies than her brother did.

"When Ondun created all the creatures," Ciarlo read aloud, struggling with a few of the words, "He also made the Leviathan, a giant and hungry creature with a cavernous mouth, tentacles, a single glowing eye, and a blowhole that belches poison. But when Ondun saw how monstrous the creature was, He wisely decided not to make a mate for it."

He looked up at Prester Fennan, who nodded in encouragement. He continued reading. "For if the Leviathan were to propagate, its progeny would devour all the fish in the sea. So now the world remains intact, but the Leviathan is lonely and angry, for it is the only one of its kind."

Adrea pressed her lips together. She was terribly lonely, too, but *she* didn't feel angry and destructive. She only wanted Criston to come home....

She lost herself in the memory of him on the last night before the *Luminara*'s departure, those sweet hours aboard the *Cindon* with the portholes open to let in the fresh night air. Adrea and Criston were alone in the small private world they made for themselves. Outside, the darkness was lit by thousands of lanterns and candles aboard boats and ships, bright windows of dockside taverns and inns, torches carried by watchmen and revelers. She and Criston had no interest in going out to experience the bustling nightlife of Calay; they wanted only to hold each other.

It seemed as if Adrea had known him forever, that they had always belonged together, and yet—on that final night, confined in the hot and stuffy cabin with a gentle breeze whispering in — it felt as if they were discovering each other for the first time. While her brother snored softly out on the deck, letting them have privacy in the small cabin, Adrea had held Criston, warm skin touching warm skin, and fingers meeting each other with a sense of wonder. She was sure that was when she had conceived his child.

"I wish I could go with you, Criston."

"You will be with me — in my heart . . . all the way to the edge of the world." He kissed her ear, her neck.

"To the edge of the world — *and back.*"

"Of course I'll be back." He pulled her down onto the bunk so abruptly she let out a laugh. "And think of the stories I'll be able to tell you! Just you wait."

That night had been more than lovemaking; rather, it was a heartfelt goodbye, a collecting and treasuring of memories that would have to last for a year. . . .

Now, months later, Adrea savored the memory.

That night, after Prester Fennan departed, Adrea lay awake in bed, smiling, wondering what Criston was doing. Despite her loneliness, she was content and not afraid. Everything seemed right with the world . . . except for the fact that he wasn't with her.

25 *Olabar*

Once again, Hannes awoke as a prisoner of burning, bandages, and pain. He had no idea how much time had passed, or where he was. He could see nothing because of the coverings on his eyes. He didn't know how often he had struggled back to acid-stained consciousness, only to be confused and overwhelmed by agony before diving deep into the blackness, clinging to the anchor of his faith.

Each time, like a tempting seductress, he had heard the sweet woman's voice, her soothing songs, the delicate music. He felt cool water on his lips, tasted lightly spiced food, sweet fruit juices, figs covered with honey. He wanted to believe this was his reward for a lifetime of devotion, but for now he had to believe this was a trick. He could not let down his guard.

Finally when the nightmares subsided, leaving him with the staccato firing of raw nerves and furious itching of scabs on his skin, he listened carefully to the voice. He was so familiar with the language that he did not at first realize she was speaking Uraban. "I know you're awake. Come back to me. I took care of you," she whispered close to his ear. "Come back to me."

Only rough animalistic sounds came out of his throat. His mouth was dry, and he felt fingers touch his chin, part his lips. Lukewarm tea slithered into his throat, and he swallowed, then coughed.

The woman wiped his mouth and said, "Rest. I see you growing stronger every day."

He tried to talk again, but could not find the right words. Language was a confusion in his mind, but he seized upon one word. "Where?" Then he asked again, gaining strength, building confidence. "Where am I?"

"With me—Asha. You are safe here. I rescued you from the fire."

He tried to see, but his vision could not penetrate the bandages over his eyes. He felt a touch of cool, moist cloths; she was bathing him, wiping his rough cheeks, his hands and arms. He could hear birds singing and a breeze rustling fanlike leaves—palms?—outside an open window.

"Why can't I see?" Hannes spoke Uraban, just as the woman did.

"It's time I removed your bandages. Just wait; it will get better. The doctors say your vision should be safe. For a while they thought you were blinded, but I didn't lose faith."

Hannes felt the cloth pull away with an extra tug. Blood, scabs, and salves had fused the threads to his face, but that little pain was nothing compared to what he had already endured. Asha gently peeled away the gauze, flooding his eyes with light.

He could see nothing but a blinding whiteness so different from the awful orange flames that had consumed him. Colors seeped into his awareness, but he was slow to focus; everything was blurry and shifting. Then a dim figure — the woman Asha — dabbed a cloth against his stinging eyes. "You are crying!" she said, her voice touched with awe.

In the background, Hannes heard barking dogs, the rustle of birds in cages, and now he sensed perfumes and flowers. Smoke and soot had filled his nostrils for so long that he'd been able to smell nothing but the burning, but now his whole body seemed to be awakening.

Hannes was wary, even more suspicious that this might be a trick. If he were indeed in heaven, why did the woman speak *Uraban?* Blinking and blinking, he began to discern the hangings in the chamber, saw the ewer of water, a tray of food. Bird cages hung on either side of his bed.

The woman was beautiful, in the Urecari way. She smiled when she saw him focus on her. "This is my private home, a villa near the soldan-shah's palace. I made him promise to let us care for you until you are better." Asha touched his cheek, then ran her hand over the brittle stubble of hair on his head. How long had he been unconscious and recovering? "We are amazed the burns did not scar you worse than they did. I applied the unguents and salves myself. And now you've come back!"

"Why?" he croaked. "Why would you do this?"

Asha held her hands together as though she revered him. "I made them care for you, because Urec himself said we must tend the sick and wounded as our human duty, but when I discovered you had saved the golden amulet, the medallion of Urec, I knew you must be a sacred man!"

She hurried to her table and returned, holding the amulet. Its edges had been blurred by the immense heat, the ancient embossings softened but still prominent. "You must have been guided by Ondun Himself to preserve the sacred relic for us. Ur-Sikara Lukai will place it here in the Olabar church. She'll want to meet you, when you feel up to it."

Hannes sat up with a jolt. *Olabar!* So she had brought him as a hostage into the heart of the Urecari continent. He felt dizzy, ready to faint. This was a terrible, ironic trick! He had stolen that amulet *away* from the church of Urec, and now it had fallen back into the hands of heretics. He should have let it burn with the rest of Ishalem.

An angular, sour-faced physician scuttled in with a basin of tepid liquid that smelled of pungent herbs. He had a sharp pointed black beard, and his head was wrapped in the pale green olba traditionally worn by Urecari scholars. Pleased to find Hannes awake, the doctor moved forward while Asha dipped cloths into the fragrant liquid, dabbed at the still-healing scabs. The physician spoke anxiously. "He can see? His vision is restored?"

"I told you his eyes were not gone. I told you I prayed," Asha said. "*I* was the first thing he looked upon."

"What is your name?" Asha prompted. She always seemed to be chattering. "Tell us who you are. Are you a pilgrim? A merchant?"

The doctor bent over him, touching, prodding, testing. Hannes flinched, but he clenched his jaw, refused to say anything. He loathed the very touch of these people! Hannes did not intend to tell them anything. Feigning deep weariness, he refused to speak, shaking his head.

The doctor scolded Asha. "He must rest, but this is truly a good sign."

Hannes lay back and closed his eyes, wanting these people to go away, *willing* himself to sink back into sleep. He preferred his own nightmares to thinking about what the Urecari might secretly have done to him.

26 *Ishalem*

The prester-marshall's expedition to Ishalem departed from Calay with great fanfare: a dozen boats and barges full of carpenters, bricklayers, stonemasons, and other artisans, holds packed with tools, forged iron nails, bricks, and glassmaking materials—everything necessary to restore the holy city.

Baine rode at the prow of the lead ship, which sailed down the Tierran coast until they reached the ugly black blot that had once been Ishalem. When he saw all that was left of the magnificent city, he wept. Dry winds whipped across the isthmus, and blown ash left a lingering gray fog in the air. He could not tear his eyes from the shockingly barren and empty hilltop where no sign of the sacred Arkship remained. The tears on his cheeks left tracks in the light dusting of ashes that clung to his face.

But he drew strength from his faith, quoted aloud from the Book of Aiden, and granted himself only a few moments of personal sorrow. When Baine watched the somber mood spread among the workers and sailors, he stepped up on the forecastle and spread his arms. His raised voice carried to the other boats that edged closer to the shore.

"The fire has swept Ishalem clean, and we have a blank canvas. Our mission, as all the faithful know, is to improve the world by the grace of Ondun. Has there ever been a more clear challenge for the devout? We have brought our tools, our materials, and our willing bodies. Shall we make Ishalem a glorious city again?" He listened to the resounding cheer, then called even louder, "When this task is completed, even Ondun Himself will take notice. Perhaps He will find our offering worthy and He will return to us."

The small construction fleet painstakingly worked their way through the sunken wrecks in the harbor. Ships had burned down to the waterline; the piers and wharves were nothing more than twisted black planks, and lonely pilings thrust up from the waters. Some of the workers, desperate to set foot in the holy land—especially now that they saw the wounds of Ishalem—lowered themselves over the sides and swam to shore, while dinghies shuttled more volunteers. Workers offloaded heavy materials onto flat rafts and poled them to shore.

The Iborian shipwright, a weathered and meticulous man named Kjelnar, directed the establishment of a construction camp after leaving instructions for the placement of the drifting fresh-cut pine logs that he had ushered all the way from the northern forests. His first command was to erect the sawmills so that he and his burly northmen could process the logs into lumber.

Kjelnar spoke in a low accented voice to Baine as they watched crowds swarm into the wreckage of the city to see what they could salvage. "The volunteers are anxious to get to work,

Prester-Marshall, but if we are going to rebuild a city, we should start with a plan."

"Ishalem originally rose without a plan," Baine pointed out. "Houses and churches sprang up around the Arkship atop the hill. Pilgrims came and settled over the centuries."

Kjelnar raised his bushy ash-blond eyebrows. "Yes, and those people stripped all the wood from the surrounding hills, which has left the area barren and eroded. The dwellings they built were cramped, and the place was a firetrap. This time, we'll do better. We can improve it. Isn't that what the Book of Aiden says to do?"

Baine took heart from Kjelnar's confidence. "You are the master builder. You create ships—now create a city that will be the ship of our faith. May the Compass guide you."

The shipwright gazed up at the hills, the blackened streets, the maze of pathways and canals that were now choked with debris and charred timbers, and the tumble of skeletal frameworks that had once been houses and kirks. Kjelnar squared his shoulders, hesitated for a moment, then nodded. "As you command, Prester-Marshall."

Their volunteers cleared out the old wells, and soon had fresh water to drink. Every day, people cast nets for fish or walked among the rocks below Aiden's Lighthouse to harvest mussels and catch crabs. Without trade, Ishalem had no other food supply.

A handful of original inhabitants lingered like ghosts at the site of the obliterated city; many had fled into the surrounding hills, living like hermits, with little to eat. Prester-Marshall Baine determined that they were scavengers who had remained to pick through the wreckage. They fled whenever members of the reconstruction crew came near.

The ruins were full of bodies, blackened horrors trapped by

the blaze, their clothes and features torn away by fire and leaving only bones and staring skulls. Whether Aidenist or Urecari, they all looked the same. Workers gathered all the corpses they found, dragged them off to a barren hillside that they made into a cemetery, and gave each one an Aidenist burial in a separate grave. The prester-marshall felt it was best to be safe and give them all the correct blessings.

For days, while bricks and tools were unloaded from the waiting ships, the people rebuilt the piers so that the Tierran ships could dock. Some pilgrims went to the top of the hill, hoping to find remnants of the Arkship, but though they returned with blackened lumps of old wood, no one could say if those were the true remains of the Arkship, or other fallen timbers.

One dedicated work party excavated the wreckage of the Aidenist kirk, which had burned to its foundations, and Prester-Marshall Baine decided that they would rebuild the kirk first. Sawmills began to whine, cutting the Iborian lumber....

During the first month, the crew made a great deal of progress, and the prester-marshall was pleased with what he saw. Fresh pine frameworks outlined the walls of a new kirk. The temporary camp tents were replaced by new barracks and a communal hall, so that the volunteers could live comfortably after an exhausting day at work. Each dawn, the prester-marshall gathered the workers and praised Ondun. Ishalem began to rise from the ashes.

Then the Urecari raiding party swept down upon them.

Fifty lean soldiers, covered with dust and riding powerful horses, charged up the coast from Outer Wahilir. Across their chests, they wore bright red battle sashes emblazoned with the unfurling fern symbol of Urec; white silk olbas covered their heads to reflect the hot sun. Seeing the encampment, the new buildings, and the unarmed workers, the raiders let out a howl of challenge, drew their long sharp swords, and rode in. Soldan Attar himself, the leader of Outer Wahilir, rode at the front of the scouting party, damning the Aidenists for returning like parasites to the city they had burned.

Prester-Marshall Baine understood some of the Uraban language, but not enough to speak it. It was clear, though, that Attar had no interest in communicating as his men encircled the camp.

The prester-marshall stepped up to the soldan, a sour-faced man with a thin scar on one cheek and deep wrinkles around his dark eyes, who sat high on his black horse. Baine touched the fishhook pendant at his throat and raised his hand in a gesture of peace. He spoke slowly, pointing to the new buildings and the piled fresh lumber and stacks of bricks. "We came to build, not to harm."

Astride his horse, Soldan Attar gave no sign that he understood.

"Not to harm," Baine repeated. "To *build.*"

The volunteer workers had gathered close, either offering protection or seeking reassurance. Other men, seeing the group of mounted soldiers, rushed down from the site of the half-constructed kirk, clutching their hammers, shovels, and axes, though they were not fighters.

The prester-marshall spread his hands, a pleading expression on his face. "You can help us," he continued in his most soothing voice. "Your men can help restore Ishalem for the glory of Ondun—Aidenist and Urecari together."

Wearing a sneer of disgust, Soldan Attar raised his sword, turned the blade flat, and brought it down hard on the prester-marshall's forehead. As he collapsed in an explosion of pain, Baine heard screaming, the horses neighing, the charge of hooves—and more screaming. Then he sank into blackness.

*   *   *

He did not awaken until most of the slaughter was already done.

Blood crusted his forehead and eyes, and he choked on a stench in the air as thick and as foul as the Butchers' District on a hot summer afternoon. His hands were tied, but he could turn his head to see red-splattered bodies all around him: severed limbs, stumps of necks, lifeless eyes staring from loose heads that had been piled on the ground.

Baine made a strangled noise. What had they done? He heard a pounding sound against wood, as though workers were driving piles for a new pier. He saw that he had been dragged to the construction site of the new kirk.

Laughing, their fine uniforms covered with blood, the Urecari soldiers were erecting posts in the ground, at least fifty of them. They had used logs of Iborian pine brought in from the harbor. That wood had been meant for new buildings, but the prester-marshall felt ice in his chest as he saw other captives and guessed what lay in store for them. They moaned and wept, each one as bound and helpless as he was.

Unbidden, tears flowed down his cheeks, and he felt an even greater sorrow than he had experienced upon seeing the burned city. The fire could have been an accident, flames blown out of control by the winds. But this massacre was deliberate, the work of human hands.

"Why are you doing this?" Baine said, his voice a dry croak, as if his throat had filled with ashes. Nobody answered. The soldan's men gave no sign that they understood him.

With their horses tethered, the Urecari raiders walked about kicking dead bodies out of the way. Baine made a rough count of the corpses and the remaining captives, and realized that many of his people must have escaped, either into the hills or on the ships in the harbor. But not all of them.

He turned his gaze toward the coast, looking at the bright sunlight that flashed on the Oceansea, and saw one of the Iborian boats—Kjelnar's craft—withdrawing from the harbor. Soldan Attar's soldiers stood on the newly built piers and fired flaming arrows that fell short of the ship.

"Ondun protect us," Baine muttered. He hoped the shipwright had gotten away. Maybe he would make it back to Calay and tell King Korastine what had happened here....

When all the wooden posts were erected in a circle around the framework of the kirk, Soldan Attar walked among the prisoners, shouting at them. He took Prester-Marshall Baine first, grabbed him by the collar and dragged him to his feet. He spoke in an angry tone, but Baine understood little of what Attar said.

"We wanted to build," Baine said, his voice carrying an immense weight of weariness.

The soldan brought one of his soldiers forward. The man spoke in barely comprehensible Tierran. "We want no Aidenist help. You destroyed Ishalem. Heretics must be punished."

Using blacksmiths' tools and anvils that the reconstruction crew had brought from Calay, Attar's people had previously fashioned thick, sharp fishhooks in a cruel mockery of the Aidenist symbol, each the size of a man's hand, which they strung with rope.

Carrying the captives forward to the fresh posts pounded into the ground, the Urecari raiders suspended the poor victims on the hooks, jabbing barbed points into throats and letting the bodies dangle against the posts, struggling and gurgling briefly.

Baine begged the soldan to not kill any more of his people, but Attar pretended not to understand. Another captive was hooked through the throat and suspended with feet just barely touching the ground, then another and another. Some of the victims died immediately, but as the Urecari soldiers grew more practiced in their torture, they were able to keep the luckless captives alive for longer.

They saved Baine for last, making him watch. Soldan Attar's men were very careful as they thrust the sharpened hook under his jaw, avoiding his major blood vessels, catching the barb on his bones. Then they hoisted him up and tied off the ropes. Slow blood flowed down his chest in a thick stream, and he dangled, kicking his feet, twitching like a hooked fish.

Baine knew he would be a long time dying. And though his voice would no longer work, he mouthed a prayer for forgiveness, a hope that Ondun would welcome these poor Aidenist souls who had never imagined they might become martyrs. Against the wooden post, his back was to the partially built kirk and the hill that had once held the Arkship. He could not turn his head, could not even look back to what he most wanted to see.

Instead he simply stared with burning eyes, and all he could see were the ashes of Ishalem.

27 *Olabar*

In the center of Olabar, crowds gathered to answer the priestess's strident call. The humid air made the sunlight sparkle off of whitewashed buildings and cobblestoned streets. Clad in brilliant red robes, Ur-Sikara Lukai raised her arms and finished her benediction. Her loud and angry prayer made the crowd even more restless. Everyone felt the pain of Ishalem, the outrage and fervor against the Aidenists.

Soldan-Shah Imir wished it had not come to this.

He stood with his son Omra in the shadow of the towering bronze statue. The handsome and muscular figure of Oenar, Imir's great-grandfather (and probably not an accurate representation of the man's features), stood as tall as three men. As a leader of Uraba, the former soldan-shah's only memorable accomplishment had been to commission this giant statue of himself, a towering work of cast bronze eclipsed only by the statue of Urec on the other side of Olabar's central square. Urec's statue was an arm's length taller, since it would be blasphemy for any soldan-shah to elevate himself above Urec.

Imir had never paid much attention to the grandiose statue, the shape of Oenar's nose, the stylized beard, the metal draping of his regal robes. Even so, all of Olabar was going to miss it once it was melted down.

Ur-Sikara Lukai turned to bless the giant metal figure. "This statue was a gift so that we might remember a great man and our great heritage. Now it is another gift, a gift that will serve in the cause of war, a gift that will grant us a thousand swords!" The people cheered.

"We will need more than a thousand swords," Zarif Omra muttered, just loudly enough for his father to hear. The soldan-shah knew his son was right, especially after the news he'd recently heard. He'd been outraged to learn what Soldan Attar had done to the Aidenist reconstruction crew in Ishalem. Attar had crowed about his accomplishment, expecting cheers and praise…and many Urabans had rejoiced at the first decisive blow being struck against the enemy.

Imir, however, thought it an indescribably foolish thing to do. Attar had always been a hothead, and he'd wanted any excuse to take revenge on the Aidenists for killing his equally foolish brother Fillok at the beginning of this mess. Now, thanks to the provocative act — made even worse by the fact that one of the victims was Prester-Marshall Baine himself—Imir had to prepare a full-scale army for the conflict that would likely escalate.

As soldan-shah, he had expected to rule a rich land in times of prosperity, facing and solving problems that were by no means insurmountable. He did not want to fight a war, although his people, his priestesses, his advisers all cried out for blood, excited by the *idea* of a crusade against the Aidenists without guessing the harsh reality of it.

After a courier had brought news of the massacre in Ishalem, Imir raged against Attar privately in his quarters, smashing pots, tearing down hangings, shouting at the walls. When he had finally calmed enough to consider the possibilities, he summoned Giladen, the ambassador who had already helped to broker the Edict treaty with King Korastine. After Fillok's ill-considered attack on a Tierran trading ship, the Aidenist ruler would have been within his rights to go to war, and yet Korastine had been willing to stop the sparks of hatred before they burst into a raging fire. The burning of Ishalem, an even greater conflagration, was now eclipsed by the slaughter of those Aidenists, including the leader of their church. Imir's stomach lurched at the thought of it.

But he had to hope there was still a chance for peace. Giladen rushed off to present himself in Calay, insisting that the Urabans did not want a war, that Soldan Attar had acted on his own... begging the Tierrans not to retaliate. If the price of peace included Attar's head on a pike, then Imir was willing to pay it.

Though he looked doubtful, Giladen had read the soldan-shah's written plea and nodded. "Korastine is a reasonable man, Soldan-Shah. He will hear your words, though I cannot guarantee what he will decide. His people will certainly be outraged about the massacre."

"As am I," Imir said. "Make sure Korastine knows that."

After Ambassador Giladen departed with the carefully worded parchment, Zarif Omra had come to Imir in his quarters. In the month since his marriage to Cliaparia, the zarif had gradually emerged from his depression; time and personal strength had more to do with the change, however, than his new wife did.

After learning of the slaughtered Aidenists and his father's attempt to salvage the disaster, Omra had finally shown the hardness the soldan-shah always knew his son possessed. The zarif stood before him, jaw clenched. "If this does not work, Father, we need to be ready for the worst. If there is to be war, then it must be *our* war. We must prepare to do more than just defend ourselves — we've got to make certain that we *win*."

The soldan-shah knew his son was right.

Equipping an army required more than just anger and enthusiasm. Across the five soldanates, he could find plenty of willing fighters and warhorses, but the continent had very little metal for swords and armor. Bordered by the desert and the sea, Uraba had always counted on trade. All of their copper, tin, and iron came from Tierra, but now that trade had been cut off, Soldan-Shah Imir did not have sufficient resources to equip the army that this war would require. Uraba needed metal. They had to take it, somehow.

A decade earlier, across the wide Middlesea on the northern shoreline of stark cliffs, the Urabans had established secret mining operations at Gremurr. The coast was part of Tierra, the far edge of Corag Reach, but the forbidding mountains made the region inaccessible from the north. Since Tierrans could not cross Corag to the Middlesea, they were completely unaware of the Gremurr mines. After the signing of the Edict, it was even more vital that the Uraban presence remain undiscovered. With the advent of war, the soldan-shah would have to turn those mines into a far more extensive operation.

Now, in the crowded square, Zarif Omra wore a pained, hungry look as he stared at the sunlight reflected from the bronze statue. Bare-chested workers came forward to throw ropes up around Oenar's proud figure, securing loops to the metal arms and neck. The crowds drew back to allow room, and Imir could do nothing but stand and watch.

With straining muscles and taut ropes, the labor teams pulled down the huge statue, balancing it with ropes and pulleys. When the enormous bronze figure lay on the ground, blacksmiths and metalworkers set up an incredible clamor as they broke apart the statue, which they would melt down and recast into swords, shields, and armor plate.

It made Imir sad to see such a piece of Olabar's heritage lost, but he did not hesitate to give the order. This one statue would yield enough weapons to win an entire battle, perhaps capture a city. It was the right thing to do.

Out of the corner of his eye, though, he saw his son staring at the even taller bronze statue of Urec with a calculating look. Melting down the other figure had not yet been suggested. However, if battles continued longer than expected and Uraba's need increased, Soldan-Shah Imir knew he might soon have to make another extremely difficult choice.

28 *Calay*

When King Korastine heard Kjelnar describe what the Urecari raiders had done to Prester-Marshall Baine and the innocent workers in Ishalem, he felt physically ill. He turned white, his hands clenched, and his eyes burned, but he said nothing. He had no words.

Marching up from the wharf in the Royal District, the Iborian shipwright had refused to speak to anyone until he saw the king himself. The audience in the throne room gasped and moaned; some dashed out into the halls, spreading the horrendous news.

This was truly the end of the world. Prophecies from the Book of Aiden resounded in his head, and he no longer had Prester-Marshall Baine to advise him. Were these the end times? Had Ondun decided to abandon humanity after all? The king closed his eyes. He could think of no other answer.

Finished with his tale, Kjelnar bowed, obviously shaken. "With your permission, Majesty, I will return to Iboria and tell this sad news to Destrar Broeck, so that Iboria can begin to prepare."

Korastine raised his head heavily. "Prepare?"

"We will summon our shipbuilders. We will cut down many trees. We must arm all existing Tierran ships and build new war vessels."

Korastine nodded. Of course he was right.

The leader of Alamont Reach, Destrar Shenro, was already in Calay on other business. When he presented himself at the castle that same afternoon, he demanded an immediate private audience with King Korastine. The king knew what the man was bound to say.

Alamont was the only landlocked reach of the five that comprised Tierra. A spacious land of rolling hills that received plenty of rain, Alamont was perfect for raising crops. The everyday people were well-muscled from their work in the fields, and Destrar Shenro had often made the comparison that wielding a scythe was little different from wielding a sword.

At Shenro's request, the two men met in the castle armory. Destrar Shenro, a thin man in his late twenties and decidedly lankier than most Alamont farmers, had a wife and three healthy sons. His storehouses and treasury were well stocked—yet he was an impatient man, always feeling incensed, looking for something suspicious. With a tablet in hand, Shenro had already begun making a tally of the swords, halberds, spears, and shields available to the Tierran army. He shook his head as Korastine arrived. "This won't be enough."

The armory chamber was dim and cramped. It smelled of oil, leather, and metal. Outside, sparks flew from a grinding wheel as one of the city blacksmiths sharpened a long-unused sword. His mop-headed young apprentice sported a colorfully bruised black eye that had swollen so nearly shut that he had to squint at the daggers in his hands as he used a whetstone.

"We have enough weapons for all of our trained soldiers," Korastine said. "That is all we have needed."

"Then we don't have enough soldiers," Shenro said gravely.

"In both, you are probably correct."

"Good. Then you agree we should increase our conscription? Alamont will double its number of soldier-volunteers. All the other reaches are bound to do the same once they hear Kjelnar's report."

The king's first instinct was to wait, to send an angry ambassador to demand apologies and reparations from the soldan-shah. But Korastine couldn't think of any concession that would prove adequate, and he doubted his outraged people would ever believe Urecari promises anyway.

"Again you are right, Destrar. Better to have a large army and not need it, than to be caught defenseless."

Every year, in order to maintain Tierra's standing army, five hundred conscripts came from each of the five reaches, and one hundred from the district of Calay; the mixed groups served one year in each reach, so that at the end of five years they completed their tour of Tierra in Calay as part of the city guard.

The military training camps in Alamont were larger than in other reaches, not because Shenro had plans to go to war with his neighbors, but because he had what Korastine called "soldier dreams." Shenro listened to tales and songs of battles, studied his military history, and glorified heroic warriors. Because Alamont was landlocked, Shenro and his people could not simply sail off to sea, although the call of the wind and waves was in the blood of every Aidenist. That, Korastine thought, must be the reason Shenro felt so frustrated.

As they talked about plans for defense, Destrar Shenro continued to set aside swords, marveling at the intricate metalwork done by Corag swordmakers, while the blades fashioned by Calay blacksmiths looked sturdy but plain. Shenro made a disappointed sound. "We should dispatch messengers to Corag, tell Destrar Siescu that we will need many, many more blades."

Korastine was about to step off a cliff, but once the fire had consumed Ishalem—and even more so, now that Prester-Marshall Baine and his followers had been martyred—Tierra had gone over the brink, and now they were all falling headlong into infinity.

"I will call the other destrars," Korastine said. "Because we all represent Tierra, we must all make sacrifices and fight the Urabans together. Before the sun sets today, I will issue a decree calling for twice the number of soldier-volunteers from the people of Tierra. We must build our army immediately."

Since her mother's death, Anjine had rarely gone into Queen Sena's quarters. But a year had passed, and she and Mateo decided to open the doors and windows, to clear the dust. She wasn't sure whether or not her father would be angry at the intrusion.

Inside the queen's chamber, the red drapes, red cushions on the furniture, and red diamond-shaped panes in the windows were all marks of Queen Sena. Some had called her the Crimson Queen during her life. Anjine missed her mother, as any child would, though Sena had always treated the girl more as an embodiment of expectations and obligations than as a beloved daughter. Korastine, though, treated her as a real person, someone he genuinely liked.

When she was younger, Anjine's upbringing had been a source of friction between the king and queen. The king had let her and Mateo run about the castle, play with the staff, spend days out in the city, while Sena wanted her brought up like a proper lady. Korastine had always assumed that there was no need to rush the princess into her responsibilities. . . .

Now Anjine and Mateo opened the leaded windows to let the breezes in. She picked up one of the cushions and pounded it, sending up a dust cloud that made her cough.

"Tolli," Mateo said, using her nickname since they were alone, "do you think your father will ever marry again?"

Anjine had pondered the question herself many times. "That depends on whether he falls in love."

"Did he fall in love the first time?" Mateo had known Sena too; in fact, Anjine's mother had often looked frowningly at him, certain the young man — who was not even of noble blood — was a bad influence on her daughter.

Anjine answered his question with a shrug. Political reasons usually trumped romantic ones. She was sure that the destrars had been urging King Korastine to marry again, though to no avail thus far.

Sena had not shown an overabundance of warmth toward her daughter, nor toward Korastine, as far as Anjine could tell, but she had thoroughly accepted her role of helping the royal heir to be trained as a leader. Anjine carried the blood of Aiden in her veins, and her mother wanted to make sure the girl lived up to her expectations. Sena showed a glimmer of pride when Anjine completed each portion of her studies: religious education, history, politics, and geographical knowledge.

Queen Sena had always considered it unseemly for a ruler to learn the rough dialects of the far reaches. "They are your subjects, Anjine," Sena once said in a scolding tone, as if the answer should have been obvious. "It is *their* obligation to speak formal Tierran, or to send an ambassador who can."

Anjine knew that her father, contrary to Sena's objections, had tried to become conversant in several dialects, but had learned only a smattering of words. At his age, tackling a new tongue was a daunting prospect.

Sena had been the younger sister of Mayvar, an influential noble from Alamont, and her selection as queen had been the result of many convoluted political wranglings. Korastine had been in a rush to take a wife to cement his hold on Tierra after his father's death. The marriage to Sena was the choice least likely to cause frictions, and the aged prester-marshall had blessed the union so wholeheartedly that he quashed any grumbling before it could gain strength.

Not quite overbearing but certainly protective, Sena did not appreciate the king's loose attitude of letting their only daughter enjoy part of her childhood *as* a child. Conceptually, at least, Sena respected the king's promise to raise Ereo Bornan's son, Mateo, in the castle, but she disapproved of the boy's close friendship with Anjine and the casually paternal warmth that Korastine extended toward him.

Mateo and Anjine had continued to dress up as the street scamps Tycho and Tolli, to make up their own adventures in the streets of Calay. Though Queen Sena knew about this, the two were nimble enough to evade her, and often came back excited and dirty, much to Sena's consternation.

The queen barely tolerated Mateo's presence in her daughter's classes, even though Korastine insisted he should be allowed to participate. "You may listen and you may learn, young man," she had said, frowning, "but the knowledge will do you little good. Anjine will rule Tierra, but your aspirations must be much more limited. The best you can hope for is to be captain of the royal guard."

Sena had expected Mateo to be crestfallen, but he had simply grinned. "No, the best I can hope for is to be the *smartest* captain of the royal guard."

Destined to be the next queen, Anjine supposed she would be flooded with marriage offers herself when she was older, though Tierran nobility tended to marry late. She knew the choice of a particular husband wouldn't entirely be hers, but she expected at least to be consulted in the matter. She thought of the giggly women at court who swooned over any handsome guard who deigned to smile at them. She promised herself she would never be like that.

Now Anjine turned, startled to see her father at the doorway to Sena's chambers. Korastine's expression was unreadable, his eyes red. She didn't know how long he had been there, watching the two of them. Mateo quickly spun, ready to defend Anjine if trouble threatened, but he relaxed quickly when he saw who it was.

"They told me I'd find you here," Korastine said evenly. "We have to talk."

Anjine blurted, "We just wanted to let some fresh air into Mother's room. We were thinking of her, honoring her memory."

Mateo interjected, "Please don't be angry with us, Majesty."

Korastine looked slowly at the young man. Anjine realized that her father had barely noticed where they were at all. "I'm not angry...not with you. There has been terrible news from Ishalem."

"Ishalem?" Anjine shook her head—the city had already burned down. What could be worse?

Korastine told them.

"I came to speak with both of you, because today our lives have changed. I foolishly hoped that tempers would die down and cooler heads would prevail as the leaders realized how much we all have to lose. I always considered the soldan-shah to be a wise man, and I believed he respected me. But now we have no choice." He heaved a long, cold sigh that sounded like a winter wind. "Mateo, your father was one of my bravest soldiers, a captain of the royal guard—and I daresay, even a friend. I promised him I would raise you in a way that would make him proud. Now it is time for you to make all of us proud."

Anjine had heard the story many times and at first assumed that Mateo was embellishing it, but her father insisted it was true. Despite the hurt Mateo had suffered, Anjine was glad that it had brought them together.

Ereo had been the captain of King Korastine's personal guard. After the death of King Kiracle, while people thought Korastine was weak, several merchant families demanded to have their taxes reduced and certain types of shipping declared tariff free. Korastine refused, and the incensed merchants set a trap for him in the streets on his way back from the launch of a diplomatic ship. They hired thugs dressed as Urecari sailors to assassinate the king.

Ereo fought like a whirlwind to defend his ruler. Two other royal guards were killed. Though Ereo managed to defeat the last of the would-be assassins, he suffered a mortal wound himself. While he lay dying in the street, Ereo begged Korastine to take care of his five-year-old son, Mateo, whose mother had died three years earlier from fever. The grateful king swore to do so.

Despite their disguises, the assassins turned out to be local Calay men, and the plot of the merchants was exposed. Korastine had them all executed and seized their assets, and Mateo grew up in a special position in the castle. Though not a noble, he had the king's blessing.

Mateo looked much older now as he glanced at Princess Anjine, then turned back to the king. "How do you need me to serve, Majesty?"

"I always thought you were too young, but that is because I saw you as the boy you were, not the man you are becoming. You are old enough." He looked at his daughter. "You are both old enough. I'm afraid you'll have to become adults sooner than I intended. From this day forth, Mateo, you must be a soldier. And you, Anjine"—Korastine wrapped his arms around her—"you must prepare to be queen."

29 *The* Luminara

That night, on calm seas, Criston drew the deck watch. It had been months since they'd seen any sign of land.

Although there seemed little chance the *Luminara* would strike rocks or a reef out in the middle of nowhere, this was uncharted territory. On this moonless night, Captain Shay had ordered the sails tied up, and the ship drifted gently for hours. Most of the crew was asleep. Up in the night sky, Criston saw constellations that did not match the star patterns he had long ago memorized.

Carrying a whale-oil lantern, he slowly made a circuit of the ship, always alert. He peered overboard at the ghostly outlines of waves, but no sea monsters came up to feed at night. He had seen many wonders since the beginning of the voyage and couldn't wait to get home and tell Adrea all about them. Now he placed the lantern atop a barrel, sat down on a crate, and took out a sheet of paper Captain Shay had torn from one of his journal books. With a lead stylus, Criston scratched out a letter — the twelfth one he had written since his departure from Calay.

On the paper he expressed his thoughts, his love, writing for Adrea's eyes alone; he would trust the merciful tides to bring the letter to her. Orico, the cook, relinquished empty glass bottles to Criston for his odd obsession.

True to his parting promise, Criston filled his letter with the things he had seen, the places the *Luminara* had gone. So far, he had discovered that the empty ocean was anything but empty. Right now the night-dappled sea was aglow with luminous plankton that skirled just beneath the surface like a silvery blue storm, an ethereal light that drifted and twitched, flushed into intense brightness in the ship's wake.

A glowing swarm of bubble jellyfish drifted alongside the *Luminara*. Whenever the jellyfish bumped into each other, they released a crackling spark in a discharge that drove them apart again. The creatures had floated along with them for the past three nights, sinking to the darker depths when the sun rose.

Criston wrote about them, imagining Adrea was there beside him. "Captain Shay was so excited the first time he saw the jellyfish that he ordered specimens drawn up in a bucket, but the moment he touched the creature's membrane, his hand was so severely stung that he still wears a bandage, days later."

After he filled the page, telling Adrea again how much he missed her, how much he hoped that she was safe and healthy—and that he hoped she thought of him as often as he thought of her—Criston rolled the letter and slipped it into the empty bottle. Before sealing the cork to the end, he carefully withdrew a single strand of Adrea's golden-brown hair from the lock she had given him, which he kept protected in his pocket at all times. He pushed the strand in with the letter, blew gently inside, and whispered, "Find your way back to her." Sympathetic magic would reunite the hair with its owner ... or so the legends said. He had to trust it to the sea.

Criston went to the port-side rail, closed his eyes, and pictured Adrea as vividly as he could, then tossed the bottle overboard. He heard the faint splash and saw the bobbing glass glint in the starlight, drifting away as the *Luminara* moved on. Of his twelve letters so far, at least one of them had to find its way to her.

Feeling tired but not sleepy, he walked toward the stern where the captain's wheel stood next to the two compasses on their stands. Another hour remained on his watch. The magnetic compass showed that the *Luminara,* after a long trip west, was heading south now, having picked up a strong current, like a river in the Oceansea. Since Captain Shay had no particular course in mind other than to explore the unexplored, he had let the current guide them. The Captain's Compass, as always, pointed its needle back toward Calay, just like the legendary compass Ondun had given Aiden before the first voyage.

Following its pointer, Criston looked off to sea, imagining Tierra, Calay, Windcatch ... and Adrea, somewhere beyond the horizon.

Prester Jerard joined him so silently that he startled Criston. Since the old man often had trouble sleeping, he came to keep Criston company and tell him stories. The two men stood by the wheel, listening to the creak of the rigging, the whisper-slosh of waves against the hull, the snoring of a dozen sailors who preferred to sleep on deck rather than in the stuffy bunks below.

"I saw you throw another bottle overboard," Jerard said. "A letter to your sweetheart?"

"It always is. How much farther do you think we will sail?"

"How much farther *can* we sail? Ondun is great, my friend, but even I never imagined Him capable of creating a world so vast. Any day now, I expect to hear the roar of falling water, feel the whoosh of spray, and see the edge of the world. But it's just more and more open sea. I come out at night hoping to see a distant spark, a glimmer of the beacon. Then at least we'll know where we are."

"A beacon?"

Jerard stroked his long beard. "The Lighthouse at the end of the world."

Criston frowned. "I don't know that story. Is it from the Book of Aiden?"

"In some texts. Others include it as part of the Apocrypha. It's just a story, maybe no less true than all the rest." Criston waited for the prester to continue.

Jerard touched his fishhook pendant and looked out to sea. They began to walk slowly around the deck. "The Lighthouse was built on a tiny island, far from Terravitae, to hold an exiled man who committed a terrible crime. Holy Joron sentenced him to live for all eternity, so that he could keep watch for Ondun's return. When God comes home, the cursed man must be the first to see Him and ask for forgiveness. And so, the Lighthouse keeper shines his light across the ocean and waits and watches, peering through his giant lens so he can see everything that happens in the world, everything that is denied him."

Criston gazed out at the waves, but saw no glimmer of light other than the ethereal luminescence of the plankton. "If we see the beacon, that means we're close to Terravitae?"

Jerard smiled. "If we see it, that means many things...not the least of which is that the story itself is true." The old man touched the pendant and with the same finger touched Criston's forehead. "You have faith. I have seen it. Every time you write a letter to your beloved and throw the bottle overboard, you show your faith."

Criston smiled wistfully back at the old prester. "I have a certain amount of faith in the ocean currents, but I have complete faith in Adrea."

30 *Windcatch*

At the beginning of each autumn, migratory seaweed arrived in Windcatch, carried on warm currents and blown by changing winds. Three days earlier, fishermen returning to port had seen the approaching kelp, and the villagers bustled to prepare for the year's harvest. Fishermen tied up their boats and stayed ashore, some grumbling about the fine weather they were missing out at sea, while others were glad for the change in the daily routine.

Windcatch had been built around a small harbor bordered by steep hills. With the approach of autumn, the wind and water patterns formed a gentle whirlpool that drew in the drifting seaweed.

All the villagers came together to meet it, since the harvest provided much of their yearly income. Men went inland and loaded carts with wood for shoreside bonfires; others scrubbed out huge cauldrons to prepare for the rendering. Women set large baskets out on the piers, and eager captains emptied their boats, anxious to take the first haul of seaweed up to the Calay markets. Bottle makers washed their brown glass bottles to hold the distilled kelp liquor.

Adrea, Telha, and Ciarlo were ready for the chores. Criston would have been there beside them, with the *Cindon* scrubbed and ready for a profitable trip, and Adrea realized with a pang that this was the first year she had harvested the seaweed without him.

Dressed in a brief swimming shift, Adrea waded out from the gravelly shore beside her brother. Both of them carried baskets slung over their necks and shoulders. Buoyed by the water, Ciarlo's limp no longer bothered him. When they met the outlying tendrils of the seaweed, they withdrew long knives and pushed their hands among the leathery, greenish brown straps to find the bulbous bladders, which they sliced off. The kelp nodules were the first and most valuable part of the harvest, but the villagers also used everything else.

She and Ciarlo kept a count, each trying to outdo the other's tally. As Adrea waded deeper into the seaweed tangle, the thin fabric of her wet dress pressed against the rounding curve of her belly. Her pregnancy had started to show, but she did not let that slow her.

Ciarlo cut off a pink kelplily and presented it to her with a flourish. Its petals stretched out wider than the span of Adrea's hands. "Since your young sailor isn't here, allow me to give you this bouquet."

She wrinkled her nose. "It smells like fish."

"When the seaweed starts rotting, you'll think this smells like a moss rose by comparison."

Having filled their baskets, they sloshed back to the shore, where chattering workers punctured the bladders and squeezed out the liquid, which was easily fermentable into a briny, strong drink for which Windcatch was well known.

As migratory seaweed filled Windcatch harbor, the warm calm waters triggered its reproductive cycle. Kelplilies bloomed in great rafts of color, and floating pollens fertilized the seaweed. Seedlings floated free, and the rest of the large mass died and broke apart. Over the next month, as the seaweed rotted, most villagers remained inside their homes, burning candles and incense to mask the stench. When the weather changed and the autumn storms picked up, currents pulled the decaying seaweed back out into the ocean. At sea, the drifting seedlings would form new clusters and grow into larger rafts, circulating in the currents before returning the following year to continue the cycle.

Hard-muscled fishermen dragged large nets full of thick kelp fronds back to the shore. The tender fleshy ends would be sliced and salted. When eaten fresh, the seaweed was delicious; when dried and preserved, it formed a long-term staple of the Windcatch diet, though most people were sick of it by the time summer came. The fibrous remnants of kelp fronds could be beaten and felted into a durable fabric — another item for which Windcatch was famous.

Old Telha decided that she'd spent too many years of her life doing the messy work. This year, she set up a reed chair in some shade and readied a flat rock and mallet, so she could beat the kelp fronds to prepare the fibers for cloth making. She talked with the other fishermens' wives and widows, gossiping, laughing, complaining. Children splashed in the water, eager to help, while their young mothers tried to work on the harvest.

The same as every year.

With her basket emptied and her brother limping back into the waves, Adrea waded out once more, always looking at the open Oceansea. Shielding her eyes, she gazed toward the horizon, thinking of Criston and wondering what he was doing just then. She hoped he was thinking of her.

31 *Off the Coast of Uraba*

The sturdy, thick-hulled ships of Soeland Reach were designed for rugged seas and cold storms, but they had sleek lines, the better to pursue and kill whales. Now, though, the Soeland ships hunted an entirely different quarry.

Destrar Tavishel clung to a slick shroud rope as cold spray splashed him and dripped from his square-cut beard. Ignoring the wet and the chill, he wiped the mist away from his eyes so he could see. They were closing in on the Urecari ship.

"Looks like a diplomatic vessel," Tavishel yelled out in his rough voice. "No match for us, men!"

One of his well-muscled sailors came up to him, also drenched. He held a battered spyglass. "No sign of any military escort, Tav—but we're in Uraban waters. They probably think they're safe. Hah!"

"If there's a military escort, we'll sink them just the same." Tavishel had to shout above the rolling roar of the waves. "We have harpoons to spare."

The silken sail of the enemy ship billowed, the Eye of Urec staring out from the scarlet fabric. If nothing else, Tavishel wanted to gouge out that hated mark and blind the ship. And that would only be the first step in their revenge for what the Urecari animals had done to Prester-Marshall Baine and the innocents who had gone to rebuild Ishalem.

The hearty and self-sufficient Soelanders were distant from the politics of Calay. They swore their fealty to King Korastine, provided volunteers to the Tierran army, and trained recruits each year, but not until he learned of Baine's martyrdom did Destrar Tavishel understand what it meant to be part of a larger, unified land. His people were members of a fold so much greater than one reach. Now, as he envisioned the prester-marshall slowly dying on a fishhook, he felt the greater glory of surrendering to the needs of the kirk for the benefit of all Tierrans, not just people from the Land of Sunken Mountains.

And because of their zeal from this new revelation, Tavishel and his Soeland fighters would not let the heinous Urecari remain unpunished. The destrar had decided it was his holy mission to shed the blood of those vile monsters. Korastine would be pleased when Tavishel sent his report of their accomplishments here off the coast of Tenér.

Foregoing fishing and whaling, the Soeland ships had sailed away from their islands in order to hunt Urecari below the Edict Line. And now they had intercepted this single diplomatic ship working its way up the coast toward Tierra. A worthy prize!

The foreigners had no chance against the bulky Soeland ships that closed in. Destrar Tavishel shouted orders for his zealous men to arm themselves with the stunning clubs and harpoons that they used to kill giant whales before butchering and rendering them. The Soelanders stopped the enemy vessel, threw ropes and grappling hooks, and swarmed aboard the lone ship.

One of the Urecari, who wore ornate robes of green and blue, looked like a diplomat of some sort. His shaved head glistened with both aromatic oils and nervous perspiration. The foreign ship's captain tried to make a defense as Tavishel's men surged onto the deck, but the soldiers aboard were merely an honor guard—enough for show but not enough for war. The captain shouted in his gibberish language until one of Tavishel's men thankfully struck him on the head with a club, cracking the man's skull.

The colorfully robed diplomat was beside himself with panic and desperation. He gathered his voice and spoke in erudite Tierran. "No, no—*peace mission!* I am ambassador. Giladen! My name is *Giladen!* I go to speak with King Korastine! We sail for Calay!"

"You will never get there," Tavishel growled.

Giladen fumbled with a rolled parchment tied to the braided belt at his waist. "No, no! Listen!" He unrolled the document, which was covered with neat words in formal Tierran as well as the birdlike footprints of Uraban writing. "Negotiate! We come to negotiate on behalf of Soldan-Shah Imir! No war!" He waved the document. "I bring message to your king!"

But Tavishel could not banish the image in his mind of the holy prester-marshall strung up on a hook…of the ruthless Urecari spilling more Aidenist blood on the already sullied ground of Ishalem. It was all he needed to remember.

He withdrew his curved gutting knife and slashed across Ambassador Giladen's plump throat, putting an end to his trickster words. The rolled treaty fell to the deck boards from his limp and quivering fingers.

Tavishel raised the bloody knife and shouted to his men, "They deserve no more mercy than they showed Prester-Marshall Baine! Kill them all!"

The Urecari sailors fought back, but they were outnumbered. The Soeland men had long experience butchering whales in a huge mess of blood, slime, and grease, with bubbling rendering pots and decks slick with gore. When they finished, the Urecari ambassadorial vessel was covered with just as much thick red fluid as there would have been after a whale hunt. To Tavishel, it seemed fitting.

After the killing was done, the destrar remained aboard the Urecari ship with a skeleton crew, turning it about and sailing on favorable winds back toward Tenér, the nearest Urecari port. One of his young crew members clambered up the mainmast to the yardarm, where he dangled on a rope, took a dagger, and cut a hole in the sail, gouging out the Eye of Urec. The ship sailed onward like a blinded cyclops.

Soon the group of ships was within sight of the bustling harbor city. Tavishel and his men kept close watch, but the only ships they saw were far off. The colorful sail of Giladen's diplomatic ship would have drawn no attention in these waters, regardless.

As he guided the ship closer to the foreign port, Tavishel made preparations. Dismembered enemy corpses lay strewn about the deck, beginning to bloat and stink in the warm sun. He had his men tie the ambassador's body to the mast, and the Urecari captain's body dangled from a hook on the bow. This was a death ship, a slaughterhouse. He would give the Urecari a sight they would never forget.

One of his Soeland ships pulled close alongside, so that the men could jump back across, ready to sail away. Alone aboard the foreign vessel, Tavishel unrolled the document that Giladen had been so desperate to deliver to King Korastine, spread it on the deck in the midst of a large bloodstain, and skewered it to the boards with his gutting knife, so that the dead, glassy eyes of the Urecari ambassador could forever stare upon it.

The uncrewed diplomatic ship caught the currents and began to drift toward the harbor, and Tenér drew closer each moment. As a last rude gesture, Tavishel dropped his trousers, squatted, and left a steaming pile in the middle of the parchment, obscuring the words the Soldan-Shah had written. Let the Urecari read that!

Finished, Tavishel swung back aboard his own ship and took command, while the ghost ship sailed onward to Tenér, crewed only by corpses. Unguided, it would crash into the docks.

Destrar Tavishel smiled as his two ships sailed northward to the safe waters of home.

32 *Corag Reach*

As Aldo na-Curic made his way up the ever-steepening path (which the locals called a "road"), the Corag mountains became ever more magnificent around him. All his life he had gazed out to sea and imagined far-off lands, but he had never thought to look inland.

The alpine meadows were bedecked with bright flowers and silvery streams. The cliffs and peaks seemed to grin with jagged teeth of gray rock whose couloirs held snow even late in the summer. In Calay, Aldo had never seen snow.

The people were hardy and independent, renowned across Tierra as talented workers of gold, silver, and iron. They extracted, smelted, and worked ores from their metal-rich mountains, then delivered completed work to the rivermen, who sold it to Calay merchants.

Deep in the trackless highlands, many tribes and villages had never been counted in any census or labeled on any map — a fact that intrigued Aldo. These isolated people paid no taxes to King Korastine, and the Corag destrar left them alone. On the other side of the impassable mountains lay the Middlesea itself, but if any Corag native had ever found the route, it was not widely reported.

For four days he trudged past villages and accepted local hospitality, on his way to Stoneholm, the reach's largest city and the seat of the Corag destrar. Aldo arrived at the mountain city at sunset, clutching his satchel of possessions and blueprints as he stared at the sight.

Stoneholm was surrounded by tall granite cliffs that provided shelter from the worst blizzards. The front of the city was built into an elbow of rock, a huge overhang above the stone-block facades. Under the cliff overhang, fine stonework graced the building fronts: hideous gargoyles, scaled sirens, and beautiful women—all iconic figures from the Book of Aiden. A benevolent-looking stone man held out a fishhook, Sapier himself. The city's interior penetrated the mountain, with streets and chambers tunneled deep, converting the original mine network into a well-settled, and well-fortified, metropolis.

Three men in high-collared black woolen jackets lined with thick white fur came out to greet him as the dusk deepened. "The destrar sent us," said one. His voice had an odd accent, the consonants harder, the vowels more nasal and flat, than typical Calay speech. "He is anxious to hear why you have come on such a long journey. You're not one of the usual merchants."

Aldo was surprised. "How did he know I was coming?"

The men smiled and glanced at one another. "Word travels quickly. We've been waiting for you."

The great stone house of Destrar Siescu was fronted with giant hewn blocks, then the back was expanded into a man-made grotto that penetrated the cliffside. Ventilation shafts had been drilled upward, and cold air circulated with a thin whistling sound. Colorful rugs and thick pelts covered the bare stone floor in the main chamber.

Against the wall, Siescu sat in a large chair from which he could look across his great hall. A fireplace enormous enough to hold an entire ox crackled with a roaring fire made from several thick logs. The enclosed chamber felt extremely hot to Aldo, but Siescu wore thick furs and covered himself with a woolen blanket. The destrar was not an old man, but his translucent skin was stretched tight across the bones of his face. His eyes were set deep in their sockets.

Seeing Aldo, Siescu sat up straighter and removed his hands from beneath the blanket. Aldo saw that he also wore leather gloves. "You are a curious visitor. A Saedran?"

"Yes, sir. From Calay."

"Come closer to the warmth so that you're more comfortable." The destrar gestured to Aldo. "It always feels so cold here in the mountains."

Until now, Aldo had not believed the stories he'd heard about this man. In one legend, Siescu had been wounded in a practice session with a fine Corag sword, and when his skin was cut, ice water ran out rather than blood. An old miner in an outlying village Aldo had visited whispered that Destrar Siescu kept ordering his men to dig tunnels deeper and deeper into the mountain, hoping to find the embers of the Earth, the dying fire of Creation, so that he could at last be warm.

Aldo bowed formally, made his greetings, and thanked the destrar for his hospitality. "I am here to commission work from your best metalworkers."

"Are there no metalworkers in Calay?"

"Not *Corag* metalworkers. I wanted the best and most precise work done. These devices cannot tolerate even the slightest error."

Aldo's comment elicited a proud smile from the destrar. Siescu leaned forward, and (reluctantly, it seemed) peeled off his leather gloves. He rubbed his hands together briskly. "Let us look at your drawings. I want to see this great challenge you have for my metalworkers."

Aldo unrolled the plans and briefly explained the purpose of the navigation devices and the sealed clock. Siescu made a gruff sound. "We have made Saedran instruments before. We can do it again." He narrowed his eyes. "It will be expensive."

"I have money." Aldo hoped it was enough.

The destrar shouted four names, promising Aldo that these were the best craftsmen in the reach. The young man felt relieved and pleased. "How long will it take, do you think?"

When the destrar frowned, the lines deepened on his face. "Your devices will be finished when our artisans are satisfied. You did ask for accuracy, did you not? Or are you in a hurry? Which is it?"

Sen Leo had not told Aldo how soon he must return. He bowed again nervously. "I will give your people all the time they need. And while I wait, I would like to explore Corag Reach."

"Oh, there is not time to see all of it. Our craftsmen are not so slow."

Aldo was surprised that the sullen-looking destrar actually had a sense of humor. "Then, when I am not overseeing the work, I'll try to see as much as I can."

33 *Unnamed Island*

For the first time in months, the *Luminara* sighted land.

High up in the lookout nest, Criston spotted clustered clouds on the horizon that suggested a landmass. His unexpected shout startled the listless men below. The sharper-eyed members of the crew rushed to the sides and squinted into the distance. High up in the sky, someone saw a bird.

Within two hours, there was no doubt that a shoreline lay ahead. The conversation thrummed with speculation that this hitherto-undiscovered land could be Terravitae itself. First Mate Willin, stern and businesslike as usual, tried to keep the now-excited sailors concentrating on their duties. Soon, however, it became apparent that this was merely a heavily forested island.

Criston wondered if it was an outlying island in a whole archipelago, like Soeland, or an entirely isolated speck in the middle of the Oceansea.

Since his mission was to explore the world, Captain Shay intended to go ashore himself. Prester Jerard would serve as a representative of Aiden to speak with any natives and learn what they knew about Ondun and his sons. The Saedran chartsman also insisted upon observing the details, so that he could mentally record the interior topography of the island.

For more pragmatic reasons, the cook Orico asked to go ashore and acquire victuals. The *Luminara* still had many stores of salted meats and preserved biscuits, and they had supplemented their diet with the daily catch of fish, but fresh game, vegetables, and fruit would be a welcome addition and necessary for the health of the crew. Rainstorms had replenished the *Luminara*'s drinking water, but the casks could certainly do with refilling from island springs. Captain Shay would take the ship's two boats ashore with several parties to hunt, forage, collect fresh water, and explore.

The *Luminara* cruised along the coastline, looking for a place to anchor, but found only inlets bounded by abrupt cliffs that made the interior inaccessible. The crew spotted many rushing waterfalls, fresh streams that spilled directly into the surf. They remained alert for smoke from villages, any signs of life. Criston hoped the natives would speak Tierran, and dreaded that they might be followers of Urec.

The *Luminara* sailed halfway around the island until at last, startlingly, they encountered a stark sign of human habitation: a towering stone wall, built from immense volcanic blocks. The sailors chattered amongst themselves, some superstitious, some merely puzzled. Captain Shay stared, amazed. "It must be twelve feet tall!"

"Fourteen," Sen Nikol corrected.

The wall reached all the way down to the waterline, where combers crashed against the rocks, and extended inland to where the lush jungle had already overgrown many of the blocks. As the ship cruised slowly past, they saw no footpaths, no break in the jungle on either side. Though the captain was deeply intrigued, he saw no place for the *Luminara* to put in, or where her two boats could safely reach the shore.

"We will keep sailing, circumnavigate the island," Shay announced to First Mate Willin, who directed the crew to heel around the tip of the island and head down the windward side. But the terrain remained unchanged. Still they saw no fishing boats, no harbors, no docks. By late afternoon, they discovered the opposite end of the wall, which lay like a sash across the waistline of the island. The man-made barrier neatly cut the landmass in half—but why?

A few miles beyond this, the *Luminara* finally found a natural cove with a rushing stream that tumbled down from the jungle. The sun loomed large and orange upon the horizon like an ember about to be extinguished in the sea. Night would fall swiftly, as it always did out on the ocean, and Captain Shay called for the crew to drop the fishhook anchor for the night.

All the crew was anxious to go ashore the next morning, and Criston got little sleep. With the first light of dawn, men lowered the two small boats over the side for the members of the exploratory teams. Criston rode with Captain Shay, accompanied by

Prester Jerard, who had combed his long gray beard and donned his best robes as Aiden's ambassador. Sen Nikol na-Fenda seemed amused and intrigued, but kept to himself on the bench.

The cook also joined them in the boat, carrying empty cloth sacks for gathering fruits, berries, and roots, expecting a cornucopia of island delights. Four other sailors came along, armed with swords and ready to fight wild animals or suspicious natives.

The second scout party came ashore with empty casks; they would spend the day shuttling fresh water back to the *Luminara*. Hunting parties with spears and crossbows would try to acquire fresh meat. Shay, though, turned his gaze inland, and Criston knew what their destination would be. The captain wanted to see the wall.

After they put ashore and the two groups parted, Shay took the lead, pushing through the dense undergrowth in the direction of the wall, then directing the four burly sailors to clear a path with their swords. The jungle resisted their efforts, and the party made slow progress. Each man took a turn wielding a blade.

Along the way, Captain Shay had ample opportunity to study flowers and colorful beetles, and he collected several specimens. Orico plucked mushrooms, sniffed them, but did not risk taking the unusual species back to the *Luminara*'s larder. He found a bush filled with bright purple berries, tasted one, and spat it out. "It's either poison, or it's so bitter it may as well be." The cook did, however, find a tree laden with bright orange fruit. When he peeled the thick rind and bit into the juicy pulp, he pronounced the fruit good to eat. Criston and the others filled their bags with the harvest and foraged on.

They saw the first skeleton when they were less than an hour from the wall.

Picked clean of flesh, the bones lay like a collection of ivory pieces in the undergrowth. Oddly, though, the rib cage was not entangled with weeds and vines, as if someone had recently dumped the skeleton there. The bones still wore a kind of leather uniform studded with tarnished metal bossets. The armor was nicked and scraped, as though the skeletal soldier had seen many great battles. The skull's empty eye sockets stared upward, its teeth green with a dusting of moss. The rusty sword in its bony fingers had been notched many times.

Criston bent down to pick up the sword, but the skeleton would not release its grip. "It looks ancient. How did it get here?" Nobody could offer him an explanation.

Prester Jerard muttered a quick prayer, and they pressed on until they reached the wall, where great blocks of chiseled volcanic rock towered higher than any person could scale. At the base of the barrier, the jungle undergrowth was packed and trampled.

And the ground was strewn with hundreds of additional skeletons. Each one carried a sword and each wore the same foreign-looking armor.

"There must have been a great battle," Captain Shay said. "But who, or what, were they fighting?"

Complex friezes and hieroglyphics adorned the blocks, but the written language was not comprehensible to either Prester Jerard or Sen Nikol; neither saw any resemblance to known languages. The prester shook his head. "These were not carved by children of either Aiden or Urec."

"Or Saedrans," the chartsman added.

They had spent most of the day fighting through the vegetation, and now it was late afternoon. Because the captain wanted to poke further into the mystery of the inhabitants, he suggested that they make camp and spend the night. They chose a spot not far from the wall, away from the fallen skeletons.

Two of the sailors joined them at their camp, having shot a large bird similar to a turkey, much to the cook's delight. Orico built a fire and began plucking feathers, preparing to roast the bird for dinner.

As the sun sank toward the horizon and a nearly full moon began to climb the eastern sky, a breeze rustled the jungle foliage. Several strange birds set up a raucous din and winged away from the wall, leaving the area shrouded in eerie silence. In such a lush jungle, Criston thought, the night should have been alive with buzzing insects.

Weary from the day's efforts, the men settled down to rest. When Orico pronounced the bird roasted and ready, Prester Jerard intoned a quick prayer, the Saedran chartsman muttered his own blessing, and they all sat together to eat. The moon grew bright as the sky deepened to indigo. A few silver stars began to sparkle overhead.

A faint clatter came from the shadows of the ancient battlefield. Criston heard the scrape of a rusty blade, a hollow sound of bones clacking, hard leather armor shifting over dry bones. The skeleton warriors came alive.

The sailors cried out, jumping to their feet. Prester Jerard grasped his fishhook pendant. "What sort of magic is this?"

Captain Shay commanded them all to silence. "Watch yourselves, and be on your guard! Look!" He pointed toward the skeleton warriors, and Criston calmed himself long enough to notice that the corpse-soldiers were not preparing to attack them. In fact, the skeletons paid no attention to the newcomers at all.

Instead, they lifted swords, adjusted shields and body armor, and formed ranks facing the wall, blank eye sockets staring toward the top of the barrier. Mandibles clacked open and shut in a silent shout of defiance, a challenge that was impossible to hear because the long-dead warriors had no vocal cords, no breath.

"What are they waiting for?" Criston whispered.

With a bizarre and frightening clatter, another group of skeletal warriors scrambled up the wall from the opposite side and stood on the top, waving their own swords and shields. The new wave of warriors wore a different style of armor and had different markings on their shields—obviously an opposing army.

The bony fighters leaped from the high barrier upon the first group, and with a great clamor, swords and shields crashed together. Skulls were lopped off of vertebrae, arm bones severed. Criston could hear the loud crack of bones—but no other sound.

Prester Jerard swallowed hard. "They must have built the wall to separate themselves, but that did not stop them from fighting."

"But if they're all dead—" Criston started.

"Their bodies may be dead, but their hatred is not," Captain Shay said.

The Saedran considered for a moment, then made a dry pronouncement. "This is fascinating. We saw no other settlements on this island. Their civilization must be extinct—yet they still fight."

"I don't think we should be here," muttered Orico. "This isn't our war. We don't want any part of it."

"I believe you're right," the captain said. "Why is it that a cook should have to state the obvious? Let's go, quickly! If they notice us, they may decide to fight anyone who gets in the way."

They abandoned the rest of the roasted bird, and Criston kicked dirt and ashes over the fire. Then they ran, stumbling through the underbrush by the light of the bright moon. Though the shadows were deeper and they tripped often, they still made better time now that a path had already been cut through the jungle.

Before long, they came upon the first skeleton warrior they had found, all alone, far out in the jungle. As the moonlight filtered through the thick canopy, the ancient soldier also rose up and lifted its notched sword. Orico was in the lead, pushing his way forward at a fast run. When he came upon the warrior, startled, the undead soldier thrust its notched and rusty sword deep into the cook's belly.

Orico's momentum drove the blade in to the hilt. He fell forward, knocking the flimsy skeleton to the ground. Criston and Jerard cried out and rolled Orico away. The skeleton pulled the blood-slick sword from the cook's belly and clambered to its feet to fight again. But before it could regain its tottering balance, Criston knocked it to the ground once more and, without thinking, delivered a sharp kick to the skull, knocking it loose from the spine, so that it flew off into the weeds. The two sailors behind him fell upon the rest of the skeleton with their swords, smashing ribs and hacking the arm bones.

Prester Jerard and the Saedran knelt over the moaning cook and studied the wound. Sen Nikol shook his head. "We take him with us regardless," Captain Shay commanded. "Get him up and drag him along. We've got to get back to the boats."

Orico was in extraordinary pain and bleeding profusely. None of the men spoke. Criston threw one of the cook's meaty arms over his shoulder and another sailor took the other arm. Together, they stumbled onward. The journey seemed endless.

By the time they reached the cove, the second exploratory group had returned to shore and built a large bonfire while waiting for the captain and his party. When they spotted Criston and the other sailor hauling the blood-covered cook, they held torches high and set up an alarm. Orico's legs barely moved now, and he had stopped moaning, but still clung to his last few breaths of life.

"Into the boats!" Captain Shay shouted. "We have to leave this island, now!"

Already spooked by the quiet and mysterious island, the sailors rushed to obey the captain's order without asking questions. Criston and his companion lifted the cook into the nearest boat and settled him, while Sen Nikol and Prester Jerard jumped aboard. The others, just as eager to be away from the strange island, pushed the boat into the deeper water as soon as the captain stepped aboard. Scrambling in, they took up the oars and plied them with all their strength. The second boat was already making its way toward where the *Luminara* lay anchored, peacefully unaware of what had happened.

Criston realized that the cook would be dead before they reached the ship, but the sailors grimly pulled at the oars. The dark silhouette of the macabre island was ominous and weirdly silent behind them.

Orico twitched, spasmed, coughed once. His last breath came out in a long gurgling rattle. Prester Jerard clutched the fishhook pendant and said a quiet prayer. The captain sat astern, like a statue. Orico was the first crewman they had lost on their long voyage.

"Keep moving," Shay said.

In the moonlight, they could see the stark line of the barrier wall, like the backbone of a gigantic fossil draped across the island. Though it might have been his imagination, Criston thought he could see the skeletons scuttling about, still fighting. He felt safer with every oar stroke that drew them farther from the cursed island.

Sen Nikol let out a yelp of surprise, an uncontrolled reaction that startled Criston. Though the cook was drenched in blood and his body had lain motionless in death, he now jerked and twitched. His elbows bent, and both hands rose up as if to flail at imaginary enemies.

"He's alive!" Criston said. "Captain—Orico is alive!"

But the cook's hemorrhaged eyes were blank. Thick dark

blood still oozed from the wound in his stomach. The dead man sat up and grasped the gunwale with one hand.

Prester Jerard blessed himself. "He was dead. I'm sure of it!"

"He still is," Sen Nikol mumbled. "The island calls him."

Criston tried to pull Orico back down; one of the sailors released his oar and grabbed the cook's other arm, but Orico shook them off with inhuman strength, pulled himself to his knees and then to his feet, nearly capsizing the boat.

"What is he doing? Stop him!"

But the dead man did not hear them. He saw nothing but the island, and the wall, and the skeleton armies there. He threw himself over the side of the boat with a great splash. Criston shouted after him.

Orico bobbed to the surface again and began to swim, making his way back to the strange shore, mindlessly determined.

With the oars stilled, the boat drifted and the men sat in uneasy silence, terrified and not sure what to do. Criston felt the sticky blood on his hands and clothes. Shay clenched and unclenched his fists, staring into the water. "The island has him now."

"It's not the island that has him," Sen Nikol corrected. "It's the war. He is part of that endless battle now. He will never rest."

34 *Khenara, Outer Wahilir*

On the Uraban coastline south of Ishalem, Zarif Omra inspected the new and heavily armed bireme war galleys being constructed in Khenara. The attack ships could not be built fast enough, as far as he was concerned. The Aidenists' appalling response to Ambassador Giladen's peace overture could not be ignored.

Long oars extended from the sides of each war galley. Beaten sheets of bronze plated the hulls. The melted-down statue of Oenar had provided enough metal for sixteen ships and two hundred curved swords. A sharp bronze beak thrust forward from each prow, ready to splinter the hull of any enemy vessel. Brightly dyed square sails of reinforced Yuarej silk were emblazoned with the Eye of Urec, which was no longer a benevolent guide, but the angry eye of a vengeful demigod.

Praying together and interpreting one another's dreams, the sikaras said they had received clear guidance, granting them not only Urec's permission but his *blessing* to melt down the second giant statue in Olabar. The spirit of Urec would live within the metal — so their dreams said — to guide the resulting weapons to shed Aidenist blood. Crowding the churches for sunset services, Urabans cheered and gave thanks, but Omra watched them in cynical silence. He knew the priestesses were simply being practical in announcing their revelations. Uraban armies needed the metal.

The surreptitious Gremurr mining operations had also been dramatically expanded and stocked with hundreds of new slaves. Iron from the mines was used to make adequate steel, which would produce the best swords.

In order to launch this swift attack fleet from Khenara, Omra had ridden long and hard from the capital city, following the caravan route from Inner Wahilir, over the pass, and down to Outer Wahilir, where Soldan Attar was still drunk with self-satisfaction at how he had "defeated and punished" the Aidenist pilgrims in the ruins of Ishalem.

Omra despised the other leader for that stupid act. Inexorable tides had thrown Urecari and Aidenist against one another in this deadly clash, but Attar had forced Uraba into battle before they had time to prepare adequately. Fool!

Pointing to the offense against Ambassador Giladen, Attar felt vindicated in his actions. "You see—they are all animals!" All Urabans had recoiled at the story of how the emissary had been murdered, the proposed peace document skewered to the deck and covered in excrement, the corpse-filled ship left to crash clumsily into the harbor of Tenér. The Tierrans had given their answer.

Though his father was sickened by the news, Omra had found the inner steel to make the necessary decision. "You tried, Father, but now a new course has been set for us. If this is to be war, we have no alternative but to crush the Aidenists. In the name of Urec and Ondun, we have to wipe them out. All of them."

He gathered his armies and departed from Olabar immediately, leaving his wife, Cliaparia, behind in the palace, barely remembering to say farewell to her. For several months, she had doted on him and given him gifts, but she had not secured a place in either his heart or his mind. Though a skilled lover and certainly beautiful, Cliaparia lived only in his peripheral vision.

Omra occupied his thoughts with war, violence, bloodshed; it was the surest way to distract himself from the loss of Istar. In the past, whenever he'd had to leave sweet Istar behind, their parting had been difficult, and he had missed her every day. By contrast, although he had not seen Cliaparia in weeks, it took him a moment to recall exactly what she looked like. . . .

Soldan Attar came up to him, accompanied by sixteen guards that made him appear important. After giving a formal bow, the leader of Outer Wahilir gestured toward the harbor, where the warships were being provisioned. "We can launch by the next full moon, Zarif. The autumn winds will pick up, but the storms will not yet have set in. We can overwhelm the Aidenists."

"I believe that this war will not be won by a mere clash of

weapons and soldiers," Omra said. "The Tierrans have armies too, but we must be smarter. We must follow my plan."

He was not naïve enough to think that their enemies would surrender easily or be defeated within the first year — or even the first five years. Urec's Log stated that each life had more than one possible course, and the bravest navigator considered all paths. So Omra had already developed an unusual scheme. When raiding the coastal villages of Tierra, his soldiers had very explicit orders.

"Our men are trained and ready," Attar continued. "All those who rode with me to Ishalem, who helped to punish the Aidenist prester-marshall and his followers, wish to join this attack and bring pain and ruin to Tierra. I, myself, shall captain one of the ships." The soldan's chest swelled. "Thus I avenge my brother's death."

"You have had your revenge," Omra said icily. "You will stay here."

"It is my right! These are my ships."

Omra did not raise his voice, but it was as sharp as a newly forged sword. "These ships belong to the soldan-shah, my father. They will serve the cause in whatever way I see fit. You are the soldan of Outer Wahilir. You will stay here and manage your lands, operate your shipyards, and prepare to receive the hostages we bring back from Tierra. *That* is the course I have set for you. If you cannot follow the map, then perhaps Outer Wahilir should have a new soldan."

Attar took an involuntary step backward, quickly raising his hands. "Please forgive me, Zarif! My emotions run high with thoughts of battle, and I forget myself."

Omra was sincere when he added in a faintly conciliatory tone, "This is but the first battle — the first of many, Soldan.

Before this war is over, there will be enough blood spilled to slake the greatest thirst. That is my promise."

He did not add that his prediction was also his greatest fear.

35 *Calay*

After the Urecari atrocities, Mateo knew it was time for him to become an adult. Once he entered the Tierran army, he would leave his current life and set a new course, far from everything he'd ever known—from Calay, from the castle, from Anjine.

Before returning home, he would have to complete a year of service and instruction in each of the five reaches. By the time he finished five years of training, he would be almost eighteen. That seemed so far off, he wondered if Anjine would still remember him.

Mateo spent the next several days in the Military District watching the royal guard drill. He saw the soldiers' families, watched their children playing around the barracks. No matter how hard he tried, he could not imagine what his life would soon be like. Although he had always dreamed of serving as a uniformed member of the royal guard and protecting King Korastine, just as his father had done, he had never given much thought to the training process.

His thoughts were interrupted by a tiny, plaintive squeak. Glancing around, he spotted a stray kitten in an alley, looking up at him and mewing. Mateo bent down to play with the kitten, whose mud-crusted fur was mostly white, with large patches of black and highlights of tan. Its ears were nearly as large as its oversized head. The kitten appeared very young, very alone, and very hungry. It could not have been weaned for more than a few weeks—if that. Yet when he bent down and extended a hand, the kitten seemed to burst with joy, butting Mateo's palm with its head, rubbing against him, and purring with great exuberance. It mewed with a shrill, earnest plaintiveness.

"What are you doing here? Where's your mother?" He picked up the kitten, and it curled against him, settling into a perfect pocket between his arm and chest. It showed no intention of ever detaching itself from him. Since Mateo would soon depart for training, he could not keep a pet. But he knew exactly what to do with it.

Cradling the kitten in the crook of his arm, he made his way back to the castle. There, in the kitchens, he scrounged a bowl of milk from the cook staff. While they all adored the cute kitten, two flour-dusted women commented that the scrawny thing would not live another week. But the kitten ravenously slurped the milk, then finished a second bowl more slowly before it licked its chops, immensely satisfied with itself.

The kitten was less pleased, however, when Mateo scrubbed at the caked mud with a wet rag. After it was nearly clean, the kitten took over and contentedly groomed itself. When the kitten—a male—was fully presentable, Mateo carried him off to Anjine, where she sat at her studies in the solarium of the castle.

"My going-away gift to you." Mateo felt strangely awkward. "*Someone* has to watch over you and keep you entertained while I'm gone."

With an indrawn breath of delight, Anjine accepted the kitten, which seemed as contented to be in her hands as in Mateo's. She scratched the back of its head until the kitten released another burst of loud purring. "What's his name?" The castle had plenty of cats to keep down the mouse and rat population, but Anjine had never adopted one as her own.

With a mischievous wink and his best courtly bow, Mateo said, "The honor of naming His Royal Furriness is yours, Princess Tolli."

Anjine grinned, regarded the kitten with its black, white, and light tan fur for a moment, then touched its little pink nose. He batted her finger with a paw. She giggled and gave Mateo a warm smile. "Since *you're* going away, I'm going to call him *Tycho*. He and I will have to make our own adventures while you're gone."

A warmth spread through his chest. "I wanted to give you something to help you remember me...."

"Of course I'll remember you!" She gave him a quick kiss on the cheek, and he blushed furiously, but Anjine, engrossed in playing with Tycho, seemed to think no more of it.

In the large Soldiers' Hall in the Military District, Mateo joined the other new recruits—the first hundred young men gathered from the districts of Calay. The call for new soldiers had gone out across the five reaches, and more recruits would be trickling in soon.

A square-jawed man with a long shock of gray hair that looked like the crest atop a warrior's helmet bellowed for them all to be silent. Comdar Delnas, who had been in charge of the Tierran military for many years of relative peace, bellowed, "You must serve a year in each of the five reaches, and at the end of that time some of you may wish to sign up for a further year of service in the Calay city guard. By moving from one end of the continent to the other, you will become familiar with every land and every people, every hardship and living condition. Not only is this good for you, it is good for Tierra, for in this way our continent's army is perfectly mixed, and every battalion understands that we are five reaches but one kingdom."

Mateo observed the recruits around him. Some of the young

men were nervous, some excited; most wore prominent fishhook pendants at their throats. Two young boys argued in whispers about whether they preferred to go to Erietta or Alamont first. The general consensus was that Soeland and Corag were the most miserable reaches. Since he would have to serve in each place, Mateo didn't particularly care where he started.

Two veteran soldiers came forward with stiff steps. One man held a tablet and stylus, the other a large beaten-copper pot. Delnas announced, "Each of the five chits inside this pot is inscribed with the name of a reach. Come forward, speak your name so it may be recorded, then draw a chit, which will tell you your first assignment."

Though many of the soldiers had known his father, Ereo Bornan, Mateo expected no special treatment, nor did he receive any. As a soldier, he might eventually distinguish himself by his own skills or bravery, but for now he was the same as all the others.

The young men formed a line and came forward, each speaking his name for the first veteran to inscribe on the tablet, and reached into the pot to withdraw a chit. After all five disks had been withdrawn, they were thrown back in and the process started again. Occasionally, one of the young men cheered or grumbled about his assignment.

Mateo drew Alamont. He nodded without comment. He was issued a standard pack and a weapon. The Alamont destrar would provide the armor and uniform during his year of service there.

Now that he knew his assignment, Mateo had one day to get his things in order. Returning to the castle at dusk, he found Anjine playing with Tycho, who already seemed much healthier. She had fashioned a toy from a scrap of cloth tied to a length of string, which she wiggled above the kitten's head. Tycho seemed to find it endlessly entertaining, jumping again and again to catch his "prey." Princess Anjine smiled uncertainly at Mateo. "When do you leave?"

"Tomorrow—for Alamont."

She shook her head, marveling at him. "My friend Mateo...a brave soldier." He thought he saw a shimmer of tears welling in her eyes.

He gave her a wry smile. "I do it for my king, and for you—my friend and future queen." He winked. "Long live Queen Tolli."

36 *Corag Reach*

Inside the workshops of Stoneholm, Aldo watched the finest Corag metalsmiths use tweezers, delicate saws edged with diamond chips, and fine files to fashion intricate gears and precisely measured gauges, following each step exactly according to the blueprints. Sen Leo had given him an important charge, and the young man insisted on monitoring each step of the progress—making a pest of himself—even though it gave him precious little time to explore the Corag countryside.

The craftsmen grudgingly tolerated his presence. Hovering over them, Aldo peered through their magnifying lenses, wanting to inspect everything. Finally, in his enthusiasm, he bumped a metalsmith who was attempting to slide a tiny axle into a minute hinge. The man spoke to Aldo with little anger, but implacable certainty. "Leave. We will deliver these instruments when they are done, and we do not wish to see you again before then."

"But I'm paying for it!"

"Yes, you are the customer, and we are the craftsmen," said

the man. "You do your part, which is to pay us. We will do our part, which is to create the finest possible instruments—without interference."

Since he was only a guest among these gruff and isolated people, Aldo had no choice but to obey. He was far from his people, his parents, his home; to the best of his knowledge, there was no Saedran temple in this entire reach. Standing beyond the cliff overhang outside of Stoneholm, he looked westward, imagining the rivers and the Oceansea, picturing it all on the Mappa Mundi. Destrar Siescu had given him leave to explore wherever he wished. It would be foolish not to take advantage of his great opportunity.

While the metalworkers continued the fabrication project in their underground workrooms, Aldo had spent some of his remaining coins to buy a sheet of paper and a lead stylus, and then he went outside.

The mountain air was cold with a stiff breeze, but the shining sun offered enough heat that he could stay outside for a short while without shivering too much. He climbed a well-worn path to the huge stone Ship's Prow chiseled out of the living rock. During an evening meal of hot soup and warm bread, Destrar Siescu had told Aldo that generations of workmen had carved that gigantic sculpture to remind them of their origins from Aiden's Arkship.

Now, from the cold platform of the granite forecastle on the immense prow, Aldo had the best view of the rugged mountain range. He smoothed the sheet of paper, weighted down the corners with small rocks, and studied the craggy landscape. He carefully aligned key marks with specific reference points and meticulously began to draw the nearby peaks. Across the dirty patches of snow, he saw thin and winding paths that spread out toward other high meadows and lost villages.

Concerned with the sea, Saedran chartsmen had little need to understand deep and mostly uninhabited mountainous terrain, but now he saw the subtleties of low passes, steep couloirs, snow-filled cirques, hanging valleys, avalanche chutes, high alpine meadows, and sheltered basins. The details of the Corag wilderness and possible paths to the Middlesea beyond that barrier of crags were not on the Mappa Mundi. Though Sen Leo had sent him here on a specific mission, Aldo could accomplish more than simply obtaining new navigation instruments.

Excited by his new project, he went inside and bundled up in warm clothing before returning to his sketching platform, where with intense care, he charted all the peaks in sight. Each mountaintop was distinctive, with a special character all its own... like an unexplored island.

He was so intent on his drawing that he did not notice the man approaching the stone Ship's Prow. He was surprised when Destrar Siescu, wrapped in a bulk of thick furs with a hood and padded mittens, appeared beside him. "My Saedran friend, they tell me you enjoy staring at our mountains."

"I am mapping them." Aldo couldn't recall that he had ever seen Siescu outside his sheltered city, certainly not so far from a roaring fire. The man looked painfully cold out in the open. "I'll explore this range, just as sailors explore the sea."

Siescu stared out at the mountains and drew in a breath of the thin mountain air. "We don't need the ocean. Our people are descendants of Aiden's crew, but just as Aiden sailed away from Terravitae, so we have left the sea and come ashore on this rugged new land. Some might see a place of harsh rocks, but I see the beauty of these mountains. Each of those peaks has a name, you know." Siescu pointed with his mitten vaguely toward one of the mountains. "That is the Raven's Head. To the left is the Sentinel. To the left of that is Thunder Crag. The three tall-est mountains are named after the brothers—Aiden, Joron, and Urec. Those over there are named after the five reaches."

This sort of information was exactly what Aldo needed. "I'd like to know the names and any information about the paths and passes. Has anyone reached the Middlesea from here?"

Siescu rubbed his mittened hands together. "Oh, there have been explorers, shepherds, travelers who made their way to the cliffs. Some say there are difficult paths that lead down to the water, but why would we want to go there? The people of Corag left the sea behind. We are content here."

The destrar shivered, though Aldo didn't feel particularly cold in the bright sunshine. Siescu said, "I will send men here to help you identify the mountains. We know to respect your people, since Saedran knowledge has saved many ships from being destroyed against the rocks or lost at sea."

He paused in his shivering, turned his face up to the sky, then back to the giant stone prow. "King Korastine has announced plans to go to war and asked for many more soldier-volunteers from Corag. I will see that he gets them. When you go back to Calay, tell them that we are loyal Aidenists and furious at what the evil Urecari have done."

Pulling his furs tight, Siescu trudged away, leaving Aldo both excited and unsettled. Within an hour, a gruff old miner came to stand with him, looking at the sketched map and comparing it to the distant peaks. As Aldo added details, the miner pointed out hidden paths, canyons, villages, roadways.

The next day, a different man came and offered additional details. Aldo was thrilled with the sheer amount of information he was compiling. He took extra time to embellish his drawing, adding detail lines, drawing birds in the sky, fluffy clouds, rush-ing torrents along the slopes. This was more than mere information; it was a work of art. He had never seen such a gloriously beautiful—and accurate—map.

He lost track of time and was surprised when, within a week, the metalsmiths announced that they had completed all of the instruments according to the blueprint specifications. Aldo inspected the ornate clock, the astrolabe, sextant, and the combination instruments, and pronounced each one satisfactory.

The instruments were packed in crates to protect them from damage in transit. Aldo sealed and preserved his map, rolling it tightly to fit in the specially locked cylinder that had held the original blueprints. Aldo wanted to make sure the embellished map was not damaged, torn, or waterstained en route. With the tube's clever seals, Aldo knew that if anything happened to him, the Corag map could be opened only by one of his people.

When he was ready to go, Destrar Siescu offered him a guide and two shaggy pack ponies to carry the boxes down out of the mountains to the river, where Aldo waited to catch the next boat, anxious to return to Calay.

37   *The* Luminara

The great storm built for two days before it threw its full fury against the *Luminara*.

The seas turned gray, and the clouds overhead became a clotted blackness, like smoke over Ishalem. The waves grew higher than the cliffs around the harbor that sheltered the village of Windcatch.

Early yesterday, Captain Shay had ordered the sails tied up and the crates and barrels battened down. The ship climbed the rolling waves, teetered, then crashed down into the troughs. Spray washed over the decks. Most of the crewmen huddling belowdecks were knocked against bulkheads or beams. Barrels and kegs broke loose from their ties and rolled across the floor. Loose objects became projectiles.

Up in the lookout nest, strapped to the mast so he wouldn't be flung to his death by the tossing vessel, Criston tried to peer through the sheeting rain and upflung spray. Despite the limited visibility, he kept watch for swaths of white foam that might indicate reefs or rocky shoals, but even if he sighted something, he doubted his warning shout would be heard above the din.

Lightning crackled overhead, flashing like a momentary torch across the churning waves. The ship's masts swayed like inverted pendulums, dipping toward the water until he was sure the *Luminara* would capsize, but each time her well-built hull righted itself, and she pushed on for her very survival.

Since clouds had blocked the sky for two days, Sen Nikol had not been able to use the stars and his instruments to determine their position. During those two days, the current had whisked them along in one direction, while the breezes pushed them at an angle. At times they had made enormous speed, while at other times Criston thought they were being pushed back the way they had come. They had sailed in a great circle—west, then south, and now east again. As the bad weather continued, crewmen had struggled to cast nets overboard for the daily catch—but inexplicably all the nets came up empty. It was as though all the fish in the Oceansea had vanished.

Pelted by rain and shivering, Criston remembered tales the sailors had exchanged about the Leviathan, a single creature so enormous and deadly that even Ondun had feared to create a mate for it. According to legend, all fish fled in terror when the Leviathan was near.

Down on the deck, spray continued to gush over the rails and a limited crew of deck workers held fast to their ropes. Captain Shay clung to the wheel, trying to keep the *Luminara* under his control, wrestling with the course. The frightened sailors sent Prester Jerard topside, so he could pray to Ondun for their safety. The old man did so with great vehemence, but Criston saw no slackening of the ferocious weather.

Sen Nikol staggered across the deck, the winds blowing his pale robes. Holding one of his navigation instruments, he struggled toward the captain's wheel, where he studied the magnetic compass to get his bearings to north, then the Captain's Compass to align their direction to Calay. But the *Luminara* was thrown up and down so wildly that both compass needles wavered, making them virtually useless.

With his instruments, the Saedran chartsman made his way to the side of the ship and tried to find any star that might provide a position. A tall curling wave capped with a crest of white rose silently, like a predator, smashed across the deck of the *Luminara*, and swept Sen Nikol overboard into the turbulent waves.

Criston screamed down to the wheel, and Captain Shay bellowed for help. But none of the sailors could leave their ropes. Sen Nikol was gone. A smaller wave curled over the rail where the Saedran had stood, washing away even his lingering footprints from the wet deck.

The deck crew was in a panic at the loss of the chartsman. Without Sen Nikol, they would not know where they were or where they had gone.

Captain Shay held fast to the wheel, soaked, battered by the driving rain. Criston heard a loud *crack*, and saw the top of the mizzen mast snap, then tumble over in a tangle of rigging. The bunched sails sagged, and under the weight, the second yardarm broke free.

The ship heeled about and bore the brunt of the waves amidships. The captain could no longer steer. Criston had to tighten his lashings to keep from being thrown out of the lookout nest; at any moment even the mainmast could break in half, and he would crash to his death — or vanish into the water.

Terrified, he suddenly understood what his father must have felt just before his fishing boat sank. He thought of Adrea and hoped she was safe.

But in his instant of greatest despair, Criston saw a glimmer of light off in the distance. It grew brighter, then dimmed, then brightened again…like a beacon. The dazzling light stabbed through the furious storm, and Criston pointed and shouted, "A light! A light!" over the howl of the wind, but he didn't think anyone heard him.

Could this be the Lighthouse at the end of the world, from the story Prester Jerard had told? Where the cursed man kept endless watch for Ondun's return? If the *Luminara* could reach that place, they would be saved. The island with the Lighthouse was not far from Terravitae!

He called out again but could not make himself heard. Captain Shay needed to know about this. Criston unlashed himself and swung down, clinging to ratlines that were slick from the pounding rain. With hands that were strong and callused, he worked his way to the first yardarm, hooked his arm through the ropes for stability, and looked out again. Yes, the beacon was still there — and brighter now. Surely other crewmen had noticed it! He stared, yearning for that light, knowing what it represented. He wasn't looking down at the sea. Even if he could have sounded an alarm, it was far too late.

The monster that rose from the black depths was impervious to the storm, greater than ten sea serpents. Its bullet-shaped head was as large as the *Luminara*'s prow, and when it opened its maw, Criston saw row upon row of sharp teeth, each one as long as an oar. It had a single round squidlike eye in the center of its forehead, and spines like a mane around its neck and ringing its gills. Armfuls of tentacles sprouted from each side, lined with wet suckers, each with a barb in its center. The tentacle ends were blind sea serpents, opening to show fang-filled mouths.

For a moment, Criston could not speak, could not breathe. He found his voice and bellowed with all his strength and all his soul, projecting his voice with enough power to call the attention of the sailors on deck. *"Leviathan!"*

Alongside the *Luminara,* the Leviathan rode the waves as though they were mere ripples. Lightning lanced out, flashing an otherworldly white glow upon its scales. The monstrous tentacles smashed into the foremast, breaking away the yardarms with unreal ease, plucking the white canvas sail like a petal from a flower before casting it into the water. The tentacles' fanged mouths snapped down, splintering the ship's rail. Two snakelike appendages snatched hapless crewmen and tossed them into the Leviathan's maw.

Captain Shay charged to the prow and grabbed a harpoon from its hooks. While other sailors were screaming, Shay stared at the monster as though mentally cataloguing its interesting aspects, then hurled the harpoon directly at its single eye. Criston had seen him throw a harpoon many months ago, skewering the Uraban pirate Fillok, but because of the ship's lurching, his aim was not true. The harpoon's jagged iron tip struck the side of the milky eye and glanced off, skittering along the scales with a flash of unexpected sparks. Captain Shay cursed the beast, raising his fists in the air.

The Leviathan reared high, opened its great mouth, and bit down, splintering wood, taking the *Luminara*'s bow—and swallowing Captain Shay along with it.

Fighting for balance, desperate not to lose his grip, Criston struggled down the mast. Belatedly, sailors on deck sprang back into action. They ran to the other harpoons to attack the Leviathan. The monster's fanged tentacles lifted crew members into the rain-whipped air and tore them apart.

When a hastily thrown harpoon stuck in one of the Leviathan's heaving gill slits, the creature let out an unholy roar, halfway between the sound of thunder and the bellow of a hundred dying whales. It submerged, but it did not go away. After a few tense seconds, it rose again, this time smashing the *Luminara* from below, fatally breaking her keel and lifting the entire hull from the water. Planks sheared off like chaff in a thresher.

Crewmen screamed. Many fell overboard, while others, still struggling up through the hatches to join the fight, were smashed or seized by tentacles. First Mate Willin finally made it to the deck, only to be crushed by a falling yardarm.

Criston could barely hold on. He grabbed a rope, still trying to make his way down to the deck, while the monster continued its attack.

Water poured into the large holes in the hull. The ship's foremast was uprooted like a weed. The Leviathan broke the deck and folded the mortally wounded *Luminara* in half. The great sailing ship fell into pieces on the sea.

Finally losing his grip on the rain-slick rope, Criston was thrown into the churning waves, which lifted him high and pounded him back down again. Choking, spitting water, he struggled to the surface, but the rushing sea whisked him far from the wreck. He could still hear the other crewmen screaming.

A yardarm floated by, tangled with thick rope and a scrap of sail. Criston clung to the wood, holding on with the desperate instinct of survival, but he knew he would be dead soon. As the

Luminara sank and the Leviathan hunted the last few screaming, struggling sailors, the currents and the storm swept him away.

38 *Off the Coast of Tierra*

With sixteen armored war galleys and hundreds of angry warriors at his command, Zarif Omra launched the raiding party from the docks in Khenara. All sails were set to show the vengeful Eye of Urec. Their journey past the blackened scar of Ishalem only served to motivate the fighters further. When they entered Tierran waters, the fighters continued up the coast in search of Aidenist fishing villages. They attacked every one they found.

With such an overwhelming force against undefended towns, each Urecari strike was more a massacre than a military engagement. Their scimitars were invincible and their victories dramatic, and the zarif learned that his most effective weapon was despair. The Aidenists could not deny that the followers of Urec were far stronger, that their faith was an anchor that held Omra and his men, while the rival religion was cast adrift.

After two easy conquests that left smoking towns and destroyed harbors behind them, Omra had lost only five fighters, and their bodies had been wrapped up and cast overboard with proper ceremony. The murdered villagers were simply left behind to rot. Captive Tierran children already filled the hold of one of the war galleys. The crew of that ship complained about babysitting when they should have been fighting, but a stern reprimand from Omra silenced their talk.

Gliding farther up the coast, the war galleys encountered and attacked two fishing boats. Omra put every Aidenist crew member to the sword, then scuttled the boats before sailing onward. He left no one alive to spread a warning as his fleet moved along like hunting sharks.

Omra spied an opening in the coastline guarded by a low wall of rock that formed a small natural harbor. With the breeze in his face, the zarif could smell the lingering stench of rotting seaweed. As he stared at the village nestled within the cove, he ordered the war ships to blockade the harbor. According to the questionable maps Uraban traders had provided, the name of this place was Windcatch.

From the broad open windows of his kirk, which sat on a small rise on the outskirts of the village, Prester Fennan spotted the approach of foreign war galleys. He grasped the rope and furiously clanged the bronze bell normally used to call worshippers to his dawn services.

Urecari attack boats swarmed into the harbor, and raiders disembarked at the town docks or sloshed onto the shingle beach. The men set fire to overturned dinghies, slashed fishing nets hung out to dry, then surged into the small village.

Fennan continued to ring the bell, hoping that some of the people would stand and fight, knowing that others would flee into the hills. Either way, he had raised the alarm.

That morning, Ciarlo had been studying with the prester inside the kirk, helping him prepare for the next dawn's prayers. Immediately upon seeing the sign of Urec on the raiders' bright sails, however, they both knew the Aidenist kirk would be a target. Fires had already been started down by the wharves, and black smoke rose from boathouses and the harbormaster's office shanty.

From the hill, Ciarlo watched dock workers grabbing boat

poles or oars to defend themselves, but the attackers struck them down with scimitars and moved onward, attacking everyone from old women to overweight shopkeepers.

"They are coming here, Prester. We have to fight for the kirk!"

"The Urecari will not respect the fishhook, boy. They'll burn this place down," Fennan said, still panting from his bell ringing. "You have to survive. We can rebuild the kirk, but they can't destroy our faith."

Frustrated, Ciarlo moved away from the altar with an exaggerated limp. "I'm not going to be running very far."

"Go into my office. Look for a trapdoor beneath my writing table. We keep our service wine there and some precious artifacts down in the root cellar. You will be safe enough."

"No—I will fight with you!"

"This is not a fight we can win, boy. And you"—Fennan glanced at Ciarlo's damaged leg—"you are not a warrior."

"You aren't a warrior, either—you're a prester! I'll stand with you and die with you, if we both must die."

"But we both don't have to die. Go and take shelter."

"You don't have to die either."

Loud shouts rang out in the yard in front of the kirk. Fennan ran to the wooden main door and pressed his shoulder against it just as heavy fists began pounding. He threw his weight to stop the raiders from crashing inside, but it wouldn't hold long. As a kirk, it did not have a crossbar to lock the door.

"Go! Ciarlo, go now—I can't delay them more than a few minutes." Wrestling with his thoughts, Ciarlo lurched toward the door to help Fennan, but the prester roared at him. "Do as I say! I am giving you a chance."

"No!"

Fennan strained against the door that rattled and shuddered

as the Urecari men threw themselves against it. One of the planks cracked. "I command it! You are my acolyte—obey me!"

Biting back a useless response, Ciarlo staggered off, still defiantly trying to show that he could run, but failing miserably. Prester Fennan was right. He got to the back room, found the hidden trapdoor underneath the table, and used the fingerholes to lift it.

The Urecari raiders hammered the door with the hilts of their scimitars and smashed the colored windows, hurling curses in their looping, glottal language. Prester Fennan yelled as the kirk doors splintered open, and a swarm of Urecari men rushed inside, bowling him over. Terrified, Ciarlo ducked into the back room just in time, as a freezing chill washed through his bones. Those men would murder Prester Fennan, and they would destroy the kirk.

We can rebuild the kirk, but we can't rebuild our faith.

Fennan was still trying to buy him time, knowing that Ciarlo could not move swiftly. In the back room, struggling to get into the hiding place, the young man cursed himself, cursed his old injury.

Backing to the altar, the village prester seized his thick Book of Aiden and lifted it as a shield, but one of the foreign invaders struck him down with two brutal blows of a scimitar. Then they began to ransack the kirk.

Terrified, Ciarlo understood now that fighting the Urecari here could serve no purpose and would only get him killed. He dropped into the dark root cellar beneath the kirk and pulled the trapdoor shut, praying he wouldn't be found.

He heard battering sounds above, the clomp of booted feet, shouts, smashing glass and splintering wood. After a long moment, they fell silent.

Then Ciarlo smelled smoke.

*   *   *

Running through the streets of Windcatch, Adrea pulled Criston's mother with her toward their home, hoping to barricade themselves inside. The raiders were smashing into shops, setting roofs on fire, seizing screaming children and dragging them back to their boats, killing virtually everyone else.

Her pregnancy was showing now. It would be another two months or more before Adrea delivered her baby, and her swollen belly made it difficult to run or fight. Telha was a scrappy woman, yes, but she would be easy prey for these awful men — Adrea had just seen well-muscled fishermen and strong dockworkers fall under a flurry of flashing swords. She and the old woman had no chance.

And the invaders kept coming. Another boatload of raiders landed on the beach, and large warships bottled up the harbor.

Ciarlo was with Prester Fennan, and the kirk was one of the sturdiest buildings in Windcatch, but as she reached the house, Adrea looked up the hill and saw the kirk burning. She felt a stabbing pain in her heart, knowing her brother was probably trapped, and he might already be dead. Telha abruptly pushed her daughter-in-law into the shelter of their house. "Whether he's alive or dead, you can't do anything for Ciarlo now." She slammed the door, and Adrea helped pile furniture against it. They built additional barricades by the windows, breathing heavily, listening to the sounds outside, looking at each other's fearful eyes.

Summoning her determination and hatred against these strangers who had come like a storm to her village, Adrea took up a heavy cast-iron pan and a long gutting knife. Telha grabbed another pan and a broomstick that she could wield as a club.

They waited together, praying that the raiders would lose interest and return to their ships. But parties of men were systematically going through the streets of Windcatch, smashing doors and murdering everyone they found. At the beginning of the raid, Adrea had seen villagers abandon their homes and flee into the hills; now she wished that she and Telha had done the same, for the raiders were on all sides.

Adrea brandished her makeshift weapons as men hammered on the plank door, shouting in a language she didn't understand. Hearing no answer, the raiders crashed through, splitting the hinges and pushing their way inside.

Telha thrust her broomstick into the gut of the first one, knocking the wind out of him. As he staggered forward, she used the heavy pan to split his skull, and he dropped to the floor. Three more men surged in, raising their scimitars. Emboldened by her first victory, Telha let out a yell and swung the pan at another man's face.

But this seasoned warrior had no compunction about killing an old woman. He thrust the sword point directly into her chest, just below the heart, paused, then rammed the blade all the way through, up to the hilt. He jerked the sword free and let Telha drop to the floor.

Adrea let out an animalistic scream, vowing to sell her life dearly. She flailed with the pan, slashed with the gutting knife, and cut a severe gash in a man's arm. A fighter wrenched the pan out of her hand, and she whirled to cut him as well.

Another Urecari man entered, and she saw he was dressed in the finery of a prince, but he too was spattered in blood — Windcatch blood. Blinded by her rage and despair, Adrea thought only of killing him.

Omra had witnessed enough death and destruction in one day to make him stop seeing it all. He had decreed that these people must die, and he moved methodically to witness the purge of this Aidenist village. He didn't count the deaths; instead, he counted the number of children taken away as trophies, but he felt only a faint glimmer of satisfaction. It had been a long time since he'd felt any real passion. Not since the death of Istar.

As his fighters burst into one particular home, he saw a young woman, her old mother killed before her eyes. She fought like a desert cougar, her fear abandoned. His soldiers overwhelmed her, wrested the cast-iron pan from her hand, and ducked her slashing knife (though two men were cut).

Something about her spirit moved him—and when he suddenly realized that she was pregnant, and further along than Istar had been when the miscarriage had claimed both her and his unborn son, Omra was stunned into unexpected paralysis. He could not drive away the bright image of sweet Istar and their lost child.

"Stop!" he shouted before the raiders could kill her. The woman wielded her knife and had raised her chin, ready to die. "*Stop*, I said!" Omra moved to intervene. "Take her with us." They had already gathered a few other women from the previous raided villages, either to be sold as slaves or to tend the captive children.

One of his men, a brash soldier from Soldan Attar's army with adrenaline-bright eyes, challenged him. "She is one of *them*. She's already cut—"

Omra wasted no time with hesitation and no breath on threats. He drew his own dagger and in a swift arc, as if slicing open a fish, he slashed the other man's throat, opening wide a second mouth beneath his jaw. The man staggered back, eyes wide, palms going to the wound as if he could catch the gushing scarlet fluid and push it back into his veins.

"Who else questions my orders?" Omra glared at the others.

The dying man collapsed with a wet thud on the floor, still twitching, still pouring out blood. The pregnant woman did not stare in shock at the murdered raider. Instead, her gaze was cold but uncertain; she didn't tear her eyes from Omra's.

He looked at her face rather than her rounded belly, confused as to why he had done this. "This woman is to be spared, I said. Take her back to the boats with the other prisoners."

As the raiders seized her, the woman struggled. As far as Omra could tell, she was not particularly pleased that he had saved her life.

39 *Calay*

As reports of Urecari depredations reached Calay, Anjine realized just how unprepared Tierra was for war. The Iborian shipwrights had only just begun to construct a full-fledged navy, and all seasoned soldiers were being rushed aboard any military ship that Tierra could muster.

Four coastal towns had been attacked, people slaughtered, homes burned, boats sunk. Survivors claimed that the Urecari had taken many children and some women as prisoners, dragging them off to their war galleys. Some believed the children would be roasted and eaten in heathen rituals, since the followers of Urec were said to love the taste of tender young flesh. Anjine had never heard such stories before, despite reading the Book of Aiden and listening to the sermons of presters. Now, however, those tales had become common knowledge.

After Mateo departed on a riverboat for his military training in Alamont Reach, Anjine had too much time to herself, and she missed having Mateo around to keep her company. No more adventures disguised as Tycho and Tolli, no more childhood.

King Korastine wanted to spend many hours patiently instructing her in statecraft, but one emergency after another sapped his energies. Every day, her father looked more weary and red-eyed as he planned his response to the latest Urecari outrages. He was convinced that the world had only begun to see the first droplets of a much larger storm.

Anjine made her way through the castle looking for her kitten. "Tycho!" But he did not yet know his name, and the castle offered a wealth of rooms and crannies for him to explore. The kitten had become extremely energetic, and he discovered countless hiding places. Each time she found him, he let out a thin, delighted meow and sprang toward her with gold-green eyes bright, ears pricked, and tail aloft. As she held him and petted him, Tycho set up a loud purr until he became restless again, squirmed out of her arms, and raced off to play.

Now she couldn't find him, and she worried he might have gotten hurt. "Tycho!" she called again, heading up the steps to the higher levels of the castle. Each riser was tall, but the kitten could bound up one step after another, until he reached the next floor, where he would find new hiding places.

Anjine discovered Tycho in the tower room where she'd once met with the king, Sen Leo na-Hadra, and Prester-Marshall Baine, when they had decided to send a reconstruction crew to Ishalem. "There you are, little mischief-maker!" She gathered the kitten, scratched under his chin, stroked the top of his head. Tycho looked at her with a curious expression, as if wondering why she had taken so long to find him. Anjine laughed at how silly he looked.

Then her gaze lifted to the shelf, where the detailed sympathetic model of the *Luminara* rested. The replica lay destroyed, smashed to splinters.

Tycho squirmed in her arms and jumped down to the floor, wanting to play, but Anjine stared dumbly at the model. Everything was broken apart. The *Luminara* had been wrecked!

She raced from the chamber and bounded down the stone stairs three at a time. She had to tell her father the awful news.

40 *Olabar*

Recovering his strength by faith and sheer force of will, Prester Hannes had healed sufficiently that he could get out of bed. But he did not let Asha know how strong he had become. Every day trapped in Olabar, and tended by the soldan-shah's wife, pained him like a knife tip worrying at his wounds.

Asha treated him like one of her pets: coddling him, feeding him. She prayed over his bed, expecting Hannes to join in as she attempted to sell his soul to a false god. He bided his time.

When she left him alone in the beautifully appointed chambers of her residence (along with three cages of birds that would not stop singing), Hannes climbed out of bed and found a loose green robe among other garments in the room. Hissing in pain but clamping his lips together to stifle any sound, he struggled to get dressed. He had no thought for what he would do beyond escaping. Nothing else mattered now.

Hannes whispered a heartfelt prayer, asking Aiden for deliverance from this place, then grasped the bedpost and swayed, gathering his energy. Yes, his body did function. Yes, he could get out of here.

Then Asha bustled into the room, saw what he was doing, and

let out a gasp of worry and delight. She rushed forward to take his arm. "Let me help you! I'm so glad you're up. Come with me to the balcony."

Despite his reluctance, he leaned on her, and they walked with small, slow steps across the tiled floor. He felt his muscles reawakening from long dormancy. His vision seemed blurred by the burns and the healing salve; his left upper eyelid had healed awkwardly, heavy with scar tissue, but it worked well enough.

Asha tugged the loose hangings aside to let Hannes step into the bright sunshine and fresh air. Much too bright. From her private villa, he gazed at the foreign city's towers, cupolas, and minarets, the winding streets that led down to the crowded marketplace near the docks, the long low ships that filled the harbor. The many-turreted palace of the soldan-shah stood not far away. Immediately beneath the balcony, Hannes saw Asha's personal gardens, colorful flowers and a small orchard of mulberry trees.

"You are still such a mystery to me. We found you in Ishalem, but we don't know where you came from." Asha paused, waiting for him to answer, but Hannes remained silent. She continued to chatter. "You've been through a terrible ordeal, but you're so much stronger now. What is your name? When do you think you can tell me more about yourself? I want to know it all! Soon Soldan-Shah Imir will invite us to the palace. I told him about the man I rescued—a holy man." She beamed at him, her dark eyes sparkling. "All the priestesses are praising you for rescuing the amulet of Urec. You have done a great service to the church."

What foolish assumptions Asha was making—or perhaps it was all part of a carefully planned deception. Hannes seethed, barely able to control himself; his vision turned red.

Suddenly Asha looked worried, as if she sensed his volatile mood. "The joy of Ondun must be filling you right now, but please do not strain yourself. Let me take you back to bed. After the sunset services, I will return with your meal. We'll talk some more then." She guided him back across the floor.

He didn't want to collapse onto the cushions piled on the bed; he wanted to strike Asha and curse her for what she had done to him. "Until evening," he managed to say. His words came out in a croak, and he suddenly realized that speaking Uraban had become even more natural to him than his own Tierran tongue.

She left him a pot of sweet mint tea and a dish of cut oranges with rosewater. "This afternoon the soldan-shah has asked me to attend him as he tells of Zarif Omra's wonderful raids against the Aidenists, and after that we will attend the sunset services. In the meantime, a sikara could read with you, pray with you. Shall I send one to minister to you?" Oh, Asha was so devious!

Hannes could be devious, too. "No. Only you," he said, and Asha brightened at that. He lay back to lull her suspicions. Without revealing any important details about himself, he tricked her into telling him things about Olabar, about the Urecari preparations for war. Unfortunately, the soldan-shah's wife knew and cared little about politics, and she could give him few specifics about what had happened in far-off lands.

After she departed, he had several hours to plan.

At sunset, he heard shrill bells ringing from the many churches in Olabar. He was surrounded by enemies, perhaps the only faithful Aidenist in this entire city. This must be a test of his faith, an ordeal he would have to endure. And he vowed to show his strength and do what was necessary. Even now, he knew that the soldan-shah and his wives would be finishing their heretical worship services.

When Asha returned, she wore colorful scarves draped around formal garments; her face had been painted, and a smell of sandalwood incense clung to her. Looking breathless, as if she had rushed, she entered the room carrying a golden plate upon which rested a goblet and small strips of translucent paper. A tray of food sat on the side table.

"I wish you could have gone with me," she said. "Ur-Sikara Lukai wants to give you her personal blessings."

Hannes sat up in bed as Asha curled onto the sheets, setting the golden plate next to him. The balanced goblet was half full of a dark red wine. Hannes looked down suspiciously, and she explained. "I've brought you the Sacraments. How fine it will be to have you awake for them! You weren't aware of what was happening, all those other times."

All those other times?

From a bedside table, Asha withdrew the ever-present copy of Urec's Log and flipped open its illuminated pages. She ran her fingers down the lines of looping Uraban text until she found the verses she wanted.

"What did you mean, I wasn't aware of what was happening?"

Asha blinked at him, then smiled once more. "Oh, while you were unconscious, we had to minister to you. We prayed over you. Though you slept, we presented the Wine and the Name." Asha read her verses and picked up one of the pieces of tissue-thin paper, upon which had been written the name of Urec. "Swallow this, and take the spirit of Urec inside you."

A thrill of disgust went up Hannes's back like a line traced by a hot spike as he realized what she had done. While he had lain writhing in delirium, struggling through the pain of his horrific burns, she had pried open his lips, forced the abominable thing into his mouth, made him swallow. "You gave this to me while I was...sleeping?"

"Four times," Asha soothed gently. "We were very diligent;

fear not. We did not let you miss any of the holy days." She lifted the goblet of wine to him. "We safeguarded your soul."

Rage overwhelmed him. He wanted to vomit out all of the hateful corruption she had forced into his body, but he was already damned. She had stolen his soul during his nightmares.

He slapped at the goblet, splashing its contents in her face. Startled, Asha drew back. Her hair and swirling scarves dripped with bloodred wine. "What is it? What have I done?"

Hannes had tested himself that afternoon, lifting objects, walking around the room, flexing his muscles. He was much stronger than Asha suspected, and now he knocked aside the platter with the scraps of paper bearing the name of Urec. He threw himself upon Asha, grabbing her scarves and wrapping them around her thin, smooth throat. "You defiled me!"

She beat at him with hands that fluttered like the birds in their cages. He needed to kill this demon masquerading as a benevolent woman. She had tricked him, forced him to participate in rituals that were anathema to him.

He twisted and tightened the scarves until Asha's eyes bulged and her tongue protruded from her mouth. Her wine-damp hair clung to one cheek. She shuddered, her struggles more feeble now. *Just a little more.* Her right ankle twitched in a last spasm, faintly jingling the tiny silver bangles there.

Hannes's heart pounded, and sweat trickled from his pores. The songbirds were agitated in their cages, chirping, fluttering around. He had listened to their incessant noise for too long. They never stopped—*never.* He opened the cages and killed each of the birds, strictly out of spite.

The time had come to leave Asha's villa and get away from Olabar. Hoping that no one had heard the noise of their struggle, Hannes quickly dressed himself, then ate the food Asha had brought with her. He had to hurry, and he had to be smart. He would need money to survive.

With a vicious yank, he tore off Asha's silver anklet, searched her body and stripped away her jewels. With one of her scarves that lay loose by her head, he formed a makeshift satchel, which he filled with other useful items from the chamber.

The balcony butted up against a low hill that descended into the gardens. With slow, painful moves, Hannes swung himself off the balcony and stole away into the shadows of the mulberry trees. Finding an unwatched gate at the garden wall, he darted through. Soon, he found himself in the tangled streets and anonymity of the Uraban capital.

By the time he heard the first wails of grief and cries of alarm ring out, he had already reached one of the many alleys. Asha's pet hounds set up a loud baying. Hannes glanced at the commotion and smiled, content with what he had done as he vanished into the city streets.

41 *Position Unknown*

Drifting among the wreckage, Criston awoke coughing and shaking, soaked in salt water—but alive.

The sky above him was mockingly clear and blue. The waves were calm, as though the storm's fury had been spent once the Leviathan destroyed the *Luminara*. Apart from the sloshing of waves and slap of water on debris, the world around him was utterly silent.

He was alone.

Criston clung to a splintered yardarm tangled with ropes and a scrap of sail. All around him the water was cluttered with flotsam and jetsam from the smashed ship: hull planks, sailcloth, leaking crates, bobbing kegs. And bodies. His shipmates.

"Hello!" He listened in the watery stillness for any response. *"Hello?"*

The debris was spreading apart, drifting away, and Criston realized that if he was to survive—even for a little longer—he had to gather whatever he could. Something out there might be vital.

Releasing the yardarm that had held him afloat throughout the stormy night, he swam to the nearest crate, grasped it and, kicking and splashing, pushed it back toward the yardarm, to which he secured it with a length of waterlogged rope. He swam out again, farther this time, and retrieved a keg of salted meat. Next, to his great relief, he found an intact cask of water; thirst would be his worst enemy out here...unless the Leviathan came back.

Criston kept calling out as he swam in wider and wider circles, but he heard no answer.

The corpses floating facedown were sailors with whom he had worked during the long months of the voyage. Many bodies were smashed and battered, their faces bloated; a few had already been gnawed by predatory fish. Unfortunately, he recognized all of the men.

He retrieved another yardarm and another long tangle of rope, to which a grappling hook was secured. He brought everything back to his ever-growing cluster of salvage, including a waterlogged package wrapped in oilcloth. Back on his meager floating shelter, Criston gingerly unfolded the coverings and found a leather-bound book: the journal in which Captain Shay had made his notes and drawings of sea serpents.

Criston stared at the smeared ink on the pages, not even realizing that he was sobbing. He rewrapped the volume and set it among the pile of rescued possessions. Then he set out on his search again.

At last, he did find one survivor—Prester Jerard. The old man was caught in a torn sheet of sailcloth and a splintered spar just buoyant enough to keep his head above water. Jerard was stunned, groggy, but he responded when Criston clasped him. "Prester! You're alive!"

The old man coughed, spat out water, and ran trembling hands through his tangled gray beard. "For now."

Criston wrapped his hands under the prester's arms and stroked back toward his makeshift raft. After Jerard balanced himself aboard two adjacent crates, he gazed about, taking a long time to realize where he was. "Where are the other survivors?"

Criston hung his head. "*I* am the other survivor."

Jerard touched the fishhook pendant at his neck and uttered a quick, automatic prayer. The old man came out of his daze long enough to note—in a distracted way—that he had a broken wrist and a deep cut on his forearm. With a strip of cloth, Criston bound the prester's wound and set the broken wrist as best he could.

But the scent of blood and bodies had sent out a silent call in the sea, and sharp gray dorsal fins appeared among the wreckage. With splashing and tearing sounds the circling sharks continued to devour the floating corpses of the *Luminara*'s crew. They had plenty to feed on. Criston and Jerard could only huddle together, and watch, and listen to the sickening sounds as darkness began to fall. The makeshift raft drifted along throughout the endless night.

The *Luminara* had sailed far beyond all known charts. Criston and Jerard had no hope of returning to any place they knew, even the empty island of skeleton warriors. In recent weeks, the swift currents had carried the ship in a great circle, and the storm winds had driven them blindly eastward. But they were still *nowhere*. Their only chance was to stumble upon another shore.

At the height of the storm's fury, Criston had spotted a beacon that might have been the Lighthouse at the edge of the world, but he had seen no further sign of it since. He had no way of finding it again... if indeed the vision had been more than his imagination.

The two ate sparingly of the food Criston had recovered. The next morning he lashed the components of the raft together securely with pieces of frayed rope. The grappling hook tied to a long, loose cord proved particularly useful, for he could cast it to nearby pieces of wreckage and haul them in, like a fisherman. With so many sharks circling now, he did not want to swim about as he had done the day before.

For his own sanity, Prester Jerard told stories and recited from the Book of Aiden as they huddled under a makeshift shade that Criston fashioned from a piece of sail and a thin spar. The wound in his arm continued to soak the salt-encrusted bandage. Criston changed the dressing, but the prester was in such pain from his broken wrist that he could not pull the bindings tight.

As the sun dazzled overhead, Criston kept an attentive watch over the waters around him, looking for any sign of land on the distant horizon, maybe some last miracle from the *Luminara*. Most of the flotsam had drifted far away by now, but Criston spotted a reflected glint floating in the water that was probably something made of glass. He stared for the better part of an hour, but the intriguing object drifted no closer, apparently pacing them.

Finally, curiosity so consumed Criston that he dove off the raft and swam toward the object. Jerard kept a sharp eye out for triangular dorsal fins, while the young sailor retrieved the object—a glass bottle, firmly corked. He grabbed it and stroked back toward the raft.

The prester cried, "Shark! Shark!" Criston swam faster, not daring to look, until he finally reached the questionable safety of the raft and threw himself aboard, swinging his feet onto the wet crates and thick yardarms. Panting, blinking bitter water out of his eyes, he glanced back to see a large shark veering off, having lost its quarry.

As his heartbeat slowed, Criston picked up his prize, hoping it would be something useful. The glass was dirty. Drops of water sloshed around inside from a leak where a piece of the cork had broken off. He uncorked the bottle, withdrew a tightly rolled letter: one of the messages he had written to Adrea and cast into the sea. The last time he had thrown a letter in a bottle overboard had been the day before the storm...and it had drifted back here.

Criston extracted the golden strand of her hair and just stared at it, longing for her. He still had the remnants of her lock of hair tucked into his pocket, secured there with a brass clip. He was sure now that would be all he'd ever see of her again....

Over the next two days, more sharks gathered, their knifelike fins gutting the surface of the sea, endlessly circling. Criston and Prester Jerard could do nothing more than watch.

He read the water-stained letter again and again, thinking of Adrea, remembering what he had thought when he'd written it. Everything was different now. He would not be coming home as he had promised....

On the fourth day, most of the circling sharks disappeared, their fins vanishing into the depths. Criston stood on their wobbly raft, scanning the water, wondering what could explain this odd new change.

Suddenly, with a tremendous splash, the dragonlike head of a sea serpent rose up, scarlet fins extended, spines outthrust. It snapped up a large gray shark that wriggled in its fang-filled jaw like a minnow seized by a pelican. The sea serpent tossed the shark into the air, opened its maw wide, and gulped it down.

Looming high, dripping runnels of water, the creature looked down upon the raft and the helpless men, but it did not attack. After a blast of steam from its blowhole, the serpent gradually submerged. Criston and Jerard blinked at each other in awe.

For the rest of that day, no shark returned, but a second sea serpent rose up to regard them. It was joined by a third, then a fourth. The scaly monsters hissed and hooted at one another, contemplating this intriguing object. With an ache in his chest, Criston thought that Captain Shay would have taken copious notes in his journal.

The serpents circled the raft, drawing closer…just like the hunting sharks, but worse.

42 *Urecari Slave Ship*

Despite her circumstances and her despair, Adrea refused to think of herself as a captive. But that did not mean she was free.

The ruthless Urecari raiders had shouted at her, threatened her. They tied her arms and threw her aboard one of their long-boats, along with many captured children from the village. They rowed out to the war galleys waiting at the mouth of Windcatch Harbor.

The children wailed and shuddered, cowed into submission after having seen their parents murdered. The few female captives from other villages were frantic, begging their unresponsive captors for mercy. Adrea, though, didn't say a word. She didn't think she had any words left in her, so she sat back with her lips pressed together, refusing to make a sound. When the whole world was out of control, this was one thing Adrea *could* control. She would not give them the satisfaction of hearing her say anything.

The Urecari men didn't seem to notice, or care, whether or not she spoke.

Watching her village recede, Adrea recalled how the day had dawned so brightly. Now it ended in smoke, blood, and pain. She saw the smoldering kirk on the hill, and realized that Ciarlo must indeed be dead along with Prester Fennan. She had watched these men murder Telha, and if it weren't for the baby she carried, she would rather they had killed her as well. She would live for the child, but even if she escaped, even if she returned home to wait for Criston in the ruins of Windcatch, how could she ever tell him that his mother had been slain? She could have done more, fought harder, run faster.

The men put all the new captives aboard the nearest war galley, where Adrea again saw the haughty Uraban prince who had killed one of his own soldiers and commanded that she be taken alive. He shouted orders from a captain's platform. Only a few women had been taken from other villages, and none but herself from Windcatch. She didn't understand why he had singled her out, why he had taken her alive, but Adrea did not let herself believe that she was safe; the man must have something far worse in store for her.

With the colorful sails stretched taut and the oars pulling against the current, the war galleys moved off. Adrea trapped a silent moan at the bottom of her throat. When Criston returned, he would never be able to find her. . . .

*   *   *

Satisfied with the destruction they had caused, the Urabans turned south again. Seeing the ruins of Ishalem, Adrea realized that they had left Tierra and entered enemy territory. Now she truly knew that she would be a prisoner forever.

The other captive women whispered to one another, imagining worse and worse fates. Adrea held her rounded belly, felt the baby there; the thought that her child would be born in enemy hands terrified her more than anything else. Criston's son or daughter would either be killed at birth, clubbed to death because the Urabans didn't want it, or raised among the enemy. Adrea wasn't sure which was worse.

She couldn't understand why the Uraban prince wanted so many captive Ticrran boys and girls. With their light complexions and blond, red, or brown hair, they would never fit in among the other Urabans. She feared they were all doomed to a life of slavery.

The mysterious prince had come to see her only once. He stood tall over her and spoke in Uraban. Though Adrea recognized a few words derived from the old language, which Prester Fennan had taught, and caught the gist of his expressions and sentences, she did not answer him. She gave no sign that she comprehended. She refused to speak.

Later, one of the swarthy crewmen spoke to her in a gruff voice, using heavily accented Tierran. "Zarif Omra demands to know your name."

Adrea merely stared at him, renewing her resolve. *Zarif Omra.* So that was the prince's name. She clamped her lips shut.

"Name!" he shouted. She turned her head away. He slapped her. Her head jerked to one side, but she gave him only a murderous glare in reply. She actually welcomed the pain, which was trivial compared to the suffering the rest of her village had endured. She had survived relatively unscathed. So far.

The crewman raised his hand to strike her again, and seemed disappointed when she did not flinch. "Omra says you must live, but he did not say I can't hurt you." The sailor gave her a cold smile. Adrea turned away, ignoring him. He struck her on the back of the head so hard that her teeth clacked together. She clamped her jaws and refused to speak. Angry, the sailor stalked off. The other captives stared at her, but Adrea focused only on her own thoughts.

At night, she huddled close to her miserable companions, listening to them moan and beg. She expected the raiders to drag the women one by one to an open area of the deck, rape them repeatedly, then throw their abused bodies overboard. But they did not touch the women, or the children.

Making sure none of the Urecari men saw her, Adrea lowered her voice to a bare whisper, trying to find out who had been taken from Windcatch, which other villages had been raided. Already, her voice sounded hoarse and strange to her. She learned little from the other women, and sailors came by, growling at the captives to keep them quiet.

During the fifth day out of Windcatch, one of the women threw herself overboard, taking a young child with her, and both vanished into the water. From that day forward Zarif Omra ordered all the women and children to be tied together and secured to iron rings on the deck. Adrea hunkered down and returned to her defiant silence.

The war galleys finally docked in a coastal city south of Ishalem. Adrea heard the name Khenara spoken, a place out of exotic stories. Now she was actually seeing it. She hated the sight.

The buildings were strange and foreign-looking. The people spoke a language she could not understand, though again she recognized a few words. Shouting sailors ordered all of them to disembark from the war galleys. Standing with her fellow captives on the sandy beach of Khenara, Adrea wondered if they would be sold here in a slave market, until she realized that this city was not their final destination. The raiders hastily built an extensive camp and prepared for a much longer overland journey.

The air was warm and dusty, and the women and children slept out in the open on grassy slopes leading down to the beach. They rested for a day while Omra and his men rounded up horses and pack animals for a caravan.

Looking at the sea, Adrea wanted to call out to Criston, who was out there, far beyond the horizon, but her voice would not come. She simply sent her beseeching thoughts out to him.

The next day their captors led them away from the Oceansea, away from Tierra, and hopelessly far from anything Adrea had ever known.

43 *Olabar Palace*

Since Asha was preoccupied with her latest project—not a bird with a broken wing or a stray cat this time, but an injured man she'd recovered from Ishalem—Soldan-Shah Imir had his choice of returning to the quarters of his second wife, Villiki, or spending the night alone.

While Villiki was pleased to have more of his time and attention, she often found excuses to avoid his physical advances, suggesting a game of *xaries* or just conversations about court gossip (along with her advice on how he should handle certain political matters). Still, it was better than spending the night alone in a cold bed.

Imir went to her quarters and lounged on the cushions while Villiki ordered her handmaidens to bring him tea, which she would probably lace with soporific herbs so he would be too sleepy to attempt a drawn-out seduction. Villiki was still a fine-looking woman, despite her age. (Imir knew he wasn't being entirely fair, since he himself was seven years older than she.) She took great care to maintain her beauty, preserve her skin, and wear perfectly fitting clothes.

Before he could relax in her presence, a servant came to the door, delivering a letter with due deference. The soldan-shah frowned to see that it was the latest missive from Lithio, brought in by a horseman from Missinia.

Seeing the letter from his first wife, Villiki turned cold, and Imir felt his chances for sex vanish in an instant. With a sigh, he read the letter, knowing what Lithio would say — how much she missed him, though she had never much cared for his company when she had it. She asked again when he would come to visit her and bring their son, Omra. Imir knew she really didn't *want* to see him, and she knew he wouldn't make the journey; by making her request, she merely made him feel guilty. Her letter went on for more than two pages with descriptions of her thorn hedges and flower gardens, a fountain that had broken, new well-blooded yearlings that had just been brought to the Arikara stables. None of the news was the least bit interesting to him.

When Villiki rubbed his shoulders invitingly, he knew that she wanted something. Maybe he could negotiate a better night after all. . . . But before she could utter her request, a red-faced guard burst into the chamber. The last time Imir had seen one of his soldiers so distraught, Ishalem had been on fire.

"It is Asha! Lady Asha! She's been murdered!"

Imir lurched up from the cushions, not sure he'd heard properly. "Asha? But she's —"

"Strangled. Someone murdered her in her villa, then fled."

Disbelief erupted in his heart and mind. He felt as though someone had struck him in the head with a heavy club. Who would kill Asha? Why would anyone *want* to hurt Asha—sweet, beautiful Asha, who cared only about everyone and everything else, every lost cause? "Who? Who has done this?"

"We think it was the man in her care, Soldan-Shah. The burned man who came from Ishalem."

Imir moaned, knowing only too well how she took care of her pets. Asha would have wanted to tend the man herself, as though he were the child she had never had.

"Oh, Asha!" He fell back on his automatic response, not daring to think further. He was the soldan-shah of all Uraba; he should be able to solve any problem. "Call Kel Rovik call all of my guards! I want horsemen in the streets, men to search every house, door to door! Who was this man? What does he look like? What is his name?"

"We have no description, Soldan-Shah. He told no one his name. Even the doctors only saw him burned, covered with salves, bandaged. Asha gave him the Sacraments herself, and fed him."

No name, no appearance...the man had been a nameless victim from the city fire. A sudden chill went through his heart, freezing even the horror and outrage. "What if he is a shadow-man, an evil spirit unleashed in the burning of Ishalem? What if he still wanders Olabar, seeking other victims?"

Villiki strode over and yanked a cloak about herself. "I will go immediately to the church, have all the sikaras write and burn prayer strips."

A second thought fell into place for Imir—not supernatural, but just as frightening. "Or he could be an Aidenist assassin, sent to infiltrate us so he could kill my wife—my *wives*. How many disguised murderers did King Korastine unleash among us after he killed Ambassador Giladen? We must find them!"

Kel Rovik burst into the room, accompanied by ten of his guards, all with scimitars drawn and ready.

"Hunt him down, Rovik!" Imir's voice cracked. "Hunt down the murderer, bring him to justice! But don't kill him — I must question him." After pacing around the room, Imir sank back to the cushions and placed his hands over his face as grief thundered through him. "Oh, my Asha!"

Villiki was at his side with a whisper in his ear. "My love, my Imir. I am not afraid. You still have me. I will always —"

It took every scrap of his control to keep from striking her. Imir pushed her roughly away, then staggered out of her quarters. He needed to be with his guards, hunting through the streets for the murderer.

44 *Position Unknown*

During a brief squall on their fifth day adrift, Criston feared that another horrific storm would whip up and smash the makeshift raft to pieces, that the Leviathan itself would chase away the sea serpents and devour them in a single gulp. A drenching rain fell.

Pockets in the bunched sailcloth captured water, with which they refilled the small keg. Criston and Prester Jerard scrambled to fill an empty cask — and even the glass bottle that had held Criston's letter to Adrea — with fresh water. They turned their faces to the sky, mouths agape like hungry hatchlings, soothing their parched throats and drinking their fill. The rain passed by midday.

The men ate the last of the food Criston had retrieved, then created makeshift nets from pockets of cloth to catch a few small wriggling fish, which they ate raw and whole. Jerard even dangled his fishhook pendant over the side of the raft with a scrap of bloodied bandage as bait. Though the symbolic hook was not sharp, they caught several fish that way, but when the thread grew frayed, the prester feared he would lose his beloved pendant and placed it back around his neck.

The old man's face was gaunt, his eyes shadowed with ever-worsening pain; Jerard shied away from changing the bandages, but Criston finally removed the cloth and saw that the wound was swollen, bulging with pus and black strands of gangrene working their way up Jerard's arm. Criston said nothing, nor did the prester, but they both knew the old man would not survive long.

Keeping his face turned away from Jerard, Criston tightened the ropes because parts of the raft had begun to loosen, leaking water. He still had the rope and the iron grappling hook, but nothing to fasten it to. To distract himself and the old prester, he took out Captain Shay's journal and studied the sketches and descriptions, but they offered no help, merely a reminder of the captain's thoughts and dreams.

Criston could see nothing in any direction as baking sun reflected off the waves, and the monotonous light began to make him delirious. He tried to sleep, but the cool shelter of night seemed far away. He came back to his thoughts, confused and disoriented.

Fumbling with one hand, Prester Jerard slid the fishhook pendant over Criston's head. The old man patted him, pressing the symbol against his chest. "Take this. I don't want the Leviathan to have it."

"The Leviathan? What do you mean?" Criston blinked. "What are you doing?"

Jerard muttered a brief benediction. "You have a long journey ahead, but mine is at its end. I have longed to see Terravitae all my life, and now I realize that I cannot get there by any earthly ship. I will find a different route to the land of Holy Joron."

He rolled himself off the side of the raft and into the water.

With a shout, Criston lurched after him and nearly fell off the creaking structure.

"May the Compass guide you," the old man called as he stroked away. Reeling, Criston prepared to jump in and retrieve him.

As though Jerard had summoned it, a huge black sea serpent rose from the water, mottled with swirling patterns of golden scales. It opened its mouth and made a sound that was partly a bark, partly a bellow. Steam whistled from its blowhole. Jerard raised his hands from the water as if to fend it off—or to pray.

Criston yelled, trying to draw the serpent's attention, but it had seen its prey. Like a striking viper, the sea serpent flashed down to the water, mouth open wide. It grabbed the prester in its jaws and swallowed the old man in a single gulp.

Crying out in horror, Criston hurled the glass bottle, which shattered against the black scales, making the sea serpent flinch. The monster twisted around, its gills flaring, its sharpened fins rising like bristling fur on the back of a cat.

Seeking something else to use as a weapon, Criston seized the grappling hook and twirled it over his head, letting the rope play through his palms. He threw the sharp hook at the serpent, hating the creature for what it had done to his friend and companion.

The serpent turned away, and the sharp iron hook caught and snagged in its blowhole. Startled, the serpent thrashed, which only set the barbs deeper—then bolted, trying to flee. With the hooks in place, dug into the opening on the back of its head, the creature could not submerge.

The rope paid out, burning Criston's palms, but he could not hold the serpent back. Astonished, Criston recalled the story of Sapier and his sea serpent....

Working urgently, he found the other end of the rope and secured it to the yardarm at the heart of the raft, gambling all his hope on this one perilous possibility. If he were going to die, he might as well choose the time and place. The slack in the rope suddenly ran out, slamming tight and making the whole raft shudder. Criston grabbed the edge to keep from being thrown overboard.

The frantic sea monster reared up out of the water, keeping its blowhole above the surface, black and gold scales glittering in the afternoon sun. With a great roar, the serpent plunged forward, churning up a furious wake and tugging the raft along at breakneck speed.

45 *Calay, Saedran District*

Returning from the high mountains of Corag Reach, Aldo looked with a new eye upon the once-familiar buildings, waterways, and bridges of Calay. He had not previously realized how seeing new landscapes could give him a different perspective on everyday things.

When he arrived in the Saedran District with his crated navigational instruments, Aldo gave a young boy one of his few remaining copper coins and told him to go find Biento and Yura na-Curic with the news that he had returned from Corag.

Knowing his main duty, he set off for the Saedran temple, eager to deliver the new instruments to Sen Leo. Inside, the scholar came forward with a gleam in his eye. "So my young chartsman has passed the first test. You reached your destination, found workers to do your bidding, managed the project to its culmination, and…paid a fair price, I presume?"

Sen Leo led them through the secret doorway, down the narrow steps, and into the vaulted underground chamber. Once they were in the Mappa Mundi room, he helped Aldo to pry open the small crates, pulled aside the packing, and looked at the fine devices. "I see the Corag craftsmen have outdone themselves. Again."

"The fabricators wouldn't allow me to look over their shoulders to monitor their work. They said I was disturbing them."

"No doubt you were." Sen Leo removed the first delicate instrument, adjusted the hemispherical gauges, and aligned the Saedran markings. "Mmm, the armature moves smoothly. The calibration lines match perfectly." He adjusted a lens, sighted along a graduated line, and nodded. He set down the instrument and chose the sealed clock instead. "We will test this one against our own perfect clock in Calay for months before we allow a chartsman to take it aboard a ship."

Just then, his father bustled through the door of the upper temple. Glad to see his son, Biento threw his arms around Aldo, patting him heavily on the back. "I missed you! Wen and Ilna have been constant pests since you've been gone. Your mother could barely keep her sanity."

"I missed all of you, too, but I saw many wonderful things, and now I can add my observations to the Saedran library." He looked up at the great map of the known world drawn on the temple walls and ceiling. Aldo saw the sparse details of Corag Reach, where the sketched mountain peaks were symbolic rather than topographic.

Very pleased with himself, Aldo unslung the cylinder, deftly worked the combination seal, and reached inside to pull out the rolled paper on which he had drawn all of the known mountain peaks, gorges, valleys, passes, and villages. "These are new details. Let us compare them to the Mappa Mundi."

His map of Corag was exceptionally beautiful, perhaps even worthy of gilding. He had scribed the labels in perfect penmanship, the artwork so detailed it looked like a painting of the landscape. He was sure his father would be proud of his artistic skill.

Aldo offered the paper to his father. "I took careful measurements, aided by the Corag destrar. I spoke to the people in the mountains and learned the names of every peak." Grinning, he pointed to the Mappa Mundi on the wall. "*This* is not accurate enough. I have filled in the blanks."

Sen Leo frowned, deep in thought. "It's true, Saedrans have sent explorers far out to sea, hoping to find some sign of our sunken homeland, but we have not given equal attention to looking inland." He tapped the mountains Aldo had drawn with such lush detail. "This could be vital information."

"'Knowledge is always vital,'"Aldo quoted. "Isn't that what you taught me in one of our first lessons?"

The scholar chuckled. "So you were listening even then."

Biento traced the details of Aldo's map with a fingernail, committing everything to his perfect memory. "Aldo, you haven't even made your first seagoing voyage yet, and already you have added to the Mappa Mundi." He pulled over a stepstool and a measuring line, then used a charcoal stick to sketch in the topography his son had brought back. He did not need to refer to the drawn map again.

Aldo beamed. He could tell Sen Leo was pleased with what he had accomplished, both in obtaining the instruments and making these observations. The old scholar took the paper with the meticulously drawn details and lavish artwork. He rolled it up, handing it back to Aldo. "There. It has served its purpose. Now take it to the brazier over there." He pointed to a brass dish on a thin pedestal. "Burn it."

Shocked, Aldo thought of how much time he had spent, how much effort he had put into capturing all the lines and details. The art, the calligraphy, the landscape details, the perspectives. "But I worked—"

Sen Leo cut him off. "Do not forget that the chartsman *is* the map. It must reside in your head and nowhere else. If we leave items such as this"—he pushed the map into Aldo's hand—"others might gain access to our knowledge. We commit nothing permanently to paper. The knowledge is what matters, not the...frippery."

Aldo hung his head. "I understand."

Sad and disturbed, he went to the empty brazier, where he crumpled the map and used a sulfur-tipped match to set fire to the edges. While the yellow flames turned the paper brown, Aldo could not tear his gaze away as the paper curled and the ashes fell away.

46 *Olabar*

After killing Asha, Prester Hannes moved like an oily shadow through the streets of the Urecari capital. His heart pounded, and his instincts screamed at him to *run*.

But nobody knew his name, and few people could identify him. The soldan-shah's wife had kept him in a separate part of her villa; the physicians and sikara priestesses had seen him wrapped in bandages. Asha had tended him herself, washing him, applying salves and perfumes, administering the vile Sacraments. Hannes had never felt so filthy in his life.

Fortunately, she was dead now. Her soul would face Aiden and the truth before being sent to damnation.

Hannes slipped through the bent and twisted alleys. Most of the people were asleep, but some came to their windows to see the cause of all the commotion back at the villa, where lantern-carrying guards hunted through Asha's gardens. Two riders clattered past on the cobblestoned streets, heading to the soldan-shah's palace.

Hannes hoped the death of Asha would be a great blow to Imir, but he doubted it. Heretical Urecari beliefs allowed a man to own as many wives as he liked, as though they were no more than pairs of shoes. Hannes had done Asha a favor, freeing her from that sin.

He found a street of merchant shops that were shuttered for the night, their awnings withdrawn, their flimsy doors barred. At an olive seller's stall, Hannes splintered the weakest plank so he could undo the door latch. Inside the dark shop, clay jars full of olives lined the shelves. He scooped out handfuls and ate ravenously, spitting out the pits. He took some preserved lemons from a large jar, then a handful of dates from another tub, eating a few now and filling his pockets; he also carried off a small jar of olives. A ragged brown robe hung on a peg beside the door, and Prester Hannes took that as well, adding to his disguise.

Leaving the broken door wide open, he scuttled through the streets, ducking into doorways whenever he heard approaching voices or footsteps. He kept moving, though he had no idea where he might go. His knowledge of the world's geography—particularly here—was sparse. He did not know the city's layout, which sections were dangerous, which would be safe places to hide.

The alleyway opened into a wider street, from which he had a good view of Asha's villa. All the windows were alight, and he saw figures moving about. The soldan-shah's palace was also lit up, as the alarm was sounded.

Prester Hannes found a sheltered stone step and sat out of sight, where he could watch. Asha had shaved him every day, but now he scratched the stubble on his chin and decided to grow a beard, made patchy by the waxy burn scars on his cheeks. Feeling content and safe for the first time since he'd awakened, glad to be free from the clutches of that woman, Hannes ate a few more dates, then casually plucked olives from the jar, sucking the tender salty flesh and spitting out the sharp pits.

He didn't think about the charity Asha had shown in rescuing him from the fires, in nursing him back to health. He had not *asked* to be placed under that obligation, and he knew that Asha must have had some devilish scheme in mind. She had given him the Urecari Sacraments when he could not fight back, when he could not defend himself. He felt no remorse over killing her.

Ever since Prester Baine had taken him as an acolyte and taught him his mission in life, Hannes had attempted to be pure and devout. Now, though, in the eyes of Ondun, he was corrupt. He cursed Asha for contaminating his soul.

A rider clattered by in the street outside the alley where Hannes hunkered on the stone step, wearing his nondescript stolen clothes. Nobody noticed him. He ate another olive. He wanted to flee Olabar, make his way out of this cursed land, and return to Ishalem and Tierra. He and Prester-Marshall Baine could pray together and begin the work of cleansing his soul.

Suddenly Hannes realized that he wasn't seeing the greater picture. Such grand events did not happen by accident. There must be a purpose. Ondun and Aiden would not have made him suffer so unless they had a plan for him.

He straightened in the darkness as he realized that, yes, there must be a way to redeem himself. Aiden loved him. Prester-

Marshall Baine had set him on this course, explaining how he must infiltrate the enemy and understand them to improve the fight for Aidenism. His heart swelled with joy.

Maybe the role he was meant to play did not bring him immediately back to Tierra after all. The more he thought about it, the more he was convinced that Ondun had an important mission in mind for him here.

47 *Position Unknown*

As the frenzied sea serpent pulled him across the waves, Criston lay lashed to his makeshift raft. Like a wild bull dragging a broken cart, the black-and-gold creature hurtled along at great speed. The hook caught in its breathing hole still prevented it from submerging—thankfully, or else it could have dived deep, taking Criston with it. He hung on, helpless, and the journey went on endlessly, throughout the dark night and the next day. And he endured.

Criston was sickened, bruised, and also starving. He had a little fresh water left in one of the casks, and when he fumbled himself free enough to move, he drank it. As the raft surged and crashed along, frightened fish were thrown onto the tangled wreckage—and he grabbed them and ate them raw. When it rained that afternoon, he captured a little more water. He thought of Adrea, and when that became too painful, he thought of nothing at all.

He lost track of the burning days and black nights. The sea serpent continued its headlong plunge toward the rising sun, growing more and more sluggish, obviously exhausted, maybe dying, but it could not dislodge the grappling hook.

Finally, so unexpectedly that Criston was not sure what had happened, the hook tore free, leaving a bloody gash down the monster's back like a sucking wound. The sea serpent thrashed and splashed, glad to be free; then it dove far out of sight beneath the waves, putting as much distance as possible between itself and the raft.

Criston untied himself from the raft and collapsed, weeping. He had no idea where he was or how far he had come, and now without the sea serpent pulling him along like Sapier in the legend, he was cast adrift, still in the middle of the empty Ocean-sea, with no land in sight.

And this time he was entirely alone. He had hated the black-and-gold creature because it had killed Prester Jerard, but now that it was gone and he sat becalmed, Criston almost longed for the serpent to come back.

The breeze picked up, and he realized he was in a current, still drifting in the direction the sea monster had taken him. He used the cloth that had shaded them from the sun and rigged a sail to catch the wind, pushing him onward....

He slept.

The raft continued to drift, caught in a current that pulled him silently along. On the open water, Criston had no reference point, no way of judging how fast he drifted or where he might be heading. He was lost.

He pulled in the rope and grappling hook and saw a gobbet of flesh torn free from the edge of the sea serpent's blowhole. Ravenous, Criston devoured the meat, but it was pungent, salty, and unsatisfying. His queasy stomach tried to reject the meal, but he managed to hold it down, knowing he needed the meager nutrition. He cast out the hook once more, letting it trail behind the raft. He yanked and jerked, in hopes that he might be lucky. The hook snagged a few strands of seaweed, which he ate, remembering the annual harvest at Windcatch....

He drifted into nightfall and looked up at the sparkling stars that pierced the darkness in diamondlike patterns that, he realized with a start, were familiar again. The constellations hung lower in the sky, but he recognized the Fountain, the Compass Needle, and the nebulous patch of Sapier's Beard. Maybe he was drifting closer to home after all... or maybe it was some sort of cosmic trick.

He remembered sitting with Adrea on the beach after they'd built a fire and baked a bucketful of fresh-dug clams. Content in each other's company, they had walked along the rocky shore, then out onto one of the empty Windcatch docks. They let their feet dangle as they stared up into the night sky. Criston had pointed out the constellations to her, explaining how the stars were guideposts for sailors. "They can always bring you back home." As she'd stared upward, he was more interested in the stars sparkling in her eyes.

Like a chartsman with a carefully plotted course, Criston had set his sights on Adrea. He had known her as a gangly girl in the village, along with her good-natured but limping brother. Criston had never paid much attention to her until one day he noticed she'd matured into a young woman. Thunderstruck, Criston realized she was the most beautiful girl in all of Windcatch.

Adrea's father had been a crewman on a merchant ship, and he spent many months away from home. When he did come back from his trips, he often fought with Adrea's mother... and then one year, he simply didn't return home. The village gossip was undecided as to whether he'd been lost at sea or simply chose a different port—and a different family—for himself. Whatever the answer, Adrea's mother was always miserable when he was home, and also miserable now that he was gone.

To make a living, she baked bread and sold it to the villagers, but only intermittently. She barely had enough wherewithal to feed herself and her children, which basically left Adrea and Ciarlo to fend for themselves.

As soon as he was old enough, Criston worked aboard local fishing boats, sometimes with his father, sometimes by himself. After they came back at sunset, Criston sorted through the catch. One evening, realizing that the catch was more than his family needed, he took the two best fish to Adrea's home. Holding them like trophies, smiling with embarrassment, he offered them to Adrea. "We had extra. I thought maybe you could use them."

A frown creased her brow. "Are we beggars now?"

"No, but you're practical. You need to eat."

And she had smiled. "Yes, Criston Vora, I am practical." She thanked him, took the fish, and Criston had found himself standing outside with the door closed in his face, not sure whether to feel elated or discouraged.

As often as he dared, but not so often as to make an obvious habit of it, Criston brought fish to Adrea's family. As far as he could tell, her mother never knew where the meals came from. The older woman drank too much kelpwine in the village taverns, and Adrea prepared the meals for the family. Her mother merely accepted the fish as part of "Aiden's bounty."

Before long, though, neither Adrea nor Criston could deny the obvious fact that he was courting her. And she let him continue.

One day, a merchant ship sailed into Windcatch, unloading its goods for the villagers. Seeing that the vessel was one of the ships on which her husband had served, Adrea's mother ran out to greet the crew. But he was not aboard, and none of the crew even remembered the man.

Afterward, her mother grew deeply depressed and drank more than before. Two weeks later, during a storm, she left their house in the middle of the night, and next morning was found floating facedown in the harbor, tangled in a few early strands of migratory seaweed. Nobody knew what had happened to her, though many had their guesses.

A week later, Criston had asked Adrea to marry him. She understood him, understood what he had to offer, and knew he would be a good husband. But she also recognized the call of the sea in his eyes and knew he would forever look outward. Adrea had always known what she was agreeing to. Criston was sure of that.

Until now, Criston hadn't seen how brave *she* was to stay home and wait for him, never knowing whether he would come back. Criston had always been so confident, so cocky, giving insufficient deference to the dangers of the sea. And now he was floating, lost, a sole survivor in the middle of nowhere....

His heart ached as he thought of Adrea looking out to sea every day, just as her mother had done, hopeful each time a ship came to port. Would she wait and wait...for years?

Because Criston did not believe he would ever hold her in his arms again, he became resigned to knowing that the merciless sea would be his last embrace. He forced himself to think of Adrea as he closed his eyes, hoping she would come to him in his dreams.

But he slept the sound sleep of exhaustion. If her spirit kissed him while he slumbered, he did not wake to it.

The following dawn, as he leaned over the side to splash salty water on his face, he looked up and saw the tiny but distinctive shape of a sail in the distance.

Criston stared in disbelief for many minutes, before he stretched his makeshift cloth as tight as he could, catching the breeze, and used a flat piece of plank as a rudder to steer toward the sail. When he tried to shout, his voice was so hoarse that sound barely came out. But his raft did move closer, and the sailing ship was no illusion. He prayed to Aiden that someone would notice him, that his course would intersect that of the other vessel.

He could tell that it was a large black-hulled whaling boat rigged with a bright sail. He flailed a scrap of white cloth to and fro, still trying to shout, hoping one of the whaler's crew would see him.

At last, he discerned tiny figures on deck. He saw them set the sail and turn toward him, and Criston collapsed to the uneven surface of the raft, having no further energy. Soon he could hear the answering calls of shouting crewmen. Three burly whalers jumped overboard and swam toward him.

It had been so long since Criston had seen another human being that they seemed strange to him. "Who are you? What ship are you from?" one of the sailors asked as he pulled himself up onto the raft, speaking Tierran with a strong Soeland accent.

The men had brought a flask of water with them, and Criston drank deeply, gaining strength. "I am Criston Vora...all that's left of the *Luminara* expedition."

The whalers were shocked to hear this. After he was taken aboard and fed an indescribably delicious fish stew, Criston gained enough strength to tell his story, and listen to theirs. He showed them Captain Shay's journal with the drawings of fantastical sea serpents; these men had seen enough on their own voyages that they did not doubt him.

They were a long-range whaling crew, sailing beyond the boundaries of Tierra, past the last islands in Soeland Reach and heading south in search of rich waters. They had a hold full of rendered blubber, barrels of whale oil, and had been about to turn back when they saw the drifting raft.

Criston closed his eyes and touched the fishhook pendant at his throat, seeing the hand of Aiden in it all.

While he rode with the whalers, seeing that their course would take him to the southern coast and Windcatch, Criston borrowed sheets of paper from the captain, torn from his cargo ledger. He wrote, *My name is Criston Vora from the village of Windcatch. I am the only survivor of the* Luminara *expedition.*

He filled the pages with descriptions of places they had sailed, the island with the battling skeletons, the new sea monsters, the months of empty ocean as they sailed for league upon league, and how the Leviathan had destroyed them all... then, as with Sapier himself, how the sea serpent had pulled Criston back into local waters.

"Please have this delivered to King Korastine." He handed the folded sheet to the whaling captain. "That is all the information he needs to know. Someday, I may go to Calay to tell the story in person, but I cannot promise it."

He could not promise anything, until he saw Adrea again.

"He may not believe you," the captain remarked. "*I* find it improbable, and I've seen your raft. I've looked into your haunted eyes."

"Just tell the king where you found me adrift. Let him draw his own conclusions."

48 *Alamont Reach*

Mateo rode with his fellow soldier-recruits on the river barge for the trip upstream to Bora's Bastion, the central city of Alamont Reach. As they traveled toward the destrar's capital and stronghold, he admired the lush grassy hills dotted with grazing sheep. Cornfields spread out in long rectangles, the orderly stalks nearly chest high. He saw fruit orchards, nut orchards, even a few vineyards. Alamont wine had never been particularly prized, since the best vintages came from Uraba; now, however, this wine was all Tierrans would have to drink.

These were the lands he must defend.

When they neared Bora's Bastion, the recruits grew restless to see their new home. Around the destrar's city, large areas of fertile cropland had been cleared to serve as training fields for practice maneuvers, marching exercises, and military parades. As the boat eased past, Mateo saw soldiers in matching uniforms with swords at their sides marching in perfect ranks around the empty fields. Rows of archers followed foot soldiers, while cavalrymen rode in the front. Mateo realized this performance was likely for the benefit of the new recruits, to let them see how well the Alamont destrar ran his contingent of the Tierran army.

Overlooking the river, Destrar Shenro's main house had high battlements and thick walls, though Mateo could not conceive of an attack occurring so far inland. Blacksmiths with riverside forges fashioned more swords with a constant rhythmic clang. Leatherworkers stretched hides over wooden frames for shields, then added metal plates for protection. All of the workers glanced up as the barge pulled up to the main dock.

The recruits began to disembark, led by their training instructors. The destrar had come down to greet them, wearing a military uniform of his own. Standing on the dock, Shenro measured the trainees with a calculating eye, then leaned over to whisper questions to the training instructors. The destrar walked the lines of new recruits, assessing them. He stopped before Mateo and regarded the young man for a long, uncomfortable moment, then said, almost accusingly, "You are the favorite of King Korastine?"

"I am a soldier-recruit for the Tierran army," Mateo answered.

"Good. Then I am happy to receive you, soldier-recruit."

The destrar turned away and issued orders for the quartermasters and supply sergeants to direct the young men to where lines and lines of tents had been pitched on the open cleared fields. One of those would be Mateo's home for the next year.

For the next two weeks the soldiers exercised until their bodies ached, then they exercised more, since recruits needed to have physical strength before they could acquire skill with weapons. For hours each day, they observed the older soldiers fighting mock combats; they watched the play of master swordsmen. In the evenings, Mateo tried to find time to write letters to Anjine, but so far he had completed only one; he was simply too exhausted to think of anything interesting to say.

In the rare times when the recruits were allowed to go into the town of Bora's Bastion, some of the older soldiers introduced Mateo and his fellows to the drinking establishments, places for musical performances, interesting local games; several strikingly lovely young ladies caught Mateo's eye, but he had never been very good at flirting.

Destrar Shenro also insisted that a good soldier needed to know the details of military history, to memorize the significant battles that had taken place in Tierra's history. Shenro taught this portion of the curriculum himself. Instead of discussing tactics and time lines as concise facts, he related the historical events as though he were a prester or storyteller, enamored of adventure tales.

In Tierra, occasional feuds had occurred between reaches, destrar fighting destrar. Alamont and Erietta in particular shared a great deal of rivalry. But the first major skirmish—a genuine insurrection against the king in Calay—had happened many centuries ago, when the Corag destrar attempted to declare independence from the other reaches and from King Yaradin.

"The other destrars were horrified," Shenro said from his open-air teaching platform. "They viewed Corag's rebellion as a *mutiny against the captain* of their government. Such a thing had never occurred before, and King Yaradin knew that he must change the relationships between the destrars and their fealty to him. He was a strong king, and he took on the mantle of captain, reminding them of his direct blood connection to Aiden."

Mateo and his fellow recruits stood in ranks, sweating and weary under the hot sun. By now, they had learned to remain at attention for hours without being restless, just waiting.

Shenro leaned forward, engrossed in his own story. "Yaradin unified the destrars, so that they all marched on rebellious Destrar Olacu and ousted him, replacing him with his nephew Miros, who swore loyalty to the king, to Calay, and to Aiden. To prove his sincerity, Miros ordered his uncle hurled from a cliff, so that his body was dashed on the rocks far below. Afterward, as added insurance, many of Destrar Miros's family members were sent to live among the other destrars as hostages. No further trouble occurred."

Shenro nodded to himself as if thinking through his lecture. "King Yaradin was wise enough to study the root cause of the Corag destrar's rebellion. Olacu was not just a power-mad man who had flagrantly abandoned centuries of tradition and law. Corag Reach was isolated, receiving little benefit from the taxes it paid to the rest of the kingdom. Olacu had not considered the ruler in Calay to be necessary or relevant. And he was not entirely wrong — Yaradin saw that.

"The king decided to increase trade among the reaches. He concluded — correctly — that if all the destrars were prosperous, they would want to maintain the status quo. Thus, Yaradin forged a much stronger kingdom, rather than a loose collection of allied regions."

As he listened to Destrar Shenro's lecture, Mateo realized he had never heard such a blunt interpretation of history before. He knew the facts, and the legends, but had never looked for the subtleties or underlying principles. Mateo had always been taught that the king was a royal personage whose throne came by divine right, but Shenro had a compelling way of describing the concepts. Mateo decided he needed to think about it for a while.

When the destrar finished his tale, he gazed out at the recruits and raised his voice so that even the back rows could hear him clearly. "I have told you a story. You all know many stories, and you will hear plenty more during your instruction. But your training is no longer a theoretical exercise.

"You must be the first of a new breed of soldiers. The threat to Tierra is real. The followers of Urec have demonstrated their brutality. We watched them burn Ishalem, and we know how they martyred Prester-Marshall Baine." He paused to shudder, then continued in a hoarser voice. "Understand that as soon as you are trained, you may be called upon at any moment to spill the blood of the Urecari. And you must do it without hesitation."

49 *Windcatch*

Resting and recovering aboard the Soeland whaling ship, Criston finally felt human again. At last, the big vessel arrived at a fishing village well north of Windcatch. After suggesting once again, unsuccessfully, that he go directly to King Korastine with his story, his rescuers bade him farewell. Criston could think only of Adrea, and his duty was to her first. With a wry smile, the whaler captain gave him a small amount of money—a fraction of the profits from the catch—to help him book passage home. They all wished him luck.

Criston's heart tugged him southward. Though battered and weary, he drew strength from thoughts of Adrea, Telha, and Ciarlo.

When he arrived at Windcatch, though, everything had changed. Half of the familiar buildings were gone. Some were only burned-out shells; others had been torn down completely, and no attempt had been made to reconstruct them. Something terrible had happened here.

A sick dread filled Criston as he disembarked from the small ship that had given him passage; he hurried along the docks, past the oddly subdued and quiet merchant wharves. He ran, breathless, not wanting to waste a second. He stopped no one on the streets, couldn't bear to ask for an explanation. As he approached the whitewashed half-timbered home where he had lived much of his life, he called out.

Finding the door of his house broken and hanging off its hinges, he rushed inside, trying to see in the dimness. "Adrea! Mother! Ciarlo!"

The house was silent. Cupboards had been smashed. Some of the shelves had been torn down and scattered across the floor. He saw bloodstains, dust, but no sign of his family. Nobody had been here for a long time.

He stumbled back out of the house and walked away in a daze, making his way through the strange streets. Belatedly, he noticed that the kirk had burned down as well.

On the outskirts of town, covering an area more than twice its former size, the village cemetery had sprouted dozens of new grave markers. He stopped, stunned, to look at all the new stones, reading names that he recognized—friends and acquaintances, shopkeepers, fishermen, wives, bachelors—people he had always known. All of the new grave markers bore the same date.

Criston could not grasp what he was seeing—so many dead at once? He could only think that it must have been a horrific plague or a fire. But that wouldn't account for the additional destruction he had seen, or the blood.

One of the markers bore the name of Telha Vora. The sight of it hit him like a physical blow to his stomach, and his shoulders sagged. He found it hard to breathe, and words would not come out of his mouth. His mother was among the dead. After losing all of his crewmates on the *Luminara*, and Captain Shay, and Prester Jerard . . . he had come home to this.

His heart began to pound in panic. He looked around frantically, scanning the additional markers and dreading what he would find. Name after name, some of them scrawled with paint, some lovingly chiseled into the rock. The graves were staggered and haphazard, as if the burials had been rushed, the diggers overwhelmed. Too many bodies.

Then, at the edge of the cemetery he saw a group of wooden posts set too closely together, without enough room between them to bury a body. A fishhook had been carved into each wooden post, letters scratched but not deeply, as if the carver had grown too weary of a seemingly endless task.

On one post, the letters spelled out Adrea's name.

He stopped there in the dirt, his legs as stiff as old masts, and after what felt like hours, he crumpled to his knees. Though tears washed in like the tide, even his blurred vision did not change her name on the marker.

Other people noticed him now, and several came up from the town to see him. The cemetery held many mourners who walked among the markers, reciting the names of the fallen as if afraid to forget them.

After his own ordeal, Criston had changed as much as they had. His expression was drawn, his face etched with many lines. He had trimmed but not shaved his beard. Even so, several people recognized him; his return from the long voyage seemed no more impossible than the events that had already taken place around them. "What happened?" he finally brought himself to ask. He raised his voice to a shout and demanded answers. And they told him of the Urecari raid in scattered recollections, disjointed snippets.

"Ciarlo is alive," said an old woman who had been a friend of his mother's. "Up at the new kirk. He can tell you more."

Leaving the graveyard, Criston ran up the hill toward the foundations of the ruined kirk, to where a small new building had been erected. A man limped out, wearing the robes of a prester, though they fit him poorly. He looked up—a young man with very old eyes—without recognition.

"Ciarlo, it's *Criston*." He stood there, his knees locked, but still swaying. "The *Luminara* was shipwrecked, but I made it home." When Ciarlo merely blinked at him, Criston could not hold his questions inside any longer. "Where's Adrea? What happened to her? What happened to *you*?"

The young man took a deep breath. "I'm Prester Ciarlo now. Prester Fennan was killed in the raid. He made me hide in the root cellar, and now I'm the only one who knows the services. I do the best I can." He absently touched the patched loose robes. "These were Prester Fennan's old robes that he had stored in the cellar. I didn't have any of my own. Windcatch had nobody else. So I became the new prester. I had to."

Criston seized Ciarlo by the shoulders. "Tell me." He felt his voice grow dead, afraid to hear the answer. *"Tell me, Ciarlo* —what happened to Adrea?" Her brother nearly collapsed, but Criston held him up, hugging him. "Tell me," he said again in a hoarse whisper. Ciarlo began to sob.

50 *Uraba*

The caravan made slow progress as they left the port of Khenara and followed a track up into the hills, passing across the isthmus from Outer Wahilir to Inner Wahilir. The younger children were placed on pack animals or in carts that jostled along the well-traveled road; the older ones had to walk. The few women and all of the children had been fed, but Adrea's pregnancy often made her feel ill, sluggish, and clumsy.

As they moved onward, day after day, she maintained her silence whenever the captors could hear her. She would not give them the satisfaction of hearing her beg... or hearing her speak at all. While other women moaned in fear and despair, Adrea just felt angry. These raiders had destroyed or taken everything she knew. She would never see her husband again, nor her brother, nor her home. Even if she survived long enough for the baby to be born, Criston would never see his child.

Twice more, the gruff Uraban sailor tried to talk with her on the zarif's behalf, but she gave no response, further infuriating him. The sailor asked other prisoners about her, but apart from the young captive children, Adrea was the only female prisoner from Windcatch in their group. Because she had not shared her name or background with her fellow captives, no one could tell him who she was, and Adrea hoped the rude man would receive punishment for his failure to learn more. Before long, though, Zarif Omra apparently lost interest in her.

As they traveled overland, she listened intently and learned what she could. When she could safely whisper to the other women without being observed, she tried to make a connection, but most of them were paralyzed with despair. The children, having lost everything, huddled in shock. Adrea turned her attention to her captors, watching them, gleaning information. She quickly picked up words in their strange language, though she gave no outward sign of understanding.

After journeying inland for five days, the track began to wind downward, and the terrain opened up. Looking ahead, Adrea saw a broad blue expanse of water that had a different color and character than the Oceansea. The Middlesea.

The shoreline was white and sandy, the water turquoise. At another port town — Sioara, she heard someone call it — the Urecari soldiers herded their captives into a large enclosure that had obviously been built for horses. When strangely garbed people from Sioara came to stare at the Tierrans — cursing, spitting, throwing things—Adrea ignored them. The prisoners slept out in the open, without shade, and she forced herself to rest.

Next morning, when faint colors of dawn tinged the sky, guttural-voiced soldiers rousted the prisoners out of the corral enclosure and led them down to the harbor, herding them toward another group of ships, single-masted galleys that looked entirely different from the normal sea vessels with which she was so familiar. The Middlesea ships had a shallower draft and a broader deck made to carry people out in the open rather than heavy cargo in the hold.

Their captors marched them double file up the gangplanks, filling first one galley, then two more, mingling the children and women. Adrea followed without speaking and found herself on the same ship as Omra. The zarif had bathed and obtained fresh garments in Sioara; she still felt filthy, her dress torn and stained. Whenever he looked at her, she glanced away so he would not see the poison in her blue eyes.

Uraban men took their places on benches, each grasping an oar, and rowed the galleys away from Sioara. Once they reached open water, they unfurled the sails, the center of each showing the Eye of Urec. Gentle easterly breezes pushed them onward. When she looked over the side into the Middlesea, Adrea saw fish darting alongside the hull.

They never left sight of the coast. With each stroke of the oars, each gust of wind, they were propelled farther and farther from Windcatch, and from Criston....

After three days' voyage, they reached a large and beautiful city boasting tall towers and white buildings constructed of limestone and marble, rooftops that were tiled instead of thatched. The sunshine was so bright that the foreign skyline seemed to sparkle with haze.

The galleys slid toward the docks and tied up against waiting wharves. The prisoners were herded out, destined for a slave market, Adrea was sure. But Zarif Omra separated her from the rest, keeping her on deck after the others had left. He stood at her side and pointed to the city and the tall palace in the center. "Olabar," he said. "*Olabar.* Your home now."

She comprehended what he said, but didn't respond to him, refused to break that bargain with herself.

"You will work in the palace. Do you understand? In the palace." He searched her face, but Adrea averted her eyes. She flinched with a twinge of surprise as the baby kicked inside her.

Omra saw it, and showed a glint of something that seemed almost like compassion. "You are home now," he repeated.

Adrea would not acknowledge him.

51 *Windcatch*

Criston felt as hollow as an abandoned ship.

He stayed in Windcatch and tried to sleep in his own home, but nightmares haunted him. After surviving the Leviathan attack and being preyed upon by sea serpents, the silence and shadows and ghosts inside his house were too much to bear.

Ciarlo had explained what he remembered, what he knew. The Urecari had attacked the village without warning or mercy, burning buildings, cutting down men and women with their scimitars. Telha's body had been found in the house, alone, without Adrea.

"We never found her, not for sure, but there were so many burned ones in the streets and inside buildings, we didn't always know who…" Ciarlo hung his head. "Many people ran into the hills and escaped, but Adrea never came back. So we put her name on a post and said the evening prayers for her. The worst part is all the missing children, dragged off to the Urecari warships."

"Why would they take children?" Criston asked, but all of the horrors now blended together, sounding like thunder rumbling in the distance.

"Nobody knows, but they're gone. Maybe the Urecari captured some of our women, too, but... I don't know."

Criston caught his breath. "Could Adrea have been one of them? Could she still be a prisoner?" He knew how achingly beautiful she was. The thought of those monstrous men taking her—

"I don't know!" Ciarlo's ragged cry showed he had been haunted by that question for a long time. "I don't know... And would that have been better? It's more merciful to think that she's *not* alive. At the time of the raid, her pregnancy was showing. Maybe they wanted the baby."

"Baby?" Criston lurched to his feet. "She was with child?"

Ciarlo began to sob again.

Windcatch was empty for Criston. His home was no longer home. How could he make a life in this place again? He wished the Leviathan had simply swallowed him as well.

He heard that the predatory war galleys had ventured up the coast, and several other fishing towns had been ruined. In Calay, King Korastine was using Tierra's resources to build his navy and arm his soldiers, launching patrols to stop further Urecari raids. The stricken villages scrambled to rebuild.

By now, Criston knew that the Soeland whalers would have delivered his letter, telling King Korastine of the *Luminara*'s fate, but he felt no desire to go to the capital city. The king would be preoccupied by the war, and Captain Shay's voyage seemed irrelevant now. All of Criston's dreams to see exotic far-off lands had turned to ash.

As a seasoned sailor, he considered enlisting in the Tierran navy, to fight against the Urecari, but he wasn't driven by vengeance or bloodlust. The people of Windcatch were trying to rebuild, struggling to recover from their shock and grief in the smoky wake of the raid. They tried to put the nightmares behind them, to erase the scars of the attack, and move forward. They wanted him to do the same. He looked at the once-familiar faces, now all stricken.

While Ciarlo toiled daily to finish the small kirk, Criston helped him, though neither man spoke much. A third of the town's population had been lost in the massacre. Most of their supplies were gone, and they had little with which to pay visiting traders. Eleven fishing boats had vanished that day, presumably sunk by the Urecari, and the daily catch was drastically reduced. Windcatch was on its own, and the people required his help. They needed the extra set of strong arms. He had to stay here, at least for a little while.

When the villagers offered him a boat free and clear and asked him to take up his old trade, Criston realized how much had changed inside him. He had gone to the edge of the world and back; he had survived by clinging to his love for Adrea — all for nothing. He didn't dare to imagine that Adrea could still be alive . . . but it was the only hope he had left. The call of the sea that had once been so strong, the tug that made him look out to the water, had vanished within him. Criston was no longer a man of the ocean; he was immune to it.

Nevertheless, he and a small crew went out fishing each day, bringing back a catch to be distributed to the villagers. On land, workers tore down the wrecked shops and dock buildings, then reconstructed them. Whitewashed walls were repainted; roofs were rethatched. His boat returned each sunset, and men hauled out the nets. He always had enough to eat. He remembered his courtship, when he had brought fish to feed Adrea, Ciarlo, and their mother.

How could he ever have thought that sailing the uncharted sea was more important than staying with his beloved wife? He had gone away for adventure, to secure his future with Adrea...only to lose her entirely.

He lay awake at night, staring into the darkness, dead to the sea. He felt like a piece of driftwood that had once floated on the waves and now lay discarded by a high tide, cast up on a shore.

Day after day, he did the same thing, beginning to fall into a routine. After several months of hard work, the villagers managed to rebuild Windcatch. To a casual observer, the town looked the same as it always had. Life was getting back to normal. The people—his friends and acquaintances—had an aversion to talking about the raid, as if they wanted to forget it all.

Criston found himself falling into the same trap, and one night he woke in a cold sweat, shouting into the empty house. *Never!* He would never forget!

The next morning, packing only a few possessions, he trudged off to the kirk to say goodbye to Ciarlo. "I'm going inland. The ocean has nothing for me anymore. Windcatch doesn't need me."

Ciarlo was shocked. "But this is your home!"

"No...not anymore. Give the fishing boat to the crew. They know how to use it."

He needed solid ground under his feet, not a swaying deck. He needed to be far from the waves, from the smell of salt, from the cold winds and storm clouds that blew in from the ocean. He did not care if he ever looked upon the waves again. The sea had lured him away and taken everything from him — his home, his hope, his love. . . .

Criston shouldered his pack and looked eastward to the hills that extended as far as he could see, knowing that he could find open land there, unexplored mountains, a place where he could be by himself, to heal . . . or at least to survive.

The rutted road out of town was dotted with puddles from a thunderstorm that had passed two days earlier. He stopped once to look back at the harbor and ocean for the last time, but he felt no glimmer of regret, no need to reconsider. He was still a young man, with his whole life ahead of him, but his heart felt incredibly old.

Woodcutters and farmers brought laden carts down to the Windcatch markets. Word had spread inland, and producers brought supplies to the coast, hoping to help. On the lonely, winding track Criston encountered a man riding a cart full of apples, pulled by a shaggy horse. Criston felt obligated to stop and talk with him, though he was in no mood for conversation. He answered the man's questions, told him that Windcatch did indeed need the food. "But I am leaving," he said. "I'm going far into the mountains, to find a place somewhere for myself."

The farmer seemed sad to hear this. "All alone?"

"Yes . . . I'm all alone."

Brightening, the man reached behind him to pull aside a woolen blanket that covered a basket in which four puppies had curled up together. Exposed to the light, they blinked and lifted their heads curiously. One gave an extraordinarily large yawn.

"If you're a man alone, you need companionship. I was planning to give away these puppies in town, but you need one. I can see it in your eyes."

"No. I have a long way to go."

"You said you didn't know where you're going."

The puppy that had yawned got to its feet and wobbled, leaning forward to sniff Criston's hand. Then it began to wag not just its tail, but its entire body.

"No man should be alone," the farmer reiterated. "Trust me. This puppy will make all the difference now, and the dog he grows into will be a more faithful companion than you've ever had. They're fully weaned—you won't regret it." The farmer scooped up the puppy and thrust it into Criston's arms, refusing to hear any protestations.

Criston reluctantly held it, and the puppy licked his face. He tried to hand it back, but the dog seemed to call to him. With his life spent on boats, going out to sea every day, he'd never owned a pet, and now he didn't know quite what to do.

"He is obviously yours," the farmer said with a nod. "You just don't realize it yet."

For some reason, this observation made perfect sense to Criston, and he found himself agreeing. "I'll take him." Criston thanked the man, who clucked at the shaggy horse, and the cart rolled slowly down the path toward Windcatch.

Holding the puppy in one arm and his satchel of belongings over his shoulder, Criston walked on, turning his back on the village, on the shore, and the sea.

Part III

Four Years Later

*Five Years After the
Burning of Ishalem*

52 *Ondun's Lightning*

Four years after his return from Corag Reach, fully accepted as a Saedran chartsman, Aldo na-Curic set off on another sea voyage — his twelfth. The young man had proven himself to be a reliable navigator; he understood the workings of complex astronomical instruments, and his mind held a detailed map of all known ocean currents. Once he knew the captain's desired destination, Aldo could plot the best course far from shore where the ship would find favorable winds and swift currents, trimming days off their expected travel time. Merchants bid for his services, and he guided their ships to far-off ports.

He would always return home to his parents, his brother, and his sister. By tradition, Saedran chartsmen remained unmarried until later in life. It was their duty to serve aboard ships for many years, guiding numerous voyages and adding wealth to the treasury. Given the respect Aldo earned with his wide travels, many young women had taken an interest in him, flashing flirtatious glances in his direction, though they'd never looked twice at him before. Someday, he supposed he would choose a wife and have a family, but for now, he wanted to see the world.

Currently, rather than exploring unmarked territories and expanding the Mappa Mundi, Aldo drew his excitement from running dangerous waters and avoiding Uraban pirates. He assisted brash Tierran captains who dared to sail below the Edict Line and trade illegally with the coastal cities of Outer Wahilir.

For this twelfth voyage, Aldo served aboard a small fast ship,

Ondun's Lightning, loaded with leather goods from Erietta, finely worked jewelry from Corag, and mammoth ivory and scrimshaw work from snowy Iboria. Such items commanded a premium in the distant south, since they could be obtained only from privateers and blockade runners willing to ignore the Edict and risk the wrath of Ondun. A single successful voyage could make a captain and crew fabulously wealthy.

The *Lightning's* captain, Jan Rennert, had already returned from two successful voyages, but wanted more. He had a contact in Ouroussa deep in Uraban territory, a merchant who was just as hungry for the easy profits, and the two men had an arrangement to distribute a shipload of luxury items.

But a ship that hugged the shoreline could easily be seen and attacked by Uraban corsairs. Therefore, Captain Rennert needed a chartsman's help. Taking the risk again, Rennert had offered Aldo an extravagant amount of money to guide him, to plot a clever course safely far away from coastal raiders. Ouroussa was halfway down the coast of Outer Wahilir, well beyond any journey Aldo had ever made.

"Because it is so far away," Captain Rennert pointed out, "our profits will be larger. I've already laid the groundwork—you'll see."

So Aldo guided the *Lightning* out to sea, following currents he had memorized from the Saedran records. Many leagues below Ishalem, the winds became hot, and the ocean turned silty and shallow. Over the next week, four sailors fell sick with a fever they were sure came from poison fish, strange ugly things that had supplemented their meals. Heading farther southward to the fabled city of Lahjar would have been unconscionable, even to Rennert, despite the obvious profits.

Aldo directed the captain to tack east toward shore where, if his calculations were correct, they would catch a swift current to bring them in to Ouroussa from the south. As expected, and to the cheers and thanks of the crew, the ship did approach the reefs on the outskirts of the foreign city at dusk, and Captain Rennert contemplated how best to go ashore and sell their valuable cargo. The crew was in a celebratory mood.

Two swift Uraban war galleys appeared unexpectedly, bearing down on them with long oars extended and drumbeats pounding. Captain Rennert sounded the alarm. "I had hoped to be discreet about this," he said, his expression tight. "My merchant friend must have sold us out." He ordered the sails set, planning to run out to sea. "Can you get us out of this, chartsman?"

"Those warships are between us and the best course, Captain, but I'll try to find another way." Aldo closed his eyes and summoned up his knowledge about the reef hazards around the Ouroussa coastline, but details were sparse. He didn't see a way out. The obstacle course of shoals now cut them off.

Another warship came toward them, dispatched from the city harbor itself. Then two more. *Ondun's Lightning* tried to beat a hasty retreat, but came up against a line of submerged rocks that even Aldo hadn't known about, and only a frantic heeling to port kept them from shearing open their hull.

Familiar with the local hazards, the Uraban corsairs boxed them in against the reefs. With a sick feeling in his stomach, Aldo watched the vessels closing in, cutting off all hope of escape. Captain Rennert ordered his men to arm themselves and stand ready. As the sun sank to the horizon, the outcome seemed inevitable.

It was nightfall by the time the ships came together in the anticipated clash. Uraban rowers brought their war galleys alongside *Ondun's Lightning*, and fighters threw grappling hooks to secure the vessels. "They don't look as if they intend to take prisoners," Rennert said, seeing the curved silver scimitars. Before the first enemy boarding party could leap onto their deck, the captain howled for the battle to begin.

Corsairs swarmed aboard, their colorful outfits making them easy to differentiate from the drab garments of the *Lightning*'s crew, even in the fading light. With swords, clubs, axes, and harpoons, the Tierrans fought furiously to protect their cargo and save their lives.

But the numbers against them were overwhelming. Instead of running for safety belowdecks, Aldo seized a sword from a dead sailor's hand and brandished it to defend himself. The bloody mayhem on the deck of the ship was the most terrifying thing he had ever seen.

One of the corsair captains spotted Aldo and bellowed in Uraban, which the young man had learned in his studies, "Save the Saedran chartsman—he's valuable!" Aldo swung his borrowed sword gracelessly from side to side, trying to keep them at bay. He called out for help, jabbing and slashing at the men as they advanced on him.

Out of the corner of his eye, he saw Captain Rennert go down, clubbed unconscious by a crowd of fighting men. In dismay, Aldo let his attention flicker for just a moment, and the largest Uraban fighter struck the confiscated sword, numbing his wrist. The hilt slipped out of his fingers, and the sword clattered to the deck. He balled his fists to fight, but the pirates surged forward to grab his arms and tie him up.

Dragged to the side of the boat and bound to a rail, Aldo was forced to watch as the attackers hauled a groggy Captain Rennert to his feet. Without ceremony or accusations, one of the Uraban captains ran him through with a scimitar, then tossed his body overboard. Aldo vomited, then tore his gaze away as the first officer was also executed and dumped unceremoniously into the water to feed the fish.

A few closely guarded and terrified Tierran deckhands were forced to wash the blood from the deck, and a small crew took control of *Ondun's Lightning*. After being put in irons, the rest of the Aidenist captives were transferred to one of the Uraban galleys, where they would be sold as slaves.

But it seemed the Urabans considered Aldo a prize even more significant than the Tierran ship. He felt dazed and miserable as the Urabans dragged him aboard their lead war galley and separated him from his companions.

53 *Uraba*

The Teacher stood as tall as Zarif Omra, but opaque black robes covered his entire body, black gloves wrapped his hands, and a featureless silver mask sheathed his face, leaving only slits for eyes and mouth. Since disguise was the nature of his work, the Teacher shielded his identity from everyone. But the students in this isolated camp would wear no masks; rather, they would hide in plain sight until it was time for them to strike.

The Teacher's voice was muffled and genderless behind the mask. "They are prepared for their first test, Zarif."

Omra stood with the dark figure on the outskirts of a hidden settlement an hour's ride outside of Olabar. "It has been four years, Teacher. Time for more than a demonstration."

"Patience is a weapon as mighty as the sword. Observe." The Teacher gestured with a gloved hand, and one of the male tenders down in the village let out a shrill whistle.

The village was a perfect replica of a Tierran town. The houses were half-timbered cottages with white plaster walls, brick porches, thatched roofs. A stone-lined well stood at the middle of a gathering square. The bell inside the town's Aidenist kirk began to toll in response to the man's whistle.

Figures emerged from doorways to stand in well-practiced lines out on the dirt streets. All were children, many of them teens, laughing and joking with one another. Their Tierran clothing was a motley of browns, blacks, and even a few dirt-smeared whites; most of the children did not wear shoes. Tousled blond, coppery, or brown hair hung moplike from their heads, though a few of the girls had tied their hair into ponytails with strips of cloth. They spoke perfect Tierran. For four years, the captives had remained here in a world that the Teacher kept carefully separate from the rest of Uraba.

"Have they completed their exercises for the day?" Omra asked.

The Teacher nodded again. "And they were exceptional. I am confident in how they will serve you."

Two lagging boys fell into a tussle in the dirt, then sprang to their feet and ran to meet the others in the square. The older teenagers kept the younger children in line, scolding the rambunctiousness; all were perfectly aware of the Teacher's presence. When the black-robed man lifted a gloved hand, they all fell silent, as though in awe.

The Teacher called out to them in his own language, "They are your first test. Are you ready?" Laughing, the children shouted their answer, and the Teacher turned his silver mask toward Omra. "You may call your guests forward now, Zarif."

Guards on horseback ushered in four Tierran sailors who had been held out of sight of the village, pulling them by ropes bound to their wrists. Omra explained to the Teacher, "These are surviving crewmen from an illicit trader recently captured off the coast of Ouroussa. The captain and officers were slain, but we did manage to seize a Saedran chartsman. My father will make use of him." Omra smiled coldly as he turned to watch the proceedings. "These sailors, though, are for you. Show me what you have achieved."

When the beaten and exhausted captives saw the familiar-looking village, they brightened. One man praised Aiden, and the offended guards cuffed him. Omra's men slashed the bonds around their wrists and pushed the men forward.

The four captives hurried into the village, where the pale-skinned children greeted them enthusiastically, calling the men farther into the square. The captured sailors, laughing or weeping with joy, threw their arms around the Tierran children and stood, heaving great breaths.

The Teacher shouted a single order in Uraban.

The children moved like a dance troupe, their reactions perfectly coordinated. From their ragged clothes they produced knives. Each child, down to the smallest boy and girl, was armed.

The captive sailors were surprised, perplexed. One blurted out a question. The children fell upon them in a frenzy of stabbing, pushing forward, flashing their knives, each one wanting to feel the bite of a sharp blade into flesh and bone. Before long, the four dead sailors were no longer recognizable as human.

"No hesitation," the Teacher pointed out. "They are completely loyal, completely trained. They may have been born in Tierra, but their hearts belong to Urec. Your plan will succeed, Zarif."

Unable to tear his eyes away Omra felt great satisfaction. "We will call them *ra'virs*." Omra took the name from a rare bird, the *ra'vir*, which had a habit of laying its eggs in another bird's nest, so that its offspring would be raised among other species. But *ra'virs* often killed their fellows to eliminate competition.

"An excellent name."

Omra's *ra'virs,* these captive children, would look and act exactly like Aidenists, but would always be loyal to Uraba, ready to perform destructive missions when they received orders.

"I'm pleased with this demonstration, Teacher. Continue your work. Soon we can start sending them north to infiltrate Tierran society."

54 *Olabar Palace*

Inside the Olabar palace, Adrea worked silently, unobtrusively. Some days, the guards let her out into the gardens to scrub flag-stones and pull weeds. Today, she toiled in the spacious quarters of Soldan-Shah Imir's third wife, Villiki. Using rags and brushes, she scoured dust and dirt from cracks in the tile floor. She polished statues, cleaning the stone faces of arrogant-looking men whose names she did not know. She used her spit to moisten the rag. A fresh dove dropping stood out on the man's sculpted head, and she took pleasure in smearing it all over the implacable face before wiping the filth away.

Uraban handmaidens with gaudy clothes and ripe perfumes twittered as they moved from room to room, fawning upon the soldan-shah's wife. Imir's second wife had been murdered four years ago, not long before Adrea was brought here, and the first wife—Omra's mother—had lived apart from her husband for more than a decade.

Like creatures settling into a fresh tide pool, a group of scheming handmaidens surrounded Zarif Omra's only wife, Cliaparia.

Cliaparia was Adrea's age, dark-haired and beautiful, though with an arrogant self-absorption that diminished her charm.

As a mere palace slave, Adrea was immune to all politics. To the members of the court, she was invisible, a disguise she had carefully cultivated during her years here. When she was first captured, she had expected to be raped and abused, passed from one Uraban soldier to another, regardless of her pregnancy. At the very least, she had been sure she'd be forced into Omra's personal harem, since a Urecari man could supposedly take as many wives as he pleased. But to her surprise, she had not been harmed; in fact, Adrea had been given her own simple quarters, and was fed and clothed.

When it was time for her baby to be born, a Uraban midwife tended her, spoke soothingly, gave her medicines and herbal tea to ease the delivery. Without Criston at her side, Adrea had given birth to a baby boy, whom she named Saan. She had even been allowed to keep him, to raise him.

Adrea didn't understand these people.

Saan was now four years old, a perfect blond-haired, blue-eyed boy, and his face showed hints of her beloved husband. Every time she saw her son, she ached for what she had lost in Windcatch — Criston, her family, her life. By now, he must have long since returned home from his voyage. She imagined the *Luminara* sailing into Calay Harbor in triumph. Criston had likely received a fortune for serving on such a brave expedition . . . only to come home to a devastated Windcatch, his mother dead, Adrea gone. In the fire and slaughter and confusion, she doubted anyone had seen her captured. If anyone *had* seen it, they had probably perished that day as well.

How could Criston not assume she was dead? Her heart felt heavy as she wondered if he had married again. Criston would still be young and handsome. He would probably never learn that she had carried his child—much less that the boy was alive....

Now, as she worked to make the marble of the statue gleam, tears sparkled in her eyes, but she wiped them away before anyone could see. In all her time here, she had refused to let her Uraban captors see a hint of emotion from her, and she had not uttered a word to them. They all believed she was mute, nothing more than a beast of burden—and a rather stupid one at that. Such attitudes worked to her advantage, and she clung to her shield of silence while she did her tasks in the soldan-shah's palace.

Although Adrea had no desire to please her captors, she worked hard because she couldn't risk being punished. She had too much to lose. In her precarious position, if anything happened to her, then Saan would pay the price. Adrea knew she could no longer count on Zarif Omra's help; over the past several years, he had paid little attention to her. By eavesdropping, she had long ago learned that Omra's first wife died during a miscarriage, and she concluded that a moment of weakness had caused Omra to protect her. Perhaps he had felt some empathy for her and her unborn son. But not anymore.

Each morning before Adrea left her quarters, Saan was taken away to a nursery school in one wing of the palace. She could not object, but it disturbed her to know that her son was being indoctrinated in Urec's Log, taught things that she found hateful.

Her own protective silence had laid a trap for her. Though Adrea longed to teach him his own language and heritage, Saan spoke only Uraban. The four-year-old did not understand his situation. Even when she held him in their quarters at night, clinging to him like one last possession that couldn't be taken from her, she feared that if she gave him words in his own language, told him the name of his father, described the village of Windcatch and the wonders she had seen in Calay, Saan might blurt something to his teachers, and her secret would be exposed.

So when she whispered to him in the night, soothing him, making him feel loved and comforted, Adrea spoke in Uraban, but made him swear never to tell anyone that she could talk. The boy had given her his word with all the earnestness of a child and for four years she felt as if she had been holding her breath.

Each day, when she finished her work in Villiki's quarters and most Urecari were preparing to go to their churches for sunset ceremonies, Adrea waited for Saan to be released from the school and led back to their quarters.

Out in the long, open-air corridor, she moved on to the next statue, polishing it in the daylight that filtered through the corridor's vine-covered windows. Bees buzzed around the trumpet-shaped yellow flowers.

She looked up, hearing a rustle of sandals and robes.

While Adrea disliked ambitious Villiki, the mother of Imir's second son, she had come to resent the Urecari priestesses even more. Ur-Sikara Lukai flaunted her superiority over any Aidenist captive, but since Adrea did her assigned tasks reliably, the sikara heaped scorn on her merely out of habit.

Today, red-robed Lukai herself brought the boy out, clutching his small hand. Adrea knew something was wrong. The priestess smiled at her with a face as hard as the statues Adrea had seen all day. Out of habit, Adrea lowered her head respectfully.

Ur-Sikara Lukai spoke in broken Tierran, sure that Saan couldn't understand her. "Your son...soon he will change. When he is five years old, we take him from you. We train him."

Adrea looked up, suppressed an involuntary cry of alarm, bit back the words she wanted to hurl after her.

Lukai seemed to enjoy her reaction. "He have the honor of being trained among *ra'vir*." Adrea didn't know what that meant, but she grabbed Saan and pulled him close. The sikara laughed. "Soon now, he is old enough."

The priestess turned with a sweep of her red gown and stalked away. Saan had no idea why his mother was so emotional. She held him, her thoughts in turmoil, at a loss as to how she could protect her son.

55 *Corag Highlands*

High in a mountain meadow at the edge of Corag Reach, Criston Vora sat on a lichen-spattered boulder. The black and gray peaks above the meadows were frosted with thick snow that would not melt even at the height of summer.

He watched his small flock of sheep graze contentedly on the lush spring grasses. Magenta, white, and yellow flowers splashed color like daubs of paint across the greenery. Silvery meltwater streams trickled down from the highlands, gathering into larger brooks, all of which flowed into valleys and eventually to the sea.

But he no longer thought about the sea. Criston preferred the solidity of the mountains to the rocking deck of a ship.

His dog, full grown now, bounded after a rusty-furred marmot. The pudgy rodent clambered up a lump of rock, out of reach, while the barking dog circled. The marmot slipped into a crack to safety, though the dog would persist for hours, without losing hope or interest, though still remaining aware of the sheep all around the meadow.

At the edge of the sparse forest stood two enormous talus boulders beside a cozy cottage built from fieldstone, timbered with wood he had cut from the patchy trees below. On sunny days like this, he left the plank door and window shutters open, so the breeze would air out the lingering smoke from his fireplace.

Criston sat in silence, comfortable and reasonably content. These days, he asked for nothing more. He no longer expected to be *happy*. The world seemed quiet and still around him, and that was enough.

He whistled. "Jerard! Come!" The dog let out a disappointed bark, looked back at the boulders where the marmot was hiding, then bounded across the meadow to his master.

For the first year, Criston had called him nothing more than "Dog," but since this steadfast creature was his only friend here in the wilderness, he eventually decided the animal deserved a name. So he named it after Prester Jerard.

Now an experienced sheepdog, Jerard came up to him, tongue lolling. Criston patted the dog's head and rubbed his muzzle, then turned him loose to circle the meadow once more, ensuring that the aimless sheep did not stray.

In the four years since leaving his old life behind, Criston had become skilled at avoiding his thoughts. He walled off his memories and could sit for hours watching his sheep, thinking of *nothing*. Now he pondered only what he would have for dinner. Perhaps he could go down to the stream and catch a trout or two; he had discovered that freshwater fish had an entirely different taste, and many more bones, than ocean fish. Criston kept a vegetable garden near the cottage, and knew where to find mushrooms and wild onions nearby. The dog might even catch that marmot, which would provide gamey but satisfactory meat.

With the nearest village a day's walk away, Criston's routine was unharried and unambitious. He had stepped off the path of life and now watched the rest of the world from the sidelines.

Sitting on his favorite boulder, he took up his knife and

began to whittle a chunk of wood. The sunshine was warm, and his fingers were nimble. When he first began carving his small sculptures, he had let the shape of the twisted wood determine his subjects: his dog, birds, indistinct humans. Soon he branched out into sea serpents, mermaids, fierce-looking sharks, and the exotic fish that Captain Shay had studied. He based many of his designs on sketches in the captain's battered scientific journal, which he kept close at hand to read in the long, solitary evenings.

Eventually, Criston's creativity drifted toward the creation of small ships. He carved models of boat after boat, though he didn't know why. He did not want to think of those days, but the wood seemed to speak to him. He crafted little vessels that reminded him of fishing craft from Windcatch, or of the *Cindon*. Getting more ambitious, he re-created the *Luminara*, adding twigs for masts.

When he finished another small carving, he realized it was already late afternoon. He whistled for the dog, which expertly rounded up the sheep. Criston had completed more than a dozen new carvings; it was time to make a trek to the village....

The following morning, with his whittled sculptures gathered into a square of cloth, he set off with Jerard trotting beside him, leaving the sheep to graze in the open meadow. They would be all right for two days until he returned.

The high mountain village in Corag Reach was isolated and self-sufficient, located beside a deep, cold glacial lake that sparkled an uncanny shade of turquoise in the sunlight. During his first year, the villagers had regarded him with suspicion, not knowing why Criston was there or where he had come from. But he was quiet and friendly, offering no threat, and eventually they accepted him. He obtained a handcart, with which he carried wool sheared from his sheep to trade in the village. He also began trading his carvings for salt, flour, and other essentials. He had enough to get by.

Now, when he arrived in the village, people came forward to see what he had to offer. The children stared at his wood carvings with delight as he produced them from his makeshift sack and handed them out for inspection. Since the villagers had spent their entire lives far from the sea, surrounded by mountains and trees, the ships were strange, exotic objects to them.

Criston distributed his carvings, and the boys took the boats to the lakeshore to set them afloat. The dog also splashed in the water, barking happily, chasing some of the floating craft and scaring up water birds.

The villagers traded Criston the supplies he needed. Though only yesterday he had felt a need for human company, after a few hours Criston needed to be by himself again. And so he whistled for Jerard, took his pack with the items for which he'd traded, and set off for home once more.

56 *Iboria*

The northern ice fields of Iboria stretched out in front of Mateo. Fog curled from his mouth when he exhaled. The sky was an empty, crackling blue. Everything else was painfully white, in spite of the landscape's rugged lines, fissures, and hills. The only breaks in the monotony were pale blue shadows in the deep ice, the sparkle of blown dry snow.

Somehow, he and his fellow soldier-recruits kept their bearings. Mateo still didn't know where the group was going, but they followed hearty, bearded Destrar Broeck, who seemed far more at home out on the frozen wasteland than back in Calavik, his stockade-surrounded town nestled in the dark pine forests.

Broeck raised a mittened hand, and the trainees stopped their slow march. The destrar sniffed the cold air, squinted into the bright sunlight, then grinned, showing teeth nearly as white as the snow. "We are close. I can sense the ice dragon." He trudged off in fur-lined boots toward a distant line of sheer ice cliffs.

Many trainees gasped in awe, though the destrar had made similar claims four other times. Mateo saw no difference in the landscape they had been looking at for days.

He was seventeen now, much tougher and stronger than when he went to Alamont Reach in his first year of service. After twelve months with Destrar Shenro, he spent his second year at Farport in Soeland Reach, where he served on different islands, facing cruel storms that blew across the Oceansea, learning how to swim in cold waters, how to perform sea rescues. He had stroked his way from one island to the next as his final test. Three of his fellow trainees had drowned in the passage, but the rest had emerged more prepared for naval warfare.

When any of the young men grumbled about the hazards of the training, Destrar Tavishel had reminded them of what the Urecari had done to the reconstruction crew in Ishalem. He remained unrepentant about how he had responded to the soldan-shah's ambassador.

After Soeland, Mateo went to mountainous Corag, learning to scale cliffs and find his way across rugged alpine passes. Then he spent a year in the scrubby rangeland of Erietta, best for raising cattle, where he learned horsemanship, how to find water in the desert, how to survive the heat, and how to make rope from the tall, woody-stemmed species of hemp, since the demand for strong rope had increased so sharply during the hostilities between Tierra and Uraba.

Over the years, he sent regular letters to Anjine, telling her of his progress, expressing his admiration for Tierra's military, though he left out certain harsh parts of his experiences, such as the time he caught a severe fever and lay delirious for four days, or when he received a long gash in sword training and needed to grit his teeth while a surgeon sewed up the cut. He didn't want her to worry about him.

During his year in Soeland he had fallen deeply in love with a fisherman's daughter—every girl in the islands was a fisherman's daughter, it seemed— and he had spent his days in a dreamy state, thinking about her. *Uishel.* Long, light brown hair that hung to her waist in thin, tight braids like fine ropes, a funny smile, bright blue eyes. He had daydreamed about her so much that his training had slipped, his fighting skills plummeted, and he broke his wrist in a stupid accident because he could not focus on his work. The training commander, recognizing the debilitating symptoms of a first love, had restricted Mateo to the military camp during the entire time it took for his wrist to heal and until he caught up on his training. Afterward, when he came out to find her, Uishel had already set her heart on someone else.

Devastated, Mateo had written Anjine all about it, pouring out his heart. He didn't ask for her advice, but she wrote back and consoled him anyway. He had eventually gotten over Uishel and found another young woman who caught his fancy in Erietta, and again in Corag.

When Anjine's missives found their way to him, he devoured the words about home, imagining her voice when he read the letters. She spent more time talking about the cat Tycho than she dwelled on the politics of the kingdom. She also explained that, without him there to keep her company, she had taken it upon herself to turn a few of her handmaidens into true companions, particularly Smolla and Kemm, but that the girls had very little curiosity for its own sake. They didn't see how learning new things would ever help them marry a young guard. He could tell that Anjine was frustrated.

Mateo had two months left in Iboria, the northernmost reach, where much of the wilderness was covered with dense pine forests. Since Iboria was in no danger of Uraban attack, Destrar Broeck used the soldier-trainees as a ready labor force. Instead of training with his sword, Mateo wielded both ax and saw, cutting down the tall trees, which were then dragged downslope to the rivers.

The Iborians had domesticated woolly mammoths from the open steppes to the north, and the gigantic russet-colored beasts could haul even the mightiest trees down to the frozen water; when the ice thawed in spring, the logs floated downstream to the open bay. From there, "log herders" used coastal currents to usher timber rafts down to the lumber markets in Calay.

Now Mateo was one of a dozen young men chosen to accompany Destrar Broeck far to the north, on what the bearded leader called a "vision quest."

"I have been on twelve of these in my life," Broeck had stated. "There's nothing like it. Out in the emptiness, you are forced to depend on your own skills and strength." He grinned at the trainees. "I have chosen you, because I think you will relish it as much as I do."

Mateo and his companions wore thick furs and carried heavy packs; each young man grasped an ivory-tipped spear for hunting. After years of training—especially the months of hard labor in the dense Iborian forests—he had developed significant body strength.

Broeck had provided them with the best furs, tools, and weapons before they set off from Calavik. In the settled forests of Iboria, the people rode plodding musk oxen, but after the destrar took them up to the edge of the snow fields, they used large sleds pulled by dog teams, which carried them many, many miles beyond the trees. The sled drivers let them off at the edge of a crevasse, then turned and raced back home.

Mateo had never felt so alone, but over the next few days of plodding and shivering, he realized that he did feel exhilarated. During the few hours of darkness each day, the aurora sparkled overhead, shimmering silken curtains of light that danced hypnotically as the constellations circled around their cosmic pivot point.

Broeck taught the recruits how to find stable ice. They crossed a deep blue lake by riding on broken ice floes to the opposite shore, from which point they could see a herd of wild mammoths thundering across the distant tundra. Even Destrar Broeck seemed intimidated by the immense beasts.

They hunted seals and ate the fresh meat, which Mateo found disgusting but nourishing. With no fuel to build a fire, they were forced to consume everything raw and cold. Water sacks inside their thick coats melted ice to provide liquid water.

Broeck had raised his left hand to show that two of his fingers were gone. For some time, the trainees had imagined the battles or monsters that had cost him his digits, but finally, as though revealing a grand joke, Broeck admitted that he had lost his fingers to frostbite while out hunting narwhals.

"Dangers don't have to be exciting to be dangerous," he said. "And don't underestimate the cold. The blowing snow here is hungry, and the wind can eat you alive. I lost my wife in a snowstorm that came up on a clear blue day. She went out to pick frostberries in the bogs and didn't see the blizzard coming. She never came home. . . ."

Mateo looked at the white expanse all around him, thinking of how swiftly the weather could turn. The bleakness offered little shelter.

He knew some of his companions were miserable, but he was enjoying the adventure himself. Destrar Broeck sensed it and spent more time with him. Even so, Mateo was greatly looking forward to returning to Calay, where he would volunteer to serve a final year in the city guard. He also wanted to see Anjine again....

Now, as the group neared the line of blue-white cliffs, the destrar stepped more cautiously, holding his ivory-tipped spear in one hand. He knelt and spread his other palm flat to the ground as if he could sense vibrations.

"Yes...yes, the ice dragon is nearby." He raised his voice to shout a challenge. "Raathgir! We have come to see your horn!"

The young soldiers muttered. One rapped the butt of his spear on the snowy ground. "We have all been trained in fighting, Destrar. Together we can kill the ice dragon and take a fine trophy to the king!"

Broeck turned in quick anger, his bushy eyebrows drawn together; frost lined his beard. His chapped lips showed no hint of a smile. "You want to kill the ice dragon?" He let out a loud laugh. "Nobody has ever killed an ice dragon. Don't be a fool—the ice dragon provides protection. His horn is blessed, and he shields Iboria. Do they not teach you the stories down in Calay?

"Raathgir was once a sea serpent who came close to Aiden's ship, but Aiden reached out from the prow and touched the monster's horn, saying, 'Do not delay me in my voyage. If you leave the sea and do not harm me and my people, I will give you a new land.' So Raathgir swam away and came up here to the ice, where he swims inside the frozen glaciers rather than the oceans. And because Aiden touched his horn, it still carries his magic. Some say that Raathgir's horn could protect any ship from sea monsters . . . but I would rather keep this protection in Iboria. We certainly aren't going to kill him!"

"Then why have we brought these spears? Why were we trained—"

"The spears are for you to protect *yourselves,* and to hunt. But the ice dragon . . . no, we won't be killing him. Save your bloodlust for the Urecari, when you get your chance to fight them."

As he studied his surroundings, Mateo saw light glinting in the smooth ice of the cliff face, possibly a reflection from high scudding clouds. Mateo wasn't entirely convinced that the ice dragon existed at all, suspecting instead that it was just a story Broeck liked to tell.

The ground beneath their feet began to vibrate, building to a larger rumble. The soldier-trainees scattered, looking to the destrar for answers or orders. Broeck had a childlike smile on his face. "I was right!"

The shaking grew more intense, and Mateo feared the ice would split at their feet. Heavy chunks of petrified snow calved off of the frozen bulwarks, dropping in a slow roaring avalanche that sprayed snow crystals like mist to expose a clean, unblemished vertical sheet of ice like a watery window.

Broeck stepped back and raised his mittened hand. His voice sounded small, blanketed in awe. "Behold what few men have ever seen."

Behind the prismatic wall of ice, Mateo saw a glint of silver and white, a flash of green scales. The angled planes of the frozen cliff might have distorted the view, but he did discern an enormous slithering body behind the ice wall.

"A tunneling ice dragon!" Broeck cried, "and a big one at that! Ho, Raathgir!"

None of the trainees now suggested killing the creature. The rumbling stopped, and the gliding serpentine form slipped away, leaving a hollow cavity in the wake of its passage. The packed ground became still, and no further ice chunks sloughed from the cliff.

"Even I have seen that only once in my life," Broeck whispered. "Consider yourselves blessed."

The thirteen of them remained silent for a long time; then Broeck turned abruptly, coming to a decision. "Come. It is time to go home."

Back at Calavik, they passed through the towering gates in the stockade wall, where villagers greeted them in their complex northern dialect, which Mateo still did not understand even after almost a year in Iboria. A domesticated mammoth stacked trimmed logs outside the fence to replace those that had been damaged by heavy snow drifts the previous winter. Barking dogs ran up and down the muddy streets. Blue-gray woodsmoke curled from the stone chimneys of the closely packed cottages inside the stockade wall.

The destrar's main house was a structure of dark lapped wooden shingles and rough planks carved with an intricate repeating pattern of fishhooks. A rustic steepled kirk had been built beside the main building. Destrar Broeck strode toward his home, leading the select trainees on their triumphant return.

The dark plank doors opened, and Broeck's daughter, Ilrida—a beautiful young woman, twenty-seven years old— came out smiling. Ilrida had hair so fair and blond it looked like silvery snow. Her skin seemed translucent, her eyes the palest blue, like the glacier wall behind which the ice dragon had tunneled.

For her own part, Ilrida could not speak standard Tierran, and Mateo didn't at first grasp the news that had made her so excited, but Broeck was certainly grinning. Mateo heard the others talking, picked up something about Calay and the king, and finally the destrar raised his voice so that all the soldier-trainees could hear.

"We announce a betrothal!" Broeck raised his daughter's delicate hand in the air. Ilrida's silvery-blond hair blew in the faint breeze, and she looked very content. "Six years after the death of Queen Sena, King Korastine has finally agreed to wed again — and he has chosen my beautiful daughter to be his wife." The destrar wrapped his arms around the young woman, swallowing her slim form in a large hug. "King Korastine is kind and wise, my dear. I know he will make you happy."

Broeck stalked toward Mateo and pounded the young man on the back. "It is time for you to go back to Calay. Your training here is finished. As your last duty, I ask that you be part of the escort to bring my dear Ilrida to her new home in Calay."

57 *Olabar, Asha's Villa*

After four years of living a shadowy existence in Olabar, Prester Hannes knew all the back streets, tangled alleys, and souk labyrinths. He had found the best places to steal food and beg, the public wells and fountains that provided fresh water. Most of all, he remained invisible.

Though he could have stolen finer clothes, he preferred the rags and hood that let him pose as a beggar or, worse, a leper. The patches of healed but slightly waxy burn scars on his hands and cheek furthered that impression. Few people looked twice at a miserable man they did not particularly want to see.

Obligated to demonstrate charity, the devout Urecari gave him brass coins, even an occasional *cuar*, and he gladly took their money. He made a habit of showing his scars, adjusting his filthy hood so that the burned part of his face showed, while carefully hiding the unblemished skin, and he silently mocked the Urabans for their gullibility.

Each day he hoped for a sign from Aiden, while he watched for weaknesses that he could use against the enemy. No other Tierran knew so much about the followers of Urec, their cities, their culture—or their blind spots—as Hannes did. Part of him wanted to rush back to Calay to tell Prester-Marshall Baine everything he had learned. But not yet. He still felt that Ondun had far more important work for him to do.

His favorite spot to sleep, both for its abundant comforts and for the sheer irony of it, was Asha's abandoned villa. He bedded down under the overgrown mulberry trees where she had once kept her tentworms.

After Hannes killed her and fled, the grieving soldan-shah had ordered her private villa boarded up, and Imir had never set foot in the place again. The superstitious Urecari now believed the place to be a haven for ghosts and evil spirits, and even squatters avoided it. Asha's home would never be purged of its demons . . . and Hannes felt he might never be clean, either, after what that woman had done to him.

Hannes had always tried to lead his life as Aiden would have wished, but it was difficult in this foreign place, with the entire culture against him. Asha had contaminated him with Sacraments that he could not vomit out, though he had tried—finding emetics in an apothecary shop and puking until he was so weak he could barely stand. He still felt the stain from within.

All alone in the moonlit mulberry orchard, he tore a thorny branch from one of Asha's dying rosebushes and shed his cloak to bare his back. Breathing hard, he leaned forward and thrashed with the thorny branch. He winced and hissed and struck harder, whipping repeatedly. He could feel the blood running down his back, but he thrashed again and again. By flagellating himself, he could at least show his heartfelt desire to be cleansed.

In all these years here, and previously in Ishalem, Hannes had been quiet and furtive, as Prester-Marshall Baine had instructed him. But now he wondered if he had truly done enough to improve the world by the grace of Ondun, as the Book of Aiden's Rule of Rules instructed.

He whipped himself until blood flowed so freely and the pain was so great he became delirious. Even then he did not stop. Feverish, swimming in his thoughts, listening to the pain and silent screams in his head, Hannes continued to beg for forgiveness. He hoped that his dripping blood would purify this ground, make Asha's villa a tiny foothold for Aiden against the heresy of Urec. Hannes knew he remained tainted. If he was so corrupted, maybe his blood was poisoned too, and Ondun would never accept this sacrifice.

But he could try, and he could hope. Somehow he would know.

When he was weak almost to the point of unconsciousness, Hannes cast aside the mangled rose branch and sank into a pain-filled stupor beneath the mulberry trees. Fearing sleep but needing it, he clung to his faith and hoped that one day he would fulfill his mission and serve Ondun in the way he was meant to.

58 *Olabar Palace*

Tukar, the half-brother of Zarif Omra, watched his mother's glee when she sank his ship. "Diagonal move," she said. "War galley rams cargo ship." She snatched an intricately carved piece from the game board. "You need to watch more carefully, my son. You always fail to prepare for the unexpected."

"I didn't know that move was allowed," Tukar said, abashed.

"Then you should spend more time learning the rules. Spend more time learning *everything*. You're the son of the soldan-shah, not a normal man."

Tukar assessed his remaining pieces: He had his captain, six sailors, and a small dromond warship, but Villiki still possessed her coveted sea serpent, a rogue piece that could attack whatever and whenever it wished.

Xaries had complicated rules, and though Tukar had played dozens of games with his mother, he had never won. She scolded him for his lack of strategic prowess; she had even slapped Tukar once when he dared to suggest that *xaries* was only a game, and that winning and losing mattered little. "It is not a game. It is a *test*—which you keep failing miserably."

Tukar would rather have been outside watching Uraban soldiers drill, the mounted warriors racing about the field in mock skirmishes. Soldan-Shah Imir continued to build his armies against the Aidenists, though thus far he had been reluctant to launch them all in a full-scale crusade. Shipments of armor plating, spear heads, arrow tips, and sharp swords arrived regularly from the Gremurr mines on the north coast of the Middlesea. This morning, when the heavily laden barges had docked, Tukar had gone to help unload the swords, planning to take one weapon as his own. But the curved blades with rough hilts were brutish weapons, mass produced by the hundreds and "utterly unbefitting a prince," his mother said.

Afterward, Tukar had spent the morning on a hunt in the forested hills south of Olabar, running with the hounds he had claimed as his own after Asha's murder. Tukar liked to occupy himself away from the palace...away from Villiki. His mother had expectations and demands for him that he did not have for himself.

"You still smell like those dogs," she said, finding something else to criticize. "And you're sweaty. From now on, before you play *xaries* with me, please bathe yourself."

"Yes, Mother."

Before marrying Soldan-Shah Imir, Villiki had been a sikara dedicated to the church of Urec. Priestesses often took many anonymous lovers, calling it a part of rejoicing, but they rarely married. In deciding to take Sikara Villiki as his third wife, Imir had caused something of an uproar. Everyone knew that sikaras were almost certainly not virgins, and by tradition the soldan-shah was expected to take a virgin bride. But Imir had found something intriguing about Villiki, so he insisted. And when the soldan-shah insisted, that was the law. Deaf to the protests of his advisers, he pointed out, "My wife is not getting a virgin husband, either, so we approach this marriage on equal footing." The Urecari Church had blessed the union, mainly because the priestesses acquired greater influence by having a sikara wed the soldan-shah.

In the years since the burning of Ishalem, the sikaras had been using their leverage to demand a violent response to the Aidenists. Now they complained—primarily through Ur-Sikara Lukai but also through Villiki—that Imir was not prosecuting the war with enough enthusiasm.

The soldan-shah had responded by requesting clear guidance from God, and the sikaras scribbled a flurry of questions on strips of paper, which they set blowing through the streets and out to sea. They wrote bold inquiries to Ondun and Urec on long ribbons, which they flew from the towers of the churches, so the ribbons could flutter in the brisk winds to be read by divine eyes. Though Tukar had dutifully studied Urec's Log and listened to the sikaras, he didn't recall that any such question had ever been answered directly and clearly. Priestesses were good at raising questions, but offered few answers. Imir must have realized the same thing.

By sending His two sons to explore the world, Ondun had meant to test them. Aiden and Urec had been ordered to accomplish a certain unknown task…which apparently had not yet been achieved. Had Ondun sent the brothers out because He was disappointed in them? Had He wanted the two to find something—a new Terravitae, perhaps? The Key to Creation? What had their goal been? For generations, the Urecari had seen signs everywhere, in an oddly shaped cloud, a freak storm, or an unusual fish pulled up in the nets. But no one really knew the answer.

Now, studying the *xaries* board with more intensity than he felt, Tukar picked up his dromond warship and aligned it to protect his remaining captain and sailor pieces. He planned his next several moves and developed an excellent strategy, but Villiki grew bored and impatient. She picked up the sea serpent piece and devoured his captain, abruptly ending the game.

"Learn that you cannot plan for disasters." She always found a way to lecture him. "Though some disasters can work to your advantage. Be prepared to become the next soldan-shah, no matter what."

"Zarif Omra will be the next soldan-shah," Tukar said.

"As I said," Villiki retorted, her voice as harsh as a desert wind, "you cannot plan for disasters."

It was no secret that the time rapidly approached when Imir would hand over the rule to his elder son. Since Omra's wife, Cliaparia, remained childless, the political machinations inside the Olabar palace were becoming more intense. Even Tukar had noticed the shift, though he remained assiduously aloof from such things, despite his mother's demands. Tukar did not want to become soldan-shah, and took no part in his mother's scheming. He admired his half-brother and felt that Omra would be a good leader.

Weary of her constant berating, Tukar stood from the game table, ignoring the scattered pieces on the *xaries* board. "I know who I am, Mother, and I accept my place. I am content with my lot. Why can't you—"

Villiki lurched to her feet and slapped him, a sharp, vicious strike that made a sound like cracking wood. "Only the lower classes can afford to be content. As the son of the soldan-shah, you are not meant to be content. You are meant to strive. I have done so much for you, and yet you continue to fail me!"

Villiki knocked the *xaries* board to the tiled floor in disgust. The bejeweled pieces clinked and bounced away as though fleeing her wrath. "While you amuse yourself with hunting dogs, I am planning great things on your behalf. Someone has to do it, or you will never get your due." Her eyes were smoldering coals fanned to life by a gust of wind. "And you, Tukar, better be ready to act when it is time."

59 *Iboria*

At the mouth of the wide river near Calavik, Kjelnar and his dedicated shipwrights worked to adorn a special wedding ship for Destrar Broeck's daughter. Using chisels, mallets, and rasps, the Iborians carved a benevolent bearded face on the prow: Holy Joron. The wondrous stories about Ondun's last son and the tropical land of Terravitae had always been Ilrida's favorites.

Since Mateo and his fellow trainees were neither skilled wood-carvers nor artisans, Broeck recruited them to tie ribbons on the masts and yardarms, sweep sawdust and wood shavings from the wedding ship's deck, paint the balustrades and cabin doors, and polish the stylized fishhook anchor.

Wood-cutters from the thick forests cut hundreds of pine trees and floated the logs downriver to the Calavik bay and the waiting wedding ship. Log herders would guide the cluster of Iborian pines to Calay as his daughter's dowry.

When the wedding ship was decorated to his satisfaction, the destrar walked the decks and inspected the well-appointed cabin where Ilrida would spend the passage and the clean but crowded berths reserved for the returning soldier-trainees.

When Broeck pronounced the ship ready to depart, his daughter came forward, preceded by five young female companions. Bearded Iborian men pounded on round-bellied kettle drums, making a thunderous sound like charging mammoths. Broeck proudly took Ilrida's arm and accompanied her across the gangplank to stand on deck. The young woman expressed her delight in the beautiful ship, the colorful ribbons, and the painted carvings, talking quickly in the northern dialect, still unable to speak formal Tierran. In Calavik, Ilrida lived among locals who were fluent in the Iborian tongue, and she had never found a knack for languages.

Mateo, placed in charge of the young soldiers who would return to Calay as the wedding escort, let out a sharp whistle and marched his men on deck. In short order, the ropes were cast off, the sails were unfurled, and the barge rode the current out of the bay into the cold northern sea, with a train of pine logs in its wake. The strong southerly current would sweep them down to Calay.

As they entered the Oceansea, a brisk wind gathered gray clouds that presaged rain, turning the coastline into a dim blur. Mateo stood on deck with the destrar as cold droplets splashed down on them. Mateo pulled up his hood for warmth, but the big destrar let his hair blow back in the breeze and smiled into the sloppy sleet. Ilrida joined them, watching the gray-shrouded shore slide by. Though at first glance she appeared as delicate as an ivory carving, the cold and wet didn't bother her, either.

The ocean remained choppy for three days, and the rocking of the ship made many of the recruits sick. Broeck urged them to come out in the open, but they huddled belowdecks, vomiting and groaning. When the weather calmed as they sailed past Erietta Reach, the recruits finally emerged on deck looking gray and shaken, breathing gulps of fresh salt air in an attempt to recover. Unafflicted by seasickness, Mateo preferred to be out in the cold open breeze, rather than in the close vile-smelling hold below.

Kjelnar, who had also accompanied them aboard the wedding ship, kept an anxious watch on his raft of logs. After the days of rough seas ended, he lowered a rope ladder over the side and dropped down onto one of the floating logs. From there, he skipped from one floating trunk to another, inspecting the chains that held key logs together. Mateo watched him incredulously, knowing that any slip would bring the shipwright between the logs, where he would be crushed. But Kjelnar did not slip.

During the storm, some of the outlying pines had broken loose and drifted free, and Kjelnar barked instructions for Iborian workers to lower the ship's boat over the side and row out to retrieve them. Not only were these pines valuable, but any rogue logs would pose a sailing hazard for future ships. Besides, he intended to use all the wood for constructing new warships in Calay Harbor. After what he had seen the Urecari do to Prester-Marshall Baine and his crew in Ishalem, Kjelnar did not ever want to stop building attack ships.

Ilrida stood on deck all day long, her pale blue eyes wide with wonder. Broeck's daughter was twelve years Mateo's senior, yet she seemed more innocent than he was, having lived a sheltered existence in Calavik ... possibly because the destrar was afraid of losing her, as he had lost his wife in a snowstorm.

Broeck told Mateo to keep her company, which Mateo did awkwardly, since he was not fluent in the northern dialect. "Talk to her in Tierran," the destrar suggested with a shrug. "She'll have to learn it sooner or later."

And so the young man stood with her on the open deck, telling her stories, describing Calay. He talked about the kitten he had given Anjine as a going-away present. He also shared snippets from Anjine's letters about how she had raised Tycho as a veritable feline prince. Most important, Mateo told Ilrida how kind and generous King Korastine was. He described how Korastine had given his word to Mateo's dying father and had never turned from his vow. "He will be a good husband, I promise you."

Looking wistfully at the coast, Mateo smiled. "And wait until you meet Anjine. She will make you feel at home. I'm sure you'll be great friends." He told her the stories of the things the two of them had done together as younger children. He laughed aloud at the memories.

Ilrida smiled at him, but Mateo could tell by her puzzled expression that she didn't understand much of what he said. Still, she seemed to enjoy his company and his voice, and he knew she picked up some basic words. Telling these stories had increased Mateo's own homesickness. He watched the coastline and knew they were almost home.

60 *Olabar, Saedran District*

Under house arrest in Olabar, Aldo na-Curic was considered a particularly valuable captive. The barred windows of his small, sparsely furnished cottage afforded him a view of the soldan-shah's palace and the nearby Urecari church. He still didn't know what would happen to him or what the Urecari wanted from him. Two guards were posted outside the main door, another in the rear, although Aldo had made no attempt to escape. Where would he go?

Each day, as he paced his room, his thoughts knotted as well as his stomach, he listened to the sikaras sing their call to the sunset services. He heard a cacophony of merchants shouting to customers who were bidding against one another, which made Aldo conclude that he must be near the main souks. He missed his parents, his brother and sister, and stern old Sen Leo.

No one seemed surprised that Aldo could speak passable Uraban, and he concluded that Saedran chartsmen were so rare here on the foreign continent that they seemed like sorcerers. As he brooded in his locked home, Aldo considered how to use that perception to his advantage. Maybe he could bargain his way home, or at least to freedom.

After a week of not-unpleasant captivity, during which Aldo realized he was more curious than terrified about his future, he resigned himself to learn what he could from his strange situation. Even in Sen Leo's large library, descriptions of Olabar and the Uraban interior were sketchy at best, the details unverified. After his ordeal, if he did get away, Aldo was determined to return to Calay with a useful report. It would make all his tribulations worthwhile if he could sketch in another blank area on the great Mappa Mundi.

On the morning of his sixteenth day, after being fed a lovely breakfast of papaya and fire-roasted eggs, Aldo was surprised when a quartet of flatulent-sounding Uraban horns blasted a fanfare in the street outside his house. The guards yanked open the door for a bald, plump man who wore orange robes, decorative golden chains, and a bright yellow sash tied across his belly.

"I am Imir, Uraba's soldan of soldans," he said. "Welcome to my lovely city of Olabar. It is not often we have Saedran chartsmen as our guests."

The soldan-shah's words took Aldo aback, and he could not stop himself from blurting, "Your guest? My ship was attacked, my crewmates killed by Uraban pirates, and I was kidnapped. We were just peaceful traders!"

Imir's expression turned sour. "Your captain was a black marketeer running cargo in our territory south of the sacred Edict Line. You're no fool, Saedran. If a Uraban ship were to sail north and secretly trade with Tierran coastal villages, King Korastine's navy would attack us, capture or kill our crews, and sink our ships." He took a seat at the small table, sliding aside the dishes that held the remnants of Aldo's breakfast. "We could just as easily have let you join the others, but you can help us." His full lips curved in an ingratiating smile. "We'll make it worth your while."

Aldo was too upset to be tactful. "My services aren't for sale."

"Of course they are. And I am your new customer. We need to have a conversation, you and I." A servant hurried in from the street, carrying an ornate silver tea set and left again just as quickly. "As a Saedran, you have no stake in the religious clash between Urecari and Aidenists. Why show them any more loyalty than you would to me? I wish to hire you as a chartsman. Help our merchants and sailors, maybe even our navy. As a Saedran chartsman, you should be objective."

Flustered, Aldo sat at the table. Imir regarded the tea service as if wondering whether to wait for some servant to fill their cups, then picked up the silver pot and splashed steaming minty liquid into the cups, serving himself first. "Although Uraba has plenty of wealth, we do not have a large population of Saedrans. Very few are chartsmen. You know about Tierran waters, the coastline, the cities, the winds, the currents. You'd be very much appreciated among us. Why not settle down here? We'll find you a wife, pay you well, give you anything you need."

Aldo reached forward to take his cup of tea, unconvinced. "I'd rather go home to my own family."

Imir's brow wrinkled. "You already have a wife? You seem quite young."

"I have a mother and father, a sister and a brother."

The soldan-shah made a quick, dismissive gesture. "They will be fine without you."

"They must be worried sick about me! Everyone knows what the Urecari do to their enemies."

Imir slurped his tea, burned his tongue, and quickly set his cup down on the table. "You aren't the only one who has endured tragedies, young man. Tierran pirates have attacked coastal vil-

lages in Outer Wahilir. They sank our ships, stole our cargoes."
He stopped himself and sighed. "Ah well, I thought you might be
intractable, so I brought someone who can tell you more about
us and our lands, and our needs." He signaled to the guards at
the open door.

A broad-hipped woman stepped tentatively into the house,
wearing a Saedran-style dress and traditional scarves tied at
her neck. In her late forties, with curly sepia hair that fell to the
small of her back, she had generous lips, kind eyes, and a studi-
ous demeanor.

With a warm smile and a bow in her direction, Imir said,
"This is my dear friend and companion, Sen Sherufa na-Oa,
one of Olabar's most prized scholars and a chartsman, though
an untraveled one. I'm one of the few who recognizes both her
intelligence and talents. I cannot fathom why men do not line up
at her door with marriage proposals."

"I turned them down," Sherufa said. "I've got too many other
things to do." She turned her attention to Aldo. "However, I am
delighted to see a fellow Saedran chartsman. I may not have
made voyages of my own, but I have read plenty of books. We
can learn much from each other."

"I'm more interested in what you can learn from him, my
dear." Imir leaned forward to kiss Sen Sherufa on the cheek, and
she flushed. The guards studiously turned their backs, staring into
the street as though an invasion might be about to happen. "I'll
leave you two alone." He pulled out a chair for Sherufa. "Have
some tea, get to know each other. Offer him anything...within
reason. He could be very useful to us."

The soldan-shah strode out, leaving the two Saedrans together,
and Sen Sherufa seemed as embarrassed as Aldo. "This is interesting," she said.

"And unexpected." Aldo cautiously studied her to see if he

could read any hidden agendas. "I have nothing against you, ma'am, but after watching them capture my ship and murder my captain and crew, I am not... objective about the Urabans."

"Oh, you've got nothing to fear from me." Sherufa picked up the soldan-shah's half-finished cup of tea and drained it. "And Imir is right in one respect—Saedrans don't have to choose between Aidenists and Urecari. We do have a lot to learn from each other."

61 *Olabar Palace*

Saan was gone.

On his fifth birthday, her son was seized and taken away, exactly as Ur-Sikara Lukai had threatened. The priestess arrived with six palace guards, all of them armed, as if they expected her to resist, but Adrea knew how useless that would be. Turning her head aside, Adrea bottled up her tears and allowed herself one last wordless embrace with her son before they pulled the surprised and upset Saan away with them.

"He will be taken care of," Lukai promised in heavily accented Tierran. "He will serve the followers of Urec. Be proud of him."

With great effort, Adrea held her tongue and kept her expression stony. Ur-Sikara Lukai swirled her red gowns and followed the guards ushering the boy away. Adrea could hear the echoes of Saan crying down the halls....

In the following days, from the blank expression on Adrea's face, no one in the Olabar palace could have guessed the depths of her fury. For more than five years of slavery, she had endured in silence, remained in her place, and performed her duties—all to keep her son safe.

Now, given the slightest opportunity, she would have poisoned them all, from the soldan-shah himself to the lowliest Uraban servant. She considered stealing a knife from a serving tray and going from room to room in the dead of night, slaying as many Urabans as she could before someone stopped her.

Only the slender hope of doing something for Saan restrained her. Without Adrea, the boy would be utterly lost. She needed to find some way to fight back, or he would be forever trapped in his fate.

She had failed him, and she had failed her beloved Criston. Saan might even be turned into a soldier against Aidenists—unless she could find a way to free him. If anything happened to Saan, if she learned that he'd been harmed in any way, then nothing would stop her. Adrea *would* kill them all.

For now, she would bide her time, always alert, playing the role of the silent servant.

Adrea entered Villiki's quarters carrying a tray with the evening meal: skewers of roasted songbirds smothered in honey and sesame seeds and a salad of bright flower petals. She was tempted to spit on the food before bringing it to Imir's scheming wife, but if she were caught doing that, she would be severely punished. Adrea was not afraid to surrender her life if it meant freedom for Saan, but she wouldn't do it for an empty gesture. No, she would act only when she was certain she could accomplish something.

Inside the chamber, Villiki and Ur-Sikara Lukai lounged on cushions, facing each other across a low table. Intent on their conversation, the two women began to eat without so much as acknowledging Adrea. She unobtrusively went on with her work, tying back the silk hangings around Villiki's bed, preparing Villiki's pillows for evening, watering each of Villiki's eleven potted ferns, whose fronds unfurled in a perfect embodiment of the Urecari religious symbol. The two women continued to speak in low tones, hushed but intense, and quickly forgot her presence.

"It will be easy to administer the poison," Lukai said.

Bending over a potted fern, Adrea froze, then forced herself to keep going through the motions of her task.

"Cliaparia's so desperate for his affections that she continues to buy aphrodisiacs, hoping to ensnare Omra's love." The ur-sikara's tone was rich with scorn. "She'll administer our poison without even realizing it. She'll think it's another love potion."

Villiki lounged back on her cushion, chuckling in her rich, deep voice. "Wonderful! That way, Cliaparia will be blamed for Omra's death since she will give him the poison, an added benefit. But we've got to move soon. Any day now, she could claim to be pregnant, and then Tukar's challenge to become heir would be even weaker." She snorted. "And it is weak enough as it is."

The two women ate their meal, crunching the delicate bones of the skewered birds. Villiki looked up and took notice of Adrea. "You, slave! Bring us some figs."

Adrea blinked unresponsively, pretending not to understand. Lukai let out a loud disgusted sigh, muttering in Uraban. "She is as stupid as a stone." She raised her voice in rough Tierran. "Figs! Bring them. We command it."

Adrea hurried toward the door of Villiki's chambers.

"When Omra returns from Yuarej in three days, Cliaparia will insist on spending the night with him," Villiki said. "Can you do your part by then?"

The sikara chuckled. "Oh, that will be a simple matter. She has already asked Fyiri for assistance. I had Fyiri tell Cliaparia that this new love potion must be added to every dish of food."

Adrea slipped through the door, ostensibly to fetch figs from the kitchens. She had heard everything she needed to know, and it gave her a spring in her step and hope in her heart. She had a weapon.

This was going to be a dangerous game. Villiki would murder her if she discovered what Adrea had in mind—but Adrea would take the gamble. She did not intend to be caught. These women had much to learn about the lengths to which a desperate Tierran mother would go. Their schemes were amateurish in comparison.

62 *Calay*

On the day the wedding party was due to arrive from Iboria, Anjine was glad to see excitement in her father's face for the first time in years. Though he had previously seen only a small plate painted with Ilrida's likeness (in the pose of a young female crewman on Aiden's ship, naturally), Korastine was infatuated with her. Destrar Broeck had described his daughter with any proud father's lack of objectivity, and the king trusted him.

This was not strictly a political marriage, Anjine knew; Korastine honestly wanted to be happy. After her mother's death, he often asked Anjine to sit next to him by the fire and read aloud from the Book of Aiden. When he thanked her with tear-filled eyes, she could see the heavy hunger of loneliness within him.

While they waited for the wedding ship to pull into the harbor, Anjine helped to finish the banquet preparations inside the castle, inspecting the platters of roast sturgeon, the herbed root vegetables, soups made from dried peas, and dozens of sweet quince tarts. Her cat, Tycho, insisted on following her, wanting her attention—as well as some of the fish. Her two handmaidens, Smolla and Kemm, fussed about with colors and banners and flowers.

The flagstoned floor of the banquet hall had been swept clean, and lace-edged linen tablecloths were spread out on the long plank dining tables. The tables were set with a wedding gift from the Corag destrar, new pewter goblets that bore the specific crest of each destrar.

The Iborian wedding ship arrived on schedule, trailed by a raft of valuable pine logs. A runner came to inform King Korastine that the passengers had disembarked and were making their way through the Royal District. Her father came to fetch Anjine, grinning and anxious. Side by side, the two emerged through the castle's arched gates, where they waited to receive the wedding party.

Tumblers and jugglers rushed out for an impromptu show, followed by musicians with flutes and tambourines. Nothing about their performance was coordinated, but the diversions were colorful and entertaining. Each of the entertainers longed to be singled out as a court performer.

But King Korastine had eyes only for Ilrida as she approached, holding the arm of her bearlike father. The destrar's ethereal daughter looked captivating and sweet, halfway between Anjine's age and Sena's. Korastine went forward to greet his bride-to-be, bowing deeply.

Behind them, Anjine saw a familiar but barely recognizable face—Mateo, tall and mature. His dark hair had recently been shorn, and his Iborian-style uniform looked a bit small for him. Why, he looked grown up! Anjine realized that she herself had flowered into womanhood since she had last seen her best friend. She was no longer an eleven-year-old girl, and he not a young boy. The gulf of years and puberty had changed them greatly.

Anjine drew herself up to look as regal as she could, while Mateo stood at attention at the head of the soldier-trainees, his face unreadable. Their eyes met and locked, and Anjine could no longer contain herself. Her lips curved in a grin, just as Mateo smiled, showing her a flash of his boyhood again, and it warmed her heart.

The group moved inside the castle amidst a welcoming chatter. While the party members were escorted to their rooms by castle retainers, the returning soldiers set off for their barracks in the Military District, where many of them would be fitted with the uniforms of the city guard for one last year of service. Mateo had already written her that he'd decided to opt for enlisting in the city guard, anxious to stay closer to home.

Anjine whispered in her father's ear, pulling his attention from Ilrida. "May I have Mateo help me with preparations for this evening? The city guard can get by without him for an afternoon."

The king was startled, as if he hadn't realized who the young man was. "Mateo! Welcome back to us. Military service has certainly matured you!" He embraced the young man. "Go with Anjine. I'm sure the two of you have much to talk about."

The pair slipped away from the hubbub of visiting dignitaries. Mateo looked around him, as if seeing the castle's familiar halls and chambers for the first time. "So much has changed in Calay. When was the old Tinkers' Bridge torn down?"

"It collapsed when a barge full of cut limestone hit the pilings," Anjine said. "People have had to walk all around the bay or take ferry boats for months, but it'll be rebuilt in the next year."

Mateo continued in a rush of words; he seemed to have so much to say. "And when our ship sailed in, I saw that the military barracks have expanded all the way up the spit of land. Looks like they'll soon edge out part of the Butchers' District. And I've never seen so many warships on patrol at the mouth of the harbor!"

"With good reason." Her voice turned hard. "You know what the Urecari have done to our villages." She led him into a west-facing upper room where afternoon sunlight streamed in to warm the velvet-upholstered window seat. There she found Tycho sprawled out to sun himself. The cat lifted his head, glanced at Mateo, and gave a curious meow, obviously not remembering the young man from so many years ago. Nevertheless, Matteo went over to scratch Tycho's chin.

"It'll be different now," Mateo said. "While I'm serving in the city guard, at least we can talk in person, so we don't have to write so many letters." She had enjoyed his letters, though . . . read each one dozens of times.

"Unless you go out on a patrol boat. Some of the city guard are being assigned as crew."

"Makes sense. There's more trouble on the sea than in Calay."

She hoped, though, that he would stay here in the city.

The two fell into an awkward silence. They hadn't seen each other for five years — during which Mateo had served in all five reaches, and Anjine had learned more about politics and leadership than most *men* learned in a lifetime. There was so much to tell that neither of them could think of how to begin.

In the weeks after the wedding, Queen Ilrida adapted to her new life and happily settled in as the wife of the king. Korastine adored the Iborian princess from the moment he first saw her, and Anjine was glad to see that her father seemed young again, as if a hard decade had melted off his face.

Destrar Broeck remained in Calay for as long as he could make excuses to do so, but eventually he had to head north before the weather changed. Kjelnar remained behind with the new shipment of logs, and King Korastine put him in charge of the entire shipbuilding district for constructing naval ships.

Anjine took her new stepmother under her wing, making sure Ilrida felt welcome and comfortable. Although the Iborian woman was full of wonder and definitely wanted to please, she had great difficulty speaking the Tierran language. Anjine knew that while children acquired languages easily, many adults were not so adept at it. She asked Smolla and Kemm to work with Ilrida on her letters (secretly hoping that the two handmaidens would learn something as well). Anjine longed for more intelligent conversation in the castle.

Right away, she helped Ilrida memorize a few key words and phrases, and sat with the other woman in her own rooms; while her Iborian ladies-in-waiting snipped lace or sewed garments, she told stories about Queen Sena, assuming that Ilrida would want to know more about Korastine's first wife. The Iborian ladies were already fitting into their new home, a few even flirting unabashedly with the castle guards.

One day, when Anjine joined her in a private drawing room, Ilrida reverently opened a locked wooden chest, rustled among fabrics and garments, and withdrew an object that she obviously valued greatly. The pale Iborian woman held up a round icon in a frame the size of a small plate. The image had been assembled from minute pieces of colored tile and polished stone, a detailed mosaic of a bearded man, his head surrounded by a golden halo, his face filled with peace and compassion.

"Holy Joron...is my favorite story," Ilrida said. The words sounded rough and unnatural when she spoke them, but she seemed proud of her ability to communicate. She had worked hard to memorize the names of the tales.

"You like the story of Holy Joron and the land of Terravitae?" Anjine asked.

Ilrida smiled and nodded. "He wait for Ondun."

"I know many Joron stories—the Silver Waterfall, the talking storm, and the lost flock of sheep in the whispering grove. Let me tell them to you to help you learn our language."

Ilrida listened with rapt attention as Anjine related the familiar descriptions of the calm animals, the orchards laden with fruit, the streams so full of fish that a person could cross by stepping on the backs of trout. She didn't think Ilrida's eyes would ever stop sparkling.

63 *Olabar, Saedran District*

Though he was released to accompany Sen Sherufa na-Oa, Aldo found it hard to believe he was no longer a prisoner. He glanced about furtively as Sherufa guided him through Olabar's Saedran District, sure there must be eyes watching him, to inform Soldan-Shah Imir of his every move. If Aldo bolted toward the harbor and stowed away on a ship bound for the far shores of the Middlesea, would they cut him down in these strange, foreign streets?

But nobody paid him any particular attention. The guards were gone.

Aldo couldn't believe it. "I won't be going back to the prison house?"

Sherufa's brow furrowed. "Why, no. Imir released you to me. He wants me to talk with you and learn from you."

"Just like that?"

"Just like that. Imir trusts me." She chuckled. "Besides, if you run, where could you go? You're on a different continent, among strangers. Since you're a chartsman, I assume you are an intelligent and logical person. Your best choice is to stay here with me.

I always have a spare room. Everyone in the district knows it, and I've had more than my share of unexpected guests."

"Other captives like me?"

She laughed. "Oh, no! More often it's angry wives who stay with me to leave their husbands with a cold bed for a few nights. Sometimes it's out-of-town travelers with nowhere else to stay. They're always welcome, so long as they're courteous and can offer some interesting conversation."

Sherufa strolled ahead of him as though this were any other day and she had simply gone to the market — to pick out a Saedran chartsman rather than fresh fish or a sack of grain.

"Is there a library here?" he asked. "I'd like to study your volumes. They must be different from the ones that Sen Leo used to teach me."

"It wouldn't be much of a Saedran District without a library, now, would it?" She shrugged and he sensed that she was slightly introverted and quite a bit more curious about him than she wanted to show. "All of the volumes belong to me, however, so you can read them from my own shelves. I'd love to share them with someone. Chartsmen are rare here, and the soldan-shah needs them for his warships. Most are taken overland to the Oceansea. Chartsmen don't stay here in Olabar — except for me."

The streets and dwellings around Aldo had a familiar look of Saedran architecture and decorations: apothecary shops, alchemists, portrait painters, physicians and astrologers, all of the usual professions. The people wore familiar garments, as well.

"I have the perfect memory, and I've studied records, charts, and tales of the Traveler, but I've never actually left Olabar. I prefer to travel in my imagination, safe at home."

Remembering the dreams from his youth, Aldo could not understand a person uninterested in seeing the wonders of the world. Why, he had practically begged Sen Leo for his first assignment. But perhaps Saedrans were different here in Uraba, surrounded by an altogether different culture.

Seeing Sherufa in the street, groups of children ran toward her, calling out together in a good-natured harmony, asking for sweets. Aldo didn't know what to do, but the children were uninterested in him. From pockets hidden in the folds in her skirt, Sherufa brought out wrapped candies and tossed them into the air with flickering birdlike movements. The children jumped and scrambled to catch them. She beamed contentedly.

Aldo's people kept a culture unto themselves, and the Saedrans in Uraba were as insular as they were everywhere else. Here, they lived in the shadow of Urecari churches rather than Aidenist kirks, but their situation was similar. It was true — as the soldan-shah had declared — that Saedrans had neither Aidenist nor Urecari sympathies. The goal of all trained Saedran scholars was to complete the Mappa Mundi. By fulfilling that destiny, his people would be allowed to return to their sunken homeland that had vanished long ago.

They reached the door of a small stuccoed house with a tile roof, her residence. On her stoop, someone had left a basket of bread and three fresh eggs tucked into a folded cloth. She picked up the food without wonder or surprise and opened the door to her home, stepping aside so Aldo could enter first, as an honored guest. He had nothing of his own.

"You have no garments? No belongings?" she asked.

"I didn't have much chance to pack while the Urabans were attacking my ship," he said with a bitter edge in his voice.

"I'll put out the call. Don't worry. We'll find everything you need. We take care of our own."

Sen Sherufa certainly seemed warm-hearted, charming, and well liked, though she had never married. When he asked her about it, she said, "I spent too much time with my nose in books, documents, and chronicles. I rarely looked up long enough to take notice of a potential husband, and I never felt the need to have children."

Aldo chuckled. "You don't need a family of your own. Everyone here treats you like a favorite aunt."

Inside her home, Sherufa showed him her library, the valued books she kept on her shelves. Aldo studied the spines and read the titles. Sen Sherufa owned quite an eclectic mix of tomes, and he knew he could offer her a great deal of information...if he decided he could trust her.

"Because I kept to myself, always studying, but never flaunting my knowledge, no one discovered until relatively late in my life that I had the perfect recall," Sherufa explained. "Belatedly, I memorized maps, constellations, and stories. My mind is full of details about things I've never seen, places I've never visited." She smiled—wistfully, it seemed. "When the soldan-shah learned of my skills, he brought me into his palace."

"Why did he need a chartsman in the palace?" Aldo slid another volume back onto the shelf and removed the next one, which was not a proper book at all but merely a ledger of all the merchant ships that had come into port over a five-year period.

"Imir wanted to hear my stories. He would sit back with his eyes closed, a goblet of wine in his hand, and ask me for one tale after another after another." She took a seat, turning her chair so she could look at him. "I'm good at recounting other people's adventures. I just don't wish to have any of my own."

"It's not the same," Aldo said in a low voice. "I promise you that."

"Maybe so, but so it is."

"And that's how you came to be friends with the soldan-shah?"

Sen Sherufa's gaze was distant. "He wanted to take me as his wife—his fourth, I believe—but I refused."

Aldo didn't know whether to be more surprised that the soldan-shah wanted a Saedran wife or that Sen Sherufa had turned him down. "Was he angry with you?"

"Oh, Imir still maintains his hope, and I let him keep that hope, but my calling is elsewhere. Because I remain a virgin, the sikaras find me laughable, but what does their derision matter to me? They'd have no respect for a Saedran woman even if I were promiscuous!"

Aldo could see how Imir would find her attractive, though Sherufa did not bother to make herself traditionally beautiful. Her skirts were trimmed with color and fitted just tightly enough to show some of her generous figure, but not in a seductive way. The fact that she was exotic and unattainable had probably made her even more intriguing to the soldan-shah.

"Imir grants me anything I ask of him...but then, I've never made any difficult requests. He knew that I'd love to speak with another chartsman. I think he was more glad for your capture because it would put the two of us together, and make me happy, than because of any strategic knowledge you might have."

"But he does expect you to pump me for information." It wasn't a question.

"Maybe." Sen Sherufa walked into the kitchen, where she poured them each a drink from a water pitcher in which floated sliced lemons and flower petals. "He wants you to tell me stories, so I'll have more tales to entertain him."

"I'd like to learn something as well," Aldo said cautiously. "We can exchange information. Do you have...any maps of Uraba?"

"Maps." Sen Sherufa's eyes lit up. She met Aldo's gaze as she handed him a glass. "Oh, you mean the Mappa Mundi?"

"You know of the Mappa Mundi? The great project?"

"I'm a Saedran, am I not? A chartsman, even if I don't travel—I told you that. Because we are so isolated, I'm sure my poor map is quite out of date. I have little opportunity to gain more information."

Aldo's heart pounded. "Now you have that opportunity. We both do."

Sherufa went to one of her cupboards and furtively removed a stack of fired clay plates and bowls to expose a wooden backing. "Nobody else knows about this...well, not many. Since I'm the only scholar and chartsman here, I keep my own copy so that I can make tentative additions and corrections as I read my books."

She slid out the thin boards so she could unfasten a broad sheet of yellowed paper. On it, Aldo saw the outlines of the world, intricately detailed landforms, the coastline, rivers and hills, Uraban villages, the boundaries of all the soldanates. In one quick glimpse, Aldo learned more about Uraba than he had ever known before.

The northern half of the map, however, showing the continent of Tierra, was both sketchy and inaccurate. Some features of the coastline were exaggerated, others nonexistent, particularly in the isolated reaches of Iboria and Soeland.

Aldo drank in the lines and markings, reading the Saedran characters, committing every detail to memory. He followed the outlines of the Middlesea, and was surprised by the especially thorough mapping of the northern coast, which was blocked from Tierran exploration by the rugged Corag mountains, as he had seen himself. Aldo marveled as he meshed these details with what he already knew.

The soldan-shah had hoped Sen Sherufa would make Aldo want to stay in Olabar and offer his services. Seeing this version of the map, however, produced the opposite reaction. He felt a fiery determination to get back to Calay. He *had* to bring this knowledge to Sen Leo!

But he also had an obligation to Sherufa, to share his knowledge with the ultimate goal of completing the Mappa Mundi. Aidenist and Urecari politics did not matter to them.

"I can help you fill in the blanks," he said. "Together you and I can make the most complete map of the world that Saedrans have ever produced."

64 *Olabar Palace*

Though Adrea averted her gaze, as a slave should, her heart was determined. She carried a lacquered tray bearing a bowl of cool yogurt mixed with mashed mango to the zarif's chambers. Few people in the palace recalled that Zarif Omra had shown her favor years ago during the raid on Windcatch, and he had paid no special attention to her since then.

Now, though, she prayed that he remembered. She was risking everything.

She walked forward with silent grace, maintaining the appearance that she belonged here. It would be a long while before anyone noticed that she had abandoned her regular tasks.

Having just returned from an expedition to the Yuarej soldanate where he inspected military encampments and staging fields, Omra now sequestered himself in a private chamber to look over military maps and tally his troops, ships, and weapons. Adrea knew that Cliaparia planned to hold a private feast for him that evening. The zarif's wife would oversee the preparations and had given very specific instructions to the kitchen staff. This would be Adrea's one chance.

She entered with the tray and set it on the low table beside his desk. Without looking up, Omra merely gestured her away as he scribbled his figures, added his sums, but she remained, her throat working, her lips moving as she tried to remember what it felt like to *form words* and speak openly after so long.

Omra glanced at her, his dark eyes narrowed with impatience; then he paused as recognition flickered across his face. After five years, he still remembered her.

Before he could say anything, Adrea astonished him by speaking in perfect Uraban. "There is a plot to kill you, Zarif Omra. You will die tonight, unless you listen to me." Her voice sounded completely foreign to her, but it strengthened with every word.

Omra stared at her and stroked his dark, pointed beard. "So you *can* speak, after all."

"More importantly, I can listen. A slave overhears things. I know all about the plot."

Omra seemed more amused than frightened. "Very well, tell me."

Adrea shook her head. "Not yet. I will reveal what I know only if you grant me something in return."

His brows lifted in amusement. "Really?" He laughed. "I remember how scrappy you were when we captured you. I suppose I shouldn't be surprised that your spirit was never broken, no matter how well you've cooperated during your time here."

"I require something from you, Zarif," she repeated coldly. "If you don't agree, then they can kill you, for all I care. You have the blood of my friends—my family—on your hands."

Intrigued now, he leaned back, pushing his papers aside. "Then why bother to save me at all?"

"Because I *do* have a great love for my son. He has been taken away, and I want him back. You can help me. I want your guarantee that he will stay with me. Is that worth your life?"

He crossed his arms, regarding her, but Adrea didn't flinch.

"Tell me what you know," Omra said. "Then I will decide."

"No. Your word first."

"And how much is my word worth, if it is given only to a slave?"

"The word of the soldan-shah's son should be worth a great deal to whomever it is given."

"Very well, then I give you my word." He smiled thinly. "But I will decide whether to *keep* my promise after you reveal what you know." He seemed to be toying with her, but not in a cruel way. He was amused by her boldness.

Dismayed, but knowing this was the best promise she was likely to get, Adrea had to push forward. So she explained how Villiki intended to poison him that evening, how the drug was to be administered in a "love potion" his wife, Cliaparia, would put into the food. She watched Omra's expression darken, for her words had the ring of truth.

"I know of Cliaparia's love potions, because they often make me ill. I also know how much Villiki wants her own son to take my place." Omra fell silent as thoughts rushed through his head, colliding, making him more and more angry. "Which priestess was she scheming with?"

"Ur-Sikara Lukai." She answered without hesitation, without regret. Though the lead priestess had taken too much pleasure in tearing Saan away from her, Adrea did this not for revenge, but for her son.

He nodded. "And is Cliaparia involved? Does she want me dead?"

"I saw no evidence of that. What would she have to gain? I

think the others mean for her to be blamed, if their poisoning plot succeeds."

The zarif rose, his expression dark. "It's best you leave now. I must speak with my father."

But Adrea made no move. She waited, silent and expectant. Preoccupied as he was, it took Omra a few moments to remember her request. He took a breath and nodded. "Yes. If this is true, then it is indeed worth the price of your son."

65 *Uraba, Abilan Soldanate*

Improving the world, by the grace of Ondun.

Prester Hannes had lived those words all his life: the Rule of Rules that God had given his sons, and that they in turn had given their followers. Such a task would never end, and all good Aidenists had to look for ways to follow the rule, to please Ondun.

But for all his contemplation on that command, Hannes had never before understood the breadth of the charge. He hadn't felt the genuine meaning of that instruction—*improving the world*—until now. It had become his mission in life.

After so many years in Olabar, preying upon the enemy in small ways, he slipped out of the capital city and made his way along the southern coast of the Middlesea, following a path that would eventually take him back to Tierra. But he was in no hurry. He had work to do on the way.

The Urecari were willful heretics. Before the burning of Ishalem, Aidenist missionaries had traveled across the isthmus to Urecari settlements to spread the word. But these people knowingly followed the wrong path, stubbornly refused to listen. Why, then, should Prester Hannes have any sympathy for them? Though the Book of Aiden was widely available, they ignored the truth, and so they had to face the consequences. The world could not be pure again while so many followers of arrogant Urec lived, and Ondun would not return until the blight was removed.

It was so obvious.

After walking for days on a stony road across an open grassy landscape, Hannes arrived at a small coastal village. The locals were tanned, the men shirtless, and they all moved about in an unhurried fashion, gathering mussels and oysters from beds along the breakwater. Fishing boats plied the calm shallow seas, their crews spearing sharks or netting sardines. In evenings, with a festive air they roasted their catch in great ember-filled beds, with smoky dry-seaweed fires right on the beach.

At the small church in the center of the village, the old half-blind sikara spotted Hannes as he entered town at dusk. She moved forward, favoring her left leg, and asked him to join them in the communal meal on the beach. He hesitated at first, but he was very hungry and finally came forward to accept a pile of black mussels from the ash bed. The shells yawned open, and as soon as they were cool enough to touch, he slurped out the rubbery meat.

He explained that he came from Olabar, but refused to answer more, though the sikara pressed him for details. She offered him shelter, saying that he could sleep in the church if he wished, but Hannes was not willing to do that. In this temperate climate, he would be comfortable sleeping outside.

He was sure that the compassion of the half-blind priestess was just an act, and he detected a buried hauteur beneath her manner. Like any sikara, she probably wanted to corrupt him. As Asha had done. He kept his distance.

The village housed its consumable stores inside a large permanent tent. Salt and spices were sealed in clay jars. Casks of lamp oil were stacked high.

Hannes watched these people furtively for more than a day, but the community was so small and tight-knit it was hard for him to remain unobtrusive. The sikara invited him to join them for their sunset services, but he begged off, pretending to be polite, knowing what the woman really wanted.

The sikara sang out her call in a reedy voice that projected far. The fishermen had tied up their boats and joined their families, and everyone came to the church building that was made of clay, stones, and driftwood. The sikara announced that she would provide the Sacraments that night.

Hannes knew what he had to do. *Improving the world, by the Grace of Ondun.*

When everyone had entered the church and the old woman began intoning memorized passages from Urec's Log, Hannes stole one of the barrels of lamp oil from the storage tent and broke it open. When the unison prayer began, he used it to cover the noise of his actions as he barricaded the door from the outside.

He splashed the fragrant oil around the windows, the door, and soaked the driftwood and porous walls. With his flint and steel, he set a spark that caught on the lamp oil, and his eyes glowed as he watched the eerie blue ignition corona race across the oil's surface, all over and around the church like holy fire. Hannes stepped back from the rising heat and listened to the crackle of the flames.

The blaze grew more vigorous at the door and windows, climbing the structural walls, until it reached the sun-dried wooden roof. From inside he could hear cries of alarm that changed to frantic screaming as the people tried to get out. But with the lamp oil and the dry wood, the structure went up like a torch. In addition to the barricades he had made, flames sealed off the windows and the small back door.

The fire grew so bright that it reminded him of Ishalem. Hannes rubbed the waxy skin on his arm and cheek. His old burns were tingling again, but this time he realized that it no longer hurt.

The Urecari church had become a roaring inferno, and by contrast the screaming seemed faint, almost ethereal. Hannes thought it sounded like a choir singing praises to Aiden.

As the fire reached its crescendo and began to fade, he ate some of the stored food and sat back to watch. In this one act, he had exterminated virtually an entire Urecari village, cleansing the world of these heretics.

Improving the world, by the Grace of Ondun.

66 *Calay*

Yal Dolicar played the role well, having bought fine clothes with a goodly portion of the money he had pocketed from his last success. People were more inclined to throw money at a man who looked respectable.

Wearing a dyed purple waistcoat and black breeches, a belt with a large silver buckle, and a wide-brimmed hat to complete the disguise, Dolicar strolled down the gangway of a newly arrived ship in the Merchants' District of Calay. Assessing the men for hire sitting around the docks, he held a coin between thumb and forefinger, flashing it so that it glinted in the sun. "I need a porter to carry a very precious package."

A broad-shouldered man strode forward, knocking the others

aside, and reached for the coin, but Dolicar deftly pocketed it. "*After* the job is finished. I've been cheated before." On the deck of the ship, where his belongings were stashed, sat a small oak chest held shut with iron hinges and leather straps. "There, my good man. Carry it for me. I need to go to the market square."

The porter wrapped his arms about the chest and lifted it with no sign of strain. His footsteps were heavy as he clomped down the gangway, following Yal Dolicar, who strolled along, head held high. Dolicar had worked these docks many times before and knew the best places to set up. With his beard shorn and hair tucked beneath the hat, no one would recognize him.

A mason's cart loaded with cut stone groaned by, pulled by a plodding ox. A cobbler had set up a stand where he patched holes in boot soles or mended leather stitching. Laughter and shouts came from a crowded tavern in which a halfhearted brawl was taking place. Iborian furs were for sale, Corag metalwork, long coils of Eriettan rope, woven baskets, rolls of ribbon, and swatches of lace.

Dolicar told the porter to set his burden down at a corner of the market square outside a wine merchant's shop, where four stained, empty barrels sat waiting to be scrubbed and refilled. The empty barrels provided a ready table for Dolicar's wares. He paid the man, who took his coin and walked off, not in the least bit curious about what the chest contained.

Other people began to show interest, though, as Dolicar produced a long-shafted key from one of his pockets with a flourish and made a great show of working the lock, then unfastening the strap buckles. He pretended not to notice his audience pressing closer, concerned only with himself. He lifted the chest's lid and surveyed his treasures, intentionally blocking the view; then he looked up in feigned surprise to see so many eager onlookers.

"Ah! Would you like to see? Come close."

Refuting his own invitation, Dolicar stood with his back to the open chest, hiding the contents. With painstaking care, he reverently pulled on a pair of thin calfskin gloves as if to imply that touching the objects in the chest with his bare fingers would be a sign of disrespect.

"I am a pilgrim, just returned from the ruins of Ishalem." He raised his voice so that more people approached. "This chest contains relics I obtained at great peril to myself, for the evil Urecari have a habit of stringing up pilgrims by fishhooks." He heard the gasps, noted the shudders. He knew exactly how to play a crowd.

Bending over the chest, Dolicar removed a lump of charred wood and held it in both hands as if it were a sacrifice for the altar. "These blackened remnants come directly from the Holy Arkship—Aiden's ship, burned by the followers of Urec. Only these few scraps remain, and I've brought them here, so that good Aidenists may give them a proper home."

The people stepped back with awe. Dolicar set the first piece of wood on a barrelhead and picked up a smaller one, then a third gnarled chunk. He had seven in all, as well as ten small glass bottles filled with gray ash. "I gathered these relics and hurried back home. My five companions were killed on the journey, and only I escaped. Trust me"—he swept his gloved finger around at the onlookers with an intense, passionate gaze—"these precious objects belong in Tierra."

Of course, he had said exactly the opposite when he made his way through the soldanates of Uraba, but the Urecari were less generous—or perhaps just less gullible—than the followers of Aiden. Here he didn't even have to encourage the onlookers to begin bidding. They dug into their pouches and pockets for coins. He made a great show of distress to part with such hard-won holy trophies, but in the end he sold them all, leaving himself with an empty trunk and a fat purse. Even after running out of the real artifacts, he could always sell his ash and his charred wood as quickly as he could manufacture it.

67 *Olabar Palace*

Soldan-Shah Imir felt only deep sadness upon learning of the plot. He had expected as much from Villiki, though he had tried to convince himself that she would never do something so dangerous, so *fatal*.

After Omra reported Adrea's information, the soldan-shah demanded that the slave girl be brought discreetly before him for confirmation. He chose Rovik, the kel, or captain, of his palace guards to deliver her. Loyal and tight-lipped, Kel Rovik stood outside the door, discouraging any eavesdroppers.

When the young woman repeated her story, Imir felt a pang in his chest, knowing that he had lost another wife, this time to stupidity and ambition. "I must have proof," he said finally, his voice thick, "though I do not want it. I have to know. This is my wife we are talking about."

"Proof is easy enough to come by, Father. Cliaparia awaits me in our quarters, and the meal will be served soon."

The soldan-shah had a heavy heart. By now he felt much too old to search for other wives. How he wished that Sen Sherufa had agreed to marry him...especially now. They could have been quite a pair.

Pretending that nothing was afoot, Omra returned to his chambers. Though Cliaparia constantly tried to win his heart, he

felt no genuine affection for her. She had given him no children, but that was primarily his own fault, since he took her
to his bed so rarely. His father lectured him about his duty to
continue the dynasty and suggested that he take an additional
wife to increase his chances of having an heir. But as yet, Omra
had found no one who interested him. He still could not forget
Istar. . . .

Maintaining a bland expression, while he entered his room,
Omra observed Cliaparia as she sat across from him on a
mound of plush cushions. She had lined her eyes with dark kohl.
Fragrant—too fragrant—incense burned in the corner of the
room. Solicitous as always, she smiled and tried to be seductive.
"What can I do to please you?"

Such a large question, he thought. *Such a broad topic.* "Is there
food? I've had a long trip."

She brightened. "I chose the greatest delicacies and made a
special tea."

He did not ask questions, could not bear to. "Have them
served."

Cliaparia called for servants to bring in numerous small dishes
filled with special treats that she imagined he would like. When
the slaves departed, he sat cross-legged on his cushions, looking
at the dishes. The food did indeed look delicious. She waited for
him to take the first bite, as was traditional. But he didn't move.
"You prepared these yourself?"

She faltered, then nodded. "I was there in the kitchens. I
assisted. Nothing was done without my direct guidance."

Still he did not reach forward. "Please eat first."

"But . . ." she began in confusion; then a shy smile lit her face.
"You do me great honor, my husband." She leaned across the
table and stretched her hand toward a bowl of olives in front of
Omra.

"Stop!" He pushed her hand away from the bowl, let out a heavy sigh, then raised his voice. "Guards! I need you."

Cliaparia's pleased smile faded to a look of hurt as armed, muscular men rushed into the room, hands on the hilts of their curved swords.

Omra said in a flat voice, "Is my father nearby?"

"Yes, Zarif. He waits in the next chamber."

"Have him come in. Also call for Villiki and Tukar, as well as Ur-Sikara Lukai. Tell them they are urgently needed, but do not tell them why. If they refuse to come, drag them." The astonished guards rushed off.

"How have I displeased you?" Cliaparia was distraught. "And what need do we have for guards tonight?"

"My food is poisoned."

Cliaparia gasped, but before she could respond, the soldanshah entered with sweat glistening on his shaved scalp. His skin looked gray and his expression sagged, as though doubts consumed him.

Cliaparia finally found her voice. "Husband, what is this accusation you make? I could never poison your food—I love you!"

"I did not accuse you. Be silent now. Not a word." His look made her slump back into her cushions, where she sat like a statue, her kohl-lined eyes wide with fear.

Within moments, Villiki and Ur-Sikara Lukai ran into the zarif's quarters flushed and breathless, followed by a befuddled-looking Tukar. The two women, wearing manufactured expressions of distress, ground to an awkward halt as they saw Omra glowering at them, alive and unharmed. They recovered quickly, but not quickly enough. All the proof Soldan-Shah Imir needed had been in their faces. They had arrived fully expecting to see Omra writhing on the floor, his tongue swollen, his skin blotched. The slave girl had been right.

Tukar was genuinely confused. "Has something happened? Why did you send guards for us?"

"Is it not enough that I wish you to dine with me?" Omra gestured to the bowls of untouched food out on the table.

Neither of the women made a move, though Tukar took a seat. Villiki said, "We should not interrupt your private meal with your wife."

"I insist. This special feast should be shared."

Villiki took a step backward. "I have already eaten," Ur-Sikara Lukai protested.

Tukar sat at the table and inspected the dishes as if to choose the most appetizing one, oblivious to the throbbing tension in the air. When he reached out for a cube of bright orange papaya, Villiki bit back a hiss.

Before his half-brother could eat, Omra stopped him and stated in a loud and clear voice, "My food is poisoned, Tukar. We have uncovered a plot to kill me." The other young man dropped his piece of papaya and wiped the juice from his fingers onto a cushion.

In a panic, Cliaparia vehemently denied any involvement, but Omra already knew his wife had been duped.

Ur-Sikara Lukai looked strong and stony before him, while Villiki acted indignant. "And how do you know this? Who is the poisoner?"

"It might be you," Zarif Omra suggested, and Villiki drew back with a shaky gasp. "Or Ur-Sikara Lukai. It is clear you both are reluctant to taste my food."

"Who dares accuse me?" the priestess said.

The old soldan-shah, his face dark with wrath, clapped his hands, and Kel Rovik escorted Adrea in. She did not avert her gaze from Villiki and the Ur-Sikara, but looked satisfied, proud. "*I* accuse you," Adrea said in perfect Uraban. "Both of you."

Ur-Sikara Lukai laughed out loud, a scornful bray. "A slave girl? Who can trust the word of a slave girl? I didn't even know she was capable of speech."

"The charge is easy enough to prove or refute," Imir said coldly. "Villiki, I know you and what you're capable of. Ur-Sikara Lukai, you bring shame upon the church of Urec, if the slave girl speaks the truth. I believe that the two of you plotted to murder my son with this food, and *that* is why you refused to eat it, even before he suggested that it might be poisoned."

"My position in the church is proof enough that I could never be responsible for such a plot." A bit of perspiration sparkled on Lukai's face.

Imir looked like a changed man, as if something inside him had broken...or turned to stone. "When the life of my son and heir is at stake, I'm afraid I need more proof than that. If you did not poison the food, then the food is safe. Eat it and prove yourselves innocent."

"That proves nothing. Perhaps your precious slave girl poisoned your dinner," Villiki said. "Or your wife."

"The slave girl was under guard all afternoon, and both my wife and *your* son plainly were willing to eat. They suspected no danger, so they are guiltless."

"If you are innocent, you can eat without fear," Imir said. He waited.

They all stood frozen in intense silence. Tukar looked at his mother with an expression of mingled disgust and panic.

Finally, playing her part with all the composure she could muster, Ur-Sikara Lukai methodically took a sample from each enameled dish and ate, glaring first at the soldan-shah, then Omra, and finally at Adrea. She poured a cup of the tea, drank it with a flourish, stood back, and looked defiantly at the soldan-shah.

The truth would have come out whether or not Villiki and Lukai cooperated, of course. Soldan-Shah Imir could have made a household slave eat the food as a demonstration, and if it was poisoned, Ur-Sikara Lukai would have been executed after a long session of torture. She understood exactly what she was doing; Omra saw it in her eyes.

Within moments the priestess began to choke and vomit. After a few minutes she collapsed in spasms on the floor, and Zarif Omra said, "I believe the evidence is incontrovertible."

Cliaparia clung to her husband's arm. "I knew nothing of this! I was not involved!"

"We *know*." Omra roughly brushed her aside.

Tukar looked almost as sick, as if he too had consumed poison. "Mother, what have you done?"

Villiki threw herself at the soldan-shah's feet, but Imir turned his back on her. "I wash my hands of you, Villiki. You are no longer my wife." He had dreaded the words that he knew he must speak, but his voice was steady as it boomed the pronouncement so that all the guards could hear. Criers would carry it through the streets. "You may keep none of your possessions. You are to be stripped naked and turned out into the street with nothing."

Villiki shrieked in desperate horror. The guards grabbed her and methodically ripped her clothes, tore away the silks, snatched off her jewels. Soon, she knelt pathetic and naked on the tiled floor next to her ruined garments, debased and shamed.

Now the soldan-shah turned to Tukar with one more terrible duty to do. It seemed clear that the young man had not been involved, but the murder *had* been planned for Tukar's benefit. Imir could not allow such a threat to continue. He had to be the soldan-shah, not a father. He had to harden his heart—to the breaking point, if necessary. The compassionate part of him said it was unjust, but the leader in him knew that as soldan-shah *he* defined justice in his own way. As he did now.

"Tukar, my beloved son, the life you once knew is forfeit. From this day forward, I order you exiled to the Gremurr mines. You will spend your life there. Your mother wanted you to be a leader. You may rule in that hell."

Tukar reeled, as if someone had struck him with a club.

The guards dragged Villiki sobbing from the room and out of the palace. Imir could hear her wailing for a long time afterward as they drove her into the streets of Olabar. After Tukar was also led away, handlers came forward to drag the ur-sikara's corpse out of the room.

Throughout all this, Adrea simply stood, looking vindicated. She clung only to the fact that now she would have Saan returned to her.

When the crisis had passed, the soldan-shah stood before Omra and hung his heavy head. "I am broken and weary to the base of my soul. What sort of ruler am I, who cannot even control his own household? How can I protect my land in times like these, when I cannot protect my own son?" He had expected to wait a few more years, but now he knew it had to be tonight.

Twisting the large garnet ring of office, he removed it from his finger and set it on a table next to Omra. "Enough...I have had enough. As of tonight, I am no longer the soldan-shah. I will retire. Uraba needs you now, Omra. You are my successor."

68 *Olabar, Saedran District*

While Olabar was in an uproar, Aldo saw his chance. After the shocking events in the palace, no one was paying attention to a lone Saedran from a captured Tierran ship, and Sen Sherufa agreed that this was a perfect time for him to escape.

They had already spent several weeks fleshing out her copy of the Mappa Mundi with his knowledge. After generations of minimal progress toward completing their great map, the Saedran quest had taken a giant leap forward.

In the meantime, Sherufa had introduced him to the craftsmen and shopkeepers in the Saedran District. Knowing he was her guest, the children in the streets pestered *him* for candies, as well, until Sherufa insisted that he make a habit of carrying treats in his pockets. Each night for dinner, a seemingly endless succession of neighbors came by with meats or pastries, and all the guests sat in her main room, letting Aldo or Sherufa tell stories. Everyone was eager to hear about exotic Calay, the mountains of Corag, the rough waters of the Oceansea. The more Aldo talked about his life, the more homesick he became, the more he missed his family, and the more he wanted to leave Uraba. For Aldo, the turmoil at the palace could not have come at a better time.

"It will be a long and dangerous journey," Sherufa warned. "Are you sure you want to go? You would be safe here — and welcome."

"Calay is my *home*," he said. "My mother and father must think I'm dead by now. How can I do that to them, to my brother and sister? I don't care about the danger. I've got to make my way back to Calay. I've *got to*." The young man's dark eyes glistened with his passion. "Can you help me?"

And so Sen Sherufa spread the word from apothecary to physician, from moneylender to merchant, asking for assistance. She had always helped her neighbors when they asked, offering her advice and knowledge, so when she asked for a favor in return, the Saedrans in Olabar responded without question.

Several nights later, after a filling dinner of noodles, vegetables, and sliced sausages that an innkeeper brought to Sherufa's house, she and Aldo worked together to clean up. A knock came at her door, and Aldo recognized the thin, brown-bearded man as a cabinet maker from two streets over. Nodding at Aldo, but speaking to Sen Sherufa, he looked grave and serious, as if someone had given him a very weighty responsibility. He handed Sherufa a message written in the coded Saedran language. "This is the plan. Everything is in place."

As she scanned the scrap of paper, her lips were drawn, and the cords in her neck stood out with anxiety. "This sounds like exactly the right thing. Thank you." The cabinet maker ducked away into the dark streets.

Aldo read the letter, memorizing the names of volunteers, the route he must take, the ships that would be waiting for him at various ports, the helpers along the way all across the Abilan soldanate as he worked his way to the isthmus and back up into Tierran territory, whereupon any captain would happily take him aboard and give him passage to Calay. It might take him months, perhaps a year, but Aldo had no doubt he would eventually arrive home, see his family again, and report to Sen Leo na-Hadra. He could not hide the growing smile on his face and the joy in his heart.

Sherufa went to a cupboard, removed a dusty jar, and dumped out a small stash of coins. She wrapped them in a small cloth and handed it to him. "We can provide you with money for now. In other villages along the way our people will give you food and shelter."

Over the next two days, the neighborhood people obtained nondescript Uraban clothing for him, and he shed his traditional Saedran garb. The loose, cool robes felt strange, but comfortable; he even learned how to wrap a cloth olba around his head.

Sherufa inspected his disguise, smiling in approval. "You will pose as a metalsmith and ring maker traveling to Yuarej to visit a relative. You will carry a few appropriate tools and inexpensive rings in case you need to display your wares, but nobody should bother you. No one should notice you."

"I'll make sure that I'm not the least bit interesting."

Her expression grew more serious. "Please don't call attention to yourself. With Imir gone into seclusion, he's got no further interest in the politics and workings of Uraba. He might even forget about your existence altogether. But you still need to be careful."

Sherufa helped him pack as they waited anxiously for nightfall. In the full darkness, she and Aldo made their way down to the harbor, where he met the short-haul captain who would take him on the first leg of his journey. On the dock, before boarding the Uraban ship, Aldo turned to embrace Sen Sherufa. "Thank you for taking care of me."

With tears in her eyes, Sherufa squeezed him tightly. "And thank you for reawakening our spirit of exploration, Aldo na-Curic. Until now, I had forgotten the reason why I'm here. Now I know that the Mappa Mundi is not just a thing of academic interest."

Lanterns had been lit on the small ship, and the crew prepared to depart with the outgoing tide. The captain whistled for him to come aboard, and Sen Sherufa slipped away so that no one would recognize her. As a "Uraban metalsmith," Aldo should not let himself be seen with a Saedran woman.

Aboard the ship, he took a long breath and looked back to the sparkling city lights of Olabar. A few other travelers snored softly in out-of-the-way places, and the sailors ignored him, having their own tasks to do. Containing the excitement inside him, he found a comfortable spot at the stern and sat down beside a coil of rope. At last, he was on his way home.

69 *Calay*

As soon as he had made up his mind, King Korastine set the wheels in motion to create a special reminder of Ilrida's home, something that would show her how much he adored her. Yes, as Tierra's king, he continued to build warships and send out naval patrols to guard the coastline, but here he would spare no expense to make his new wife feel happy.

After consulting with Sen Leo na-Hadra, he commissioned a Saedran architect to design a traditional Iborian-style kirk, mimicking the appearance of the small chapel she had left behind inside the stockade walls of Calavik. He hired Aidenist artisans to provide appropriate religious trappings, symbols, and details. When complete, it would be marvelous.

Because so much construction was always taking place near the castle and in the adjoining Shipbuilders' Bay, Korastine did not find it difficult to keep Ilrida from noticing the work, but as the structure took shape, he enlisted Anjine's aid to keep the secret. Happily joining in the plot, the princess accompanied Ilrida on her trips into the city, careful to steer her away from the site of the kirk.

Following Iborian tradition, the kirk was assembled from seasoned pine, each log stained dark to enhance the grain and knots. Lapped wooden shingles covered the steep roof like the scales of a great sea monster. The shipwright Kjelnar provided two of his best wood-carvers to depict scenes from the great story along the kirk's outer walls, Ilrida's favorite tales of Holy Joron's adventures. As they set to work constructing this familiar structure, the Iborian shipbuilders began to grow homesick for the dark forests and huddled towns of the north.

As an added extravagance, King Korastine told his carpenters to use iron nails rather than wooden pegs for the entire construction, as his way of showing the permanence of his feelings for Ilrida. He couldn't wait to see the expression of delight on his young wife's face when he finally revealed the surprise.

Ilrida had not yet learned to speak Tierran very well, but the king was patient with her and managed to make himself understood. Longing to communicate, she had tried to teach him the northern language, but he found it just as baffling. Now he wished he had insisted on continuing to learn other languages despite Queen Sena's disapproval of the suggestion. Ah, how different sweet Ilrida was! Sena had been able to talk with him as much as she'd liked, and she had said little of merit; even with her few words of Tierran, however, Ilrida could express volumes of affection. Korastine learned how to tell his Iborian sweetheart that he loved her, in both languages, and that was enough.

When the kirk neared completion and the wood-carvers erected two obelisk trunks by the front door, the carpenters finally allowed King Korastine inside to view their work. Dark paneling covered the interior walls; candles stood in iron sconces, illuminating the interior with an orange glow. Traditional Iborian kirks had slit windows to block out the wind, which also denied sunlight.

Korastine had engaged the services of a well-known Saedran portrait artist, Biento na-Curic, to create icons in lustrous colors by mixing powdered gold and silver with the pigments. From above the altar, the image of Holy Joron seemed to glow in the candlelight, smiling down at the private worship area.

The king brought in the new prester-marshall, Rudio, to bless the kirk. The successor to Baine was not quite the fire-brand visionary the younger man had been. After the martyrdom of the volunteers in Ishalem, a convocation of presters chose Rudio—an older and much more traditional man than Baine had been, someone not as keen to espouse experimental new ideas, preferring instead to reinforce the old ones. At the time, Korastine had realized that the man's selection was not so much a backlash against Prester-Marshall Baine as it was a retrenching, a return to the basics of the religion. However, because Baine had died horribly for his faith, no other prester dared to dispute his controversial call to explore the world, though the distractions of the war focused Tierran resources elsewhere.

After Kjelnar completed an inspection of the new structure, he gave his wholehearted approval. "This is a true Iborian kirk, Majesty. It is as though Destrar Broeck uprooted the building whole and shipped it here. Ilrida will be delighted."

The next day, Korastine felt like a boy waiting to open his gifts on Landing Day as he took her hand and led her out of the castle. He felt as though his heart could not contain any more love for this young woman. His mood was infectious, and she gripped his arm, snuggling against him as they walked through the castle gates and down the path. She could sense his excitement.

At the base of the hill, Korastine led her along a street adjacent to the castle, rounded a corner—and Ilrida stopped with a look of astonishment on her face. Her ice-blue eyes widened, and her snow-silver hair blew about in stray breezes.

"For you." Korastine gestured toward the distinctive building, then to her. "A kirk to remind you of your home." Then he repeated it in her own language, a sentence he had worked hard to memorize.

Ilrida pulled on Korastine's hand, insisting that he come with her. "Wonderful," she exclaimed, adding many words in the northern dialect before she found another Tierran word. "Beautiful!" She paused to touch the carved obelisk posts on either side of the door, then rushed inside, delighted.

In the middle of the kirk was a wide altar made of thick pine planks held together by crossbars and iron nails. The beautiful painted icons with Holy Joron stood on display, but subordinate to the kirk's main treasure: a twisted, burned fragment of wood from the original Arkship, perhaps the most valuable object in the entire Royal District, which had recently been purchased at great expense from a pilgrim trader in the streets of Calay.

Ilrida turned to Korastine, beside herself with happiness. "Beautiful!" she said again, shaking her head with an obvious wonder far more eloquent than words. She threw her arms around his neck to kiss him. "Wonderful!" Her Iborian ladies-in-waiting would also want to come see the structure.

She took his arm again and drew him to the plank riser before the altar. When she knelt, he bent beside her, their shoulders touching. Ilrida gazed upon the benevolent face of Holy Joron in the icon. She closed her eyes, Korastine did the same, and the two of them prayed together, each in their own language.

70 *Olabar Palace*

Her new quarters in the Olabar palace felt like a different kind of captivity, and a more suspicious one. As a household slave, Adrea had cleaned these rooms many times, though she had never known to whom they belonged. Now Omra gave them to her. Adrea was no longer a slave.

At first, after all the turmoil that followed Imir's abdication, she had not believed Omra would keep his word. She waited in her rooms, alone and on tenterhooks...until an unfamiliar sikara brought her son back to her. "By the soldan-shah's command," the priestess said, bowing slightly.

Adrea rose, gazing at Saan in disbelief. Seeing his mother, the boy ran toward her, and she scooped him up in her arms. His face was sunburned, adorned with an extra splash of freckles; his hair looked bleached and tousled. It took her a moment to realize that he wore Tierran clothes, traditional garments she hadn't seen since Windcatch. Why would Saan be dressed as a Tierran *here*, in Olabar?

But the joy in her mind and heart was so great that she had no room for questions. Saan was *safe*, truly safe, and back with her. She held him, suddenly free in a way she had not felt in the more than five years since losing her home and her past. For so long she had clung to absolute silence as a defensive shield, but now there was no reason not to speak openly with Saan. She could talk with him, without reservation, and she poured out all the things she had wanted to tell him for so long. Adrea talked with him for hours, needing to make up for years and years of silence.

The five-year-old boy described the adventures he'd had after Ur-Sikara Lukai took him away to live in an entire strange village populated by children and very few adults. He tugged at his brown tunic. "They wear clothes like this. And other people there have yellow hair, like me. They speak Tierran and Uraban." Then Saan flinched when he spoke of the "Teacher"—a hooded, gloved enigma who wore a silver mask.

He described half-timbered houses with thatched roofs, and when Saan insisted that the town church "wasn't right," Adrea realized he was describing an Aidenist kirk, complete with the fishhook symbol. The concept mystified her. Why would there be an entire village of Tierran refugees, most of them children? Could they be the other captives Omra's raiders had taken all those years ago?

For the next four days, their meals were brought by servants whom she recognized, but Adrea neither saw nor heard anything from Omra. Gradually, as questions piled up, her happiness slid into concern. She knew that her fate dangled by the thinnest of threads, like a fish on a line. At any moment, the new soldan-shah could renege on his promise...or some capricious priestess could steal her son away again. With the death of Ur-Sikara Lukai, the humiliation of Villiki and the exile of Tukar, Adrea had witnessed how swiftly the palace could change.

One day, a young sikara arrived at her doorway. "I have come to ask if you would like your son to continue his instruction. I will take him back to his old classes, if you wish it."

Even though Saan clearly wanted to go with the priestess, Adrea clutched the boy's arm. "He stays with me." She was surprised when the other woman relented and left them alone, and for hours afterward she expected guards would come to enforce their will, but no one bothered her.

Every day was tense, heavy with waiting. Saan had been

taken from her once, and she had averted that disaster by only the narrowest of margins. She felt like a ship's captain, skating past treacherous rocks to escape with only a scraped hull. The image made her think of Criston, wherever he was....

Adrea spent her days thinking and planning, trying to guarantee a future for herself and her son. She would do anything to keep him safe. Because the soldan-shah had given them his protection, none of the guards, sikaras, or palace workers could harm her or Saan. By the same token, she would have no recourse, no chance for appeal, should Omra change his mind.

He surprised Adrea by inviting her to dine with him.

Three dark-haired and demure Uraban handmaidens came to her room with bundles of colorful garments and instructions to make herself presentable. Adrea knew these women, but they had never treated her as an equal, for she was a Tierran slave and they had been invited to the Olabar court. Now solicitous, they offered Adrea choices of scarves, long-sleeved gowns, and braided sashes. They fussed over her long blond hair, pulling it back and holding it in place with combs. Adrea shunned the makeup and perfumes, not wanting to look like a whore (though that might be what Omra intended for her to be). Now that he had saved her son, he probably considered her beholden to him. What if he wanted to make her serve as a different sort of slave?

Adrea felt a cold resolve. Long ago, she had expected to become a sexual plaything for the Uraban raiders, but she had remained untouched for all these years. Her only lover had been Criston Vora, whom she saw nowhere but in her dreams.

But Omra had saved her twice now. What else did he want from her?

She resigned herself to do what must be done. Long ago, though she had dearly wanted to marry Criston Vora, she refused to do so until he agreed to care for her brother as well.

Now she might have to make another bargain with Omra for the sake of Criston's son.

When the handmaidens finished properly dressing her, she appraised herself in a polished mirror. She bore a passing resemblance to a proper Uraban woman, and the idea made her stomach twist. As Criston's innocent young bride, she had been so beautiful, but that young woman of Windcatch had been left behind forever on the shores of the Oceansea. Now her features were stronger and sharper, chiseled into dramatic relief by all that she'd endured.

The handmaidens promised to watch Saan in her quarters, and she gave the boy a kiss before departing. She didn't trust these women, but if Omra wanted to take the boy away again, if he intended any treachery, he hardly needed such an elaborate plot to do so.

Adrea went to the soldan-shah's quarters, escorted by silent guards. Omra had been waiting. He smiled at her, gesturing to the comfortable cushions laid out before him. "Join me." Dishes of food were arrayed in a banquet on a low table between them.

The exotic foods were strange and puzzling, a clash of sweet scents and savory meats. He invited her to cleanse her fingers in a small basin of rosewater, apparently less interested in eating than in watching her.

He nudged a bowl of yogurt and mashed mangoes toward her. "Eat this. You'll find it a treat."

She looked at the sweet-smelling fruit and creamy dessert, so different from the bland fare she had eaten as a slave. "How do I know it's not poisoned?"

He laughed. "You did me a great service—I admit that, and I will not forget it. You saved my life. In return, I freed your son from his training among the *ra'virs,* and I released you from your duties as a household slave."

Adrea bowed her head, suspicious. "You kept your word. Thank you." She ate a delicate spoonful, and the delicious taste was like an explosion in her mouth.

"But that doesn't seem like enough for me." Omra ran a finger along his bearded chin. "I owe you more than mere gratitude."

A commotion at the doorway startled them. Omra looked up, annoyed, as Cliaparia barged in, dressed in swirling silks and jingling gold bangles. "We were supposed to dine together tonight, husband. I waited for you. I prepared—"

Omra looked at her coolly. "Can you not see that I have a guest, Cliaparia? Leave us." She gave Adrea a look of impotent hatred, but when she saw the look of dark anger on her husband's face, she knew she'd gone too far and retreated quickly.

Omra folded his hands again, returning his attention to Adrea. "My apologies. Because she is my only wife, Cliaparia feels an unseemly possessiveness toward me. She should know her place. And you can help me in this."

Adrea said nothing, instantly on her guard.

"You showed caution, patience, and cunning by remaining mute for so many years. You made a shrewd bargain to get your son back. All of these traits I admire in you, Adrea, woman of Tierra. A long time ago, I saw something when I watched you fight my raiders. You have a strength that matches your beauty." He leaned forward. "I would like to take you as my second wife."

Adrea recoiled. She had expected to become a plaything, a concubine—but a *wife?* He had just reawakened her memories of what his men had done in Windcatch, how they had murdered Telha, burned the kirk and probably killed her brother, Ciarlo. They had destroyed her village, stolen her and so many helpless children.

"I am already married, in the eyes of Ondun," she said. "Just because you took me away from my home does not mean that my bond is broken."

He waved a hand dismissively. "A marriage in the Aidenist church means nothing here."

She spoke in an icy voice. "For more than five years, I've been at your mercy. I am at your mercy now. You can inflict yourself upon my body, but you will never claim my heart or my mind."

Omra was startled by her frank reaction. "That was not my intent—that is not Urec's way. I would have your consent, or I would have nothing. My people expect me to take other wives, since Cliaparia has not yet given me a child. Many women have been offered to me, and my father urges me to take them—probably all of them—but they don't interest me. *You* interest me. I had hoped you would see the benefits in this arrangement."

And, despite her automatic revulsion, Adrea could. She understood that she could not possibly go back to her former life in Windcatch. It had been so many years; by now, her dear Criston, if he still lived, would have come home, found her gone, and presumed her dead. Surely he had remarried by now. Adrea had no past to cling to, and only a very narrow path to her future. The Urecari religion meant nothing to her, and any union made by their priestesses had no standing in the sight of God. This arrangement would not be a marriage or a breaking of her vow to Criston; it was a bargain to protect Saan.

"If you wish me to be your wife, you must do something else for me . . . for my son." She pushed aside the bowl of yogurt, left the other dishes untouched. "Convince me that my cooperation is worth something to you. Promise that Saan will never again be taken from me."

"This is not a negotiation," Omra said, but there was a glint of amusement behind his eyes.

"Isn't it?" Adrea's heart ached.

The soldan-shah reached a decision. "Very well, your son is important to you. Therefore, he should be important to me. I will do better than what you ask: I'll raise him here in the palace as my adopted son, with all the rights and privileges that entails."

Adrea caught her breath. This was far more than she would ever have dared to ask. She swallowed hard, fighting to keep her voice steady. "Then I agree." She pushed away her confusion and despair and looked across at the admittedly handsome face of Omra, the man who would become her new husband.

"Since this has become a negotiation," Omra added, without a hint of humor now, "there is one additional thing I require of you. There will be enough talk of your Tierran heritage. In order to be the wife of a soldan-shah, you must accept a Uraban name."

"And is there a specific name you've picked?" she asked, her voice finally cracking.

"*Istar.* From now on, I will call you Istar."

71 *Tierra*

Leaving the dog Jerard to guard his flock of sheep, Criston departed from his high meadows with a grim fortitude and walked downhill out of the mountains, heading back toward the sea. It was his annual pilgrimage, something he always did for Adrea...or for her memory.

He had a pack, a walking stick, and some food, but no company; he wanted none. This was a task for him to do, as he had done for the previous five years, as he intended to do every year until the end of his life.

He reached the river and followed its bank down several miles, until he came to a quiet town with a large set of docks. He camped in the forest to avoid the villagers and other waiting travelers. He showed himself only when the riverboat docked and its passengers and cargo were unloaded and loaded.

Criston made his way to the captain, one of the distinctive bearded men of the river families. "I would like to buy passage. I can pay with a few wood carvings I've made. Or, if you insist, I have a few coins left."

The captain regarded the handful of whittled carvings he produced from his pack. One of them was of the dog striking a noble pose, complete with the lines of his fur, the uplifted tail, snout extended forward questing for a scent.

"I'll take this one in trade," the riverman said. "I always wanted to have a dog, but they're not practical on a riverboat." He accepted the carving and gestured for Criston to put the others away.

"I'll work for my food, if necessary," Criston added.

The riverman brushed aside the idea. "Did I ask for more than the carving?"

The boat stopped frequently over the next four days, finally emerging from the river's mouth into the splayed harbors of Calay. The city's buildings, people, and noise now intimidated Criston, but the ice in his chest began to melt as he remembered Adrea's excitement upon seeing the same sights.

He did not want to be in the capital city. Too many people, too many questions, too many memories. So he left the harbor and struck out southward, knowing it would cost him an extra day, but he didn't mind. He needed to find an isolated, private spot.

In three previous years, he had journeyed all the way back to Windcatch on the coast, feeling the need to see Ciarlo, to walk through the town, to see how the people were faring... and to reassure himself that they could survive without him. Adrea's brother had recovered, and now seemed confident and determined. With the kirk rebuilt and a bit of practice, he had become a knowledgeable, compassionate prester, very much like Jerard. Criston was glad to see it.

Last year, no one had even recognized him when he walked quietly through the streets down to the docks, seeing the shops and boats, the fishermen bringing back their catch. The migratory seaweed had come and gone, leaving only a lingering stench.

He visited the cemetery, which had only a few more grave markers, signifying a handful of natural deaths, not another slaughter. The name on Adrea's post had been weathered to the point where it was unreadable. He stared for a long time, but did not fix it. Some part of him still clung to the tiny hope that she might be alive somewhere.

Satisfied that Windcatch was doing fine without him, Criston decided that he didn't need to come back—at least not every year....

South of Calay, he reached a windswept patch of open seashore bordered by rugged headlands. He picked his way down a steep, narrow path used by animals and a few intrepid fishermen, to reach the abrupt shore. The blue water was deep, dropping off sharply from the beach, and he saw no large, dangerous rocks. The outgoing tide would create a swift current. Yes, this was a good place.

He unshouldered his pack, undid the knot—a knot that Captain Shay had taught him how to tie—and opened the pack to withdraw a corked glass bottle. He had worked for eight nights on the lengthy letter to Adrea rolled tightly inside.

He could not forget to do this. He had made a promise, and

neglecting that promise would mean that he had given up on her. She still might be alive, and the currents and tides could find her. Criston couldn't decide whether this was truly hope, or just a remembrance ceremony that he held by the sea, in the kirk of his heart.

He removed the bottle's cork and reached into his pocket, from which he gently, lovingly pulled a worn leather pouch, in which he kept the lock of hair she had given him — the lock that was still his most precious treasure. He removed a single golden strand, which he dropped into the bottle with the letter, then sealed the cork firmly.

He closed his eyes and pictured her, hoping that thought might summon the sympathetic magic and help the golden strand of his beloved's hair find its way back to her. Then he tossed the bottle as far as he could, flinging it out into the Oceansea, where it struck with a silvery splash and bobbed upright again like a buoy. It hung there briefly until, as the currents shifted with the retreating tide, the bottle drifted out to the open sea.

His task complete, Criston stared at the lonely sea for a few minutes more and began to make his way home.

Part IV

Five Years Later

Eleven Years After the
Burning of Ishalem

72 *Uraba*

Years ago, when Prester Baine dispatched him to Ishalem to be a spy for God, young Hannes had never dreamed he would be trapped for so long in Uraba. Once he realized his new mission, though—and he understood what he was supposed to *do* here in the foreign land—Hannes embraced his work with great zeal. After setting fire to his first Urecari church, he continued his wanderings, letting Ondun choose his next destination, his next cleansing target.

His life was remarkably free. He worked his way along the southern coast of the Middlesea for years, pretending to be one of the heathen, but never forgetting his true faith. No one bothered to look at a wandering beggar. They averted their eyes and whispered after he had passed.

Of late, though, he had learned to be cautious. As he continued his work, news of his burned churches and the many people he sacrificed spread as swiftly as the smell of smoke. Because widely separated churches burned to the ground in several different soldanates, the Urecari imagined a larger scheme at work, speculating that a whole army of disguised Aidenist crusaders had infiltrated their land. Some called him a shadowman, an evil spirit.

But Prester Hannes was doing it all himself, just one man, a dedicated soldier for Aiden.

He traveled south into the hilly soldanate of Missinia until the grasses turned browner, the landscape bleaker. When he crested a rise and saw the stark and impassable Great Desert, an unending spread of hot sands, he knew he had come to the edge of the world. The heat and baking sun reminded him of the fires of Ishalem . . . and of all the Urecari churches he had burned.

Afterward, he worked his way out of Missinia, looping westward again. Unfortunately, with the spreading rumors and exaggerations, people had begun to fear all strangers. Now, when he entered a village, the once-benevolent Urecari did not immediately offer their help. Sometimes they shunned him; sometimes they threw stones to drive him away. Volunteer guards stood outside their churches during the sunset services, and some sikaras decided to worship out in the open, where they could keep watch for an attack.

So Hannes was forced to alter his plans. He set fire to their crops in the night, then ran away. He poisoned public wells or animal drinking troughs. As he left town, he imagined their wails of grief.

Hannes made his way to the small soldanate of Yuarej, a pocket of temperate forests where mists supplemented the infrequent rainfall. Large orchards of bitter green almonds, kumquats, and blood oranges gave him plenty of food for the taking.

In the gathering shadows of evening, Hannes entered a mulberry grove where gossamer webs festooned the branches, as if a giant spider had spun up the trees as its prey. Picking his way between the close-packed trunks, he listened to the eerie stirring sounds, saw the crowded tentworms, each as long and fat as an index finger, moving like maggots in the webbed trees. He could hear their tiny jaws munching incessantly, stripping the mulberry leaves. These worms reminded him of the Urecari themselves: a loathsome infestation spreading lies to destroy the faithful.

In the small village adjacent to the grove, he saw workers spinning the silk, processing it into long sheets of fabric, which were soaked in vats of colored dyes. Caravans set off with the thick rolls of tough silk, which would be used as sails for Uraban warships.

His mouth went dry with anticipation when he realized how easy it would be to set fire to this whole grove, to burn the raw silk fibers and kill the caterpillars. Before he could take out his flint and steel, he saw lanterns, heard the rustling footsteps of vigilant town guards patrolling the groves at night. When they spotted Hannes and shouted at him, he tried to run crashing through the branches, but two men intercepted him. They held their lanterns up, shining them on his face. He averted his eyes. "Please don't hurt me — I mean no harm! I'm just a simple traveler."

"You don't belong here," a gruff old man accused. "Why are you in the mulberry groves?"

"To sleep! I just needed a place to bed down for the night. When I passed through your village, no one offered me shelter or hospitality. I wanted to rest my head, then depart in the morning — that's all."

"You were given no welcome because you are not welcome." The men held sticks, and Hannes saw they were ready to strike him. They could break all of his bones, maybe even kill him and leave him here to rot. But he needed to survive if he was to continue his work.

"Please, I am just a leper! I have suffered enough. I was driven from my home." Hannes did not expect sympathy, but when he showed his burn scars, which the men mistakenly attributed to leprosy, they drew back in fear. Hannes pressed closer, making them even more uneasy. "I do not know what I did to offend Ondun, but He has decreed a long and lingering death for me. If you wish to kill me quickly here and now, I would consider it a mercy." Hannes took another step toward the gruff old man, who shrank away.

They muttered, ready to ward him off, "He could contaminate the silk, kill the worms," another man said, lifting his lamp to get a better look at Hannes's face, but the prester ducked and pulled his hood closer.

The men reached an uncertain agreement and waved their sticks at him. "Begone from here! Go far from our village and suffer somewhere else." They prodded him roughly with their sticks, enough to bruise but not to maim, and then chased him all the way into the rugged foothills. Hannes looked behind him at the lanterns; the men stood together as a grim barricade to make sure he did not return. More lanterns shone in the night as additional guards came out to walk the mulberry groves.

His heart pounded. He had survived, but he felt a deep disappointment that he was unable to strike Yuarej, as he so longed to do. Maybe he would have to return.

73 *Missinia Soldanate*

In the five years since his father had made him the leader of Uraba, Omra had fashioned his rule in a way that made Imir proud. In his retirement, the former soldan-shah kept to a separate section of the palace and avoided the politics—both external and internal—that had made him relinquish his throne. Whenever Omra asked for advice, old Imir obliged, but his heart was no longer in it.

At the start of Omra's reign, when he took Adrea, "Istar," as his wife, the other soldans—still insulted by his marriage to the original Istar, a mere merchant's daughter—complained again.

A Tierran woman! A slave, a spoil of war! But he reminded them of their constant insistence that he take a wife in addition to Cliaparia.

Omra was quite happy with Istar, and in less than three years she gave him two daughters, Adreala and Istala. Now she wore her hair plaited in three braids, one for each child...the tradition originally proposed by the first Istar. As if prosperity were in the air, Cliaparia, too, delivered a daughter, much to everyone's surprise (though she and her hairdressers were not interested in braids). Sooner or later, he would have a son and heir, but Omra was young yet and expected to rule for some time. In the meantime, he had become quite attached to his surrogate son, Saan.

Apart from continued clashes with the Tierrans—though not yet a bloody outright war, thank Ondun—Soldan-Shah Omra was quite content.

Secure and settled in his rule, he departed for Arikara, the capital city of Missinia, on a journey to meet with the soldan there, as well as his mother, whom he had not seen in some time. Omra took only a dozen advisers and courtiers, leaving his wives and children behind in Olabar, and set off on a team of fine geldings that could travel long distances.

They rode southeast from Olabar, in the direction of the Great Desert, stopped overnight in caravan camps, then pressed on. Some of the courtiers complained about the discomforts of the journey, but Omra enjoyed the challenge. He stretched out next to a campfire to sleep on the hard ground, enjoying the chance to look up at the stars. "The lack of comforts will strengthen you," he said, but his courtiers did not seem convinced. Young Saan, ten years old, would have loved the adventure....

His uncle Xivir, the soldan of Missinia, welcomed Omra to Arikara with an extravagant feast that seemed excessive after days of eating only camp food. Relieved to be back in civilization again, the courtiers ate until they were stuffed.

Omra was glad to see his cousin Burilo, who had come to the Olabar court eleven years ago to deliver the tarred head of a desert bandit. Burilo sighed. "Unfortunately, they did not take long to choose another leader, and now they attack us with renewed fury." Omra decided to dispatch additional troops to help hunt down the bandits.

Looking around the crowded banquet hall, he was surprised not to see his mother. Unlike scheming Villiki, Omra's mother did not revel in the fact that her son was now the soldan-shah; she had never been particularly enamored with Imir's power and riches either.

Lithio delayed just long enough that her entrance drew everyone's attention in the banquet hall—exactly as planned, Omra was sure. He stood from his place at the long table, embraced his mother, and kissed her on the cheek.

But they were strangers to each other. He visited Arikara only rarely, and Lithio never came to the court in Olabar. Now he smiled at his mother, regarding her as she regarded him. She wore her extra years like a fine, sheer garment that added only the subtlest of wrinkles and weight.

"Although I'm sure Xivir wants to talk business with you every waking moment," Lithio said to him, "I hope you'll let me be the doting mother." The seats next to Omra were occupied, but she chased away one of the men, telling him to find a different place. After scanning the guests, she frowned. "I don't see any beautiful women here. Where are your wives? Did you not bring them? And my granddaughters? I hear that I have three, and I've seen none of them."

"The journey was arduous, Mother." He knew she wouldn't accept the excuse. He had indeed wanted to bring Istar, but that would have required him to bring Saan — and the blond-haired, blue-eyed boy would have raised too many questions. Besides, if he brought his second wife to Missinia, then Cliaparia would also insist on coming, and she and Istar would not make good traveling companions. In fact, one of them might kill the other before journey's end. So he had left them all in the palace. Already, he missed Istar, and he had no doubt that Cliaparia was pining for him. "If you want to see them, you could always visit Olabar."

"Or you could bring them here."

He surrendered. "I will. I promise."

As the meal wound down, Soldan Xivir summoned a group of lovely female dancers and court musicians. As they began to perform, his uncle leaned forward to whisper loudly to Omra, "The four in red are my own wives, but I dressed the others in blue to let you know they are available."

"I'm not in the market for wives," Omra said.

Xivir leaned back, not convinced. "A customer in the bazaar does not always *intend* to buy — until something catches his eye."

In the middle of the dance, four Missinian guards burst into the banquet hall, shouting, "Soldan! Soldan!" The dancers stuttered to a halt in a whirling clash of blue and red silks as both Omra and Xivir rose to their feet.

Behind the first guards, a second pair supported a bedraggled stranger, a large man whose ragged clothing, shaggy hair, and sunburned skin were covered with dust and dirt. "We found this man at the edge of the Great Desert, Soldan. He is unlike anyone we have ever seen."

Xivir began to speak, but caught himself and deferred to Omra, who said, "Where did you find him? Is he one of the bandits?"

"No," Xivir answered after a mere glance. "And he doesn't look Tierran either."

The stranger's hair was a shaggy mixture of reddish brown and black. His face was broad, his eyes widely set. A long, thin mustache drooped on either side of his mouth in a style unfamiliar to Omra. The man could barely stand as they brought him into the hall. His voice came out in a croak, and his words were utterly foreign, resembling none of the dialects among the soldanates.

Xivir ordered servants to offer him food and drink. The exhausted newcomer looked at the food set before him as if he had never seen such exotic victuals, then tentatively began to eat. After his first bite, he proceeded to devour the rest of the food on the plate; one of his front teeth was missing, but the gap seemed to give him no difficulty as he ate.

The first guard continued his report. "He was crawling across the grasses when we found him. When we asked where he was from, he kept pointing back toward the dunes."

Soldan Xivir made a gruff, disbelieving sound. "No man can cross the Great Desert. Nothing lies on the other side."

Sitting beside her son, Lithio said in a matter-of-fact voice, "And yet the man is here."

Omra wanted to learn much more. "Have him bathed, given fresh clothes, and a place to sleep. We will take him with us to Olabar."

74 *Olabar Palace*

Whenever Adrea gazed upon Saan, the ten-year-old looked every bit the Uraban prince. He had been raised, trained, and presented to the public as the soldan-shah's adopted son, though his features and coloration were an unforgettable reminder that the boy was not Uraban.

By marrying a man she did not love, but whom she had grudgingly come to respect, Adrea had meant only to make sure her son was not taken from her. Omra kept his word, and Saan grew up in luxury, not slavery. He was safe, and that was all she needed. Adrea—*Istar*—could live with the bargain she had made. She even braided her hair the way Omra wanted.

Though handmaidens and palace boys were available to help Saan dress, Istar cared for him herself, since it was her job as a mother. She brushed the hair away from his forehead and kissed his cheek. "I love you."

"I love you, too."

They both spoke perfect Uraban. Saan was taught by the sikaras all his life, and Istar forced herself to learn the basic tenets of the Urecari religion. She had given up on the hope of keeping the boy's Tierran heritage alive within him and secretly instructing him in the Book of Aiden. She was no prester.

Istar and Omra's two young daughters, aged four and two, were already being eyed by the priestesses for recruitment. The girls had been provisionally accepted to become acolytes when they were older and finished with their conventional schooling; Istar dreaded the possibility that her daughters would be taken from her—not as a punishment, but simply as Uraban tradition.

Mothers brought their baby girls to the revered priestesses for careful inspection. Any infant daughter deemed perfect was marked for later consideration. Both Adreala and Istala had passed that test—not surprisingly, since no sikara would dare turn down a daughter of the soldan-shah. At the age of seven, the chosen girls were brought to the priestesses again for a second testing. The sikaras accepted only one from every dozen, the smartest and most beautiful, to be raised in the church schools. Once they reached maturity, only the best were culled to become actual sikaras, but even the rejected young women became courtesans or valued wives of noblemen; some remained with the church to serve in other ways.

Almost certainly, both of her girls would enter the church, and stay there at least until they reached marriageable age. Istar felt a pang of guilt, scolding herself to imagine that she did not care for the two daughters as much as she cared for Saan. The boy was all she had left of her true husband, of her home. Each time she looked at him, she saw echoes of dear Criston....

She deftly tied a bright orange sash around his waist, adjusted his billowy tunic, and pronounced him ready to go play in the gardens. "Are you anxious to search for the Golden Fern next month?" All the children of Olabar ran into the forested hills for the annual spring festival to search for the prized object.

"I am ready," he said, "but I'll be more ready if you tell me the story again."

Istar chuckled. "You already know the story."

"I also eat my meals every day, yet I eat again the next day. That is how I am nourished. I'd like to hear the story again." Istar could argue with neither his request nor the inexorable logic.

Prior to coming here as a captive, she had never heard the tale, though it was a key religious legend that explained the origin of the Urecari symbol. Now Istar had the tale memorized.

"When Urec was old, he gathered his children and grandchildren before him and brought out a chest that contained a special fern frond from Terravitae, which he had kept all his life. Urec told them that he intended to spread these fern spores out in the forests of Uraba, and the winds would carry them all across the land.

"Long ago on the voyage he lost the map that Ondun had given him, and the Golden Fern was the only item that remained of magical Terravitae. 'The fern will grow only once every year,' Urec said, 'and whoever finds it will be blessed by Ondun. That person will be blessed with a great destiny.' And so Urec left his family and went out to spread the fern spores. Afterward, he walked the four corners of the continent, spreading his tales as the Traveler, and we have been searching for the Golden Fern ever since."

Satisfied that his mother had told the story properly, Saan squared his shoulders with resolve. "I'm going to search and search and search. And if I find the Golden Fern, then Ondun has something special in store for me." His blue eyes sparkled. "Will that make you love me even more, Mother?"

"No, because it's not possible to love anyone more than I already love you. But I'd still be very proud of you."

75 *King Korastine's Castle*

Though Princess Anjine remained in Calay, her mind wandered to thoughts of the other reaches as the army of Tierra continued to expand. She was twenty-two now, and had been preparing all her life to lead Tierra, especially in these troubled times.

The king had once wearily told Anjine, "By avoiding contact or trade with Uraba, I hope to keep from being pushed into a full-scale genocidal war. I pray to Aiden that the soldan-shah feels the same way. Neither the Aidenists nor the Urecari can survive such a conflict."

For years, Uraban attacks had continued on coastal towns, and many Tierran ships went missing despite the increased patrols of the king's navy. Repeated sea battles took place, warships sinking warships on both sides of the Edict Line. Now Anjine thought of Mateo out there, currently assigned to one of the guardian ships, defending the continent in the name of Aiden.

King Korastine had aged visibly in the eleven years since the burning of Ishalem, but he endured, moving forward one day, one month, and one year at a time. He found joy wherever and whenever he could, particularly in his wife Ilrida and their young son.

In the spacious, well-lit playroom, Anjine sat with her two-year-old half-brother Tomas, who had very pale hair, fair skin, and a silly laugh; the boy's delight in the smallest of things was infectious. Ilrida was an exceptional mother, and Anjine found herself smitten with the boy. Tomas was such a wonderful child that she reconsidered her own doubts about having children in such a time of crisis. Old enough to be wed, Anjine had received many subtle and not-so-subtle invitations from suitors, but she'd taken none of them seriously. Right now she was more concerned about the war with the Urabans. Tierran royalty often married late, and she was in no hurry.

Tomas sat on a rug, reaching out for the carved and painted figures scattered around him: soldiers, sailors, merchants, horses, ships, and evil-looking Urecari. The boy clacked them together with abandon, holding them upside down. In recent months, he had finally given up his habit of thrusting each one into his mouth.

Tomas, the only child of King Korastine and Ilrida, was born three years after their marriage. The baby brought a much-needed sense of hope to Tierra not long after a raider attack that had cost a heavily loaded cargo ship and a navy warship. The captured Aidenist sailors had been taken to the nearest Tierran shore and strung up with fishhooks through their throats. Local fishermen found the bloated corpses pecked into horrors by hungry seabirds. After receiving the news, King Korastine had spent days locked in grim discussions with the destrars and Prester-Marshall Rudio, asking for guidance.

Like a drowning man clutching a lifeline, King Korastine came to see his little son after each council session. By playing with Tomas, he reminded himself about life and hope.

Now Anjine held up the figurines and explained to the boy what they were, though the two-year-old didn't understand much of what she said. She found it sad that at such a young age Tomas had to be prepared for the realities of a war that would probably surpass his own lifetime.

Tycho wandered in, tail upright and twitching. He strolled toward Anjine but remained an inch or two out of reach as she extended a hand to pet him. Giggling, Tomas grabbed for the cat, and Tycho patiently let the boy pound him, mess up his fur, and gently tug on his tail. Tomas tried to balance a ship figure on Tycho's back, as though it belonged there. The cat tolerated the indignity for a few moments before jumping onto a window ledge from which he stared out at the sparrows flitting around the eaves.

Anjine watched as Tomas turned a toy ship upside down, and it gave her the unsettling thought of a capsized ship. She went to the window, stroked Tycho, and looked out past the Royal District to the harbor and the Oceansea beyond. She hoped Mateo was safe, hoped his patrol ship would be sturdy, and hoped he would come home soon.

76 *Calay Harbor*

After his patrol, Mateo sailed back to Calay, looking forward to resupply and a few days' furlough. Captain Illiom — a man only four years older than Mateo — had commanded the ship that cruised up and down the coast, and they had encountered no Uraban raiders, no illicit cargo ships. Tierra was safe — for now.

The patrol ship was a shallow-draft vessel with an armored hull, designed for speed and agility. The *Raven*'s prow contained a long saw-edged point of cast iron for ramming, and oarlocks were in place so the sailors could row, increasing speed to smash into enemy vessels. Boarding grapples shaped like Sapier's fish-hook could be thrown as soon as the *Raven* came alongside a Uraban vessel. Weapons were stored on deck for quick distribution during an engagement: spears, swords, and arrows dipped in pitch.

Rain had moved in on the last day of the patrol, swathing the coastline in gray mist. The drizzle cast a pall over everything. The *Raven*'s rigging sparkled with drops of water, and the canvas sails were heavy with it, making the yardarms creak. The decks were wet, the men's clothes drenched, and the crew was happy to see the entrance of Calay Harbor.

The patrol ship passed the two lighthouses, which blazed in the fog. Entering the mouth of Calay Harbor, Illiom issued commands, though the sailors knew full well how to handle the ship. They were all anxious to get home.

As the ship sailed deeper into the harbor, the Merchants' District seemed subdued in the miserable weather, but the Military

District was busy with soldiers continuing their drills, splashing through inconvenient puddles. In Shipbuilders' Bay the cranes and buzzing sawmills were all turned to the construction of new warships.

Mateo was eager to get to his barracks and relax. He had made a list of all the things he wanted to see and do when he returned to Calay, though he had made similar lists in all of the smaller ports where the *Raven* had stopped. He had his favorite inns for food and drink, his preferred places to take a relaxing stroll on dry land, even a girlfriend or two. But nothing compared to Calay. He hoped he could see his friend Anjine before he shipped out again. He made a point of meeting with the princess each time he came home.

When he'd shipped off on his first patrol, years ago, Mateo was spoiling for a fight. All his fellow trainees had felt cocky after attacking straw-filled dummies, perfecting their swordplay under the watchful eye of veteran trainers. But straw-filled dummies didn't fight back with sharpened scimitars and faces filled with hate.

Mateo felt he had aged much more than his twenty-three years. Since that first patrol, seven members of the *Raven*'s crew, young men whom he had called friends, had been lost. They were buried at sea or left under high rock cairns on bleak shores, never to return home. Mateo's comrades killed their share of Urecari as well, and in two engagements they fended off raiders that came north of Ishalem. Once, when Captain Illiom was particularly incensed, the *Raven* had sailed south of the Edict Line and gone hunting for Urecari fishing vessels. They found three, which they had boarded and sunk. An unequivocal victory. Mateo should have felt proud of what he had done.

But he no longer believed that war consisted of glorious battles comprised of hundreds of ships. During his training, Mateo had always wondered why King Korastine didn't simply call his entire navy together, launch all his vessels, and conquer the heathens once and for all. Now he understood it wasn't that simple. Even a small clash was a horrifying affair of screams and blood, utter exhaustion and unending tension. He'd been fooling himself to think that fighting the enemy would be an exciting story-book adventure.

On each patrol, Mateo continued to write letters to Anjine, beginning them with "Dear Tolli," just as he had when he was a trainee. He brought a new batch with him, written over the four months of the patrol; they were carefully bound in a packet inside his trunk. He would hand deliver the papers and tell her to read them slowly, one at a time, but only after he was gone. For her sake, and for his own, he did not tell Anjine everything, because some things he had seen—and done—were far too painful to relive. His nightmares reminded him well enough, and far too often.

As the patrol boat sailed toward the military wharf, dripping with mists that condensed on the rigging and sails, Mateo forced himself to focus on a gentler time, memories that brought a smile to his lips. Dressed as street scamps, the pair had slipped away from the castle, resolved to test their nautical skills. Mateo suggested that "Tycho and Tolli" take an outing in their own small boat, to see the sights, so they went to a public pier where a small rowboat had been tied up for weeks, apparently unclaimed; Mateo had been watching it. Slimy green algae like mermaid hair covered the hull's bottom.

After Anjine climbed in and steadied herself on the stern bench, Mateo set the oars into the oarlocks and rowed them out into the harbor. A puddle of brown water sloshed in the bottom of the boat, and Anjine dutifully bailed so their feet would remain dry. In the main channel, Mateo struggled to dodge the busy harbor traffic. Large sailing ships and merchant galleys, fishing boats and smaller ferries plied the many fingers and bays that formed the city districts. From the shore, people waved and shouted at them; Mateo and Anjine waved back, unable to hear what they were saying.

Mateo kept rowing while Anjine sat with regal poise, gazing upon the wonders of Calay. She insisted on taking her turn at the oars, but he wouldn't let her, though his arms ached and his hands felt raw and blistered.

Mateo took her under six bridges, circled Shipbuilders' Bay, then toured the Merchants' District, where many large and exotic ships were tied up. The boat carried them to the harbor mouth, beyond which they could see the choppy expanse of the Oceansea and the gray-blue waters that vanished behind the curve of the world.

In the late afternoon, they returned to the dock below the castle in the Royal District, where they were surprised to see people crowded on the pier, who were pointing excitedly as they spied the two rowing toward them. Mateo's heart sank as he noticed two uniformed members of the city guard among them.

"We might be in trouble, Tolli," Mateo said.

She pulled off her yarn hat and shook her head to let her long hair fall free. "In that case, I'd better be Princess Anjine again."

The owner of the boat had discovered it missing and raised the alarm, calling on the city guard to find the thieves. Caught, Mateo was mortally embarrassed; he had never meant to keep the boat, and as far as he could tell, nobody had used it in some time. He would have taken all the blame upon himself so that Anjine did not suffer because of his impulsive idea.

But when she alighted from the boat, she stood proud and straight, regarding the people as if they were a reception party. She nodded toward the distraught boat owner. "I am Princess

Anjine. Thank you for allowing us the use of your boat. We will pay you handsomely for the service, or we'll simply buy the boat from you, if that's what you prefer?"

All of the man's complaints and accusations evaporated, and he bowed low. "Princess Anjine! If you had merely asked, I would have rowed you myself."

"Oh, I enjoyed the time with my friend. We're sorry for any misunderstanding." As a reward, Anjine had invited him to the next large banquet dinner hosted by King Korastine and Queen Sena. Mateo had been so proud of her....

Now the *Raven* tied up to the wharf nearest the barracks. Inns opened their doors and stretched out awnings above outside tables to ward off the rain. Mateo stood at the side of the ship so he could walk down the boarding ramp as soon as the lines were tied to the pilings.

He found his heart lightened, and he was smiling. Speaking with Anjine and handing her his letters would brighten his mood even more. He needed that before he shipped out again — before he was once more weighed down by grim stories that he could not tell her....

77 *Corag Highlands*

Because it was a wet spring, Criston Vora stayed inside his cozy stone-walled cottage and spent extra time sitting by the fire with the dog at his feet. With his sharpened knife in hand, he whittled models of ships he could see inside his mind, remembering vessels he had seen or imagining ships that had never been built.

Captain Shay's hand-drawn sea-serpent book lay open on the table, in case he needed the reference.

Intent on his work, he set aside all thought. He brushed the wood curls from the hearth into the fireplace, where they flashed and sputtered into bright coals. His focus left no room for anything but the tip of the knife, the small shavings of wood, and the shapes that appeared in his hands. Criston didn't need to think about anything else, and here he was far from his past.

When the skies cleared again after a few days, Criston found that he had fifteen finished carvings, and very few supplies in his larder. Time to go to the nearby village by the mountain lake; by now, the people had come to expect his occasional visits. The children looked forward to their wooden toys, and started pestering their parents as soon as they saw him approach.

Though the children showed such obvious joy in their new toys, he did not let himself take too much pleasure in their delight. If he allowed himself to feel happiness and satisfaction, then it was only one step away from feeling the overwhelming grief again. The same grief he had felt the day Ciarlo had told him Adrea was pregnant when the raiders came....

It was safer to keep those storms behind an emotional seawall.

The lake had risen high with meltwater from the spring run-off. A few chunks of greenish white ice still floated in the middle of the water. Taking their new model boats, the children ran to the stony shore and floated them in the chilly water, while Jerard barked and bounded along the edge, splashing in and then thinking better of it when he felt the deep cold.

The village boys used long sticks to poke the boats farther out onto the lake. As the vagaries of the stirring currents caught the models, the boats spread apart like a miniature regatta. With an odd detachment, Criston studied how his models floated, comparing their designs. In his mind's eye, he thought of the vast Oceansea, the whaling ships from Soeland, the guano barges, the fishing boats from Windcatch, and, of course, the spectacular, doomed *Luminara*.

The thin, cold breeze carried a chill from the lake, but no smell of salt, no iodine of seaweed, no pungent sourness of fish — only the mountain mineral air. Criston had almost forgotten what it was like down at the sea.

Racing ahead, one boy clambered up a rocky outcrop that extended over the lake. Holding on to the rock with one hand, he leaned out with his stick, trying to snag one of the boats before it drifted into deep water. With the mud and slush of the thaw, the stones in the outcrop were crumbly, and Criston looked up just in time to see a rock break loose. The boy's hand slipped. He scrambled for a hold, then fell into the water with a large splash. The other children stared; some laughed at the misadventure, some shouted an alarm. Though the boy gasped and flailed, the frigid lake water sapped his strength, nearly paralyzing him.

Criston didn't even realize he was moving; he acted automatically. Without a word, he ran as far as he could along the rocky shore, then dove into the water. The iciness hit him like a slap, forcing the breath out of his lungs in an involuntary whoosh. His arms felt as if they had turned to stone, but he forced himself to stroke forward, warming his shocked muscles by using them.

The boy had stopped struggling now, slowly turning over to float facedown in the water. Criston grabbed his shirt and pulled him back. The boy was pale, his lips already blue, and Criston's heart pounded like a distant kettledrum, laboring to keep warm blood moving. After a few more minutes in this frigid water, he too would be unable to move — he would sink, and he would die.

On the stony beach, Jerard howled. The yelling children had

brought a group of adults, and they stood waving their arms and shouting.

Finally Criston's leaden feet touched rocks at the lake bottom, and he struggled forward until he reached dry land. He pulled the boy out first, and several sets of arms grasped him; then Criston collapsed. One of the village men grabbed the boy, rolled him over, forced water out of his mouth. The boy started coughing and retching on the lakeshore.

Criston's teeth were chattering. "Bring blankets. Or... take the boy to a fire." He huddled into a miserable ball, wrapping his arms around his knees and shivering violently. The people rushed about, pulling the coughing boy away, carrying him off to the nearest village house. Someone threw a woolen blanket over Criston's shoulders as he sat hunched on the shore.

Gradually, like the faintest of predawn light seeping into a black sky, Criston felt the warmth return. He still couldn't bend his fingers. His teeth continued to rattle together like dice shaken in a cup.

The wide-eyed villagers showered him with thanks, and Criston could only nod. Water dripped from his hair, his beard. Plunging into the lake had shocked more memories out of where he had hidden them. His heart was pounding harder than it had in a long time, as if it had just recalled how to be alive.

What he felt in his chest now was an entirely different type of cold from the shock of the near-freezing lake. He let out another gasp, drew a deep aching breath. For the first time in many years, he heard the call of the sea that pulled a man like the tides, and realized how much he *missed* it. And with that realization, he recalled just how much he missed Adrea.

78 *Calay, Saedran District*

It took Aldo the better part of a year to make his way back to Tierra. Along the way, he received assistance from other Saedrans—food, shelter, and enough coins to reach the next stop on his long journey. When he encountered Uraban soldiers searching for Aidenist infiltrators and church burners, he expected them to seize him, but his disguise remained sufficient.

His people had helped him, and he had gotten home.

Weary, wiser, and older, Aldo made his way to a greatly changed Calay, and looked around in wonder, as if seeing it all for the first time. A new Iborian-style kirk stood in a place of honor beside the castle. A fire had destroyed an entire neighborhood in the Merchants' District, and pale pine frameworks were still being erected to replace the lost houses and shops. A new bridge had been built to replace the collapsed Tinkers' Bridge.

But Calay's Saedran District remained unchanged. As he walked the perfectly familiar streets on his way home at last, the sights and smells enfolded him in a welcoming embrace. He stared at his family home, the mossy roof, the flowerbeds in front of the door, the windows covered with curtains his mother and sister had made.

He opened the door and stood on the threshold, just staring in at the familiar rooms and furniture, breathing in the smell of bread baking in the oven and soup simmering in a pot. In the sunlit main room, he startled his father, who stood before a canvas as always, finishing another portrait. "I'm home," he said, knowing he sounded foolish. "Sorry it took me so long." He had not thought of what to say next.

Biento's face turned pale, as if he didn't even recognize his older son. In a soft voice, he called, "Yura! Come and see who's here."

She bustled out of the kitchen with their daughter, Ilna, in tow, both of them dusted with flour. Aldo's little sister had grown a foot taller, gained weight, and blossomed into full womanhood. She squealed like a child when she saw him. Yura marched forward and grabbed him in a fierce embrace. "Where have you been?"

"Everywhere, I suppose—but not by choice."

Then came the explosion of tears, hugs, and excited chatter. Aldo told his story in great detail, then told it all over again to Sen Leo inside the Saedran temple. Down in the underground vault, the old scholar looked as if he might cry as he listened to all the exciting details.

Finally, smiling with great reverence, Aldo revealed the new information he had compiled for the Mappa Mundi, including the shape and fine detail of the Uraban continent. It was a torrent of fresh and unexpected knowledge.

Later, his revelations caused quite a stir in the Saedran community. Sen Leo tested his observations, queried him, but caught Aldo in no contradictions. As best they could tell, his information was perfectly accurate. With Aldo's report, the Saedran perspective of the world drastically changed.

During his absence, Aldo's younger brother, Wen, had also studied to become a chartsman, but he had neither the talent nor the patience to memorize libraries full of data. Because Wen had wanted to go out and find Aldo, his parents were secretly relieved to know he would be staying home.

After his return, Aldo spent days with his father in the Saedran temple chamber, directing him to paint the new features on the Uraban continent and revise other imperfections in the Mappa Mundi. And when the expansive revision was finished, Biento, Aldo, and Sen Leo stood together in delighted awe.

But that was only the beginning of the work. Once Aldo deemed the main temple's map to be accurate, he and Biento traveled together to the smaller temples in Calay, then to other reaches where they shared their knowledge with the Saedran settlements there. Biento painted a revised Mappa Mundi in one temple after another, clearly proud of his son.

In each settlement, Aldo sat before large crowds during temple services and told his tale again and again. As he did so, he remembered how Sen Sherufa's neighbors—as well as the soldan-shah himself—had loved to hear her spin marvelous stories.

Aldo could have exaggerated his deeds to make them seem more exciting, but his real adventures were spectacular enough, and his sacred calling as a chartsman was to ensure *accuracy*. While he enjoyed being the center of attention, Aldo was much more interested in *having* new experiences than in talking about them.

Because of his journey to Corag as a young man, his many trips as a chartsman, his capture by the Urecari raiders, his imprisonment in Olabar, and his subsequent overland escape that had taken him across both continents, some Saedrans were already calling him a new Traveler—sometimes jokingly, sometimes not.

After all his experiences, he had definitely earned the honorific "Sen," though he was still young. Whenever people called him Sen Aldo, it took him a moment to realize they were talking to *him*.

He wasn't ready to stop his life of exploration and travel. Aldo was not yet thirty years old and still unmarried. Sen Leo na-Hadra had offered him any of his three daughters as a wife, and the young women were a logical choice, though all three of them giggled too much and read too little. But a chartsman didn't marry until he was ready to settle down, and Aldo still wanted to explore the world.

Though glad to be back in Calay and well respected among his fellow Saedrans, he was restless and didn't know what to do with himself. He had not been born to stay at home.

Plenty of blank spots remained on the Mappa Mundi. Someday, he thought, someday . . .

79 *Olabar*

Since his abrupt retirement, Imir had stayed out of politics so there could be no question that *Omra* was now the soldan-shah, the leader, the point of all decisions. Out of view in his own section of the Olabar palace, the former soldan-shah raised peacocks in his private gardens, tended small ponds of colorful fish that amused him endlessly, and played games of *xaries* with the servants and occasionally with his son Omra.

"I wish we could find an honorable way to bring Tukar back from Gremurr," Imir said, moving a game piece across the board. "He's my son, too, you know, and he was a good boy . . . but with a bad mother. We both know it wasn't his fault."

"Tukar understands full well why you sent him into exile," Omra said, his voice hard. "He was lucky to keep his head on his shoulders. His life is not overly harsh. After you insisted on having a small palace built near the mines, we even sent him a wife.

He's probably happy enough." He moved his own piece to block his father's advance.

Imir said with a heavy sigh, "I've come to discover that wives do not always make a man happy." He thought of Lithio living far away in Missinia, of Asha murdered by the shadowman, of Villiki disgraced, banished, and probably dead by now.

"You should go out and try to build a new life for yourself, Father. You were never cut out to be a hermit."

"I suppose I wasn't." He scratched his rounded cheek, which he still kept smoothly shaved. "It's time to make friends again."

Sen Sherufa na-Oa could not have been more surprised when the former soldan-shah appeared at her doorway with a bottle of Abilan wine, a vintage he had always enjoyed, though he never paid attention to how much it might cost. "Imir! I haven't seen... You haven't said a word to me in so long."

He held up the bottle, looking bashful. "It was easier to carry than a tea tray. Do you have something to eat? We can make dinner out of it. I've missed your stories. Do you think you could tell one tonight? Maybe by the second glass of wine?"

He stepped inside, and Sherufa blushed, fighting back a smile. "I always have stories. The difficulty is finding one I haven't told you already." Back in happier times she had come to him every week. She opened the bottle and poured each of them a glass. "The best stories entertain as well as instruct."

"I don't want to be lectured," Imir scoffed.

"Have I ever lectured you?"

"No, no. You're always entertaining. Please, carry on."

Sherufa gathered some cheese, olives, and bread, and they shared a simple meal. Before she could commence her tale, a quiet knock on the door interrupted them, and one of Sherufa's neighbors delivered five fresh candles. While she had the door open, several children ran across the cobblestone street to ask if she had any sweets—which she always did.

Imir smiled. "All the people in the district love you—then again, how could they not?"

She sat back down, toying with her glass of wine. He finished his much more quickly than she did. "Now, then, why don't I tell you where the Saedrans came from? It's an old story, but an important one."

"Ah, yes. Something about a sinking island and a curse? Ondun's stepchildren?"

"*I'll* tell the story, if you don't mind. Many generations ago, long after Aiden and Urec had departed in their ships, the original Saedrans left Terravitae on an expedition of their own, with the blessing of Holy Joron. They founded a new homeland on a fertile island continent, and from there, they built and sailed many ships to continue exploring the world. Eventually our people encountered Tierra and Uraba and reestablished contact with the descendants of Aiden and Urec. Civilization flourished.

"But then, in a terrible disaster, our island continent sank beneath the waves, destroying most of the Saedran civilization. The only members of our race who survive today are descendants of those sailors who were away from home at the time of its catastrophe." She looked up at the rapt face of the former soldan-shah. "According to legend, some of the native Saedrans survived by transforming themselves into a race of mer-men who now make their home beneath the surface. One day, we will find that lost sunken land and be reunited with the rest of our race."

When she was finished, Imir poured himself a third glass of wine and refilled hers. "Very fantastical! You Saedrans don't actually *believe* that, do you?"

"Why, yes, Imir, we do." Sherufa's voice was clipped.

He looked embarrassed. "I meant no offense, my dear. To an outsider your Saedran religion seems strange."

"And have you ever considered how the church of Urec appears to outsiders?"

He chuckled heartily, but then noticed that she was serious. He decided to change the subject. "Speaking of Saedrans, my dear, whatever happened to that chartsman you cared for? Did you ever convince him to serve aboard our ships? I should have checked long before now, but there was all that messy business with Villiki and Ur-Sikara Lukai. What was the young man's name . . . Aldo something?"

"He left some time ago, aboard a Uraban ship. I haven't heard from him since," she answered quickly, sure that Imir knew she wasn't giving him the complete answer. "Was I supposed to be keeping track of him?"

She grew quite self-conscious as Imir stared at her features, into her eyes; he didn't seem at all interested in what she'd just said. "Things have changed, Sherufa. I'm no longer soldan-shah, but I would still make a very good husband. And I've certainly had bad luck with my wives of late. I know I've asked you before, but won't you reconsider? We're quite well matched."

Sherufa leaned forward and put her hands over his. "I know the arguments in your favor, Imir, but if I wanted a husband, I'd have married a Saedran man years and years ago. I like being alone. I like being a scholar. I like living my own life, following my own interests. I am a better person by myself than I would be with a man."

She pressed a palm to her sternum. "Maybe it's something missing in my heart, but I've never felt the need to have babies. All the children in the neighborhood come to me, and I'm their surrogate grandmother. I have the love of my people — that's all I could ever want."

Imir looked crestfallen, and she leaned forward to kiss him on the cheek. "We *are* well matched, you and I, but you're already giving me what I want most. I want you as a friend, Imir. A close friend."

Imir took his defeat with good grace, finished off his wine, and stood. "I suppose I could use a few good friends, too. Think of more stories, please. I'll be back to see you next week." He paused at the doorway, as if something else had just occurred to him. "Oh, and I'll ask Omra to send someone else I think you'll find intriguing—another foreign stranger. The man speaks no known language, and it is said he walked across the Great Desert."

She had heard of the fellow, but had thought the reports must be exaggerated. "And what shall I do with him?"

"He is an enigma in the form of a man," Imir said. "Help us understand who he is."

80 *Gremurr Mines*

A pall of smoke and a constant racket hung over the mines at Gremurr. Around the shallow harbor, tall, stark cliffs of gray rock were laced with a verdigris of copper ore and pocked with numerous shafts like termite burrows. A maze of docks, wharves, and chutes had been built for slaves to unload ore and pile heavy cargo into barges on the Middlesea shore.

The air rang with the endless clink of picks, the rumble of metal wheels on tracks, angry shouts of slave masters, and groans of workers. Conical smelters belched black smoke. Connected to a polluted stream that ran down a sheer rock gully from above, water wheels spun conveyors that hauled coal endlessly to the furnaces.

Tukar could barely hear himself think. Outside his small "palace," under the meager shade of a green awning, he tried to concentrate on his next move on a *xaries* board. Across from him, burly Zadar, who supervised all the slave teams, completed his move and straightened. His smoke-reddened eyes never entirely stopped watching the Gremurr works for any sign of trouble. Though Tukar was theoretically the nobleman in control, Zadar kept the mine complex running efficiently.

The daily *xaries* game had become a ritual between the men. For exiled Tukar, it was a way to bring a hint of civilization to this desolate place. For his own part, Zadar enjoyed the young man's company and relished the opportunity for intelligent conversation.

In the five years since his banishment from Olabar, Tukar had accepted his situation. It had taken him a long time to recover from seeing his mother stripped and turned out into the streets, but Villiki had deserved her punishment. His father would have been well within his rights to execute her.

Tukar hadn't whined about his situation or fallen on his knees to beg forgiveness. He understood that if forgiveness were ever to come from his brother, he needed to earn it. Omra knew him well enough to understand that his mother's plans and ambitions had never been his own.

In the meantime, Tukar tried to ensure that the mines remained productive and profitable. The wife his father and brother had chosen for him was pleasant enough, though if he had any sons, they would have little future. Still, his life could have been much, much worse.

When Tukar first arrived at Gremurr and saw the harsh conditions, the dirty smoke, and the miserable slave laborers, he had been anxious to make improvements. But he had been as naïve as he was untrained. At first glance, Tukar was shocked to watch the slaves being abused and whipped, their lives worth less than the ore-rich rocks they chiseled from the mountainside.

Work master Zadar had advised against abrupt, unnecessary changes, but Tukar insisted. He wanted to be good to the poor slaves. He had announced sweeping reforms, sure that the laborers would react like household servants and court functionaries at the palace and work harder to show their gratitude.

He had been so foolish.

Exactly as Zadar had predicted, instead of showing gratitude for the improvements, the slaves had actually produced *less*. Escape attempts increased dramatically, and more than a dozen men vanished into the rugged mountains.

"Showing kindness is seen as weakness. When you show kindness, the slave workers no longer respect you," Zadar had explained.

Tukar sensed that the work master had lost respect for him, as well. To his credit, Tukar realized his error and approached Zadar, recognizing the man's knowledge and talent. "I made a mistake. You would earn my gratitude if you could help me restore Gremurr to its former production levels."

The burly work master had been surprised and pleased. "Grant me the freedom to do what I must, my lord, and our next shipment will go to Olabar without delay."

Relentless search parties had scoured the mountains and captured most of the escaped slaves (two men had already died of exposure). Although the effort they expended was greater than the benefit of retrieving a handful of workers, Zadar insisted that its psychological impact was vital. He chopped off the left hand of each escapee, which provided a valuable example for the others. Work hours were increased and rations temporarily cut, so that when the slaves once again received their full allotment, each meal seemed to be a feast.

As Zadar had promised, the next shipment departed from Gremurr on time in a large, dirty barge riding low in the Middle-sea from its heavy load of metals. Soldan-Shah Omra never even knew there had been a problem.

Tukar came to realize that Zadar's general treatment of the slaves was not unnecessarily cruel or harsh. The work master might have been gruff and inflexible, but he had the mind of a businessman. Though he possessed little compassion for the workers as human beings, he understood their value. "No farmer would survive if he treated his animals badly and they died. The only way to get the maximum work out of these people is to ensure that they are strong enough, well enough fed, and well enough behaved."

Over the years, Tukar and Zadar became more than lord and subordinate, but partners and friends. They relied upon each other. The work master refined the routine to perfect efficiency. Since he delivered raw metals, finished swords, and armor as expected, Tukar was able to obtain any additional materials or personnel he needed through polite requests to Soldan-Shah Omra....

Tukar made his next move on the *xaries* board, surprising his opponent. "That's innovative!" Zadar studied the board, brow furrowed. "You are quite a masterful player, my lord."

"My mother always beat me at *xaries*."

"She won not because you were a bad player, but because she wanted to make you lose," Zadar said. Years ago, after playing this new opponent, Tukar had been surprised, then embarrassed, then simply annoyed to learn that Villiki had defeated him all those times only because she'd been *cheating*.

Zadar studied the pieces, cautiously touched his sikara, then tipped the piece over in defeat. "Now that you know the rules of the game, you have become a worthy opponent."

Tukar drank from a small cup of tea at the edge of the table. "I admit I like it better this way."

81 *Abilan Soldanate*

Mounted on a compact dun mare, Saan turned his blue eyes to watch the military preparations on the trampled field below. In the years since the Ishalem fire, Uraban breeders had produced superior horses. Beside him, astride a larger, muscular mare, Omra regarded the blond-haired boy that he had raised as his own and felt a strong wash of feelings, even if the ten-year-old looked so different from any other Uraban.

Saan was keenly interested in the cavalry maneuvers, and Omra could tell that the boy saw more than just an exciting show of running horses and shouting men. He saw wheels turning in Saan's mind as he mentally arranged groups of soldiers like pieces on a *xaries* board. Thinking tactically. The boy often surprised him.

Saan turned to him. "When will they truly go to war, Father? Are they ready yet?"

"The world is a very large place, Saan. Bringing an army strong enough to conquer Tierra would take years of supply preparation, and possibly a year's march just to transport them."

"Is that why King Korastine hasn't sent his armies here to destroy Uraba?"

"Probably. Unless he is reluctant for some other reason."

Omra tightened his grip on the reins when the mare shifted. "Let's watch them train for a while longer."

Istar had told her son at least part of his origins, but Omra himself did not refer to the boy's Tierran heritage, though it was obvious. He did not want to think about it himself, nor did he care whether the sikaras muttered or the other soldans worried. He had neither encouraged nor discouraged Saan from calling him "Father," but at the moment, the soldan-shah had no other heir.

When he had agreed to accept and help raise Adrea's son, Omra had not expected to become attached to him. From what he had seen of Villiki's schemes for *her* son, Tukar, and knowing the palace politics and the soldans jockeying for prominence, Omra found it refreshing that the boy had no agenda at all.

At the Olabar palace, in a solarium that had been converted to a war room, Saan often studied the charts spread on tables. These were tactical maps, emphasizing terrain and roads, focusing on what the soldan-shah liked to call "military geography." The boy had a sharp mind and an intelligence enhanced by bright curiosity. Because of his fascination with far lands he had never seen, Saan quickly developed a good understanding of Uraba, the coastlines of both the Middlesea and Oceansea, and the known parts of Tierra.

On the training field below, fifty horsemen prepared to face a charge from a rival party. One group carried a set of red pennants, the other yellow, and when the pennants were lowered, the horses galloped toward each other. The two groups slammed together with a great clamor; then the riders swirled around and passed through, to re-form ranks instantly before spinning and taking up positions once more. They raised pennants to salute the soldan-shah, who watched them from the hill overlooking the field.

Saan's expression was appraising and satisfied. "When they do ride, Father, our cavalry will be invincible against the Tierran armies."

The following day, he and Saan rode out to the mock Tierran village hidden in an isolated valley not far from Olabar, where the young inhabitants spoke an unfamiliar language and pretended to worship Aiden. Saan's brow furrowed as he gazed down at the streets, the town square, the kirk, the half-timbered homes. He watched the indoctrinated children and teenagers as intently as he had studied the cavalry maneuvers. "I remember being here."

"Oh? You were only five years old."

"Does that mean I should have forgotten?" Saan smiled.

When the mysterious Teacher came to greet them, the masked figure made Saan flinch, but he summoned his courage and stood straight—clearly for Omra's sake.

Regarding the young man, the Teacher asked in a neutral voice muffled behind the silver mask, "Have you brought me another subject, Soldan-Shah?"

"No!" Omra's sudden reaction surprised him. "This one is mine, Teacher. You already had a few days with him, long ago."

The masked instructor was taken aback by the vehemence. "Ah, now I remember—the slave girl's son? All these Tierrans look alike."

"He's *my* adopted son." Omra's pulse was racing, and he felt a hint of what the boy's mother must have felt when Saan was snatched away from her and sent to this place.

The Teacher bowed deferentially. "I meant no offense."

"Can I play with them?" Saan asked. "There aren't many boys my age around the palace."

"No, stay here. Those children have another purpose."

The Teacher turned his silver mask toward the small town. "As you commanded, Soldan-Shah, thirty of our best *ra'virs* have been dispatched northward. By now, many should have made their way into Tierra, even to Calay, where they will remain quiet and hidden . . . until it is time."

Omra placed a hand on the boy's shoulder. "If it weren't for your mother, Saan, you would have been one of these *ra'virs,* dispatched on a mission, rather than living with me in the palace. But I want you in Olabar. You're too important to waste here." Omra would never have said that in earshot of Cliaparia, but he was the soldan-shah and he made his own priorities.

Saan watched the group of Tierrans, who looked so similar to him, but did not seem dismayed about the fate he had nearly suffered. "If joining them is what I needed to do for the glory of Urec, and for you, then I would do it."

Omra felt his heart swell again. "Of course you would."

82 *Calay*

Holding Tomas's hand, Anjine led the boy through the castle's main gates and down the cobblestoned street. His mother spent an hour every morning at prayer in her private kirk, so they knew exactly where to find her.

Aidenist presters traditionally performed their services at sunrise, but Ilrida preferred to go slightly later, when the risen sun sent golden light through the kirk's narrow windows. Up in her native Iboria, during the short days and long nights of winter, devotions were held later in the day.

Because Tomas could not sit still for an hour inside a kirk,

Anjine cared for the boy each morning while Ilrida prayed. His mother spent the afternoon playing with him or taking him on walks around the Royal District or down to the docks. At times, King Korastine would join them, although the king's presence turned what should have been a pleasant stroll with his family into a crowded royal procession. For the most part, Korastine spent private time with his beloved wife and son in the royal wing, where he could be a doting father and husband instead of a king.

Anxious to see his mother as they approached the kirk, Tomas pulled ahead, yanking Anjine's arm, but she kept a firm grip on his hand. The boy jumped into the air and wanted to dangle in his half-sister's embrace; Anjine let him burn off some of his energy, since he would have to be quiet when they entered the holy place.

Past the fishhook anchor and the wooden obelisks, the kirk's wooden door stood ajar to let the sunshine in. Ilrida was the only person inside her private chapel. Only twice before had Korastine allowed large groups to use the kirk, when two of Ilrida's Iborian ladies-in-waiting had married Calay guards. His silver-haired queen had been so happy to see her native friends get husbands of their own, though Ilrida told them in halting Tierran that no husband could be as good as hers.

As Anjine and Tomas entered the wooden kirk, she put a cautioning finger to her lips, and the boy mimicked her, striving to be as silent as his sister. They found Ilrida kneeling on the riser, hands extended beneath the pinewood altar. Her silvery hair hung down to the small of her back, combed so straight that it shimmered like blowing snow. Her face was turned toward the charred wood relic from the burned Arkship, her eyes closed, her expression beatific, her pale lips moving quietly as she continued her earnest prayers.

In the years since leaving the northern reach, Ilrida had learned to speak passable Tierran, though the language still fit her like a poorly sized, incorrectly cut garment. When Ilrida breathed out a word of closure, Tomas pulled his hand free from Anjine's grip and bolted toward the altar, yelling, "Mother!"

Startled by the noise, Ilrida jerked her hands from beneath the altar, then hissed with sudden pain and looked down at a deep scratch on the back of her hand. One of the iron nails protruding from the bottom of the pine altar had traced a line from her knuckles to her thumb. Ilrida saw the blood welling in the scratch and put her hand behind her back so that Tomas wouldn't be upset. Seeing Anjine's look of concern, Ilrida smiled gamely as she gathered her boy in her arms. "Just a scratch. Come, Tomas. Let us go to the kitchens and find a snack."

The boy ran out of the kirk into the sunlit streets again, and the two women followed at their own pace.

A week later, Ilrida lay on her sickbed, coated with oily sweat and writhing in pain. Anjine was at her side, unable to do anything. King Korastine knelt at the bed, clasping Ilrida's uninjured hand, squeezing his eyes shut as if he couldn't bear to see his wife in such agony.

The scratch from the rusty nail had become infected and swollen; foreboding tendrils of black and green extended up Ilrida's pale arm. Her facial muscles were drawn back in a terrible rictus, her cheeks rigid, her jaw locked. She didn't seem to know where she was. Delirious, she had not spoken a word of Tierran in the past four days. Anjine could only pray that wherever Ilrida's mind had gone, she had escaped from the pain racking her body.

Old Prester-Marshall Rudio prayed over her, and his acolytes lit strongly scented candles at the head of her bed. Other presters had come in, sure that Ilrida was possessed by some Urecari demon, but their ministrations did not help her condition. Anjine had fetched the lustrous icons of Holy Joron from the kirk, hoping they might comfort Ilrida.

The court doctors bathed her with sweet-smelling liquids and burned herbs and incense, to no effect. Though King Korastine was a devout Aidenist, he begged Sen Leo na-Hadra to send the best Saedran apothecaries and physicians, and the scholar did so. After seeing Ilrida, the men were not baffled by her condition, but neither could they help. "We have seen this malady before, Majesty," the somber physicians said to the king. "The muscles spasm, the jaws lock, the fever increases."

"Give her your best medicines," Korastine pleaded. "Give her anything. Cure her."

The four Saedrans were reluctant to pronounce their assessment, but one of them summoned the courage and shook his head. "There is no cure, Majesty. Sometimes the patients recover—we don't know why. A few of them find the strength."

"My wife is strong," Korastine insisted.

The apothecaries gave Ilrida powders to send her into deep sleep, but still her condition worsened. Seeing her father mad with fear and grief, Anjine led the Saedrans out to the private corridor as the prester-marshall engaged in another round of prayers. She faced them, demanding to know the truth. "How long does she have? How much hope is there?"

The Saedrans regarded one another soberly, then turned to her with large, weary eyes, and she *knew*. "This type of sickness is very often fatal, and always tragic, Princess."

Anjine had dreaded to hear it, but she thanked them and went back in to stay at her father's side. Grief-stricken, Korastine bowed his head with a greater sadness and despair than more than ten years of war had been able to inflict upon him.

Tomas called and called for his mother, but the servants kept him out of the sickroom. Finally, however, Anjine relented and brought the boy to Ilrida. She didn't want him to see his mother like this, but—facing the truth in a way that her father seemed incapable of doing—Anjine knew the boy would want to say goodbye. And Ilrida, wherever her delirious mind might be now, would be comforted to have Tomas at her side.

The boy ran to his mother, shocked at what he saw, not understanding at all. Anjine tried to hold the tears back, clamped her lips shut, and stood trembling, but they flowed freely down her face after all.

Korastine leaned over the bed to embrace Ilrida's spasming shoulders, sensing that she had only moments left. He refused to let go, holding her against him as she died in his arms.

83 *Calay, Merchants' District*

The *Dolphin's Wake* limped back to Calay Harbor, storm battered, its sails threadbare, its hull planks badly in need of caulking. The people who watched maritime traffic come and go in the Merchants' District greeted the ship's return with cheers of surprise and calls of disbelief. Runners bolted up and down the docks and into the district, calling out the news that the *Dolphin's Wake* had returned. The trading ship had been gone for well over a year and was presumed lost at sea.

Aldo na-Curic often lingered in the district to look at the exotic wares on newly arrived ships, reminding himself of the amazing things he had seen. He watched the *Dolphin's Wake* pull up and was one of the first to call out her name. As a chartsman, he had sold his services to Captain Osmuc three times over the years, but those had been normal trading voyages, nothing as extensive as the apparent ordeal the ship had suffered.

Ropes were thrown and planks laid across to the dock; people streamed aboard the battered ship, greeting the weary yet happy crew. The gaunt men's clothing was ragged, but nothing could erase the delight on their faces.

The man they called captain was Francosi, who had been first mate when the ship sailed. "Captain Osmuc died two months into the voyage," Francosi explained. "Not the way I expected to be promoted...but that was a year ago."

"You got the crew home," Aldo said, pushing his way forward. "That's what a real captain does."

The former first mate recognized him. "It's our Saedran chartsman! By Aiden's Compass, I would have loved for you to be aboard with us. We've desperately needed your services."

Aldo would rather have been out on an amazing voyage than home in the Saedran District, whiling away the days. "What happened to your own chartsman?" He searched his memory. "Sen Lioran, correct?"

"Now, that's a long tale," Francosi said, raising his voice, "and I'm sure these fine gentlemen will be treating me and my crew to pints of ale at the taverns so they can hear it again and again." Many of the listeners cheered and offered to buy the first pints. The last members of the crew staggered out onto the docks, searching for loved ones, looking so thin and frail that a gust might blow them over. "But you, my chartsman friend—come aboard the *Dolphin's Wake*. I have something for you and you alone."

Curious, Aldo walked up the plank to the deck. Many people bustled around him, but the captain would speak only with Aldo. "We set course for far Lahjar, the most distant city in the known world." Aldo's eyes sparkled. Few reports had been written of that mysterious, exotic city on the southern edge of Uraba, below which the silty, shallow waters grew so hot that they boiled each day at noon. "Sen Lioran guided us. We arced far out to the west, in open waters, heading into unknown territory, but our chartsman knew of certain currents."

In prior times of uneasy but unrestricted trade, Tierran ships would work their way down the coast from Khenara, to Tenér, to Ouroussa, and finally to Lahjar. Sen Lioran had taken a different, more efficient route.

"We caught a brisk southerly flowing stream that brought us around and swept us back toward Lahjar before we sailed off the edge of the world. It was about then that a rogue wave unexpectedly swept Captain Osmuc off of the bow and to his death. Nothing we could do." He shrugged. It had been a long time ago for him.

One week later, the *Dolphin's Wake* had reached the distant city. The natives had marveled at their pale skin and light brown hair, and promptly bought all the exotic items from the five reaches, exchanging them for items that would be just as valuable back in Tierra.

"We headed back for home with our cargo hold full. As we sailed far out to open sea to catch a northerly current that Sen Lioran insisted was there, the men hauled up a sea turtle in their nets. And on its shell, they found strange etched drawings, lines cut deeply into the hard plate. When Sen Lioran saw the drawings, he grew very excited. He said this was one of the most important discoveries of our time. Our men were more interested in eating meat other than fish for a change, but I let Lioran keep the shell."

Francosi led Aldo into a small cabin with many obvious Saedran trappings, where he removed a bundle wrapped in old scraps of sailcloth and handed it to a curious Aldo. "Before long, though, our chartsman had far more important concerns—powerful abdominal pains in his right side. He developed a fever, he began to vomit, and his condition grew worse."

"Sounds like his appendix," Aldo said. "A burst appendix."

"Yes, and he died. But before he became delirious at the end, Sen Lioran made me swear—made me take the fishhook in my hands and *swear*—that if I made it home, I would find a Saedran chartsman and present the turtle shell to him." He tapped the package.

Aldo pulled away the sailcloth wrappings to reveal the old hemispherical shell, turned it over to see the play of curved lines, the drawing of continents and islands. *The world.*

Recalling all too clearly the fake chart that Yal Dolicar had sold him, Aldo approached the object with skepticism. This, however, was different. Sen Lioran, an accomplished chartsman, obviously believed in its veracity, and now in his mind, Aldo matched up the lines of reefs, the known shoals, the convoluted outlines of distant islands, places that no one but a Saedran was likely to know. He held the map against his chest, barely able to contain his excitement. The map was real.

Smiling, the captain said, "Before he died, Sen Lioran also told me that I should ride the northerly current for eleven more days, and then strike due east. We eventually found the coast again, though we were still below the Edict Line, and Urecari vessels pursued us. Fortunately, we escaped them in a fog bank and kept working our way northward. Now we're home.

"The map is yours. If nothing else, it's what I owe your people."

"Sen Lioran was right," Aldo said. "This may be the most important discovery of our time."

84 *Inner Wahilir, Sioara*

Prester Hannes made his way to Inner Wahilir and the city of Sioara, the gateway to Ishalem and his way back to Tierra. Though weary, he was pleased with what he had accomplished in his years of doing Ondun's work. Now, however, he was eager to report to Prester-Marshall Baine all the progress he had made. *Improving the world, by the grace of Ondun.*

The soldanates of Inner and Outer Wahilir were ruled by cousins, Soldan Huttan and Soldan Attar. Though their lands split the isthmus in half, east and west, and thriving commerce passed between them, Hannes had learned that the cousins hated each other. Both men, apparently, had been in love with the same woman and tried to woo her, but she had died before she could choose between them; the cousins accused each other of poisoning her rather than let the other soldan win.

On the main caravan road from the Middlesea shore to the Oceansea coast, a line of guards stopped all travelers at the border, requiring them to transfer their goods to a second caravan that would lead them across the adjacent soldanate for a substantial fee. No caravan from Inner Wahilir was allowed to pass through Outer Wahilir, and vice versa. In recent years the soldan-shah had stationed his own troops at the crossing point to prevent a civil war from breaking out.

Prester Hannes did not want to be seen, inspected, and questioned by Uraban border guards. So he found another way.

Weary and footsore, looking like any other traveler who wanted to avoid paying the high toll, Hannes protected the handful of coins he had hoarded. On the outskirts of Sioara near the wide main road that led up into the Wahilir foothills, he lurked about until he spotted five men who looked like a group of thieves planning a large and risky job. Their intentions were obvious; they all needed an illicit guide. Just as he did.

Before long, a solicitous man was drawn to like-minded fellows as iron is pulled toward a lodestone. "I know a secret trail," the guide offered with a smile. "I can find invisible paths, dense trees, sheltered canyons — and a pass known only to me. I will lead you across to the Oceansea."

"That's all we need," said one of the gruff men.

"Oh, you'll need more than that, but it is all I can give you." He raised his eyebrows. "Provided you can pay."

"How much?" someone asked.

"Ten *cuars*," the guide replied with a straight face.

"For the group?"

"Apiece."

While the others groaned and complained, Hannes stayed silent, standing apart from these men. He drew out his coins. It would cost most of what he had in his purse, but he didn't care. He could always obtain more. "I will go."

The guide chuckled derisively at the hesitant men. "If a beggar can afford it, then you men can! Or maybe you don't want to go badly enough?"

"I'll go, even if I am the only one," Hannes insisted, hoping the others would indeed go along, though he did not relish the idea of close company. However, if he were alone with the guide, a servant of Urec, the man might lead him into the wilderness, murder him, and take the rest of his coins. Hannes could not make his own way through the mountains, and he didn't dare get caught by the soldan's guards. Stories of the "shadowman's" deeds had spread throughout Uraba for years.

Despite their complaints, each of the five men agreed to the price. Smiling, he told them where to meet at dusk, when they would set off into the Inner Wahilir foothills. The guide's name was Yal Dolicar.

85 *Olabar Palace*

When it was Cliaparia's evening to dine with Omra, she guarded her time jealously, always searching for some way to engage her husband's attention.

Not only did the soldan-shah continue to pine for his first wife, who had been dead for more than a decade, but Omra lavished time and attention on his other wife, a former slave girl and a *Tierran* at that! He doted on the woman's son more than he paid attention to Cliaparia's daughter, *his* own daughter, who was of noble blood. *Uraban* blood.

When Cliaparia was alone — which was too often — she sometimes stood before a looking glass, trying to imagine how Omra could find fault with her, which part of her beauty was not flawless. Oh, he cared for her as a husband should, according to the ancient rule that Fashia had laid down when she granted Urec leave to take other wives: A husband must care for them equally.

But there was no law that he must *love* them equally.

She had tried virtually everything over the years, but she still hadn't given the soldan-shah a son. Neither had Istar, thankfully.

Cliaparia made herself beautiful for the evening; three hand-maidens fixed her hair, applied her makeup, added her jewelry. The burning incense would ignite desire in a man, according to her sikara friend Fyiri, who had access to the chemicals, perfumes, and drugs that the church considered effective. After the disastrous poisoning incident with Villiki and Lukai, however, Cliaparia had been afraid to try any more potions.

It had been five years since Omra's marriage to the Tierran slave, and nearly eleven since he had wed Cliaparia. Once again the nobles and his advisers were urging him to take another wife, to increase the odds of having an heir. Despite numerous wives, the soldan-shahs in Omra's line had never been particularly successful in producing offspring. With his three wives, Imir had fathered two sons and a few daughters, and *his* father had sired only one son and a daughter.

But failure to bear an heir for Uraba wasn't Cliaparia's fault. The soldan-shah simply did not make love to her often enough — and *that* problem wouldn't be corrected by introducing a third wife into the palace. He needed to cease being preoccupied by other things.

Nevertheless, after constant pressure, Omra had recently agreed — with obvious reluctance — to marry a young girl named Naori, the daughter of a wealthy and influential family from Missinia, who had been put forward by Omra's mother. That had quieted the voices for the time being.

But not for Cliaparia. Upon learning of the new betrothal, she had felt her dreams slip from her grasp. A son of her own should be the next soldan-shah! Maybe if Omra paid more attention to *her* and less to Istar, he would already have a real Uraban heir. He wouldn't need a third wife now, but she did not know how to make Omra love her so madly and passionately that he would think of no other woman.

Such thoughts weighed on her day and night, and each special evening like this gave her a new opportunity. She refused to give up hope. While she waited for Omra to come to her, Cliaparia directed her handmaidens to arrange the table just so, then she chased them away.

She was sitting with a perfectly composed smile as her husband entered and took a seat cross-legged on the cushions she had prepared for him. She offered him a porcelain bowl of apricots, a comb of honey, cubes of marinated lamb roasted with almonds, strong coffee spiced with shaved cinnamon. Polite and cordial, Omra complimented her on the food, but little else. Preoccupied with other things, he did not look her in the eyes.

Finally, she released her exasperation. "Omra, you're right here in front of me, yet I feel your mind is far away."

"My mind *is* far away. A soldan-shah has many concerns."

"Shouldn't your wife be one of your concerns? I have always been faithful to you. I have always loved you." She leaned toward him and took his hands in hers. He twitched, but did not draw away. "Omra, I am your first wife, and I deserve prominence."

"You will never be my *first wife*," he said with a razor-edged voice, and she turned pale. After a moment, he drew a long, slow breath and continued in a reasonable, measured tone. "First Wife is merely a title you hold, not your place in my heart. That title gives you sufficient prominence. What is it you lack?"

"A son!" She tugged at her colorful sleeves and dangling bracelets. "I have many possessions, but I would like more of your time, more of your attention, and more of your heart. You give Istar more than her share."

"Because I enjoy being with Istar." He no longer looked at his food, no longer ate at all.

"And you do not enjoy being with me?"

He spoke in a calm voice. "Tell me, Cliaparia—you've been married to me for twice as many years as Istar has. Can you answer a few simple questions about me? What, for instance, is my favorite food?"

Cliaparia gestured down at the banquet spread before them. "I have made your favorite dishes."

"No, you made the most extravagant ones. You serve them to me over and over, but you never ask which ones I particularly enjoy. What is my favorite color?"

The question surprised her; they had never discussed such things before. "Gold, I assume. A royal color."

"No. The green of emeralds is my favorite. What is my favorite ballad?" He didn't wait for her to answer, but continued his quiz. "Tell me about my childhood, my friends, *anything*." Cliaparia did not know a single answer. Omra gazed at her with patient sadness. "You see? You don't really know me. You don't love me. You just love the *idea* of me."

"Is that not enough?" Her voice was so quiet she couldn't even be sure he heard her. He did not answer. She ate the rest of her meal in sullen silence, and the soldan-shah departed early, without staying the night.

Her mind made up, Cliaparia sought the only remaining path. The other alternatives had been cut off to her.

Entering the main Urecari church, as she often did to write her prayers on scraps of paper that the priestesses would scatter to the winds or burn in a fire, she met with Fyiri. The young sikara had risen in prominence since the disgraceful death of Ur-Sikara Lukai. Fyiri had also garnered political leverage by the fact that she ministered directly to the first wife of Soldan-Shah Omra. Cliaparia would help Fyiri rise even higher, so long as they helped each other.

"I have concluded that the boy Saan must die," she said bluntly.

To her credit, Sikara Fyiri did not look surprised. "That is one solution to the problem. Should you not kill Istar instead?" She stood by a brazier, smelling the aromatic smoke, lifting a basket that held numerous ribbonlike strips on which the faithful had scribbled their pleas.

"I would rather see that woman shattered and devastated when her child dies. The foreign boy is nothing special, but we can use him."

Still cautious, Fyiri lifted one of the strips of paper, scanned the brief request some supplicant had written, then tossed it into the brazier's glowing coals. "The soldan-shah dotes on the boy as though he were his own son."

"That is why he needs his own son. A blond-haired Tierran is simply not acceptable. Omra's love for the boy is...unseemly."

"It is offensive," Fyiri agreed. "And the boy's attitude toward his soldan-shah is even worse." She tossed several more prayer strips into the fire without bothering to read them.

They had made halfhearted attempts on Saan's life twice before, setting up accidents, engineering perils, but Saan was clever and deft...or perhaps just lucky. Now Cliaparia knew it was time to begin in earnest.

"When the slave girl reported the poisoning plot of Villiki and Lukai, Omra rewarded her very well." Fyiri arched her eyebrows. "Aren't you afraid I will reveal your new scheme to the soldan-shah? Maybe he would make me his next wife instead of Naori."

Cliaparia felt more annoyed than worried. "If I believed that was what you really wanted, then I might be concerned. You and I have too much to gain from each other. This alliance benefits us both."

The ambitious priestess chuckled. "Yes, better to rule a church than to share the soldan-shah's bed."

Cliaparia scowled. "Omra doesn't share a bed often, or very enthusiastically."

"Not with you, at least." The barb stung, and Cliaparia barely stopped herself from slapping the other woman. Fyiri pressed, "Have you thought this through? If the boy dies, won't Omra and his beloved Istar simply fall into each other's arms?" She frowned at another prayer strip, crumpled it in her palm, and tossed it to the floor instead of the brazier.

"Let me worry about that," Cliaparia said. "It would be best if *she* were implicated somehow."

"That might be difficult. Nevertheless, we should plan."

Cliaparia's lips were stained with a deep pomegranate dye, which made her smile look like a curve of blood. "Soon the children will go into the forest to hunt for the Golden Fern. I know Saan: He will range farther than the others, and he'll be unwatched and unprotected. That will be our best chance."

86 *Uraba*

The weather always seemed perfect during the hunt for the Golden Fern. The sikaras took credit for that, half jokingly, half seriously. As part of the celebration, the children wore brightly colored costume tunics, sashes, and hats reminiscent of the sailors of long ago, pretending to be members of Urec's crew. Saan blended in with the other Uraban boys by covering his hair with a scarlet sailor's scarf and tying a yellow bandanna around his throat.

For three years, he had been old enough to participate in the festival, but his two half-sisters were still too young to join him.

With every child in costume, Saan had a chance to play among them just likc any other boy, but he could never forget that he was different. He looked different, and even the handmaidens and palace slaves treated him differently from the other noble children.

He concluded he had a better chance of finding the Golden Fern *because* he didn't think like all those others. When he and countless children fanned into the wooded hills on the outskirts of Olabar, most would follow well-worn paths or animal trails, more interested in the festive nature of the game than in the possibility of success. But Saan intended to go where the hunters hadn't already searched. He was not afraid to leave the laughing, clumsy crowds. . . .

His mother kissed him on the cheek, adjusted his costume sash, and turned him loose. When his companions hurried down a trampled path into the forest, Saan ducked into the underbrush, wading through weeds and brambles, alert for any sign of the magical fern. Laughing to himself with delight at the feeling of freedom, he ran among tall cedars and dodged fig trees dusted with thick moss. He did not shy from steep hillsides, trudging up slopes and sliding into hollows.

To find something no one else could find, he needed to look where no one else was looking. It only made sense.

Sweeping the toe of his soft leather boot from side to side, Saan stirred thick leaves and needles on the ground, looking for the fern's tightly wound spiral. He pushed his way through tall cane that towered over his head.

He had never heard of anyone actually finding the Golden Fern, though confectioners made looping candies in the shape of fern spirals, covered with sticky honey. Many mothers made imitation ferns out of feathers and fuzz, so their children could pretend to be special. Every boy or girl was able to come home having "found" the prize.

But it wasn't real. Saan wanted to find the real Golden Fern. His mother and the soldan-shah would be so proud if he were to find the special object, thereby proving that he had an uncommon destiny and the true favor of Ondun. He would be a lucky one, a special child, and all of Olabar would celebrate. They would throw feasts in his honor, and everyone would applaud him.

However, he knew that, as an unusual child, born of a Tierran father and mother, others looked on him with suspicion, as if he were some kind of changeling. Even the soldan-shah had enemies who always looked for weaknesses, ways to harm him. Maybe it would not be a good thing for Saan to draw too much special attention.

Still, if he could find the fern...

Continuing his search, he came upon a fairy ring of mushrooms poking up from the sodden ground, then a coral-colored toadstool that looked as tempting as it was poisonous. He squished into a moist marshy area where fanlike ferns spread their fronds. But these were ordinary ferns, not magical ones. Biting gnats flurried around Saan's face.

Then with a buzz like an overly loud insect, an iron-tipped quarrel smacked with a hollow *pop* into the trunk of a rusty cedar only inches from his head.

Immediately, falling back on his training and instincts, Saan dropped to the ground as two more crossbow bolts whizzed through the tall ferns. He didn't panic, didn't freeze.

Someone had shot those deadly arrows directly at him.

As he peered through the drooping green shield of a wide fern frond, he saw shadowy figures in the trees: two men, dressed in greens and browns... a flash of one man's eyes, the hard expression on his face, the quick clockwork movement as he set another quarrel into the short crossbow and wound the tight string.

Keeping low, Saan bolted in the other direction, slapping ferns aside, then dove into the brushy-tipped cane forest. His flight made loud rustling noises, but he needed to be quick, not silent. If he could get enough distance, he would be able to hide. He could not waste time or thought wondering who these men might be, or who had hired them. He knew it had to be one of the soldan-shah's enemies. They were trying to hurt his father by hurting him.

Saan couldn't allow that.

He had experienced strange accidents before—too many near misses to be explained by clumsiness or coincidence. But these men were well-practiced killers who did not hesitate. Saan either had to outsmart or outrun them.

He realized that his colorful clothes made him painfully visible. Thinking fast, he dodged through near-impenetrable thickets, yanking off his scarlet scarf and yellow bandanna. Then he tore away his shirt, frantic to get rid of anything with bright colors. Though his skin was pale, it was better camouflage than brilliantly dyed fabrics. Soon, his bare shoulders, back, and chest were scratched and scraped, but he kept running.

The mercenaries searched noisily for him, underestimating the boy, their voices low and angry. He heard mutters of surprise, then curses when they found his discarded clothing. They had expected him to be an easy target. He flashed a hard grin.

Saan pressed his back against a tree surrounded by tall tufts of pampas grass and concentrated on the sounds of his pursuers. Suddenly he heard laughter close by, children talking, twigs breaking, an older woman—a mother or teacher—telling the children to stay together. They kept coming closer. Behind him, the hunters continued their approach.

From his shelter, Saan spotted three boys younger than himself, led by a middle-aged woman with large hips. Together, they sang a song about the Golden Fern, as though the fronds would unfurl at the very sound of the music. Saan was sure that if he asked the woman for help, the hunters would kill her, the boys, and then him. He wouldn't put these other children at risk just because of who *he* was.

Without calling attention to himself, Saan darted away, leading the hunters in a different direction. The three boys continued their search, kicking up fallen leaves, pulling down branches, not knowing how close they had come to death.

Saan came upon a large hollow log with bark sloughing off in thick curved sheets. Beetles, termites, and moss had chewed through the decaying wood. Saan pushed the bark aside to reveal a dark cavity that had been used as a shelter by some animal. He was just small enough that if he folded his shoulders together and worked his way backward, he could hide inside the tree, pull the bark up to cover his tracks, and strew the dry leaves around.

Saan pressed himself into a tight ball, feeling spiders and ants crawl over his bare back. The dust of the old wood nearly made him sneeze, and the log's rotting mulchy smell made the air difficult to breathe.

The mercenaries were still out there.

He heard crunching boots as the hunters came closer, talking in low voices, and he fell absolutely silent, hardly daring to breathe. Through a small crack, he could see two pairs of legs as the mercenaries paused to look around. Then another sound came in the distance, and the men set off again, apparently chasing another target.

Saan still didn't move, afraid it might be a trick to lure him out of hiding. He waited and waited, then closed his eyes and counted to a hundred. He still couldn't be sure he was safe, but he knew he had to go.

At last, he moved with all the stealth he could manage, shifting aside the thick pieces of curled bark. Covered with dirt, he crab-walked out of the hollow in the rotted log. Crawling forward, always alert, he kept his eyes ahead. He brushed aside some dead leaves on the ground.

And there, less than a hand width before his eyes, was a beautiful *golden* young fern, a perfect plant spiral unfurling from the underbrush.

87   *Wahilir Mountains*

The reluctant comrades followed Yal Dolicar into the hills at night, moving away from the port city of Sioara and the Middle-sea. The men did not ask questions, did not tell one another their names, did not explain their business or their reasons for wanting to make a secret crossing. Prester Hannes was glad they showed no intention of trying to become friends; he didn't want any friends, especially among these people.

The group trudged along, wreathed in self-absorbed silence as they picked out a faint trail into the mountains of Inner Wahilir. Hannes knew they were all liars and criminals, enemies of God … but since they cheated or stole from their own people, Hannes would not interfere with them. Unless he found it necessary.

They camped for three nights, working their way deeper and higher into the hills. Some of the men had brought their own food but refused to share. Yal Dolicar had brought dry pack food, which he sold to those hungry enough to pay. Hannes sat in camp with his knees drawn up to his chest, eyes open and alert, ignoring the gnaw of hunger in his stomach. He had fasted before; it made him feel pure in the eyes of Ondun.

Their cheery guide whistled songs to himself when he rose in the morning and set off along the winding trail, expecting the others to follow. Two heavyset black-market merchants complained about the pace, but Dolicar showed no sympathy. "I said I would guide you over the pass to Outer Wahilir. I didn't say I would coddle you. I have a schedule to keep."

Hannes knew that the quicker they moved, the sooner he would be able to reach Tierra.

On the fourth day, they crossed over the spine of low mountains that separated the two Wahilir soldanates. On the western side of the range, the terrain became arid, the ground cover scrubby. The hills were blanketed with golden grasses rather than green trees.

Because the track now led downhill into widening valleys and circled around sharp-elbowed drainages, the travelers were in higher spirits, while Dolicar grew visibly more impatient. Late in the afternoon, with the orange sun hovering directly in their eyes, he stopped at the summit of a foothill ridge and gestured expansively toward the deep blue Oceansea that glimmered in the distance. "There is your destination. You're already in Outer Wahilir, and this track will take you down to the coast. From this point, you're on your own."

The merchants whined. "We paid you to lead us to the other side."

"You are on the other side. Are you incapable of walking a straight path downhill? Besides, I am known down there, and it's best if you are not seen with me." Dolicar gave an unapologetic shrug of his shoulders. "I have other parties waiting for me back in Sioara."

Hannes didn't care. He took out his camp gear, deciding this was a good enough place to rest until tomorrow. The others continued to mutter, but Dolicar simply turned around and set off at a jaunty pace back up the pass the way they'd come. Within moments he had vanished into the scrub oak.

Since they had a common destination, the companions remained together for one more night in camp. Hannes planned to rise before dawn and set off at his own time and pace, leaving the others to their fates. They could find their own way.

As dusk deepened, two of the travelers gathered fallen deadwood, cleared a space in the rocky soil, and built a fire, apparently not worried about Soldan Attar's scouts seeing the light. Hannes sat at the edge of the fire's glow, watching the flames as he relived that terrible, glorious night inside the burning Urecari church in Ishalem. . . .

To ease his hunger, he chewed on some succulent stalks he'd learned were edible during his crossing of Yuarej. He listened to the sullen conversations of the two fat merchants who had apparently known each other before joining the caravan. Since it was the last night together, the reticent men loosened their tongues, believing they were about to go their separate ways.

Hannes narrowed his eyes as the merchants spun a story of how they had once found a pair of Aidenist missionaries trespassing in Uraba, foolishly trying to spread the word of Aiden. The merchants gleefully described how young men from the village had clubbed the missionaries senseless, tied them up, and thrown them — still alive — into a deep dry well.

Now, by firelight, the merchants mocked the missionaries' thin echoing cries of pain, their wails for mercy. "Oh, my legs are broken! Oh, we're dying of thirst!" The calls had wafted upward from the well for days, but far from taking pity, the people threw stones down at the holy men.

In the shadows, Prester Hannes pulled his hood forward so the men would not see the murderous hatred in his eyes. He could not pretend to laugh along with them, but they did not notice or care.

When his companions bedded down to sleep, Hannes gruffly volunteered to take the first watch, and no one argued with him. He did not feel sleepy at all. With bright eyes, he stared at the flames, watching the twigs crackle as they surrendered to the light. He hardly noticed time passing, but hours floated by until he was confident the others were sound asleep, curled up on their thin blankets. Two of the men had an odd whistling snore that Hannes had found maddening over the past several nights. At last he could silence them.

Hannes slid the razor-edged knife from his pack and, crouching low, moved to the nearest man, one of the fat merchants. He clamped his hand firmly over the man's mouth to prevent him from making a sound, then with a quick unhesitating arc, he left a deep crescent slash. The man spasmed and gurgled as a bright red beard sprouted in the middle of his throat and streamed down his dusty shirt.

When the first victim lay still, Hannes moved to the second man, then the third. He acted with cold precision. The fourth victim woke up—a man who had laughed about throwing Aidenist missionaries down the well. He lurched to his feet, flailing his arms and yelling. Hannes thrust the point of the dagger into the hollow of his throat beneath his jiggling chins, withdrew it with the speed of a scorpion's sting, then whirled to slash the neck of the last man, who had begun to stir, groggy with sleep.

The camp was still, puddled with blood. In the dying fire, the knotted wood popped with a loud noise, as if spitting at the victims. Hannes would find a creek in order to wash himself in the morning. He ransacked their packs, helped himself to their stored food and pulled out clean clothes, discarding his blood-soaked rags.

Finally, he lay down and slept more soundly than he had in months. He had improved the world a great deal this night, and Ondun would surely reward him. The next morning at dawn, he walked away from the bloody campsite, leaving the bodies to carrion animals, and made his way down to the coast.

88 *Calay*

Destrar Broeck came from Iboria for the funeral of his daughter, sailing the once-marvelous wedding ship, now transformed into a mourning vessel with black sails and black pennants. Before the arrival of the grim craft, the two lighthouses flanking the mouth of Calay Harbor were lit to shine the way for poor Ilrida's soul.

As they watched the solemn ship glide into the harbor, Anjine stood with her father, who wore black robes and a heavy crown. At the prow of the funeral vessel, the bearlike destrar wore polished armor and a fur-lined cape draped about his shoulders.

At a whistle from the squad captain, members of Korastine's royal guard formed ranks and beat deep kettledrums. Men threw guylines to tie the Iborian ship up against the royal wharf, and when the vessel came to rest, the drums stopped.

Young Tomas held a pillow of purple velvet—his mother's favorite color—on which rested the delicate crown that Ilrida would never again wear. Anjine put a reassuring hand on her little brother's shoulder, and he didn't flinch.

With his head hung low, Destrar Broeck strode down the

boarding plank, shrugged off his fur-lined cape, and formally bent his knee to Korastine. The king stared for a long, frozen moment before he came back to himself, helped Ilrida's father to his feet, and embraced him, not caring whether their shared grief would be seen as weakness before the crowds.

A loud fanfare blew, and the kettledrums began anew. Korastine and Broeck walked slowly up to the castle, followed by Anjine and Tomas, and then the crowd of followers and retainers.

The next day, Ilrida's preserved body lay stretched out atop a bed of ivory cushions on the deck of the funeral ship. Her beautiful purple gown was surrounded by a cape lined with Iborian ermine fur. Her silver-blond hair had been combed straight, her hands folded across her abdomen. Her skin was heavily powdered, for Destrar Broeck had needed several days to make the journey. Her cushions were surrounded by straw and dry kindling that had been soaked in fragrant oil. Additional oil casks were broken open to drench the deck planks.

The holy fragment of burned wood from Aiden's Arkship was taken from Ilrida's kirk and placed aboard, next to her head. Though Prester-Marshall Rudio had requested it be moved to Calay's main kirk in honor of the fallen queen, Korastine insisted that the relic belonged with her, even in this final ceremony.

Anjine could see that her father had dreaded this funeral for days. Korastine had spent the entire night kneeling in vigil on the deck, refusing even a folded cloak to cushion his knees as he prayed over Ilrida's body. As his daughter, Anjine stayed beside him, touching his shoulder, feeling the unrestrained outpouring of his grief.

"After the fires of Ishalem, then what happened to Baine and all those volunteers, the terrible raids…and now Ilrida." He shuddered, looking up at Anjine, who had also begun to weep.

"If we are truly fighting on the side of God against His enemies, then why do all these tragedies keep happening to us?"

Anjine did not pretend to have an answer for him. Not even the old prester-marshall could have given a convincing response.

At sunrise, the time for the most solemn Aidenist services, Destrar Broeck clomped with heavy bootsteps onto the deck to join him, and the two men bound by common sorrow crossed over to the royal cog, which was connected to the funeral ship by strong grappling hooks.

Even Mateo had come back from his patrol and insisted on joining the solemn group. From his time in Iboria and escorting Ilrida to Calay, he too had known the kind and ethereal queen, and Anjine had granted a special dispensation for him to don a royal guard uniform. She had not been able to speak with him further, but now she could see a sparkle of unabashed tears on his face as he stood with his fellow guards.

Weighing anchors as the day brightened, the two linked ships cast off from the royal wharf and sailed out of Calay Harbor to the open sea. When the ships passed the lighthouses on the headlands, young Tomas stared at the wondrous sight. Korastine, though, did not turn his gaze from the adjacent funeral ship and the silently resting Ilrida.

When the linked vessels reached the open water and the brisk current caught the vessels, Prester-Marshall Rudio called out a solemn prayer, both in traditional Tierran and again in the northern dialect, in honor of Ilrida's memory. Rudio had learned the phrasings specifically for this ceremony.

Mateo and the royal guard escort detached the grappling hooks to separate the vessels. The royal cog raised its sails, and the pilot turned the wheel, while the funeral ship continued on its way, drifting farther out to sea. As the separation between the vessels widened, Destrar Broeck blew a horn.

Mateo and several other well-trained archers lit pitch-covered arrows and raised them to the sky, loosing a volley that arced gently over. In unison, the arrows struck home and ignited the funeral ship's deck; two of the shafts plunged into the cushions and kindling beneath Ilrida, and within moments, her pyre was alight.

Tomas started to cry again, and Anjine held him. She didn't need to say anything. By the time the fire began to consume Ilrida's body, the ships had separated enough that Anjine could see only the flames rising above the deck rails. Her father clung to the beautifully painted icon of Holy Joron he had commissioned for Ilrida's special kirk, holding it against his heart.

His hair blowing in the sea breeze, Destrar Broeck turned to the king. "My daughter could not have asked for a better husband, or a better life." He glanced down at Tomas. "Or a better child. Although you built that kirk for her, the innocent scratch of a rusty nail has caused great tragedy. I beg your indulgence now, Sire—let me and my men tear down the kirk."

Korastine appeared broken, but his eyes sparkled with an odd wistfulness. "I have a mind to do something else, Destrar. 'It is better to fix than to break, better to stitch than to tear, better to caress than to strike, better to build than to knock down.' I command that Ilrida's kirk be remade entirely. And this time, we will use only wooden pegs and nails of fine silver...silver, like my beloved's hair."

The burly destrar seemed surprised, but satisfied. "You see clearly, Sire, and you speak wisely."

They watched the funeral ship, now entirely aflame, its black sails consumed, the masts transformed into giant torches. The ship drifted west, toward the endless watery horizon.

Korastine stroked the lustrous painted icon of Holy Joron and gazed at the shimmering illuminated eyes of the saintly man.

He whispered, as if Ilrida could hear him, "I hope you find Holy Joron and the land of Terravitae, my love." They watched the plume of smoke as the burning ship shrank into the distance.

Then the pilot heeled the cog about, and they sailed back to Calay.

Black pennants and banners hung all around the castle for the declared time of mourning, and King Korastine withdrew to his chambers. But Sen Leo was quite insistent.

Always before, the Saedran scholar had been allowed to see the king, but the royal guards were reluctant to disturb the grieving Korastine. Sen Leo stood outside in the corridor, his arms wrapped around a roughly woven sack large enough to hold a thick pillow. The sack was tied shut, showing only hints of the mysterious object within. "Tell King Korastine that I have found *hope*."

One of the guards retreated into the royal bedchambers and eventually returned, signaling for Sen Leo. Gathering himself, the Saedran scholar entered the room and stood before the king, who slumped in one of his high-backed chairs like a discarded suit of clothes.

Sen Leo and the king had held many long discussions in this room, exchanging ideas on politics and history, contemplating the war. Now the scholar took a seat opposite him, holding the sack in his lap. "Majesty, I have something very interesting here."

The king sounded incredibly weary as he regarded his visitor. "There are few things I find interesting these days, old friend."

"Nevertheless, you will want to see it." Sen Leo toyed with the string that tied the sack shut and slowly worked the knot loose. With great care, he spread apart the opening and slid out a dome-shaped object flecked with bits of dry seaweed. It was an old sea turtle shell, weathered and notched.

When King Korastine showed little excitement, the Saedran scholar reverently turned the shell to display its underside, where many lines had been carefully engraved, coastlines etched, notations made.

"There is a map etched on this shell." Sen Leo ran his finger along the lines, touching some of the blurred sections. "Look, Sire — much has been worn away or covered over with algae, but see these islands, this coastline, the details of these reefs? Believe me when I tell you, Majesty, this is an *accurate* representation of what we know, including obscure details that only Saedran chartsmen know."

Korastine leaned forward, not grasping the significance. "So someone drew a map on a turtle shell..."

Sen Leo slid his hand to the far side of the engraved map where, well beyond any familiar points on the coastline of Tierra, was marked another whole continent on the far side of the world. He lowered his voice with a genuine sense of wonder. "This, Majesty...this is *Terravitae*."

Korastine straightened with sudden interest. "The land of Holy Joron?"

"This map is clear evidence — or at least a very convincing argument — that the realm of Holy Joron is real."

"We already sent out the *Luminara*." Korastine sagged back a bit. "It was lost at sea. I received a letter, long ago, but no one ever found the man who wrote it. Still, we know from the sympathetic ship model and from the letter that the ship was destroyed..."

"Majesty, it is a sad fact, but many ships are lost at sea, especially those that embark on dangerous missions. Does that mean we should give up entirely? Years ago, Prester-Marshall Baine and I convinced you that Ondun wants his people to study the unknown parts of the world. Now, with this map" — he thumped a finger on the hard shell—"we have a much better chance of finding the lost continent from which we all came."

89 *Olabar, Saedran District*

The second foreign visitor who stayed with Sen Sherufa na-Oa proved to be stranger and far less comprehensible than Aldo had ever been. Five years ago, the young Saedran chartsman had vastly increased Sherufa's knowledge about the world, and for that she would always be grateful.

The new exotic stranger posed an entirely different sort of challenge. Unlike Aldo, this man shared no language, culture, or common experiences with her. He was said to have crossed the Great Desert from unexplored lands beyond and collapsed in the foothills of Missinia. Sherufa didn't know how she could believe that preposterous claim.

In the Olabar palace, the man had recovered from his mysterious ordeal. Sikaras prayed over him and performed the Sacraments, but he clearly didn't understand what was happening. A man so entirely unfamiliar with Urec's Log was an amazing novelty to the priestesses. Imir had suggested Sherufa to Soldan-Shah Omra, and as soon as the stranger was healthy, Omra sent him to the home of the Saedran woman, who began trying to communicate with him.

He was a large, muscular man, albeit not threatening, and seemed genuinely interested in learning the Uraban language. The man identified himself as Asaddan, but he was impatient because he didn't have enough vocabulary to describe for Sherufa the things he'd experienced, the places he'd seen.

He had a wide, flat face and tanned, weathered skin, as if he had stared into blowing winds all his life. When he smiled, a prominent gap showed where one of his front teeth had been knocked out. His hair was a dark, thick black and plaited with thin leather strands into clumps that seemed to have some kind of significance for him. His original clothes had been tattered by his journey, and his new Uraban garments looked odd on him.

For days, her neighbors stopped by to see the curious stranger, and when Asaddan saw that he frightened the children who came to see him, he released a loud storm of laughter and lured them back. Sherufa insisted to the wide-eyed boys and girls that the stranger wasn't *really* an ogre from the deep desert, but her tone sparked their imaginations. Asaddan then fascinated them by whistling through the wide gap from his missing front tooth. A young boy who had also lost a front tooth spent hours trying to emulate the sound.

Sherufa devoted every waking moment to teaching her visitor to speak Uraban, working the lessons into the tasks of daily life. Occasionally, Asaddan grew frustrated and lashed out in his own tongue sprinkled with new words, resulting in a mix that made no sense at all. As the weeks went on and the two began to understand each other better, the pieces started to fit together for Sherufa. Asaddan learned to convey increasingly complex concepts. When he couldn't express himself well enough, he snatched a piece of paper and drew a line to mark the Middle-sea, then circled Olabar. He drew his finger vaguely down in the direction of Missinia and made another mark. Then he sketched squiggly lines that Sherufa realized were meant to represent sand dunes.

"The Great Desert," she said.

"Desert," Asaddan agreed. He drew more lines to symbolize dunes that extended southward in a seemingly endless expanse.

But on the other side of the wasteland he drew hills, marked villages and more villages. He sketched strange animals that must have been herd beasts.

Sherufa couldn't believe what she was seeing. "There are no habitable lands beyond the Great Desert." He merely grunted. Near the bottom of the paper and far from the desert, Asaddan added a line meant to signify a southern coast. A new coast. An entirely new sea.

The very idea rocked Sherufa's concept of the world. The Great Desert was an endless and unbroken barrier of sand, the edge of the world, a barrier beyond which no one could go. According to Asaddan, though, the arid wasteland was just an obstruction. Once past the hot sea of dunes, new vistas opened up—whole new lands. Perhaps half of the Uraban continent remained to be explored!

In halting words, Asaddan told her that his people, a hitherto unknown race called Nunghals, populated those southern lands beyond the desert. None of the books in her library—even the tales of the Traveler—suggested such a thing! Excited, she and Asaddan worked far into the night to unlock further secrets of language so Sherufa could understand what he was saying.

Over the next few days, the Nunghal castaway described his people, who were mainly nomadic tribes that lived in the vast grasslands. The Nunghal clans herded buffalo, drank the milk, ate the meat, used the hides. Far to the south, another branch of the race—the Nunghal-Su—were seafarers who lived their lives on ships and met with their landbound brothers, the Nunghal-Ari, only once a year at large market encampments, where they exchanged goods, stories, and breeding stock.

One morning, Asaddan came to her at breakfast with weary but bright eyes. Sherufa realized that he must have stayed up all night, practicing his words. The Nunghal sat down, drank morning tea with her, then announced: "I tell story now." He grinned, and his pink tongue flicked into the space of his missing tooth.

She caught her breath. "By all means."

"I am caravan leader...in hills, villages. Storm wind." He gesticulated and blew through his lips. "Drives pack animals away...supplies, water, food, deep in desert. Winds make them..." He mimicked galloping movements with his hands. "Run. I cannot escape. Animals run into dunes, run and run."

He let out a long sigh, hanging his head. "After storm...lost. Not know where. Follow winds, travel at night. Stay with animals. Some animals die, so I eat meat. Need water...drink blood of animals. Then sand dervishes." He gesticulated more, but she didn't know what he was talking about. Sand dervishes?

"I find water...a well bandits use. I see bandits come and hide. Follow them at night to edge of desert. Your land. I walk more. I walk and walk. Then—out of desert!"

Clearly pleased at having conveyed such an epic adventure, Asaddan wolfed down his breakfast, then went into his room and collapsed into a deep sleep to make up for his restless night.

Calling one of her neighbors and handing him a note written in Uraban letters, Sherufa dispatched a message to the palace, requesting to speak with the soldan-shah, also suggesting that Imir might want to be present. He would love Asaddan's tale.

Then, after closing the door and making sure Asaddan was sound asleep, Sen Sherufa went to the back of her cupboard, removed the false panel, and looked at the expanded Mappa Mundi that Aldo na-Curic had helped her develop. She studied the known boundaries of the Great Desert and extended her imagination to encompass what she had just learned from her guest. Her finger quickly ran off the edge of the paper.

If Asaddan's story was true, then the Saedrans would need a much larger map.

90 *Olabar*

After the Festival of the Golden Fern, Saan emerged from the forest scratched and dirty, his blond hair mussed, his shirt gone, his remaining clothes torn. The afternoon sun hung low in the sky, and many families were already streaming back into the city by the time Istar saw him and came forward to greet him, smiling. Other parents greeted their children with laughter and presented them with false ferns made of golden feathers. She thought little of her son's unkempt appearance at first, since the energetic boy had spent the day running through the forested hills.

Then Istar sensed that something was wrong. Saan's eyes were unusually bright, his jaw set with determination. He seemed breathless and eager to leave. "We have to get back to the palace and the soldan-shah. I have news, Mother—important news. We're all in great danger."

Instantly on her guard, she grabbed his shoulders, looking for injuries. "What is it? Are you hurt?"

He spoke in a low voice. "No, I'm safe now, but I'm worried about my father. There is a plot, and someone tried to kill me. We have to talk with him right away." Saan pulled his mother along.

Istar, painfully familiar with convoluted plots and assassination schemes in the soldan-shah's court, looked over her shoulder for some unnamed threat until they were back at the palace. She found one of the palace guards, who ran to find Kel Rovik, who in turn informed the soldan-shah that they were coming.

When the two of them stood before Omra at his low writing table, he pushed the papers aside. Before the soldan-shah could speak, Saan blurted, "You're in danger, Father. Maybe we all are."

He rose abruptly to his feet. "What happened? Are you harmed?"

"I survived. Someone wants to hurt you, and I believe that's why I was a target." Saan went on to describe the assassins who had pursued him through the forest and how he had narrowly escaped.

Omra regarded the boy in silence, his dark eyes meeting Saan's blue gaze. "You have never lied to me before, and I hear the truth in your words now." The soldan-shah reached a quick decision. "I will move your quarters closer to mine. I will inform Kel Rovik that it is to be done."

Istar's thoughts spun, trying to think through the complex palace politics. Villiki had already tried to eliminate Omra so that her own son would be the heir. Could Tukar have plotted such a thing from the Gremurr mines? No, Istar didn't believe that for a moment. But who would see *Saan* as a threat? A blond-haired Tierran boy with no Uraban blood would never be accepted as the next soldan-shah, no matter what. It would have led to civil war among the soldanates. What could the plotters intend to accomplish by harming her son? She felt a chill. "Cliaparia," she whispered. "It might have been Cliaparia."

Omra's face darkened. "I will not have my wives squabbling. You've never shown any ambition to become First Wife, and Cliaparia knows her place."

She recognized the implacable tenor in Omra's voice. His

words were a command, and he would not change his mind. "Yes, my lord."

Even after so many years, her feelings for Omra remained conflicted. He had been responsible for the attack on Windcatch; that could never be erased. In the past eleven years, however, she had seen Omra from many perspectives. He was a wise and just leader, a caring son, and a generous brother, a kind and fair husband, and a conscientious, loving father. He worked hard, was proud without being vain, and rarely broke a promise. It had come as a surprise to Istar when, only two years into their marriage, she had realized that she actually *trusted* Omra. Not loved him... but trusted him.

True to his word, he had kept her son safe. She knew that she *should* still love Criston, her true husband, but Omra had been remarkably good to her... and especially to Saan. Her thoughts were very tangled and complex, her heartstrings tugged by memories of Criston, thoughts of Omra, love for Saan and for her two daughters... even for Olabar, where she had lived for a third of her life.

In the brief silence, Saan spoke up again. "And I have more news. I *did* find the Golden Fern. When I was hiding from the assassins, I saw it in the mulch under a log, sparkling and yellow, unlike any other fern I've ever seen."

Istar looked at him uncertainly. "You didn't tell me about this. Where is it?"

The boy straightened. "I didn't pluck it. The fern is so rare that it seemed wrong to destroy such a precious thing. So I left it where it was. But I did find it, and so now I'm blessed by Ondun."

Istar felt a sudden wash of skepticism. Was this whole crisis merely a wild adventure created by the overactive imagination of a ten-year-old? He had never been prone to exaggeration or bragging, but she did know he would do anything to impress Omra. Her tone was cautious. "Now, Saan, you know the Golden Fern is just a story for children."

"It is not just a story," Omra said with a warning edge in his voice. Istar had forgotten that these Urecari believed their legends to be the literal truth. Still, he frowned at the boy. "So you have no proof of the Golden Fern?"

"My word is my proof." Saan looked as though the soldan-shah had insulted him.

"The fern has been sought for generations," Omra said. "If you discovered it, why would you show no one?"

Saan drew himself up. "I *wanted* to show the fern to everyone, but I knew the assassins were still out there. You both taught me to think carefully before I took action, so I thought about it, Father...and then I realized it wasn't necessary. Doesn't the legend say that whoever *finds* the Golden Fern is blessed? That Ondun is watching over him? Nothing says I have to destroy the fern to be blessed. And if finding it is enough, then Ondun and Urec both know already. The fact remains a fact. I thought it was a test."

He shrugged. "So I gently covered the Golden Fern with leaves and underbrush and crept away from the fallen log. When I was sure I was safe, I ran until I found a path and followed it until I heard other people."

Now Istar feared that Omra would discount Saan's warning about the assassination attempt, that he would think it had all been the product of a young boy's enthusiastic fancy. The tale of hunters trying to kill him in the forest during the crowded festival seemed preposterous enough, and now this....

Finished, Saan awaited Omra's answer. The soldan-shah

spoke with a grave voice, a leader making a firm pronounce-ment. "As I said before, you have never lied to me, Saan. I believe you."

91 *Calay*

The loss of Ilrida left an emptiness in his life that went far deeper than when Sena had died, and King Korastine needed to cling to something.

By his command, carpenters dismantled Ilrida's Iborian-style kirk to its foundations, removed the lapped shingles, pried the pine planks from the support frame. He ordered the iron nails melted down, and then craftsmen reassembled the whole kirk using only wooden pegs and soft silver nails.

But even when the task was complete, Korastine did not feel whole. He needed something else, a noble goal that would allow him to touch his wife's lost spirit, a quest that went beyond the long-simmering war with the Urecari.

Every month brought news of some other coastal raid by the Urecari, another bloody retaliation from Tierran warships, pri-vateers on both sides claiming to fight to protect their lands, but really just in search of plunder.

For years, though the two continents had cut themselves off from each other, Korastine had stopped short of launching a full-scale crusade. If he gathered all of his naval ships, soldiers, and weapons, and sailed south past the ruins of Ishalem, he could have conquered a Uraban coastal city or two, but he could not win the war. He could never send a sufficient military force overland across the isthmus to achieve a successful attack on Olabar. Geography provided as much a defense as their respective armies in keeping the two continents apart.

Sick of death and suffering, Korastine sat alone in his bedchamber. Assuring the king that he and his chartsman had already memorized it, Sen Leo na-Hadra had left him the sea-turtle shell with the map inscribed by some lost mariner. The king held the leathery old shell and studied the unknown coastlines far across the Oceansea. The *Luminara* had tried to go there, and failed. He had seen the shattered sympathetic model with his own eyes, and read the mysterious letter from Criston Vora. Certainly, no one could deny that the ship was lost, now that a decade had passed.

Still, as he looked at the etched map, the *idea* of such far-off lands sparked his imagination — the far seas, the unexplored continents, the possibility of finding Holy Joron, the third son of Ondun. If anyone had divine powers, Joron did. If any hope remained in the world, it would be found in Terravitae. Ilrida had always been so passionate about that particular legend. And now Korastine saw a way that he could find it — for her.

Setting the sea-turtle shell on a prominent shelf in his quarters, where it would remain a precious reminder, he sat at his desk to write a proclamation. He did not need advisers for this, did not require a scribe. He wrote the words plainly, stating his desires, and then sent riders to each of the five reaches, calling the destrars to Calay.

He would ignore the Urabans and instead look outward. In a whisper, he quoted from the Book of Aiden, " 'It is better to fix than to break, better to stitch than to tear, better to caress than to strike, better to build than to knock down.' "

He would find Terravitae.

*   *   *

The king held the session in his large banquet hall, so that more people could crowd in and hear his words. For the important occasion, he had ordered a feast of fish and game, preserved fruits, and many loaves of freshly baked bread. At separate tables sat Destrar Shenro from Alamont, Destrar Broeck and the shipwright Kjelnar from Iboria, Destrar Siescu all the way from Corag, Destrar Unsul from Erietta, and Destrar Tavishel from Soeland. Comdar Delnas was there, representing the Tierran military: the land forces, the city and royal guards, and the ever-growing navy. At the head of the table, Princess Anjine tended to her brother, Tomas, neither of them knowing what their father had in mind. Many of the destrars probably thought Korastine intended to make a long-overdue announcement of Anjine's marriage, since she was twenty-two.

Korastine regarded those gathered here, noting curiosity and puzzlement on every face. Prester-Marshall Rudio invoked a long, traditional blessing for the feast, but even he didn't know what the king had planned.

The king stood, waited for silence, and picked up the royal proclamation he had written himself, unrolling the parchment for all to see. "Twelve years ago, Prester-Marshall Baine received a revelation from Aiden — that our true mission is to expand our horizons, to voyage to new and unexplored lands. To that end, we dispatched a single ship, the *Luminara*...which was destroyed." He paused, drew a deep breath. "But the loss of one ship does not mean the end of our mission! We have allowed ourselves to be distracted by this conflict with the Urecari. Our shipyards have produced only warships and patrol vessels — but we must not forget what Aiden truly wants of us."

A ripple of muttering ran up and down the tables. Korastine waved the proclamation. "I hereby decree that an allotment be made from our royal treasury, a small but vital fraction. We will build a new Arkship, one to rival Aiden's ship that was lost in the fires of Ishalem. We will design and construct a great vessel to carry our people to the edge of the world, and beyond."

The sounds of surprise and uncertainty grew louder from the destrars, courtiers, and military representatives. Korastine leaned forward, sharing a secret with all of them. "I recently came into possession of a map that shows the likely location of Terravitae."

Further gasps rang out. Anjine held herself back with visible effort.

"I may be old," Korastine continued with a deprecating smile, "but I intend to lead the expedition to Terravitae myself. I do this to honor my beloved Queen Ilrida, but I also do it for Tierra and for Aiden — to show Ondun that we have not forgotten why we were created."

Destrar Broeck pushed his plates aside, lifted his large body, and stood tall, looking just as hardened, just as determined as the king did. "Iboria will provide all the wood necessary for the ship! And I assign my master shipwright to manage the project."

Knowing the others would not like it, Korastine added, "Every destrar in every reach, every person in Tierra should be glad to help pay for this expedition."

He could tell by the mood that none of them was glad, but no one would contradict him. He sat back down, both mentally exhausted and exhilarated, and reached out to pat Anjine's hand. He handed the proclamation to one of his scribes, so that it could be copied and distributed widely. "We will find our way back to Terravitae."

A hush fell over the underground temple chamber. Aldo na-Curic held himself silent, though he was bursting with ideas, waiting to hear what Sen Leo and the gathered Saedran elders had to say in the urgent discussion. Aldo still couldn't believe he had been asked to join this prestigious meeting of elders only, but he was more widely traveled than any of these men, and they very much valued his opinion. He grinned when, during a brief roll call and opening prayer, the old scholar called him *Sen* Aldo.

"Years ago, we secretly contributed funds to make possible the voyage of the *Luminara*," Sen Leo said. "We must do so again. Now that we have seen a real map, now that there is evidence of the unfolding world, we *must explore it*. We cannot let financial bickering among the destrars delay this great quest."

The other Saedrans nodded, including Aldo's father, Biento. Aldo spoke up. "As much as we think we know, there are still so many empty spots on the map. We can't even be certain of the size of the world. Or its shape! This is a very exciting time for the Saedran people. Let's not pass it up."

"While it's true that the money belongs to all of us," Biento pointed out, "it is also true that all of us have the same goal—to complete the Mappa Mundi. Think of how much my son has contributed. This voyage could teach us even more."

"And remember how much work there is left to do," Aldo added, feeling a flush on his cheeks.

One of the other elders cautioned, "As soon as the merchants begin to see the added tariffs and the destrars look into their treasuries, their enthusiasm will be dampened. Someone may even manage to cancel the project."

Sen Leo wagged his finger. "But if we Saedrans open our coffers, then the Arkship is sure to set sail."

The elders dickered over the amounts they would contribute, but since Saedran chartsmen were paid handsomely for their services—and that payment was banked in the secret Saedran treasuries—they had saved significant sums.

"What could be more important?" Aldo thought of the Mappa Mundi on the temple walls. "This voyage is how we should invest our money. Just think—we may even discover our lost homeland. Isn't that worth more than all our accounts put together?"

"Truly, what could be more important?" Sen Leo agreed. He folded his hands. "And though such an unprecedented ship will not be completed for years, I must make the proposal now so that there will be no discussion later." He smiled at Aldo. "For that most magnificent voyage, no chartsman is more qualified than Sen Aldo na-Curic. He must be the one to sail on the new Arkship."

92 *Tenér*

After he reached Outer Wahilir, Prester Hannes worked his way up the rugged coast, following bad roads from village to village, keeping a low profile. The clothes he had stolen from his traveling companions made him look like a peddler without items for sale. Even so, he was viewed with less suspicion than if he had continued to disguise himself as a beggar.

Though he was still many months from home, he could almost taste the nearness of Ishalem.

Hannes reached the large port city of Tenér, the capital of Outer Wahilir, a large shipbuilding port that had fallen on hard times because the forested hills had been stripped of their trees for miles around. Approaching from the south, Hannes walked along the naked hillsides, saw the scars of graying stumps, the bare soil and rough washouts from erosion. Poor planning. They had done this to themselves, damaging Ondun's beautiful world. Stands of new trees had been planted much too late, and would take years to mature. Elsewhere down the coast, the Urecari were furiously chopping down wood to expand their ocean fleet for war.

Yes, Hannes thought, *these people are like locusts upon the land.*

As he trudged past the Tenér harbor, he saw numerous Uraban vessels with sails bearing the spiteful Eye of Urec, but two of the ships in port were clearly of Tierran design. He could still see the marks of the blessed fishhook symbol carved into their hulls, now defaced by the chisels and axes of heathens. With gulls wheeling overhead, he shaded his eyes and watched Uraban crewmen haul up buckets of water to scrub away bloodstains on the deck. *Murderers!*

Broad-backed men marched off the two captured ships with bundles over their shoulders or heavy crates in their arms. People crowded around, quarreling like magpies over stolen Tierran goods: preserved fruits, Eriettan beer, urns of honey, blocks of aromatic wax, intricately stamped leather items, salted meats, finely worked jewelry and knives from the famed metalsmiths of Corag.

Hannes listened to the talk around the docks that the captains of the raiding ships would have their pick of the spoils, but the bulk of the confiscated items would be given to Soldan Attar as his due. Guards hauled off the finest foodstuffs and treasures toward the lavish palace on a hill overlooking the Tenér harbor. Because Attar was a benevolent soldan (so they said), he would host a large celebratory feast for himself and his family, his most important merchants, and the pirate captains that had seized the Tierran vessels.

They would gorge themselves on the bounty of Aiden's followers — a bounty they did not deserve. Hannes tried desperately to understand what he was supposed to do. How he hated these people!

When Hannes saw red-gowned sikaras come to take their turn picking over the spoils he drew closer. The women ululated an outcry when one splintered crate spilled out ten copies of the Book of Aiden. The priestesses kicked at the books, shouting against the "lies" the Scriptures contained.

Hannes barely restrained himself from lunging forward to protect the holy books. Angry and anxious, he ran through the possibilities in his mind, trying to decide whether to attempt a grand gesture. It would make him a martyr, but it would not save the books, and he doubted that his death—at least here and now—would accomplish anything. A futile act could not be what Ondun wanted from him. This had to be another test.

The people crowded close, and the sikaras piled the books on the paving stones. The lead priestess called in a shrill voice, "Bring a torch!"

Someone handed her a flaming brand, and she made a great show of shoving the burning end against the books until all the volumes caught fire. The flames consumed page after page, erasing so many holy and beautiful thoughts that Hannes wanted to weep.

"This has put a spark in the Eye of Urec!" the sikara crowed. "Tonight, at the soldan's palace, we shall celebrate our triumph and praise the name of Urec."

Hannes backed away from the pyre, hurrying from the crowd, keeping his head down so no one would see the tears on his dusty cheeks. What he had witnessed had been painful, but it had also clarified his mission. In a way, it had been a harsh but necessary lesson from Ondun. Until this morning, he had intended just to pass through Tenér and continue north toward Khenara, the isthmus, and on into Tierra. But Tenér could not now be simply a stopping point. He had work to do here.

When all the Urecari shops closed for the sunset services, the Merchant District was vacant and quiet. Seizing his chance as dusk thickened, Hannes moved among the buildings until he found an apothecary shop. In Tierra, most physicians and pharmacists were Saedrans, but because fewer Saedrans lived here in coastal Uraba, the locals had their own shops. Hannes pried open a latch and slipped into the shop.

He searched among the jars of leaves, roots, and powders for what he needed. Like any dockside town, Tenér was infested with rats that plagued the butcher shops and grain storehouses, and apothecaries provided deadly poisons for baited traps. Hannes found an appropriate locked cabinet and stole enough poison to kill an entire army. Yes, that might be sufficient....

Up on the hill, Attar's ostentatious dwelling was an affair of domes, towers, gardens, hedges, fountains, and sandstone arches embraced by flowering vines. Because the celebratory feast was so extravagant, hundreds of workers had erected serving pavilions outside. In storehouse tents behind the brick-walled kitchens, servants unloaded delicacies stolen from the Tierran ships. Hannes managed to acquire a white bandanna and sash, so that he fit in with the similarly clothed workers. After so many years among the Urecari, he knew exactly how to be invisible, how to deflect suspicion and interest.

He slipped under the canvas tarpaulins that covered stacked wine casks taken from the hold of one of the captured ships, and wrestled the barrels upright, one by one. Sheltered from view, he worked loose the thick cork of the first one, poured in some of the poison, then pushed the cork back into place. Before he could lift the next cask, a harried-looking server rushed into the tent, glanced at him, and said, "More wine—Soldan Attar demands wine!"

Hannes pushed the tainted barrel at him. "I have already loosened the cork." The server gave him a look of gratitude, then hurried away, straining with his load. Hannes called after the man, "I'll loosen the other corks as well."

"Bless you!" the servant called, then disappeared.

Hannes went about his work, using all of his poison powder to prepare six kegs, which would be swiftly consumed. Ondun had performed a miracle, shown him the light, and opened the way for him to continue his work.

Improving the world . . .

Hannes darted behind the tents and outdoor warehouses and found a shadowed place in the hedge maze of the eastern courtyard. He relaxed on a cool stone bench where young couples might have met for assignations. From here, he could hear the raucous conversation, the singing and laughter—the gloating—of the celebrants within.

He waited.

In less than an hour he heard the sounds of revelry change to surprise, to horror, then a succession of screams.

And finally a long and satisfying silence.

93 *King Korastine's Castle*

After years of listening in council sessions, meeting with the treasurer of Calay, and poring over trade ledgers to understand the tariffs paid by all merchants, Anjine realized the magnitude of the project her father had undertaken. A whole new Arkship! It would take several years for such a vessel to be designed, for the wood to be delivered and cured, for the work crews to be assembled, for the hull construction to commence. This was no patrol ship. Korastine's Arkship would be a craft unlike any other.

And it might bankrupt Tierra. With the war expenditures, the constant destruction caused by Urecari raiders, and the curtailing of normal trade with half the world, the kingdom's coffers were already drained. And now this expensive and long-term project?

Anjine sympathized with her father and knew why he longed to do such a thing. Yes, she too dreamed of one day being reunited with Ondun's children in the land of Terravitae. She yearned for a return to peaceful times, as did everyone. She understood her father's passion. Even so, Anjine couldn't be sure he was thinking clearly. Because Korastine was her father and he loved her, she hoped she could change his mind by talking with him.

After putting Tomas to bed, she went quietly to the king's private chambers, where he sat by a tall candle that shed a pool of light across the book he was reading — a book written in the language of the northmen, a dialect he had vowed to learn, though he had not become fluent while Ilrida was with him. Now he seemed more determined than ever, though Anjine didn't know what he would gain from the obscure tongue now. He also kept the map-inscribed turtle shell on a precious shelf, so he could see it whenever he liked; a shelf nearby held the preserved, splintered fragments of the twinned *Luminara* model.

After he greeted her, Anjine pulled an ottoman forward and sat before him, as she'd done when she was a little girl. Korastine closed his book and gazed at his daughter with such deep emotion that the words caught in his throat. "Anjine, when did you grow up? You're a full-grown woman now, old enough to be a queen, a wife, a mother." He blinked. "Thank you for helping me with the burdens of leadership since Ilrida...in recent days."

"I've learned a great deal from you, Father. You have taught me, and reality has taught me." She leaned forward on the padded seat. "And I hope you will hear me now. I speak to you out of love, and also concern."

He stroked his beard. "You're worried about my plans for the Arkship."

"I am worried that it's a fool's quest, when the money and resources could better be spent to conquer the port cities of Outer Wahilir, to push back the Urecari, to rebuild Ishalem and keep our own lands safe."

Korastine nodded slowly. "That could be done, yes, although I'm not confident that we wouldn't fail, even so. This is more important."

"Think of Tomas. Think of all the soldiers, think of the villagers who are repeatedly preyed upon by Urecari raiders. Think of Mateo!"

"I always think of those things...yes, and Mateo, too." Korastine gestured toward the turtle shell. "But how can you question this map? Do you doubt the existence of Terravitae?"

She wrapped her hands around her knees. A crock of warm mulled wine sat on the table, but he had not yet poured himself a goblet. Anjine served her father and took a smaller cup for herself. "I believe in the Book of Aiden as much as anyone, Father...but I see some of the stories as parables, legends told to entertain listeners. Can all of the tales of the Traveler be true? No one believes that. Before we spend so much of our treasury on this new quest, can we be absolutely certain that the land of Terravitae isn't just one of those parables?"

"It is the truth."

She got up and went to the sea-turtle shell. "How do we know that this map is correct? Who drew it? Some sailor washed up on an unknown shore?"

"Saedran chartsmen have verified it," Korastine said. "The known details match up perfectly. That can't be an accident."

Though he was being stubborn, Anjine didn't give up. "Then, if you must launch this ship, I beg you to remain here. Tierra needs its king. Tomas needs his father. *I* need my father. This mission is a diversion we cannot afford right now."

Korastine sipped his wine and looked at his daughter with a beatific expression. She didn't understand why he was smiling. "There are things you don't know, my daughter."

Levering himself out of the tall chair, he stood straight. He seemed very old when he reached out to take her hand. "It is time you saw for yourself. Follow me." Taking a candle, he led her out of the royal chamber and down the corridor to a hanging tapestry, which he pushed aside to reveal stone blocks of a slightly different color. A hidden door.

Korastine took a heavy set of keys, thrust one into a crack in the stones, a cleverly concealed lock, and turned it until she heard the tumblers align with a *clack*. He pulled the low door open. "This way." He held the candle ahead of him as they climbed an upward-spiraling staircase to a small, isolated tower room inset with thin windows of clear glass panes.

"What is this place?"

Breathing heavily, Korastine seemed excited. "Remember the story of Aiden and Urec? Remember how Ondun sent them on their separate voyages, and how He gave each man a gift?"

Every Tierran child heard the story again and again, told by the presters in their kirks. Ondun had given Urec a special map to show him the secret pathways of the world, but the prideful man had discarded the chart, claiming he didn't need it. Aiden had received a Captain's Compass, its needle twinned to a special counterpart in Terravitae, so it would always point the course home, but that compass had been broken. When they were younger, she and Mateo had searched for the relic in obscure market stalls run by dealers of oddities.

Korastine lit a taper on the wall from his candle flame, then touched it to the wicks of oil lamps set in sconces in the stone blocks. The room was like a vault, with only a small table and one chair.

On the table lay an intricate compass, an ancient device that radiated age and power. A special compass...its crystal cover cracked, its needle bent out of alignment.

"This is Aiden's Compass, broken long ago by a spy from the ship of Urec," Korastine said. "So far from Terravitae, the sympathetic magic is weak, and the needle can barely find its way. But if we can journey to the right part of the world, if the Arkship can get close enough to Terravitae, the needle will point the way. I know it. How can Aiden's Compass not lead us home?"

Anjine cautiously leaned forward to inspect the object. She had not experienced such awe and wonder since she was a little girl. Aiden's Compass! The *actual* compass! It was one of the most miraculous artifacts in history, and her father had known of its existence all along. When he had announced his mission, his intention to build the new Arkship, he already knew the compass was here, and that it could be used to find the lost holy land.

Despite her doubts and concerns, Anjine now realized that her father was not deluded. Given the potential glories of rediscovering the land of Joron, perhaps he was thinking as clearly as ever a ruler had.

"You're right, Father," she breathed, her voice barely a whisper. "The Compass will guide us. We have to build the Arkship."

94 *The Coast of Tierra*

Waves rolled in and crashed against the black rocks on the rugged coast south of Calay. Tides pushed and pulled the currents like watery pendulums. Floating objects followed a drunkard's path, drifting close to shore before being swept far out to sea again, only to return to a different part of the coast.

As the moon waxed and waned and the tides completed the next movement of their dance, driftwood piled high on the beach, caught amongst strands of seaweed and moss.

A glass bottle, its mouth firmly sealed by a cork, rode the perilous crests and valleys, rolling forward on a whitecap's peak, then floating gently back once more as if to catch its breath. The bottle contained rolled-up sheets of paper covered with handwriting. And a single strand of golden hair.

A surging wave caught the bottle and carried it forward. The foamy crest finally toppled over, and the wave smashed against the uninhabited coast, shattering the bottle on a jagged boulder.

Sodden, the letter's pages spread apart, the ink running like dark tears. The golden hair washed away, lost in the currents.

The combers came in again, spread the glass fragments, and erased all sign of the bottle and of the note.

Part V

Two Years Later

Thirteen Years After the Burning of Ishalem

95 *Olabar*

Once the lost Nunghal wanderer became fluent enough in the Uraban language, he worked hard to convince Soldan-Shah Omra to mount an expedition that would send him home.

In two years, Asaddan had become a court sensation in Olabar, a large foreign-looking man with a wide, tanned face, thick black hair, and a gap-toothed smile. At first, he had worn familiar clothing provided by the palace, but he soon showed court tailors how to make traditional Nunghal clothing. Though he learned about Uraban culture and religion, Asaddan chose not to blend in, leveraging his strange individuality to his advantage. The people found him amusing and intriguing.

From her perspective as a similar foreigner in this land, Istar understood exactly how he felt. She had lived more than a dozen years in the Olabar palace, five as a slave and seven as a wife of the soldan-shah. Even though she wore the appropriate silks, and even though the soldan-shah had made it quite clear that she was his *wife* and must be respected, Istar did not fit in. After the attempt on Saan's life during the hunt for the Golden Fern, her quarters had been moved close to the center of the palace, but it still did not seem like home. Despite her changed name, she could never forget that she came from Tierra; she did not renounce her faith in Aiden, though she could no longer practice it. But she had survived, and her son had survived. She had done what was necessary. And now she had a different life, a different husband, and two daughters as well.

In Omra's throne room, Istar sat cross-legged on a turquoise cushion, her hair bound in four braids now, staring at the inlaid map of soldanates on the floor. She had chosen her place next to an open window where a cool breeze drifted in, carrying with it the faint cacophony of Olabar's streets. She would offer Omra her opinions about the morning's business later, if he asked for them.

On the far side of the chamber sat dark-haired Cliaparia, who devoted most of her attention to resenting Istar rather than listening to the cases that supplicants brought before the soldan-shah. Omra rarely talked with her about political matters.

As expected, Asaddan's request provided the main reason for the session. The big Nunghal, who now spoke nearly flawless Uraban, stood at the base of the soldan-shah's dais. "Soldan-Shah, I have described the hills and the herds of my homeland. I have told you of the fertile grasslands and vast plains that lie beyond the Great Desert. I beg you to send your representatives on a great and perilous journey that offers many rewards." He had learned to speak eloquently, and his passion was not feigned, though his missing tooth gave him something of a whistle when he talked. He tapped the center of his broad chest. "I can lead you there. I will be your ambassador to the khan. I long to see my homeland again." Asaddan tossed his mane of ebony hair, and the listeners muttered to one another, obviously feeling sorry for him.

Old Imir entered then, causing quite a stir, since he rarely showed any interest in the business of Uraba anymore. Omra's father had gained weight since his retirement; though he still shaved his head and chin, his features were saturnine, and he perspired more heavily. He grinned as he walked in, sandaled feet clicking on the tiled floor. "I beg you to heed this man, my son. The rest of the world awaits! Great adventures beckon!" He lowered his voice. "I will offer my personal fortune to fund this expedition, on one condition—that I accompany him."

Istar was pleased to see the courage of the plump old soldan-shah. Though this man had been the leader of the Urabans at the beginning of the war, she had never considered him her personal enemy. The old man had never really wanted war with Tierra, but the sikaras had pushed for the conflict and given him no alternative, just as many parties were now doing to Omra.

Twelve-year-old Saan sat next to his mother, fidgeting but attentive. At the mention of trekking to lands never before seen by any Uraban, his blue eyes shone. He whispered to her now, "May I join my grandfather? Please let me accompany him. Nobody has ever gone as far!"

"Asaddan has certainly gone there," she said patiently. "And all of his people live there."

"I meant *Urabans*, Mother!"

Istar's initial reaction was to insist it was too dangerous, but she knew that it was also dangerous for him to remain here in Olabar. Saan had survived too many "accidents" for them to be coincidences, and Istar had no reason to believe the threats would ever stop, short of the young man's murder. Though she had still found no proof of Cliaparia's involvement, she never let down her guard.

As if sensing her thoughts, Istar saw the other woman shoot a glance at them. Cliaparia, married to Omra for thirteen years, and just past the age of thirty, had given her husband only one daughter in all that time. She had not managed to bear the son that the soldan-shah — that *Cliaparia* — so desperately needed.

But Istar had, at last.

The baby boy, her fourth child, had been born only a month earlier, thus becoming the true firstborn son of the soldan-shah. Omra's young third wife, Naori, was also pregnant, but that didn't matter. Now that he had his heir, the line of succession was clear. Cliaparia was not part of that line.

As old Imir stood alongside the burly Nunghal, Istar acknowledged that Saan might be safer if he left Olabar, if he had his own adventure. Her son's enthusiasm reminded her of when Criston had felt the call of the sea, so passionate to serve aboard the *Luminara*, wanting to sail off to lands unknown....

Let Saan go beyond the most distant soldanate, she decided. He got along well with his surrogate grandfather, a man who liked to talk about his own amazing (and possibly fictitious) experiences as much as he enjoyed hearing new tales. Though it hurt her to say the words aloud, just as it had been difficult to say goodbye to Criston that last night in Calay, she spoke warmly. "You will go on the expedition, Saan, if it is in my power to allow it."

Inside her comfortable home, Sen Sherufa na-Oa spread out her drawings and charts, sketching in the information that Asaddan had provided. The big Nunghal sat beside Imir, his brown eyes bright with interest, while the former soldan-shah seemed particularly delighted just to be in Sherufa's presence. "And what have you found for us, my dear?"

"I am not your 'dear,' " she said teasingly, then pointed down at one of the sketches, as well as records from previous Missinia soldans. "We already knew, and Asaddan has verified, that there are strong prevailing winds over this section of the continent. They blow consistently southward for several months of the year, then reverse themselves and blow northward."

Imir frowned, his plump face florid. "Now, that might be interesting if we had sailing ships, but this is a desert—not a drop of water to be found."

"Therefore we need new kinds of ships," Sherufa said. "In perusing all the volumes in my library, I've discovered concepts developed by the greatest Saedran minds. One involves a large sack filled with heated air, which can lift heavy things. The inventor conceived this design as a sort of detached crane, a way to raise extremely large loads. I propose that if such a thing could be used to raise the framework of a ship above the ground, then you could set sail high above the dunes, as if they were water and your vessel were a sailing ship."

Imir looked down at the drawings. "A balloon? We would ride a balloon?"

"You would ride a *ship*," Sherufa gently corrected. "The balloon would simply lift it. Several layers of Yuarej silk, waterproofed and lined, should be adequate. And if the boat itself were constructed of a lightweight material—woven reeds, wicker work—it would weigh virtually nothing. The expedition could cruise across the Great Desert, riding the prevailing winds until you reach the land of the Nunghals. Half a year later, you ride the breezes back northward. The crossing should be simple."

"Not 'simple,' " Asaddan cautioned. "But possible."

"Wonderful!" Imir exclaimed. "Perfectly wonderful, my dear. I knew that if anyone could find a solution, it would be you. How I wish Uraba had more treasures such as yourself. Therefore, I have a reward for you. You have lived your life vicariously, and I have enjoyed your tales. But now I offer you the chance of a lifetime: Come with us. You and I will peel back the mysteries of the world."

Sherufa quailed at the thought; she had never even left Olabar. She read about grand quests and epic journeys, but preferred to experience them from her armchair, looking at books and maps rather than enduring storms and privation. "It is not necessary, Imir. I will help you to plan—"

He waved her off. "None of that! A twelve-year-old boy is eager to come, so it's perfectly safe. Come now, remember all those stories you told me? I know this is what you want. Believe me, you won't regret it."

Sherufa was not so certain.

Asaddan drew a breath, sounding like a blacksmith's bellows, and looked with sincere gratitude toward Imir and Sherufa. "If one man with a few animals can make the journey, certainly a flying ship with all the resources of Uraba is much better. We will be fine."

Istar lay next to Omra at night, listening to breezes stir the silk hangings at the balcony and windows. "He should go, Omra. He wants to go."

"If my father considers it safe, then I will consider it safe," Omra answered. "It will be good for the boy to experience new things. He can take care of himself—I've seen him do it. But even now that we have a new son, my heir, I insist on finding an appropriate and important place for Saan. He is..." Omra was at a loss for words.

Istar felt no edge of bitterness when she spoke. "You have always been good to Saan. I never expected that when I agreed to marry you."

She could barely see his wry smile in the shadows of the bed-chamber. "I love our two daughters, and, yes, the new baby is my only male heir. Even so, you know how I feel about Saan."

"Yes." Istar nodded. "I do.

Work crews prepared for departure on the caravan south toward Missinia. Carts were loaded with reeds harvested from marshes in the lowlands of Abilan. Pack animals were harnessed. Sikaras burned prayer strips asking for good weather and a safe journey.

Istar would stay behind in the palace to tend her new baby, assisted by her dedicated handmaiden, a doe-eyed young woman named Altiara. Istar's two daughters were now old enough to be in traditional school, and Adreala—the older one—would soon be brought to the Urecari church for her second testing, to see if she was worthy of becoming a sikara herself.

As golden morning sunlight slanted through the open windows, Saan came to say goodbye to his mother. His clothes were already packed and loaded aboard the caravan. Istar had selected the garments herself, remembering what Windcatch fishermen used to wear when they set off on long voyages. Though Saan brought one set of fine clothes in case he needed to meet with important Nunghal nobles, Istar chose the rest of his garments for durability, knowing the arduous journey that lay in store for him.

Saan proudly displayed a new medallion around his neck, toying with its leather thong. "The soldan-shah gave me this." He turned it in his fingers so that it caught the sunlight. "He told me to wear it, and to think about him, and Olabar, and Urec. We will go to these new lands and bring Urec's Log to the Nunghals. We will teach them the truth."

As always, Istar held her past close to herself, though the curling spiral of the unfurling fern often unnerved her. "*Two* brothers sailed from Terravitae. Perhaps you should also mention Aiden."

Saan scowled. "But I hate the Aidenists! We know the terrible things they've done."

In the boy's eyes, Istar saw a hint of the raiders storming the streets of Windcatch, burning the small kirk that Prester Fennan could not defend. They had killed old Telha without mercy; they had captured *her*, dragged her across half the world. "Terrible things have been done by both sides, Saan."

He seemed offended by her suggestion. "Nothing so bad as what they do to us. Think about the bloodbath in Outer Wahilir — Soldan Attar, his family, more than a hundred nobles and merchants, all poisoned by an Aidenist assassin! And all those churches burned, the villages attacked."

"Saan, you are old enough to realize there are two sides to any story. You know that I originally came from Tierra. I did not ask to be brought here."

Saan challenged his mother, staring at her in disbelief. "But you were a slave — and now you're the wife of the soldan-shah. You live in a palace. Think of all the wonders we have! My little brother is the zarif of Uraba. You were saved from a lifetime of ignorance and squalor!"

Istar picked up the baby and held him in a soft blanket in her arms. She sat back in a chair and regarded Saan. "Do not believe everything you've heard. A happy life is not necessarily based on appearances and possessions." She gazed at the peacefully sleeping baby, who was now six months old.

"You cannot deny that the soldan-shah loves you, Mother. I can see that this pleases you every time you look at him."

She nodded slowly, taking care not to show a flicker in her expression. "Yes, you're right." Yes, she had gained a measure of contentment in her life here in Uraba, with her children, her position in the palace. She could not admit that she was *happy* — a hard part of her would never allow that — but she was not as unhappy as she had tried to make herself believe for the past seven years.

Istar longed to tell Saan the truth as she stroked the infant's smooth head. She had asked Omra to name the boy Criston, and he had allowed it, not knowing what it meant to her. She had never revealed the identity of her true husband, and she had — thankfully — found an obscure reference to another sailor called "Criston" in the scripture of Urec's Log. No one else would know.

"Just remember," she told Saan. "You do not have all the information."

96 *Iboria*

The Arkship was under construction—the most magnificent vessel men had ever dared to build. Kjelnar had at first trembled at the responsibility of overseeing the project, and now he reveled in it. It was not hubris, but respect. No one had ever attempted such a titanic work to honor Ondun's creation and Aiden's quest, and every aspect of the majestic ship had to be perfect, the best.

In the dense Iborian pine forests, Kjelnar had spent all his life walking the paths, studying the trees, and marking specimens of particular interest to him. Expanses of dark evergreens covered the northern wilderness, but Kjelnar imagined that he had seen them all. With a long knotted string, he measured the circumferences of the trunks. He stared upward, using a bob and measuring stick to plumb the straightness of the trees. Only the perfect...the best.

He'd had his eye on this particular tree for much of his life, waiting to find a use sufficiently grand for such a specimen. A tree like this could not be used in just any ship, but as the main mast for King Korastine's new Arkship. There could be no greater glory.

Back in Calay, the king had cleared Shipbuilders' Bay of other projects so that the sawmills, dry dock, and cranes could be used for the Arkship. Some of the merchants' harbors and part of the Saedran District had been commandeered to continue work on refitting warships and building new ones.

Kjelnar had never before constructed such a large, ambitious vessel. He spent nearly two years bringing the enormous project to this point: drawing up the detailed plan for the Arkship, building models, supervising the construction of new dry docks, erecting superstructures, cranes, blocks and tackle, everything the giant vessel would need. Seasoned wood was floated down from Iboria, each log chosen by him and cut by the sawmills into the lumber that would be needed.

Kjelnar supervised the laying of the Arkship's keel, using the best seasoned wood. Although many Calay dockworkers volunteered their labors, Kjelnar hand-picked Iborian workmen to trim, steam, and bend the beams, then carve them to perfection. The first sets of the great ribs were set in place, so the Arkship looked like the skeleton of an enormous beast.

Satisfied with the Arkship's progress and knowing that his crews could continue their work without him, Kjelnar returned to the forests of Iboria so that these loggers could cut down the main tree.

He led a crew of burly Iborian woodcutters on an expedition deep inland, needing to be there himself, to guide the work and contribute his own sweat. Pride in workmanship allowed him to steer no other course. He and his team followed a river upstream, then branched off into a dense valley carved by a swift creek. The mainmast tree stood like a sentinel at the head of the side drainage, and even from a distance, Kjelnar admired the pine. It stood like nature's obelisk before the imagined kirk of the wilderness.

Leaving their shallow boats on the boulders at the rocky edge of the rushing creek, his men trudged through the underbrush. Wiping sweat out of his eyes, brushing mosquitoes away from his face, the shipwright guided them along winding trails used only by animals, remembering the path to his prize. When they reached the base of the kingly tree, the Iborian treecutters nodded their approval and clapped Kjelnar on his broad back.

"That is a worthy tree," said Ragnal, one of the bearded northmen.

On the hike up the basin, Kjelnar had begun calculating the best way to bring the great pine down to the main river; the wide creek was swollen with runoff, but too many large rocks and abrupt falls would hinder its passage. The men would have to guide the giant tree along the valley's edge, using the creek when possible and the bank when necessary. It would be an arduous journey, taking many days, but his men were strong. And they were doing this for Aiden.

When the group reached the end of the valley at the head-waters of the creek, Kjelnar explained his plan, and the men deferred to him, since he had more expertise in cutting and moving logs than any other Iborian. To prepare a path for the tree's passage, he told the men to cut down other trees and clear the way. The logs they felled would have been prime wood for construction; here, though, the men laid them down as rollers and guides to move the mainmast tree.

While the crew did the preparatory work, Kjelnar climbed the majestic pine until he was high above the other treetops, holding on to the trunk and looking up to the sky, the cold mountains, the extensive dark forests, marveling at the glory of Ondun. Working his way back down, he sawed off branches, and when the tree stood stripped of its boughs, it already looked like a tow-ering mast. Staring at the immense, perfect trunk, he knew he had made the right choice. It was time.

At the tree's base, the men used their axes to cut a deep gouge and then set to work with their saws. The loggers did the back-breaking work in shifts. Buckets were hauled from the stream to dump on the hot saw blades so they could keep going. They cut for nearly a full day before the giant pine teetered, then surrendered to gravity. It bent, slowly at first, then picked up speed, falling gracefully and precisely where Kjelnar had directed.

The men rushed forward, working together, muscles straining, to align the huge trunk onto the roller logs; next they began the arduous journey of moving it several feet at a time. Every step had to be done perfectly. After two days, they built a new camp, and worked again the following day, and the next. By the time the mainmast tree reached the river, the men were exhausted to the point of collapse.

But Kjelnar would not let them stop. They needed to get the tree into the water and follow it downstream with their boats. They could rest during the voyage to Calay. He admired the exceptional tree as the crew wrestled it into the deeper water, already envisioning the finished Arkship, which had haunted his dreams for two years now.

Yes, it was perfect. The best.

97 *Ishalem*

After his glorious achievement in Tenér—more than a hundred Urecari poisoned, including Soldan Attar, his two wives, and several children—Prester Hannes was in less of a hurry to return to Calay. He still had so much to accomplish.

He had remained there until he burned another Urecari church along with its sikara and its congregation. For years now, his legend had grown. Mothers told stories to their children about a shadowman who killed the "faithful," who burned churches and poisoned their leaders. There was no holy ground, no safe place for them. Hannes liked the fact that they were scared.

The delusions of their faith made them blind to what he was doing, and why. Fearful, the people turned against anyone who looked remotely Tierran, and many scapegoats were killed. But they died for a good cause.

Still, his extravagant bloodbaths in Tenér sparked such outrage that he had become exceptionally careful. He had been glimpsed too many times over the years. Though he now wore different clothes, he was still a stranger, and strangers were looked upon with suspicion and fear. Travel was dangerous for him.

He moved north past the city of Khenara until at last he reached Ishalem. Ishalem! A burned ruin...a wasteland where once a great city had stood.

Many years had passed since the great fire, but the wound had festered rather than healed. When Hannes saw the blackened hills, the outlines of streets, the fossils of collapsed buildings, his hatred for the Urecari grew beyond measure. How could Ondun ever forgive them for the damage they had done?

After more than a decade, the city remained a graveyard. Even in the best of times, the rocky soil of the isthmus had been unsuitable for growing enough crops to feed more than a small population, and only scrub brush had grown back since the fire. Anyone who came there now — with the emptiness everywhere, the ruins overgrown with thorny weeds, the land crumbly with weathered ash — would believe they had been sent to a kind of purgatory. Surely Ondun had turned His back on this place.

Worst of all was the central hill that overlooked both sides of Ishalem — a barren hill now, showing no sign of Aiden's sacred Arkship. It was gone, all gone...but his faith remained.

He wept as he recalled the city's former glory. That last night was so vivid in his mind — the bright flames, the collapsing

Urecari church, the precious amulet he had gained and then lost again — that his scars began to throb. How could Aiden have let this happen?

Hannes saw only a few huts and tents erected by the most tenacious pilgrims, widely separated from one another in different parts of what had been the great city. By now he had expected the city to be rebuilt, loyal Aidenists reclaiming the ground, constructing a new metropolis to replace what the Urecari had destroyed. Instead this was a damned place, shunned by both religions. He didn't know how long he could bear to stay here, but he knew he must.

Finding a sheltered spot without too much ash or debris, he used stones and scraps of collapsed building timbers to make a modest shelter. He kept to himself, avoiding the other pilgrims. If they were Urecari, he had no interest in talking to them; if they were Aidenists, they would look at his stolen clothing, assume he was a heretic, and surely throw rocks at him. In order to survive, he decided to steal food from other pilgrim camps, killing a few more Urecari if necessary. He would wait until nightfall.

At dusk, when the Urecari were at their sunset prayers, Hannes crept out from his shelter and was startled to see five soldiers on horseback — Uraban guards, armed with curved swords and angry expressions. Before he could duck back into hiding, they spotted him, and he heard the rumble of hooves, the snorting of horses.

Hannes stood to face the circle of riders, letting his shoulders slump, averting his face. Though his heart pounded and he felt great fear, he fell back on his false persona and blurted out his words. "I am but a faithful pilgrim, come all the way from Olabar so that I may lay my eyes on Ishalem." He had no qualms about lying, since lying to a follower of Urec was not exactly lying.

The kel of the Urecari group sneered down at him, unimpressed. "Any man may say he's a pilgrim."

"For what other purpose would I come here?" Hannes wiped his blackened hands on his pantaloons. "What else is there, but the memory of Ishalem?"

The kel had an uneven black beard, and his white uniform was now gray, ash stained and improperly washed too many times. "We have orders to arrest any beggars or lone wanderers. Such a man—or men—caused great harm across Uraba, and you fit the description."

Hannes tried to keep his voice from cracking. "A man alone, on a pilgrimage to Ishalem? That is your only description of this criminal?"

"It's good enough for us." The kel gestured to his men and spurred his horse forward.

"Wait, wait!" Hannes could not let these men take him. Only a few more miles, and he would be back in Tierra. "I received a vision in a dream to come to Ishalem. I gave up everything to make the journey. Ondun Himself must have guided me."

"Then Ondun Himself guided you into our arms," the kel said. Some of the weary and hard-bitten soldiers looked sympathetic to Hannes's story, but their captain was uninterested. "Our instructions are to take every suspicious person into custody."

Two of his soldiers slid down from their mounts, pulling out leather thongs, and though Hannes struggled, they bound his hands behind his back. "But I have done nothing. I am innocent! I live only to serve Ondun." And that was the truth.

The kel merely shrugged. Three additional riders from

the kel's scout party came up, leading five more pilgrims who had been similarly arrested. "You will be taken to a slave galley in the old Uraban harbor and be shipped across the Middlesea to work at Gremurr. You will serve Ondun—in the mines."

98 *Missinia Soldanate*

The caravan toiled across the grassy hills toward where the floating sand coracle would be built at the edge of the Great Desert. Saan was comfortable with the rocking, swaying gait of the slow-moving pack animals; he imagined it might be like the rolling deck of a ship in restless waters.

Saan had spent so much time with Omra, looking at tactical maps and picturing those far-off places in his mind. Now the world lay before him... and it certainly seemed larger than the maps implied.

Sen Sherufa na-Oa rode beside them, showing a strange mixture of excitement and anxiety for the long journey; the rolling landscape intrigued her, but Saan could tell she would rather have been home in Olabar.

His grandfather kept his horse close to the Saedran woman, always trying to engage her in conversation. Imir told many long, drawn-out stories from his years as soldan-shah. More than once, he bragged about his bravery or wisdom, telling his exploits for the Saedran woman's benefit as much as his own.

"Did I tell you about the time a great sea serpent nearly wrecked my dromond on my voyage to Ishalem to sign the Edict? It was a huge serpent." Imir stretched out his arms to their full width. "Razor-edged fins and fangs as long as your arm. It even breathed fire."

Sherufa commented wryly, "So your ship burned in the waters, then?"

"No, the flames missed us." Imir drew himself up. "I ordered the sailors to row backward and prepare their harpoons for a fight. Ur-Sikara Lukai was terrified, of course, but I stood at the helm and faced down the sea serpent."

"The beast must have sensed your great strength. You were willing to wrestle him out of the water, no doubt?"

"Of course—anything to protect my crew."

Asaddan did not like to ride in formation. The big Nunghal urged his mount forward and scouted ahead, then dropped back to speak with the other travelers, restless, anxious to be back home. Imir seemed a trifle jealous when he chatted so easily with Sen Sherufa, who had taught him the Uraban language.

After the caravan crossed the hills, Saan looked for the first time upon the endless blond expanse of barren dunes, sculpted sand like frozen waves. He stared so hard that his eyes stung from dust and sand borne on the brisk breezes.

Sen Sherufa said, "The currents are turbulent right now because the prevailing winds are about to shift. We will have several weeks to construct our sand coracle before the wind gathers its full strength."

"Plenty of time," Imir said. "We've brought along the finest laborers and materials, and your plans are no doubt brilliant, my dear."

"I did not draw the plans." Sherufa blushed. "I merely gathered them."

"That's the brilliant part—we could never have done this without you."

In a gully where a tiny seasonal stream petered out before reaching the dunes, the Missinians had already established a work camp, waiting for the caravan to arrive. Two horses cantered up to meet Imir's party as they approached, one bearing Soldan Xivir, the other with a matronly looking woman in her mid-fifties.

The soldan of Missinia raised his hand. "Imir, old friend! I brought my sister with me — I knew you two would like to spend time together."

The former soldan-shah looked awkward and uncomfortable, and suddenly Saan realized who the woman was: Lithio, the mother of Omra. Imir's first wife.

"My husband and I have much to share after all this time. He has been somewhat remiss in sending me letters." Lithio arched her eyebrows. "It's been at least eleven years, has it not, Imir?"

"I was busy."

With a glance at Sen Sherufa, Lithio gave a wry smile. "A new wife? I don't recognize this one, but I could have lost count. There was Asha after me, then Villiki—ah, but they're both gone now, aren't they? There must have been more wives in the intervening years." She didn't seem to have lost count at all.

"As I said, I have been busy." Imir was terse now.

"I am not his wife," Sherufa said. "I am a Saedran scholar brought along for this mission."

Lithio's lips pulled together in a skeptical pout. "Of course he would take probably the only female Saedran scholar in all of Uraba, and an attractive one at that."

Soldan Xivir ignored the interplay between his sister and her husband, turning his attention to Asaddan. "Nunghal, you have recovered well since I first saw you brought into my court on the verge of death."

"With all the food in Olabar, I have grown fat." He chuckled and patted his rock-hard stomach. "I hope I do not weigh down the balloon."

Xivir looked out at the expanse of sand. "I hope your tales have merit, because it sounds like you're chasing sand devils across the dunes."

"I am chasing my knowledge — and the winds."

Lithio seemed to notice Saan for the first time, and the wrinkled lines around her eyes grew tighter as her gaze narrowed. "Now, he's a strange boy. He looks as odd as a Nunghal. Does he speak our language, too?"

"It *is* my language," Saan said, a bit defensive.

Imir flushed and introduced the young man. "This is Saan, the son of Omra's second wife Istar."

"I thought his first wife was named Istar. The one that died? This boy doesn't look at all like Omra." She seemed to disapprove.

"The first Istar died in childbirth. The second Istar is Tierran, and Saan is hers." Imir drew himself straighter, standing up for the boy. "The soldan-shah adopted the boy and raised him as his own, but now Istar has given him a true son."

Lithio frowned, trying to make sense of what she'd learned. "A true son? Ah, so now this boy is no longer needed. That is why Omra is sending him on this desert journey."

Saan quirked a smile rather than taking offense. "No, he sent me because I asked to go...and so that I could meet you."

"Such a sweet boy, even if you do have a strange appearance."

Xivir interjected, getting down to business. "We can speak of court gossip and wives and children in the tents tonight. Let us unload supplies and get your workers settled in the camp."

Not far from the camp lay bitumen fields, the source of tar and black oil used for construction and fuel. Several pools of sulfurous-smelling water bubbled up nearby, ringed by carefully placed rocks. The warm pools were considered a luxury, and Lithio insisted on going there to bathe after dark. She wanted Imir to come along with her, and he insisted on bringing Sen Sherufa. The Saedran woman appeared so uncomfortable at the prospect—yet unable to turn down Imir's request—that she suggested Saan join them as well.

As they settled into the pool, Saan felt the warm waters caress his muscles. Imir sighed as he let himself sink deeper. They both wore waistcloths, and Sherufa, in a thin but concealing gown, immersed herself up to her shoulders in the murky pool. Much to the young man's surprise, Lithio stripped naked and simply climbed in. Imir's eyes widened, and he seemed embarrassed; Sherufa didn't know what to do. Saan courteously looked away from the nude woman who might have been his grandmother.

"You've gained some weight, but you are quite attractive with your head and beard shaved," Lithio said to Imir. "I remember your hair was quite curly. I loved oiling it."

"Yes, you did," Imir snapped. "That's why I shaved it off."

"And you, Sen Sherufa—you have designs on my husband? His other wives must have exhausted him, though I seem to be the only one left, and he almost never comes to see me. Someone of your ... age, might be a refreshing contrast."

Imir gave a weary sigh. "You and I never had much of a spark in our marriage, Lithio. Politics is politics. You got what you wanted."

"I still get what I want." Lithio chuckled, lounging back in the warm pool. "Oh, don't be so scandalized, Imir. I am merely teasing you. I wish you the best. I always have." She looked at Sherufa. "You should marry him — he is a good husband."

The Saedran woman climbed out of the water with a mumbled apology. As she stood dripping, drying in the warm night air, Imir stared at how the once-chaste gown now clung tightly to her chest, outlining her breasts and nipples in clear detail.

"I believe I've had enough of a soaking for now." Sherufa looked innocently at Lithio. "I wouldn't want to prune up like that. Or are those wrinkles?"

Lithio's mouth hung open as the Saedran woman walked off into the darkness. Then she began to laugh uproariously, and Imir joined in. "You see, Lithio? She keeps me humble."

"Not enough." Lithio caught Saan's gaze as he regarded her. "And what are you looking at, young man? Ogling me? Or scheming against me?"

"Just assessing whether or not you are a threat," Saan said. "It seems to me that even far from Olabar, the politics among the wives of a soldan-shah are similar."

Imir burst out laughing. "You see how perceptive the boy is?"

"Perhaps too perceptive," Lithio said in a thoughtful tone. "But it's good that he stands up for himself."

99 *Calay*

In the castle's Naval Room, numerous shelves held sympathetic models of every single ship in the Tierran navy, each replica built by a master model-maker from materials twinned to the larger vessel. Though the military strategists in Calay could do nothing to affect a ship out on patrol, the twinned models did keep Anjine and her court advisers aware of which ships remained intact and which had been damaged or sunk.

She easily located the model of the *Raven*, the fast patrol ship to which Mateo had been assigned for the past several years; she had its spot in the Naval Room memorized by now. Commanded by Captain Trawna now, the *Raven* had seen its share of sea battles. Recently, Anjine had received a long list of promotions from Comdar Delnas, who regularly moved men up in rank to replace those lost in the war. Mateo had finally been named a first officer, and his future was bright. Anjine had no doubt he'd soon become a captain in his own right. His skill counted more than his years, and his experiences at sea had already hardened him. Because she knew *him* so well, she could tell that Mateo was leaving a great many details out of his letters.

The model of the *Raven* was intact, and so the actual ship must be intact. As always, Anjine breathed easier, knowing Mateo was safe.

Alone in the Naval Room, she walked slowly along the shelves, smelling the wood, the paint, the shellac of the models. Advisers inspected the replicas every day. In the past two years, she had greatly increased the size of the display shelves and even required that models be built (after the fact) of existing Tierran merchant ships, in addition to the war vessels. Thus, Calay could more accurately monitor the casualties of the war.

In the years since the death of Queen Ilrida, King Korastine retained his crown and continued his kingly duties, but the fire in him had been quenched. He no longer burned to prosecute the war and launch massive assaults against the Urabans. The enemy had continued their harassment that caused such pain and suffering, but not to the extent of a full-fledged crusade. Anjine's father suggested that the Uraban soldan-shah might have suffered a tragedy equal to his own, and thereby also lost his heart for the war.

But she refused to gamble on that. She considered it just as likely that the Urecari were up to something. More and more, she had taken an interest — and then an active role — in watching the new warships, while her father devoted his energy and enthusiasm to his ambitious expedition to find Terravitae.

While Korastine — limping from the gout that had grown increasingly serious in his knee — spent his days with shipwright Kjelnar and Sen Leo na-Hadra planning the epic voyage, Anjine handled more of the kingdom's daily affairs. Listening to the repeated requests in Mateo's letters, she quietly ordered the construction of several more warships in different yards.

She kept all of Mateo's letters safe in a chest in her bedchamber. When she felt lonely or sad at the way the war was proceeding, she would read the old letters at random. She could imagine his voice, always telling her stories, always trying to bring a smile to her face. "Dear Tolli," each letter began. Mateo never grew tired of the old joke, and she never grew tired of hearing it.

Just two days previously, a small cargo ship coming up the coast had delivered letters to Calay, including one from Mateo. Receiving it, Anjine excused herself from a tedious tariff-negotiation meeting and withdrew to a window seat out in the corridor, where she sat with her cat. Accepting the attention as his due, Tycho curled up in her lap as she read.

"It rained last night," Mateo wrote, "a drenching downpour that went on for hours in a constant stream. Every man aboard was soaked and cold, but the seas weren't rough, and we sailed right through it. Our water barrels were filled up, and the crew came out on deck just to get a good wash. Now the decks are cleaner than they've been since we left port!

"Then — ah, you should have seen it! — after the rain passed, the clouds parted and the full moon came out. With the high mist in the air, a halo surrounded the moon. It was beautiful, Tolli. I wish you could have been here with me. After the rain, the smell was so wonderful I just wanted to laugh out loud.

"Remember the time when the two of us had to hide outside under an awning during a downpour? We just watched the water run down the roofs, through the streets and gutters. Remember how afterward everything seemed entirely washed clean?"

Anjine smiled. Of course she remembered.

"That was the time we decided to go to the Butchers' District to see the tannery vats and leather workings. It always stinks so much that we had never bothered to visit it in all the times we explored Calay. Nobody could walk the streets in that end of the city without holding a bundle of aromatic herbs to his nose. But after that big rain, we thought we could handle the stench. Of course, even the downpour couldn't wash all that away."

Mateo's letter abruptly changed subjects, and he talked about his fellow crewmen, of the fishing villages they had seen, how long it had been since they'd spotted a Urecari sail. Anjine frowned, scanning the lines again. He hadn't finished the story about the Butchers' District, but she remembered what else had happened that day. . . .

She and Mateo had been lighthearted after the rainstorm, their clothes damp and mud-stained. They ran to the Butchers' District, wanting to see what went on there. In the tannery section, hides were scraped, stretched, and then soaked in large stone vats of foul-smelling tanning chemicals. Leatherworkers cut sections for their uses; cobblers came to buy materials for boots and shoes.

Farther on, cattle and sheep made an unsettling din, lowing and crying. When Anjine and Mateo bounded around the corner to the open area of corrals, the two stumbled to a halt to see large-muscled men *wrestling* with the frantic penned animals. A man grabbed a bleating sheep by its neck and dragged it forward into a chute, where another man smashed the center of the sheep's skull with a heavy mallet. Two more men hefted the carcass and, with a flash of their knives, stripped it of its fleece, sawed the bones at the joints, and cut the meat into large bloody pieces.

Men wielded even larger mallets for the cattle, while some thrust long sharpened iron rods into the doomed animals' throats, spilling the blood into buckets and then catching the heavy beasts as they collapsed, butchering them even before they had stopped bleeding out.

While Anjine had known intellectually what happened here, she had never witnessed it herself. Mateo puked into the gutter. The two of them stumbled away from the horrific scenes, no longer laughing, no longer even able to speak.

She pushed the letter aside with a deep frown. *Why* had he brought up that story . . . and then left out the worst part? It made her wonder what other horrors Mateo was censoring from his letters. Anjine wasn't sure she wanted to know. . . .

Now, in the Naval Room, she brushed her fingertips across the ship model on its special shelf, as though by sympathetic connection she could reach out and touch Mateo onboard the *Raven.*

"Come back safe," she whispered. "Please, come back safe."

Hovering around the construction dock in Shipbuilders' Bay, Sen Leo picked up scraps from the Arkship—shavings from the deck boards, snippets of rope, tiny swatches of sailcloth—and stuffed them into a satchel. He studied each piece, memorizing its contours and committing to his mind the origin of the bits.

He had a copy of the Arkship plans back in the temple vault, and another copy in his personal library. Saedran artisans and craftsmen had offered to help him, but he wanted to do the model-building work himself. This was too important.

Up and down the docks, he heard pounding and shouting, the creak of pulleys, and the crack of wood from the Arkship's construction berth. Slowly and meticulously, the massive vessel was taking shape.

"She's a giant, isn't she?" said one of the workers, lounging under an eave where he could keep himself dry from the drizzle but still see the Arkship. "Uses as much material as ten or fifteen battleships. We'd be better off with fifteen battleships, eh?"

"It's not my place to criticize the king," Sen Leo said sharply, "nor is it yours. Who can put a price on discovery and dreams?"

The man grumbled something about Saedrans, and Sen Leo trudged away with his carefully gathered materials. Tugging the hood over his head, though his long gray hair was already damp, he crossed the bridge back to the Saedran District and took his samples to the temple.

As he walked, Sen Leo greeted people he'd known most of his life, waving to apothecaries, scribes, painters. Inside the temple, he passed through the hidden door built into the mosaic and descended to the Mappa Mundi vault. There, he lit additional lamps and emptied his satchel, spreading the tiny pieces out on the table.

Before him, the sympathetic model was nearly as complete as the Arkship itself. Since the laying of the keel, Sen Leo had taken pieces of every component, trimmed them to scale, carved each item, and assembled an exact duplicate, bit by bit. Once the Arkship sailed, this model — held in the castle — would be the only clear link with home.

Using a sharp knife, he whittled one of the wood pieces so that it fit where it belonged on the replica, on the small deck aft. Before the Arkship departed, he would also make sure to obtain locks of King Korastine's hair and Aldo's hair to strengthen the magical ties between the actual ship, the crew, and the model.

And, if possible, he would go along himself, for if the world was to be opened at last and the Saedran prophecy revealed, then Sen Leo na-Hadra intended to be there in person.

100 Raven

From the deck of the battered patrol ship, Mateo scanned the sea and the coastline for any sign of Urecari raiders. It had been more than a week since they'd glimpsed a colorful silken sail, but they all knew the enemy ships were out there, and the soldiers aboard the *Raven* were spoiling for a fight.

Ship-to-ship battle was terrifying yet energizing, and Mateo had already seen two of his captains die in seagoing engagements. He was under no illusion that his new rank as first mate would gain him riches or glory, but it did earn him respect, and he was sure that Anjine would be impressed. But what would she think if she knew how difficult it really was?

Captain Trawna used signal flags to communicate with the five other ships in the patrol group. The watchful vessels plied the southern waters where Urecari raiders were most likely to strike (although several weeks earlier a surprise enemy fleet had arced north all the way to the southern tip of Iboria).

From the lookout nest, a sailor called, "Torch! I see a signal torch!" The crewmen scrambled to the port side, gazing toward the coastline. In the distance they saw a smoky fire and bright orange flame atop the stone tower.

"Haul anchor and set sail," Captain Trawna ordered, and signal flags passed the message around the patrol group. All six small vessels stretched their canvas, caught the wind, and picked up speed. In the past six years a new network of signal towers had been built at regular intervals along the coast, even where no navigation hazards existed. Someone on the shore had issued a call for help.

The patrol group raced southward, catching the current. Mateo consulted the charts, and after marking the locations of prominent villages, guessed the site of this unexpected strike: a village called Reefspur.

When the wind tapered off and blew in a contrary direction, the six captains ordered the drums brought out, and the sailors began rowing to bring the patrol ships to their destination. They had no time to lose.

An extended reef created a calm harbor on the coast, and a thriving village had been built at the site. There, the patrol group came upon a pair of large Urecari war galleys. The enemy raiders had closed in on Reefspur, expecting little resistance from the villagers, whom they had already raided a decade earlier. Armed to the teeth, the Uraban soldiers pulled their small rowboats toward shore, but when the Tierran patrol ships hove into view, the Uraban sailors still aboard the main galleys banged alarm gongs to call their shipmates back. With a flurry, the raider rowboats turned around, but the Tierran patrol ships sliced in and cut them off at the harbor's edge.

Mateo and his exhilarated shipmates looked upon their prey with an almost savage hunger. Two Tierran ships remained in the outer waters beyond the reef to block any escape route, while the *Raven* and the other three shallow-draft vessels crowded into the Reefspur harbor, driving the two large Uraban war galleys against the coral breakwater. From the decks, the Aidenist soldiers issued a wordless cry of challenge.

Taking charge of a small squad of archers, Mateo directed them to fire a volley down into the open, overloaded rowboats, killing dozens of Urabans like penned animals in the Butchers' District. Several raiders dove overboard to get away, but the arrows pierced the clear waters, and bristling bodies soon floated to the surface.

Mateo felt no sympathy for the Urecari at all, not after what he'd seen. They deserved the pain and death they received.

Sometimes, following the worst battles, he felt sick regret as he realized how much the war had already changed him. He was now a person he had never expected to become when he first entered his military training in Alamont Reach. But he was doing this for Tierra, for his king, and for Anjine. He would die for her, and he had already killed for her — many times.

The hot-blooded Tierrans drew swords and waved their blades at the skeleton crews aboard the Uraban war galleys. Two patrol vessels pulled alongside the first foreign warship and threw fishhook grapples to secure the vessels. The Uraban fighters faced them from the decks, snarling and shouting in their incomprehensible language.

With a heart that felt as cold as Iborian ice and as hard as the steel of his sword, Mateo turned to his captain. "Sir, these men came to prey upon a defenseless fishing village. Why not treat them like the cowards they are? Why should we let them defend themselves, when they denied our people that honor?"

Captain Trawna was intrigued, a gleam of bloodlust and revenge showing in his eyes as well. "What do you have in mind?"

Mateo closed his eyes for just a moment, remembering Ilrida's funeral ship catching fire as it sailed out to open sea, toward legendary Terravitae. "I say burn them from here. They're just raiders—our archers have a much greater range. Light our arrows and torch the war galleys, then stand back and watch them roast."

"I'm sure the crew would rather take these two as prizes, capture the Urecari as slaves." Trawna was unsure of himself. "Could be a tidy profit."

But Mateo felt no greed within him, no desire for dealing with the troublesome complexities of capturing and repairing these foreign ships, crewing them, and moving them north to Calay. He could see that the seamen wanted the same thing; many of them had lost comrades and family members in raids.

"Maybe under different circumstances, Captain. This is not a business, sir, but a war. I am willing to forgo a handful of coins if it shortens the lives of these monsters. Think of what they've done to our villages, what they intended to do here."

His fellow sailors held their swords, anxious to leap across to the decks of the war galleys. The men were already disappointed to consider killing the Urecari from a safe distance, but they certainly didn't want to let the enemy live.

The captain sensed the mood immediately. "Very well, we'll watch them roast from here." He gave the order, signaling the two Tierran patrol ships to withdraw.

Tierran archers fired a volley of blazing pitch-wrapped arrows into the two helpless Uraban war galleys. The arrows clung to the decks, the masts. Burning shafts plunged through the colorful sails, which blazed quickly, turning brown, curling, and finally raining fine ashes. Flames blinded the painted Eye of Urec in the center of each sail. Though the Uraban crew scrambled to douse the fires with buckets of seawater, they could not catch the small blazes fast enough.

In his mind Mateo saw a picture of the ruthless Urecari riders in the streets of Ishalem, throwing torches, spreading the fire, cutting down Aidenists who had simply wanted to help put out the flames. "If any of those men try to surrender, butcher them like pigs."

The *Raven*'s sailors contented themselves with that prospect. Mateo watched with no small amount of pleasure as the enemy raiders died by water, by flame, by arrow, and by sword. The patrol captains ordered the Tierran ships to drop anchor outside of Reefspur so the crews could watch until the Urecari vessels were nothing more than floating charred wrecks.

101 *Olabar Palace*

Word came to Olabar that five more Uraban fishing boats off the coast of Khenara had been boarded by Aidenist privateers, the crews murdered, and the boats captured and taken back to Tierra.

The people in the streets of the capital city howled for revenge, demanding that the soldan-shah launch an immediate attack on Tierran cities. Down in the square below the palace, they chanted for the death and damnation of all Aidenists. Careful to remain out of view for the moment, Omra eased out onto the balcony high up on the white tower; he was buffeted by the swell of voices, the thunderous waves of anger. He had to respond to it all somehow.

In the well-lit, airy chamber behind him, his advisers had gathered for hours to discuss further war plans. Their words strangled him. He needed to step outside, breathe the fresh air, and see the sun reflecting off the whitewashed buildings that crowded the city center like kneeling worshippers. When Omra stepped into full view at the balustrade, the resounding wave of cheers nearly deafened him.

The jubilant sound of the populace was not just an expression of love, respect, and admiration for their soldan-shah. They wanted him to fight back; they needed him to strike. The people pushed him to show no restraint, but he didn't know if he could give them what they demanded.

Inside the chamber, dark-skinned Ur-Sikara Erima sat beside three of her high-ranking priestesses. Hailing from Lahjar, Erima had lived her life separate from the convoluted church and soldanate politics. Chosen to succeed Ur-Sikara Lukai, Erima was a woman with no known enemies in Olabar, but also few alliances. In the eight years since assuming command of the Urecari Church, the mahogany-skinned woman had stood by her beliefs and cemented new connections, while the other sikaras scrambled to fit into the power structure. To her credit, Erima did not take rash and impulsive actions. In the palace meetings she spoke little but listened intently, so that when she did comment, her words were well considered and interesting.

Also at the council meeting sat Kel Rovik, the captain of the palace guard, Kel Unwar, the leader of Omra's horse soldiers, Kel Zarouk, a veteran of dozens of naval battles, along with representatives of merchant families, town leaders, and all of the soldanates. Zarouk was grim and impatient, waiting for Omra to return from the balcony. "It is time we take this war seriously, Soldan-Shah. This is not a mating dance with endless and tentative moves of foreplay."

Omra turned sharply. "You do not believe I take this war seriously?"

"I...I did not mean that, Soldan-Shah." Zarouk flushed,

averting his eyes. "But we cannot allow the situation to continue. Think of all the Aidenist atrocities!"

"Have there not been plenty of atrocities on both sides?" Omra muttered, much to their surprise.

From where she sat at the end of the table, Ur-Sikara Erima spoke up at last. "I believe ours are *retaliations*, not atrocities."

Kel Unwar rested his fists on the tabletop. "I suggest, Soldan-Shah, that we gather all our warships and pull together a navy greater than the world has ever seen! Sail northward, blockade the Calay Harbor. We have enough soldiers. The Gremurr mines now provide us all the weapons we need. We could crush the enemy capital once and for all."

Two of the merchant leaders chimed in enthusiastically. "Yes, that would put an end to this war."

"You think so?" Omra's voice had a dangerous, razor-sharp edge. "Can you honestly believe it would be as simple as that? And afterward, what would we do? If we took over Calay Harbor and attacked their people, do you not think that all five Tierran reaches would retaliate against us? Do you seriously suggest we could conquer that entire continent with one battle in one city? We don't have the soldiers, the time, the weapons—or the fortitude. What you suggest would lead to decades of disaster. Do you not think I have tried to imagine a simple, straightforward way to victory? Do you not think that King Korastine has done the same?"

He glared at them all, disgust clear in his voice. "If we launched our navy to Calay, what would stop *their* ships from slipping into our undefended lands? They could burn every one of our ports to the ground!" Omra turned his gaze toward Ur-Sikara Erima. "They could sail unhindered all the way to far Lahjar."

The old veteran Zarouk cleared his throat. "Perhaps you are not seeing the point, Soldan-Shah."

"The *point?*" Omra pounded his fist on the table. "*I* am the point! *I* am the Soldan-Shah! *I* decide!"

"Yes, you are the point, Soldan-Shah," said Kel Rovik, speaking in an even voice. "Your people believe in you. But they also pray you will become the point...of a sword."

102 *The Edge of the Great Desert*

The Missinian work teams quickly assembled the sand coracle according to Sen Sherufa's detailed plans: A sturdy framework of hard wooden slats formed a large bowl, wide and deep enough to carry the four passengers along with water, supplies, food, clothes, and weapons.

As workers wove reeds to form the basket's walls, Soldan Xivir expressed grave doubts about the mode of transportation. "You travel to a strange land, Soldan-Shah. There could be many enemies, great armies to kill you. You should take guards and soldiers—a whole fleet of these sand coracles."

"Maybe I should," Imir answered, "but if I did, we would never be finished in time for the winds to carry us. One thing I learned during my reign is that such projects take on lives of their own. We would not depart for years! Besides, if we brought along an invading army, what would the Nunghals think?"

"We will rely on our wits," Saan said. "I always have."

Asaddan smiled, showing the gap of his missing tooth. "There are things to fear everywhere. Do not be too afraid."

"Oh, I'm not afraid," Saan said.

"Neither am I." The big Nunghal clapped the boy on the shoulder.

The large balloon sack of Yuarej silk had been stitched together and thoroughly sealed with pitch to make it both air- and water-tight. To test its integrity, workers staked out the sack in an open clearing, where they built a large fire. The hot air inflated the colorful silk bag like the bladder of some enormous beast, swelling the balloon until it strained against the ropes that kept it tethered to the ground.

Meanwhile, heavy crates of dense black coal from Missinia were loaded aboard the coracle. The coal would burn long and hot enough to keep the balloon inflated, provided that the embers did not spill out of the large iron brazier and set the wicker basket aflame.

As the sun set that evening, Saan walked with Asaddan to the edge of the dunes. The Nunghal tilted his head upward, and his nostrils flared as he sniffed the air. "The winds are already shifting. Feel the breeze picking up."

Saan wiped his stinging eyes. "Does that mean it's time?"

"Yes, it is time...time for me to go home." He gazed out at the dunes with a longing expression. "You'll get used to the grit in your teeth."

After the first night, having spoken her piece to Imir, Lithio had departed with a group of nobles, preferring her own comfortable quarters back in Arikara. Saan, though, didn't mind being away from the luxuries of the city. He was quite content to camp out in the open, making plans for the adventure to come.

After they bedded down and the last campfires burned low under the bright wilderness of stars, Saan could barely sleep. He lay on his cushions listening to the rustle of tent fabric, feeling the breezes gaining strength out in the desert, as if the dunes were calling him. Thoughts of the upcoming great journey prevented him from falling asleep, though he knew he needed to rest. He couldn't imagine it would be easy to find a comfortable spot in the coracle's cramped wicker basket.

Just as he began to doze, Saan heard a stirring outside the small tent, a rustle, then a pounding of hooves. He sat up and shook the shoulder of Imir, who slept next to him. "Grandfather, I hear—"

Whoops and screams cracked the night. Guards shouted, "Desert bandits!"

Saan scrambled out of the tent on his hands and knees, looking from right to left; Imir struggled off of his cushions, sputtering. In the dim glow from the campfires, Saan spotted a dozen veiled men on agile mares charging around the camp. Brandishing swords, they slashed at the tents and ropes. One raider snatched a log from a campfire pit and threw it, still blazing, against a tent.

Saan ducked as one of the raiders rushed by, howling. The man chopped at him with his sword, but Saan rolled and sprang back to his feet, on his guard.

Imir finally burst from the tent, arms spread out to his sides and ready to grapple any opponent. On the other side of the camp, Soldan Xivir bellowed for his guards, who were already grabbing swords and pikes to drive off the attack. The desert mares easily swirled by as the bandits stole provisions, ruined piled supplies, and set another tent on fire.

Asaddan, who slept out under the stars with no need for a tent, stood like a contained thunderstorm. He let out a shrill banshee whistle through his missing tooth, ripped out a tent pole, and used the makeshift staff to knock a bandit from his mount. Spinning around, the Nunghal thrust the blunt pole into a second bandit's stomach, making him drop his sword, and a follow-up punch knocked the invader from his horse.

Riding past, another bandit slashed the ropes of Sherufa's

tent and tossed a flaming brand onto the fabric. Still inside, the Sacdran woman cried out and struggled beneath the weight of the collapsing canvas. As the tent caught fire, the bandit thundered past and thrust his long sword into the cloth, but Sherufa squirmed away from the point.

Two bandits, grinning as they heard the female voice, converged on her tent and began cutting their way inside. One man reached in, grabbed Sherufa by the arm, and tried to drag her out. The tent was fully on fire now. The second bandit seized the woman's hair and pulled. She thrashed and fought, but she was no match for them. They tried to throw her onto the back of a horse.

With a roar, Imir snatched up a fallen sword from the ground and—without hesitation, barely looking where he was going—charged forward and thrust the curved blade right through the first bandit's back. "Leave her alone!" He shoved hard until the point emerged from beneath the desert man's sternum.

As Imir fought to pull the sword free, the second attacker knocked Sherufa back down onto the burning tent. Turning to face the former soldan-shah, he laughed at the plump old man standing there, sword drawn.

With a vicious stroke of the razor-edged blade, Imir lopped his head off.

He watched the man collapse, his neck spouting blood. Imir sniffed. "I ruled all the soldanates of Uraba. You think I don't remember how to fight?"

Imir pulled Sherufa off of the flaming tent ruins. The Saedran woman flailed at her singed hair, while he swatted out the smoldering spots on her nightclothes. When Sherufa wavered, he steadied her. "You're all right now."

But the bandit attack continued around them.

Saan grabbed a curved sword from the first man Asaddan had unhorsed and brandished the heavy scimitar, two-handed, to defend himself. Soldan-Shah Omra had trained him to be a fighter, and now that he was in a real fight, the young man felt his blood pounding, adrenaline racing through his veins. He realized he was not frightened at all. If only his father could see him now!

One bandit chuckled at the boy's audacity and swung his scimitar, but Saan met the blade with his own, surprising the man. With a parry, he slashed the bandit's inner arm, and the man yelped as blood spurted. He wheeled his horse about, pressing his other hand against the pulsing wound.

At the edge of the camp, the bandit leader shouted through the scarf that covered his face, "Take what you can, and go!" The invaders snatched food and weapons as the Missinian guards rallied to defend themselves. Xivir's men struck down two more bandits before the rest of the raiding party thundered back into the starlit dunes, leaving their fallen behind.

Three camp archers launched a flight of arrows after the retreating men. One shaft plunged into the bandit leader's meaty shoulder, and he slumped over his horse but did not fall. He kept riding.

Soldan Xivir rallied the men. "Prepare for pursuit!"

Standing protectively close to Sen Sherufa, Imir stared at the burning tents, at the damage that had been done. "Leave them! We have few enough men, and they could ambush us out there. Our priority is to protect the sand coracle."

Xivir reddened, but he obeyed without voicing a complaint.

Flushed and breathless, Asaddan waited near the wicker basket and silk balloon sack, tentpole still gripped in his hands. He had been ready to die to defend their vessel, so great was his desire to go home. Saan grinned at the Nunghal, who responded with a gap-toothed smile of his own. They understood each other.

The night wind had picked up, and Saan could feel the increasing breezes. The camp lay in disarray, many of the tents ruined, their supplies gone or scattered. But, all in all, disaster had been averted.

Imir announced, "We'd better depart as soon as the sun rises."

103 *Gremurr Mines*

Prester Hannes sat on deck in the blistering sun amid a group of huddled prisoners. The slaver dromond worked its way up the rugged northern coast of the Middlesea; even from a distance, a smear of smoke marked their destination, the Gremurr mines. The men chained beside him were sweaty, dirty, and miserable. They complained incessantly. "We are innocent! We have committed no crime!" "We do not deserve this. Free us!" "I know many nobles. The soldan-shah will punish you if you don't release me."

But they were lying. The Urecari always lied. Hannes knew that not a single person here was innocent, and they all had unforgivable heresy in their hearts. He remained quiet, watching, learning...and hating.

He had nearly made it home, within sight of Tierra...and then this setback. It could not be an accident: Ondun was showing Hannes that he had further work to do, so he did not complain. He was merely a vessel of flesh created to serve the needs of God.

Nevertheless, he did not like the idea of laboring in the mines.

As the dromond carried its prisoners toward a forbidding, rocky shore, Hannes liked the place even less. The mountains formed impenetrable bastions with sheer cliffs pockmarked by mine tunnels. Mounds of shattered rock debris and tailings lay strewn about at the base of each mine opening. Shirtless, filthy men worked with sledgehammers and pickaxes, breaking the rubble, digging out veins of ore. Heavy barges rested against the reinforced wharves, weighed down with processed ingots or finished metal sheets and swords. Additional barges lay at anchor farther out, waiting to be loaded with cargo.

Flatboats mounded with coal pulled up to smelters, where more sweaty men shoveled the black rock into bins. Hannes heard the incessant clink of tools and crack of whips. Too thick for the sea breezes to scour away, a pall of smoke clogged the air, caught in the valleys, and clung tenaciously to cliff faces. Upwind from the smoke, a small palace and several permanent-looking homes belonged to the highest-ranking officials.

On the flat rocky shore were tents and wooden shacks, squalid shelters for the prisoners and slightly better barracks for the soldier-guards. Hannes had lived in worse places, and he knew he could endure hard labor in the name of Ondun.

The slaver dromond tied up at a separate set of docks, where two men waited to meet the new arrivals. The first was a husky man of about thirty years, well dressed and with somewhat effeminate features—obviously not a man accustomed to physical work. Beside him stood a man of nearly the same height, but older and meaner looking, exuding implacability. His body was hard muscle, his face rigid.

The pampered-looking man spoke up as crewmen unlocked the prisoners' chains. "My name is Tukar, brother of Soldan-Shah Omra." He sounded proud of the fact. "I hold your lives in my hand. I am your master here. You will help us to create weapons and armor for the glory of Urec." He paused, as though expecting applause or cheers. The slave ship's captain snarled, and the prisoners mumbled their obligatory support as they shuffled toward the disembarkation ramp. Hannes made no sound at all.

The hard-looking man took one step forward. "And I am Zadar, the slave master. Tukar may hold your lives in his hands, but *I* control your level of misery. Your life in Gremurr will never be pleasant, but there are varying degrees of pain. I am the man who makes that decision. I am the one you must impress."

Hannes studied the two men and decided that Tukar was harmless; Zadar was the man to watch out for.

"Many hours of daylight remain," Tukar said. "Zadar will issue your assignments. It's time for you to get to work."

After a week, most slaves surrendered any thought of resistance. Hannes did not. He settled into a routine of exhausting labor, but a routine gave him the ability to plan. A routine allowed him to find weaknesses. He took his time. In his years in Uraba, moving from village to village, he had learned patience.

He ignored the ache in his arms as he shoveled crushed ore into the open hatch of a reinforced cargo barge. Gremurr's five smelters processed some of the metal, but they did not have the capacity to produce all the copper, tin, and iron Uraba required. Since the rugged rocky coastline offered little wood for making charcoal to fire the furnaces, heavily laden barges sailed across the Middlesea with coal mined from rich veins in Missinia.

When the day's shift ended, all the prisoners filed back to the encampment. There were no sikara priestesses here, no sunset services, no prayers to Urec — no religion whatsoever. The mines were a harsh and godless place. These people were all followers of Urec, but they had no faith—not the prisoners, not the guards, perhaps not even the administrators. Prester Hannes wondered, quite seriously, whether Aiden preferred men to be entirely godless or to follow the *wrong* religion.

In the evenings, Hannes sat at long tables with the other prisoners, who were too exhausted for conversation. He ate his bowl of watery fish stew, accepting the food without comment, but finding irony in the fact that his captors were giving him the nourishment he required in order to turn on them. When he sat to eat, Hannes always chose a bench that faced toward the mountains, so he could constantly study the cliffs and canyons, in search of possible passes that would lead him out of here.

The guards insisted that there could be no escape, that the cold and rocky wilderness would kill them. His fellow prisoners were convinced that no one could survive the impassable mountains, but those men, Hannes knew, were weak, meek, and beaten. *He* had the faith of Aiden in his heart. *He* had the strength and blessing of Ondun.

He also knew that those mountains were part of Corag Reach. On the other side lay Tierra. The crags seemed to pose an ominous challenge, but Prester Hannes had done the impossible before.

104 *Iboria*

Another vision quest in the arctic wastes—his thirteenth such journey—and this time Destrar Broeck went alone. He took his furs, mittens, and eye protection against the stinging snow and blinding whiteness; he carried dried food, and he could add snow to a water pouch inside his coat, where it would melt for drinking water. Broeck needed nothing else for his body, yet he needed so much more for his soul.

He left Calavik abruptly, having awakened at night after an unsettling dream. For most of his life, he'd been a hale and hearty man who loved people, loved noise, and loved his memories, but now Broeck realized that his heart was hibernating like a brown bear from the deep forests. So he packed his things the next morning and announced his intentions. Iborians were accustomed to a man's need to be alone and face the challenges of a self-imposed quest.

Broeck journeyed north to the tundra, where he joined a family of itinerant mammoth herders, who occasionally drove mammoths down to Calavik, where the beasts were domesticated and put to work hauling logs down to the rivers. Broeck accepted their quiet hospitality for three days before setting off for the distant white lands even farther north. He thanked the mammoth herders, then said, "I have hunting to do. A private hunt."

In all his life, Broeck had seen an ice dragon only twice. Now he stalked it. He had to hunt the monster, had to defeat it with the three long sharp iron spears strapped to his back. He trudged in fur-lined boots across the packed snow and ice, skirting ominous dark areas that hinted at fragile fissures. He knew how dangerous and unpredictable the north could be.

When his wife, Wilka, had vanished in the snowstorm, her loss took him completely by surprise. She had lived her life in Iboria, and she knew the vagaries of its weather. She should have watched the shapes of the clouds, noticed the changing taste of the winds. Broeck had never thought he needed to worry about her. Wilka...

He'd always had a fondness for frostberries, and though it was late in the season, Wilka had gone out by herself, wandering far to find unpicked bushes. She shouldn't have been so far from home, from shelter, but the anniversary of their wedding day had been nigh. That evening, when she didn't return, while Broeck had huddled in their house from the blizzard outside, holding his five-year-old daughter, he had noticed the makings of a pie that Wilka had begun. She had gone out to pick the berries for him.

Ilrida had cried in his arms as the wind howled, and he had hoped against hope that Wilka had seen the brewing storm in time and made her way to a cabin or a hunting camp. The next morning, as the storm continued, he and ten searchers—against their common sense—had trudged out through the howling white gale, shouting her name, but the words were snatched away by the jaws of the blizzard. They had not found Wilka's body until the spring thaw. . . .

Despite the legend, the ice dragon certainly hadn't protected *her.*

As he raised his daughter, Broeck had thought he would eventually heal from the emptiness. He devoted himself to ruling his reach, knowing his people, working hard in the forests, and wandering out on his vision quests. He had survived, and had gradually become himself again.

And then a single scratch from a rusty nail . . .

For three years now he'd waited for the pain of losing Ilrida to abate, for the sadness to lift from him like a freezing fog on a winter's day. He had missed his daughter when she left to marry King Korastine, but that was nothing compared to the cold wound left by her death. At first he doubted that even Korastine's anguish could match the chasm in Broeck's own heart, yet when he saw the utterly lost expression in the king's eyes, he knew he was wrong.

The ice dragon's protection no longer seemed to benefit Iboria.

By contrast, the king's new Arkship project gave them all a beacon of hope, a beacon far more significant than the safety of his cold and sparsely populated reach. Though many people complained about the enormous and costly construction project, Destrar Broeck understood the need for a ruler to create works greater than himself. If there was a chance to find the land of Holy Joron, Ilrida would have insisted on going herself.

The Arkship could not truly be completed until Broeck contributed a vital, yet mystical, part to its construction. If Raathgir's horn could indeed protect a ship from other sea monsters, then Aiden's blessing could be conferred on King Korastine's bold giant vessel. . . .

It was the time of the brief thaw in the great white north, the season when the ice dragon was most likely to surface. As he made his way toward the mountains of snow and ice, Broeck removed his mittens and knelt to touch the ground so that his sensitive fingertips might feel the vibrations. The stumps of his missing, frostbitten fingers throbbed, as if with a sympathetic connection to the cold. Concentrating, he listened for the rumble, then followed lightning-bolt cracks in the ice, tracing them to their origin.

Knowing he was close, he looked up at the snowpack, the fissures in the icy cliffs. He sipped meltwater from the pouch inside his coat, chewed on dried meat to fortify himself. When he reached a solid ice cliff, Broeck thrust his three spears, points upward, into the packed snow so they stood ready and available.

Drawing deep, cold breaths, he unslung the iron ice hammer from his waist and swung it with all his strength into the frozen wall. A spiderweb of cracks radiated from the impact point. Broeck pounded again and again, knowing the thunderous sound would attract the ice dragon. "Come to me, damn you!" he shouted into the cold wind. He slammed the mallet a final time, and the crack went deeper into the ice cliff. "Ho, Raathgir!"

Behind the smeared barrier, he saw a reptilian slither, a blue-silver blur shifting and moving. The cracks in the ice wall widened, and Broeck staggered back, seizing the first spear just as the cliff split open. Behind the crack the enormous serpentine body glided through a slick-walled tunnel, like an adder crafted from frozen metal.

Boulders of ice calved away, falling all around him. Broeck dodged and ducked, then stood his ground with the first spear, fitting it into his full-fingered grip. The ice dragon's triangular head burst out, glaring with pearl-white eyes, its fangs flashing like silver icicles. A single knurled horn protruded more than two meters from the center of its bony-plated forehead. It lunged out, breathing a gust of freezing mist. Broeck dodged, feeling the impenetrable shattering cold ripple past him.

He hurled his first spear at the base of Raathgir's throat. The sharp point smashed into the creature's hard scales, and silver and blue shards tinkled from the serpentine neck, leaving a bare patch on its throat. Roaring, the ice dragon lunged down at Broeck and sent the destrar sprawling as it smashed its head into the snow.

When Wilka was lost out in the blizzard, did the howl of the storm winds sound like the ice dragon's roar?

He scrambled up, grabbed his second spear, whirled. When the ice dragon reared up and opened its fanged mouth, Broeck threw the second spear into its throat, where it stuck.

The ice dragon thrashed in agony, smashing its head against the cliff, snapping the cold-brittle spear shaft, but leaving the iron point embedded. Broeck seized his third and last spear, spread his booted feet, and cocked his arm back, waiting for Raathgir to turn toward him. When it did, he let the spear fly directly into the naked patch on the dragon's throat.

Deadlier than a scratch from an iron nail...

Steaming black blood sprayed out. The ice dragon gave a dying roar that sounded like the harshest blizzard of the year. Broeck scrambled away, taking shelter among the blocks of ice and snow that had collapsed from the cliff, and waited while the creature thrashed in its death throes. Finally, with a great sigh, Raathgir slumped onto the packed ice. Black blood stained the pure white snow. It twitched once more, and its long snakelike body oozed the rest of the way out of its warren of cliff tunnels.

Broeck stared at the magnificent beast, feeling great sadness now as he had second thoughts about what he had done. But he hardened himself and remembered his purpose. He drew his ax and stepped forward.

The immense knurled horn of the ice dragon would be perfect for the prow of the Arkship. Iboria may have lost the aura of Raathgir's protection, but King Korastine — and the hope of all Tierra — would gain it.

105 *The Great Desert*

After the excitement and terror of the bandit attack, Saan was ready to go as soon as dawn's glow graced the desert. The southerly breezes would whip up with the rising heat of the day, and they wanted to take advantage of the strongest gusts to whisk them across the expanse of dunes.

Soldan Xivir clapped his hands to rally everyone in the camp.

"The soldan-shah has spoken. Come, let us get these travelers on their way."

"Precipitous decisions often lead to mistakes," Sen Sherufa cautioned as the men rushed about making final preparations. She was still rattled by the raid. "Are you sure you aren't being rash, Imir?"

The former soldan-shah brushed aside her concerns. "We have been ready for days, my dear. It is time to go!"

Asaddan crossed his arms over his big chest. "Yes, it is time to go." He had taken the time to replait the braids in his ebony hair, which now hung like dark ropes around his head.

While Sherufa circled the base of the coracle for a final inspection, Saan and Imir filled the iron brazier inside the basket with coal from the camp's supply; Saan lit the fire, stoking it until the black rock glowed bright orange. The heat rose, puffing breath into the colorful silken balloon tied to the basket, swelling it into a spherical shape that stretched the guy ropes and the support netting. The coracle's wicker body creaked and groaned like the rigging on a sailing ship.

Saan tested the taut hemp ropes from outside the basket. "I'm ready as soon as the balloon is."

"You'd better be." Asaddan nudged him into the basket. "The balloon will not wait for you."

Imir graciously assisted Sen Sherufa, though she seemed perfectly prepared to climb in without help. Asaddan stood, feet apart, as though savoring the last few moments of solid ground. He raised his voice to address Soldan Xivir, the guards, the camp workers as equals. "People of Uraba, I promise to keep my companions safe — with Saan's help, of course!"

"Yes, Asaddan, I will protect you, if need be." Saan quickly realized how crowded the coracle would be, at least until they consumed some of the salvaged supplies, drank the water, burned the coal.

When they were situated aboard, old Imir gave a signal, and the Missinians released the ropes from the wooden stakes. Like a freed stallion, the sand coracle leaped into the air, making its passengers clutch the wooden frame for balance. Saan felt dizzy and worried that they might keep falling up into the sky and never come down. From the basket, they waved and shouted their goodbyes, listening to the ever-fainter return cries from Xivir and the camp workers as the buoyant ship soared high. Like an oceangoing vessel leaving port, the sand coracle drifted out across the expanse of sand, pushed southward by the breezes. Saan moved from one side of the basket to the other, bumping into his fellow passengers, peering in all directions.

"Think of all the stories you'll tell about this!" Imir said to Sherufa, hoping to evoke an expression of delight identical to his own, but she appeared seasick.

Even up here, the winds spat sand and dust at them. Asaddan squinted into the glare. For the most part, because the coracle drifted on the air currents, they seemed surrounded by silence, hearing only the crackle of coal burning in the brazier. The horizon shimmered outward.

Early in the first afternoon, they passed over a sheltered dell in the dunes, an unexpected patch of greenery. Tracks extended in several directions, and Saan could see tents, tethered animals, groups of men by fire pits. "That must be where the bandits live!"

Imir made a low sound like a growl in his throat. Still shaken by her ordeal the night before, Sherufa tried to sound analytical. "An oasis in the desert—a seep of water that they've dug into a well—enough for them to survive."

Seeing the remarkable silk balloon high overhead, the bandits pointed upward, shaking their fists, and Asaddan bellowed a challenge down at the desert men. Saan just chuckled. "They can't bother us up here."

The bandits began shooting arrows, and with a soft "thunk," one struck the bottom of the sand coracle and another whizzed by. Sherufa shouted, "If those arrows puncture the silk, we'll crash."

"How do we make this thing go higher?" Imir asked.

Saan and Asaddan frantically added more coals to the brazier, and as the heat blazed brighter, the silk of the inflated balloon stretched tighter, and the sand coracle rose out of range of the arrows.

Encouraged by Asaddan, Saan whistled down at the bandits, taunting them. Great anger showed on his grandfather's face. "We must remember the position of their base. When we return, my son can send an army into the desert to wipe out those vermin."

For three days, stoking the coal in the brazier, they floated along undisturbed through sunlight and darkness. Here in the air, unlike on a sea voyage, there were no treacherous reefs or uncharted shoals to pose hazards. Because the southerly prevailing winds set their course, the passengers had nothing to do but talk and wait, amusing or distracting themselves. Asaddan insisted that the Great Desert would eventually end; Saan could see nothing but dunes upon dunes upon dunes extending to a hazy horizon. "Now I understand the ordeal you endured when you crossed that expanse on foot," Saan said to Asaddan.

"You may think you do." The Nunghal flashed him a hard smile. "I hope you never have to find out for sure."

To pass the time, Asaddan told them stories as they watched dusty whirlwinds churned up by crosscurrents blowing across the desert. "Those are sand dervishes, small demons that live in the dunes and disguise themselves as beautiful women to fool unwary travelers. They hunger for love and for flesh. They sing to men on the fringes of campfires and lure them out to the dunes. The dervishes are so desperate for love, so alone, that they embrace their victims in a cyclonic wind and bury them in sand."

With a shiver, Saan sat up straight, blinking his blue eyes. Sherufa wore a skeptical expression, and Asaddan looked at the Saedran woman. "We know this because mummified bodies are found out in the sands, all the water and life gone from them."

"We don't have to worry about them up here," Saan said.

Imir pointed behind them. "We have other things to worry about, though." From the north, a gray-brown hammer of whipped-up dust lumbered toward them; sparkles of lightning flashed inside the cloud, which moved faster than the sand coracle.

"Should we land? Find shelter down there somewhere?" Saan scanned the dunes, but could see no place to hide in the sands, no rock outcroppings, no cliffs.

"We will have to ride it out," Asaddan said. "Up here."

Sherufa could not keep the anxiety from her voice. "I suggest that we cover ourselves so we don't choke on the dust. And hold on."

Saan stoked up the brazier's coals. The looming fist of the storm closed the distance, and they were at the mercy of the wind. As the first breezes knocked against the basket, the travelers huddled down, covered their noses and mouths with scarves, and waited as the storm engulfed them. He had wanted an adventure, to see and experience things that few other people had. In the storm's embrace, he felt a thrill of fear.

The scouring winds shrieked over them, scraping against the wicker, buffeting the inflated balloon. A few loose items—an empty water pouch, one of Imir's dirty tunics, Sen Sherufa's green scarf—blew away, never to be seen again. As Saan hunkered against the wooden frame, he felt the uncertainty of the reeds beneath him that were being eaten away by the abrasive sands.

"Keep the fire burning," Sen Sherufa yelled. "If it goes out, we lose our buoyancy, and the coracle will crash." Trying to shield the edges of the brazier from the winds, they added more coal from their mostly diminished supplies.

Caught by gleeful handfuls of wind, loose embers scattered onto the wicker and began to smolder. Asaddan swept some of the hot coals over the side with his bare hands. Saan shouted and snuffed one out, burning his palm. "We're also lost if the wicker burns!"

When the storm finally began to fade the next day, leaving them battered and caked with grit, they were able to shake the dust from their clothes, from the water sacks, and from the packaged food. Saan laughed at the crusting of dirt on his grandfather's brown face that made the man's bright eyes look startlingly white against the dust. The sky turned maddeningly clear and bright.

Swirling breezes loosened dust that had clogged the wicker. Saan rubbed his stinging eyes and looked ahead to where he discerned a different color of brown against the undulating tan dunes. "Are those...hills?"

Asaddan raised both hands above his head in celebration. "The golden grasses of the steppes!" In his excitement he poked his foot against the side of the coracle, and sand-scoured reeds splintered. Saan grabbed his friend's muscular arm to steady him.

Imir brushed at the grit on his arms and face. "Tell me, Asaddan, do the Nunghals have baths?"

Limping along and losing altitude from many small leaks in the treated silk, the sand coracle crossed the last dunes and drifted over the tan hills. They added the last lumps of coal to the brazier, but the fire remained low so that the sand coracle skimmed not far above the ground now.

Scanning the landscape for familiar features, Asaddan spotted the dark shapes of a herd moving across the grasses. Below, several brown-clad men astride ponies reacted with excitement to see the strange balloon drifting overhead. The riders chased them, and Asaddan leaned over the edge of the basket, bellowing in the Nunghal language. The herders circled, shouting back. Their ponies kept up with the drifting coracle as it dropped gently to the ground.

"I know this clan!" Asaddan called.

The basket scraped the grass, but the still-buoyant balloon bounced and carried them along for another substantial distance. The Nunghal riders laughed and shouted as they chased along. Asaddan taunted them to catch him.

The wicker coracle hit the ground again, and Saan held on, careful not to be thrown overboard; his teeth clacked together in the jarring rebound. Imir said with a gasp, "I will be very glad to be on solid land again."

Finally, the sand coracle came to rest, and the Nunghal herders circled, regarding them curiously. Saan could only imagine what an odd picture their group posed: coated with dust, their facial features strange. Asaddan swung himself over the side of the basket, splintering more of the reeds. Trying to gain his balance on solid ground, the big Nunghal stumbled like a drunken man, which made the herders laugh uproariously.

They came forward to clasp hands with Asaddan, who wore an expansive grin on his face. "Welcome to the land of the Nunghals, my friends. I know these men and their clan. We are safe now, and at home."

106 *Gremurr Mines*

Prester Hannes had little difficulty escaping from the Gremurr mines. When all was said and done, he simply walked away.

Cowed by overseers' threats and the imposing snow-capped mountains, few slaves had bothered to try. Hannes, though, made his own plans, his own decisions. As he performed his daily labors, he paid attention to which guards were lax, which ones were attentive. Work master Zadar was confident that no slave would be foolish enough to defy the rules...and Hannes considered him the fool for believing this. It made his escape easier.

A fresh shipload of prisoners arrived at Gremurr, and Hannes watched as the new slaves marched off the boat. Tukar and Zadar delivered the same speech as before, threatening severe consequences if the slaves did not work, did not obey the restrictions.

The guards focused their attentions on the new arrivals, because fresh prisoners were more likely to take impulsive actions. As a consequence, they loosened their vigilance on seasoned slaves who had resigned themselves to their fates. Hannes looked for his opportunity.

The season was late spring, and streams from the high country swelled with the snowmelt. Since he knew he had a long journey ahead, Hannes did not want to miss the high summer in the mountains. He quietly prepared, telling no one else of his plans. They were, after all, Urecari. He made a habit of stealing dry lumps of bread from the trays of other prisoners who were too weary and confused to notice. He hoarded strips of cloth he could use for wrapping his hands and fingers to prevent frostbite.

Finally, one night Ondun gave him a clear sign that it was time to go. A weak old man chained to the bunk beside him died in his sleep with a low gurgle. As part of his preparations, Hannes had secreted a bent iron nail he'd found in the ground. Now he used its point to pick the lock on the shackle that bound his ankle to the bed. He stripped the clothes from the old man's corpse, stealing the dead man's blanket as well as his own. Hannes would need them for warmth in the mountainous wilderness.

The barracks door was locked with a crossbar, but the walls were made of stretched canvas. Hannes moved past the snoring, unconscious slaves and bent to the base of the far wall. He poked the nail through the cloth and made a rip large enough to fit his fingers through. The canvas tore with an unexpectedly loud sound. He froze. Other prisoners stirred but did not awaken. He squeezed his head and shoulders through the gap in the canvas and, holding the spare blankets and his stockpile of stolen bread, sprinted into the moonlight.

All around him, the Gremurr mines stank of smoke and chemicals. Reddish glows came from the banked fires of the smelters. Bright lamps lit the fine houses of Tukar and Zadar. As he took his last glimpse of this place, Hannes felt a great disappointment in his heart. Before he escaped, he was tempted to wreak such havoc here! He could set fire to the homes, damage the smelters, wreck the ore lines. By spilling oil across the decks, he could destroy the weapons barges or the ingot-laden galleys. He could kill every one of his fellow slaves in the barracks—since they were chained to their beds, he could have gone from bunk to bunk, strangling them.

But Hannes knew his most important mission was to escape, to return to Tierra. One slave slipping off into the night might not cause much furor, but if he created the holocaust he imagined, they would never let him get away. No, he had to listen to Ondun's greater calling.

He also remembered that while these people paid lip service to Urec's Log, they had no faith. Because they were not devout in the Urecari heresy, killing them would be almost like murder. And he could not do that.

So Prester Hannes merely walked off into the night. He left the slave camp behind and found a path into the rugged mountains. He had his faith as his armor and his weapon, and that was all he needed.

107 *Abilan Soldanate*

"We should never have abandoned Ishalem, Soldan-Shah," said Sikara Fyiri. "The place is not shunned by Ondun—it is *ours*." The two stood on a hill overlooking the Middlesea, watching the constant battle training below. Warm breezes blew in their faces, bringing the smell of horses and the sea.

Now that Omra had finally set plans in motion, he had expected Fyiri to relent. He was wrong. "We will make up for it, Sikara. The Aidenists will not expect such an ambitious move from us—not after thirteen years."

"Your war has wasted too much time without focus," Fyiri scolded. "Skirmishes here and there, raids of villages, acts of piracy—for years! We are like children scuffling on the beach. This is a *war*, a holy war against the Aidenists...and you are the leader of Uraba. In the name of Urec, we must crush the enemy, defeat the followers of Aiden, whom God despises, and reclaim what is rightfully ours. *Ishalem.*"

With Saan and Imir gone off on their adventurous journey, and with his new son and heir waiting in the palace, Omra realized that he did not want to leave any of them with this war. The conflict was like an aching tooth that could only be cured by the sharp pain of a complete extraction. Sitting in the bedchamber with Istar and his baby son Criston, he had cobbled together a sweeping military plan to reconquer Ishalem, writing on long rolled sheets of paper and drawing diagrams, as she looked over his shoulder, concerned. He had made up his mind. After so many years of preparations, Uraba had all the weapons, ships, soldiers, and horses they needed for this assault.

In the war room of the palace, Omra explained the war plan to his kels, showing them how he intended to take advantage of the terrain. He calculated how swiftly he could move the components of his army to converge at Ishalem for a decisive, concerted strike....

Now, in the broad fields above Abilan's open beaches, hundreds of infantry archers drew back their bows to loose flights of arrows toward targets. On the flat beaches at low tide, hundreds of mounted cavalrymen rode hard, the horses' hooves pounding the sand as they charged straw-filled dummies that had fishhook symbols painted on their ragged tunic coverings. The cavalry soldiers hacked with their scimitars as they rushed past. Kel Unwar guided them, shouting commands, criticizing every flaw in the maneuvers.

Meanwhile, Omra's new fleet of war galleys was ready in the shipyards of Ouroussa, south of Tenér, sixty armored vessels that would glide up the Oceansea coast to reach the isthmus. They would be commanded by Kel Zarouk. Groups of foot soldiers were being ferried across the Middlesea to the port city of Sioara; from there, they would march over the Wahilir pass to crew the war galleys. Very soon, Omra and Kel Unwar's cavalry would ride up the coast of Inner Wahilir and arrive on the eastern side of Ishalem at the same time as the war galleys arrived on the western shore. In an enormous pincer maneuver, they would close in on the barren holy city and recapture it in the name of Urec.

Watching the military plans finally set in motion, Sikara Fyiri looked more bloodthirsty than ever rather than satisfied. Omra regarded her out of the corner of his eye. She had dark brown hair, stained red lips, and a face as smooth as ceramic...so different from the young woman who had blessed his first wife, Istar, and their unborn child so long ago. *Terrible events have shaped us all,* Omra thought, *twisted us like driftwood into something that would have been unrecognizable to us at another time.* As Fyiri observed the training exercises now, her imagination seemed full of grand-scale battles with screaming Aidenists falling to the sword. She relished it.

"Ah, Ishalem," she said in a long breath, as if reciting a chant from church. "How I long to have the holy city under our control. Ondun must be displeased that we abandoned it, but we will soon show the power of our faith."

Omra regarded her skeptically. "Did you ever visit the city before it burned?"

Fyiri frowned. "No, but I know we belong there. That is why you must take it back."

Omra continued to press. "With the Arkship gone and the city burned to the ground, nothing is left."

Anger flashed in the sikara's dark eyes. "It is holy land! It is *our* land— *Urec's* land." That was what the people truly believed, and the sikaras had stoked their righteous anger to a blazing intensity.

And yet if they were genuinely doing Urec's bidding, in the name of Ondun, why had there been so many tragedies? Shouldn't victory be easier for the faithful? *It is not God's obligation to give us an easy victory,* he told himself. *Victory must be mine.*

"Yes, Fyiri—we will throw out the Aidenists," he promised her.

Seeing the hard look on his face, the hawkish sikara finally appeared satisfied.

Studying his tactical maps, and missing Saan's curiosity and earnest advice, Omra calculated the time it would take for all parts of his plan to come to fruition, issued a final schedule, and sent fast riders to ensure that each kel understood the importance of his own role.

Omra promised himself that by the time Saan and Imir returned from their journey across the Great Desert, he would be able to show them a clear Uraban victory in Ishalem. He launched this new phase of his crusade because it was *necessary* and *right*. He also did it because he needed to restore the future for his people. Omra knew his father would rest more quietly in his retirement if he saw a return to the calm security of his reign.

But there would be much more thunder before the storm dissipated....

After planning his troop movements and dispatching foot soldiers to meet the waiting war galleys in Ouroussa, Omra called his cavalry together in the fields outside of Olabar. When Kel Unwar summoned them, they rode overland to the capital city, where they would board the ships to Sioara. Over the past several years, Omra had positioned many *ra'virs* in Calay, and they, too, could strike during the attack on Ishalem. From all directions, this whirlwind would sweep the Aidenists away.

The operation's three prongs would strike on the night of the full moon, two months hence. All of Tierra would be thrown into turmoil, and he expected a complete Uraban victory. Afterward, he prayed this nightmare would be over.

While farriers shoed his blood-bay mare for the long overland ride, Omra dutifully went to say goodbye to Cliaparia and their daughter, Cithara. The little girl was crying, and Cliaparia was theatrically distraught to see him go. He treated both of them with courtesy and formality, kissed the little girl on the forehead, then did the same to his wife, much to Cliaparia's disappointment.

"I must remain focused on the battle plans," he said.

"I will miss you, and as First Wife I'll be the first to welcome you home. Then we will celebrate your victory together!" She clutched his loose white sleeve and fussed with the clean olba wrapped around his head. "I'll count the days until you return."

"I'll return when I've accomplished what I need to do." He could tell she wanted him to say something endearing, but he had no honest words that would have satisfied her.

Next he went to see Istar and their two daughters, as well as their baby son Criston. Adreala and Istala both hugged him. "You have everything you need?" he asked Istar. "The handmaidens and the guards will take care of you until I return." He gave her an understanding smile. "And Saan will be back soon, too. I hate to see you sad."

"How can I *not* be sad?" Her response was surprisingly stiff, reminding him of how much he had forgotten about her past— and how much she had not. "You are leaving in order to kill Tierrans. You may be killed yourself. Whatever happens, I cannot celebrate."

He remembered the attack on her village, when she had been so young, her son unborn, her life set on a different course. That woman—Adrea—remained a stranger to him. "I am only going there to win this war. When I succeed, then I can stop the bloodshed."

"But you *will* shed Aidenist blood to do it."

"Yes." He had never lied to her.

"Then at least come back alive and unharmed." This, Omra knew, she meant sincerely. She kissed him, but she seemed fragile, fighting with turbulence inside her.

Finally, in his third wife's quarters, he embraced young Naori, feeling the swell of the baby in her belly as he pressed against her. She was due in less than two months. By the time he returned from the battle of Ishalem, she would have delivered her child, maybe another son, another heir.

Yes, many things had changed in the past year. Perhaps peace and prosperity would finally dawn on the Uraban continent.

Outside the Olabar gates, crowds gathered to celebrate the army's formal departure. The soldan-shah mounted his blood-bay mare, adjusted the white olba around his hair, and raised his gloved hand to a thunderous roar of cheers.

Cliaparia and Naori waved pennants, standing close to each other. Demonstrably apart from them, Istar held the baby boy and watched Omra go, but he could not read the emotions on her face.

The soldan-shah faced west and a mounted standard-bearer raised a large scarlet flag bearing the symbol of the unfurling fern. Kel Unwar whistled, and the mounted army of Uraba set off for Ishalem.

108 *Nunghal Lands*

Saan, Imir, and Sen Sherufa spent two weeks among the nomadic Nunghals, following the buffalo herds eastward. Since Asaddan had given the travelers his approval, the nomads were friendly, boisterous, and very loud. They rose at dawn to do their work, then stayed awake late around campfires, playing a game with black and white marbles on a polished board with indentations.

Long thought dead, Asaddan was received as a hero among the Nunghal-Ari. His comrades gave him a golden earring to reward him for his wonderful stories, though they still teased him about his missing tooth (apparently he had lost it in an embarrassing accident when a buffalo kicked him in the face). Though Saan could not speak the language, he listened to Asaddan tell his tale, watching his gestures, noting the tones of his voice, and began to pick up a few words. Sherufa, having already learned some Nunghal vocabulary from her intensive time with Asaddan, used it now. For his own part, Imir had no interest in learning another language, claiming he was too old.

The breeze never stopped blowing, constantly rustling the dry blades of grass. At this time of year, the only greenery came from prickly plants that scratched Saan's bare legs when he ran. He played with Nunghal boys his age, having fun with tasks that they considered their daily chores and tending the buffalo.

For her own part, Sen Sherufa took a great interest in the Nunghal religion. She often sat preoccupied at night in her open tent, scribbling notes. Saan joined her and asked what she had learned. "The Nunghal religion is very interesting," she explained. "There are certain mythic similarities to—yet striking differences from—what is familiar to us."

"Mythic similarities? Does that mean Urecari missionaries came here in times long past?"

Sherufa smiled at him, as if he had missed the point. "Nunghals believe they are descendants of two brothers who left their paradise home long ago. When they were lost at sea, both brothers cursed God for not watching out for them, and then both of their ships crashed. One brother took his people inland—his descendants became the nomadic tribes that call themselves the Nunghal-Ari. The people from the second brother's ship built themselves new ships and boats, remained at sea, and kept their traditions. The seafaring clans call themselves the Nunghal-Su."

Saan was suspicious. "That sounds a lot like the tale of Urec and Aiden."

Sen Sherufa nodded. "There might be a single mythic foundation from which the tales were garbled over the generations."

"Then we can tell the Nunghals the tale of Urec, give them the truth, and explain the real story."

"They would not thank you for that, Saan. Besides"—Sherufa raised her eyebrows—"how do you know that *your* version of the story isn't the garbled one?"

Saan was taken aback. For that he had no answer.

The aimless buffalo herds moved in a general direction, day after day, and the animals arrived at their destination just as Asaddan's clan friends had promised.

The city of the Nunghal khan started out as a nomadic camp made of expansive tents, yurts, and colorful pavilions, but it remained in place for so long that it became a permanent city. The tents were dyed ochre, orange, and brownish green, so that the encampment looked like a traveling carnival. Fabrics stretched from pole to pole to pole, joining one section to another. Separate thick-walled yurts were private dwellings, the largest of which was reserved for Khan Jikaris himself.

When they entered the settlement, Asaddan led Imir, Sherufa, and Saan to the largest yurt. "A rider went forth yesterday to tell the khan, and he is very anxious to see you," he explained. "Jikaris probably didn't believe half of what the rider told him." The hangings jingled with a fringe of gold and brass bells as Asaddan pushed his way into the yurt.

Inside, the khan hurriedly settled himself upon a wide wooden chair upholstered in dyed hides. When they entered, he was still tugging on wrapped-leather gauntlets and adjusting his stone-encrusted crown—a crown that looked as heavy as an old kettle. Long gray hair hung to his shoulders, but atop his head, most of the hair had fallen away to leave only a bare and leathery scalp.

Khan Jikaris assumed a relaxed posture, trying to pretend that he sat slumped on his throne awaiting supplicants all day long. Though he tried to look powerful and intimidating, two plump women—presumably his wives—went about the business of straightening rugs and lighting candles as if this were any other day.

The khan eyed the visitors with a demeanor that suggested both power and boredom, as if amazing things were a regular occurrence to him. Asaddan stepped forward and gave a rapid-fire speech in his tongue, to which the khan gave a brusque response before heaving himself from his chair. Jikaris was a head shorter even than Saan's grandfather. The khan studied Imir's unusual features, then moved to Sen Sherufa with greater interest, touched her long thick hair, and spoke appreciative comments to Asaddan. When the khan's fat wives snapped at him with clear displeasure, Jikaris hurried to Saan, intrigued by the young man's blond hair and blue eyes.

"He thinks you are either an angel or a demon," Asaddan said with a chuckle. "He wants to know if someone worked a spell on you, to turn your hair to gold."

"I suggest you correct that impression," Sen Sherufa scolded, "so that no one has ideas of cutting off Saan's head to acquire a treasure."

Asaddan took the threat seriously and spoke with the khan. Showing excessive friendliness, Jikaris slapped Imir on the back, then did the same to Saan and Sherufa, startling all of them. He pushed past, threw open the jingling flap of his yurt, and shouted into the din and bustle of the large camp.

"What's happening?" Imir asked.

"Khan Jikaris announces a great celebration to show off Nunghal hospitality to his strange visitors."

Saan glanced around. A few passersby paused to listen, but the mood of the encampment changed little. "They don't seem overly curious."

Asaddan laughed aloud. "The khan orders so many celebrations, the people are no longer impressed by it."

That night the open-air feast served a main course of buffalo meat, along with heavy breads, preserves of tart purple berries and honey, and a murky, odd-tasting beverage supposedly made from fermented mare's milk. A group of deep-voiced men played clangorous musical instruments and sang songs with clashing harmonies that Saan found too strange to be enjoyable.

Another man sat at the khan's side. Though he was clearly a Nunghal, his clothing was of an entirely different cut. His tunic's billowing sleeves were cinched tight at the wrists, while most of the other Nunghals had bare arms. Rather than fur trimmings, intricate knots decorated the man's clothing like an odd sort of embroidery. His leggings were reinforced by stiff, tough-looking strips of fabric: cured sharkskin, Saan realized, as he studied it more carefully.

Asaddan talked with the khan's strange companion, then made introductions all around. "This man is Ruad, a representative of the Nunghal-Su. He has come to spend a year with the tribes of the Nunghal-Ari, to exchange information and news."

Saan could not imagine such an arrangement between Aidenists and Urecari. Asaddan lowered his voice and continued his story in the Uraban language, so that none of the other listeners could understand him. "The truth, my friends, is that Ruad was sent here as a sort of punishment. All the Nunghal-Su have their own seagoing vessels, but Ruad lost his ship in a storm. Worse, the poor man had the bad fortune to survive when most of his crew was lost. Now he is considered something of a" — Asaddan waved his hand as though trying to summon vocabulary from thin air — "an outcast among his clan.

"Ruad, as one of the many nephews of the khan of the Nunghal-Su, is supposed to be braver than other men. His clan has exiled him among the land-dwellers, herders, and wanderers whom — I shall be honest with you, my friends — the Nunghal-Su do not respect. Ruad believes that the sea spat him out onto dry land, and he must remain here until he learns his lesson."

Saan regarded the outcast, trying to gauge his mood. Ruad did not seem to be in sparkling good humor, but rather withdrawn and resigned.

Asaddan touched his chest, keeping his voice low. "I think,

however, that this incident will teach Ruad many things — things that the Nunghal-Su don't know they should value. Either way, he will be a stronger man for it when he returns to his ships. Ruad can become a valuable adviser to both Jikaris and the khan of the Nunghal-Su."

Impatient with all the talk he did not understand, the old khan interrupted Asaddan and issued an abrupt command. In the full dark of the moonless night, the people fell into an anticipatory hush.

Saan heard a hiss, then saw a streaking tail of fire rise into the sky, like an inverted shooting star, which suddenly exploded into a dazzling flower of orange, yellow, and sparkling white. The Nunghals cheered and applauded. Astounded, Saan traced the colorful light, wondering where the flames came from. Was it magic, alchemy, some sort of natural eruption? Another rocket streaked upward into an extravagant fireworks display, as if the heavens themselves were at war.

"What is that? It flies, it burns, and explodes!" Imir exclaimed.

"It is firepowder, a mixture of chemicals that makes flames." Realization dawned on Asaddan's face. "Ah, in Uraba you do not have firepowder!"

The former soldan-shah was fascinated as another rocket exploded in the sky. "This is magnificent."

Asaddan shrugged. "It is firepowder."

"I would like to learn more of this," Sen Sherufa said. "Can you show me how it's made?"

The big Nunghal laughed. "If you think these fireworks are interesting, then you should see the cannons on the ships of the Nunghal-Su."

"Cannons?" Imir said. "What are cannons?"

"You want to know everything!" Asaddan let out a loud laugh

from deep in his chest. "It is good that you will stay here for half a year."

Breathless, Imir turned to Saan and Sherufa, lowering his voice. "Think of how we could use this firepowder against the Aidenists!"

109 *Olabar Palace*

Only days after Omra departed, Cliaparia made her move.

The soldan-shah and his army would not return for months, and by then — regardless of victory or defeat — he would be long past caring about a squabble among his wives. Cliaparia had her alliances, her schemes, and her hatred for Istar, but it was her obsessive anger that made her predictable.

Istar was ready for her.

She kept to her spacious chambers in the palace, occupying the rooms closest to Omra's own, because those were the rooms the soldan-shah had chosen for her. During the afternoons, Istar taught and entertained her two young daughters, seven-year-old Adreala and her sister Istala, two years younger.

Adreala was a precocious girl, so full of questions that her mind was never filled with enough answers. The girl was also brash and impetuous, playing with the boys and enduring scrapes and bruises that would have brought any other child her age to tears. Istala, quieter than her older sister, preferred listening to stories and drawing pictures instead of roughhousing.

Istar was teaching her older daughter a simple game of colored stones that she had often liked to play in Windcatch, though she did not reveal, even to her daughters, the game's Tierran origin. Istala found amusement enough in watching her mother and sister play. Baby Criston slept in a padded basket.

Cliaparia appeared unannounced at the doorway accompanied by four grim-faced palace guards. "We have come to move you from your quarters," she said without preamble.

Istar placed herself between her daughters and the door. "By whose authority?"

"Mine—as First Wife."

"And you issue orders on behalf of the soldan-shah?" Istar's tone was even. "I think not."

Cliaparia spoke over her shoulder to the silent guards. "I told you she would be difficult."

Istar bent to speak quietly to Adreala. "Run—this is what I told you about! Find Kel Rovik and tell him to bring his men." The seven-year-old understood perfectly. She dashed into a side room, slipped out another door, and raced down the corridor.

Istar faced Cliaparia once more. "These specific rooms were given to me by Soldan-Shah Omra because he wants me closest to him. He wishes to protect me and my family."

"I am First Wife. I should be closest to him," Cliaparia said. "By the time he returns, he will be happy to see me."

"And what quarters did you have in mind for me?" Istar asked, with more curiosity than anger. Beside her, a frightened Istala clutched her leg.

The white-robed guards strode into her chambers, their scimitars obvious in sashes at their hips. The men acted intimidating, but Istar knew they would never dare touch her.

Cliaparia shrugged. "I want you out of the palace. Go stay in the haunted villa that once belonged to Asha. It's been empty for so long, you may need to help your handmaidens do the cleaning."

"I'm surprised you haven't already prepared it for me, if you're so anxious to have me gone, Cliaparia." She chuckled. "Would you have gone on your knees to scrub dirt and mildew from the tiles?"

Cliaparia bristled. In his crib, baby Criston began to cry, startling them all. Turning her back to show how unimportant she found the indignant woman, Istar went to the crib and gathered up the baby in his blankets. When she held him against her breast, he calmed immediately. "This is the soldan-shah's heir," Istar said, looking at the guards instead of Cliaparia.

"Naori is also pregnant," the other woman said. "She might have a son—a *Uraban* son."

"Will that matter to Omra?" Istar asked. How could Cliaparia know so little about her own husband? "You delude yourself."

Cliaparia was not sure what to do now that Istar had defied both her demands and the threat of the guards. Obviously, this hadn't gone the way she'd expected.

Outside in the corridor came the sounds of a commotion: the jangling of armor, the thud of boots, a swirl of cloth, and the metal whispers of drawn scimitars. "Mother, we're here!" called a girl's voice. Adreala burst in ahead of the twelve breathless guards, astonishing Cliaparia and her four men.

"What is the difficulty here?" Kel Rovik said. He flashed a glance at the four guards—his own men—standing with Cliaparia.

As kel of the palace guard, Rovik was reluctant to take sides among the soldan-shah's wives, but he did know Uraban law and traditions. While forging her alliances, Istar had never insulted his honor with bribes; instead, she had softened his stoic mood through respect and courtesy, remembering to address him by name. She had taken the time to bring baby Criston before all the guards, to let them look into the face of Omra's true heir.

Cliaparia had not thought to do any of those things. "There is no difficulty. I am First Wife. Help us move this woman's possessions out. She will find her own rooms."

"These are her rooms," Rovik stated.

"And now they are mine. I insist. I am First Wife, and you will obey me."

Avoiding the guards, Adreala ran to her mother and sister. Istar folded her into an embrace.

Rovik remained troubled. "I was present when Soldan-Shah Omra gave these chambers to Lady Istar. You are asking me to perform a deed that I know is against the soldan-shah's express wishes."

"The soldan-shah is not here. You cannot know his current wishes."

Kel Rovik was not moved. "And when I receive word from the soldan-shah himself that he has changed his mind, my men and I will be pleased to follow his command. Until then, his orders remain unchanged, and the Lady Istar remains where she is. As the soldan-shah wishes, so Urec wishes."

Cliaparia recognized that she had been defeated. Without bothering to call the four guards after her, she slipped past Kel Rovik's men like a raven frightened from a fresh carcass.

But Istar could tell that this was not over.

110 *Calay, Shipbuilders' Bay*

King Korastine's Arkship was an enormous vessel unlike any other Tierra had ever built. When the Iborian shipwright declared that his work was complete, all the riggings strung, the sails mounted, the deck boards and hull waterproofed, the bulwarks carved and painted, and the double-fishhook anchor hung, the Arkship was finally released into Shipbuilders' Bay.

Though King Korastine and Destrar Broeck had both insisted on having a place aboard the Arkship for the voyage, neither man would serve as the actual captain. After much discussion in chambers and reviewing the records of other skilled seagoing captains, Korastine had made his choice. Kjelnar himself would be the captain. No one knew more about the Arkship than he did, and King Korastine trusted no one more.

On the day of the christening, most of Calay's population lined the bridges and streets in excited celebration. The nearby docks were reserved for all of the young craftsmen who had worked on the great vessel and now gathered to watch. These young men had been drawn from all walks of life and had worked tirelessly to build, rig, paint, and supply the Arkship for its maiden voyage.

Aldo na-Curic stood among his fellow Saedrans to marvel at the glorious ship, especially since he would be joining the crew, once King Korastine set sail for parts unknown. For most of the people in Calay, the ship had a deep religious significance, an echo of the marvelous wrecked vessel that had watched over

Ishalem. And if Aiden—or Urec—could sail such a giant vessel across the empty seas from Terravitae, then surely a similar design would suffice for King Korastine's exploratory crew.

For Aldo, though, the new Arkship signified the chance to discover the mysteries Ondun had left in the world, the breathtaking possibilities that waited in the unmarked portion of the Mappa Mundi, and the chance, at last, to complete the great work of the Saedran people. And he would be the one to record it all, as the master chartsman.

More than at any previous time since the burning of Ishalem, the people of Tierra had come together on the same quest. Over the past year, the work crews in Shipbuilders' Bay had swelled with enthusiastic young men, many of them orphans; without parents and growing up on the streets of Calay, these young men wanted to do something grand and tangible with their unsettled lives, perhaps even sail off on the Arkship when it was completed.

Eager to get a better look at the beautiful ship, a vessel that would be his home for uncounted months or years, Aldo worked his way to the edge of the dock, where he could study her graceful lines. His brother and father tagged along, though Wen clearly wanted to be somewhere else. Aldo wondered whether looking at the new Arkship reminded Wen that he had not passed his chartsman examination.

The crowd cheered with a renewed roar as King Korastine ascended the gangway accompanied by Prester-Marshall Rudio. The two men walked to the prow, and the king raised his hands. Aldo strained to hear the distant words as the religious leader opened a heavy old volume of the Book of Aiden and began to recite. When Rudio finished his passage, he closed the book and shouted to the sky, "We beseech Ondun to bestow His blessing on this new ship."

In a well-rehearsed performance, Korastine called, "Help us to sail safe and true, for I am of the blood of Aiden."

The prester-marshall raised the king's hand and drew a gilded blade. "By the blood of Aiden"—he cut a small slash on the king's palm—"we ask Ondun to consecrate this ship." As blood welled up, he pressed Korastine's palm against the wood of the bow.

Korastine raised his voice to add, "And by the blood of Aiden, I beseech Ondun to help us find our way home to Terravitae."

The crowd stirred at the end of the dock as several men came forward. Aldo stood on his tiptoes to catch a glimpse of the broad-shouldered Iborians marching forward in what was obviously an unexpected addition to the christening ceremony.

Kjelnar and Destrar Broeck led a group of northerners, who strode onto the deck of the grand vessel, carrying a long fur-wrapped package. "Wait, King Korastine. We have a priceless contribution to the Arkship!" Broeck bellowed.

The king looked curiously at the package. "And what is this, Destrar?"

"*Safety,* Majesty." The bearded destrar removed the covering with a flourish to reveal a long, sharp shaft made of a milky blue substance. "This is the horn of the ice dragon Raathgir. Blessed by Aiden himself, proof against sea monsters, protection from storms. Immediately before we depart, Kjelnar will install Raathgir's horn on the Arkship's prow—a rare and fearsome ornament that will also impress Holy Joron when you see him."

The shipwright smiled. "As the captain of the ship, I agree."

Prester-Marshall Rudio touched the smooth pearlescent ivory surface. "First let me bring this back to the main kirk, where our master craftsmen can etch the five prayers of Aiden into its shaft."

King Korastine smiled. "Then the Arkship will surely be invincible."

Broeck was immensely pleased by the idea. "That gives Kjelnar time to craft a socket in the prow for the ice dragon's horn."

From the crowd, Aldo listened, curious. He had heard only obscure mentions of the ice dragon legend; now he would have to look into the Saedran libraries to discover more about the tale. As the chartsman accompanying the Arkship on its voyage, he had to know everything possible, to organize and file it in his perfect memory. Aldo would have to make the most of this journey. When he came back home, Sen Leo would probably insist that Aldo marry one of his daughters and settle down.

Beside him, his father was enthralled by the ceremony, though Wen fidgeted. Aldo could tell that Biento longed to paint a mural of this scene, though Aidenist practice forbade the creation of any artwork that did not come from the great story. Quirking his lips in a smile, Aldo leaned close to his father. "Maybe you could paint the christening of Aiden's original Arkship before its launch from Terravitae? It would look very much like this scene."

"Ah, yes," Biento nodded. "And since Korastine is of the blood of Aiden, his features must be very similar to Aiden's, wouldn't you say? The painting would look almost exactly like this."

Aldo could already see the wheels turning in his father's mind.

111 *Nunghal Lands*

Saan and his companions lived for two months as guests in the great camp of the Nunghal khan before Jikaris announced it was time to begin the procession down to the sea and the clan-gathering festival.

While learning to speak the Nunghal language passably well, the young man also participated in the sport of buffalo wrestling, a dangerous game that depended on agility and speed rather than brute strength. Saan was wiry and light on his feet, and he loved to confuse the buffalo bulls by flailing a bright red kerchief before them, his arm extended to one side so the animal attacked the wrong target. He astonished the other Nunghal boys by springing onto the beast's back and riding it briefly before dropping off and running back to safety.

He taught himself to play their games of chance, discovering a strategy that depended more on trickery and bluffing than on actual luck or skill. He even flirted with some of the girls his age, though Nunghal standards of beauty tended more toward muscular and squarish women than the willowy lovelies of the Olabar court.

During these months, Imir—with Asaddan as his interpreter—spoke to Ruad and Khan Jikaris, describing Uraba's long-standing war against the Aidenists. Ruad in particular collected these nuggets of information as if they were coins with which he could buy his way back among the Nunghal-Su. When Imir wasn't discussing a possible alliance with the Nunghals, he spent his time with Sen Sherufa.

For days before departure, the Nunghals packed their belongings and prepared their mounts, drawing lots to determine who would stay behind and who would drive the buffalo herds down to the sea. Saan asked his new friends what was happening, and they explained the clan-gathering festival, an annual event among the tribes, at which they would trade goods and arrange marriages between the Nunghal-Ari and the Nunghal-Su. In addition, the separate branches would exchange young men so that nomads would learn to sail ships, while seafarers discovered the ways of the land, hunting and herding.

Khan Jikaris would join the procession, as he always had, so he could meet with his counterpart among the Nunghal-Su, a much younger khan who had taken the place of his dying father two years prior.

Sen Sherufa spoke to the khan at yet another banquet complete with fireworks. In slow, careful Nunghal, she said, "My companions and I crossed the Great Desert to see your land after hearing Asaddan's stories. I ask now for permission to accompany your party to the south, so that we might gaze upon this vast new sea you have spoken of."

The khan slapped his hand on the table surface, jarring the goblets and rattling plates, delighted by Sherufa's boldness. "You must come! I will show the khan of the Nunghal-Su these people who fly like birds in a basket, who tell of strange lands, and whose hair is made of gold." He reached out to scrub Saan's blond hair vigorously, a gesture to which the young man had grown accustomed (though he did not particularly enjoy it). Saan always found the khan's words difficult to understand, not because his grasp of the language was weak, but because the man had a pronounced lisp.

Imir was annoyed to be left out of the joke. He asked repeatedly, "What? What's happened?" until Asaddan took pity and explained it to him.

*   *   *

The khan's procession was a great, slow-moving parade. The buffalo drovers left early and maintained a fast pace, but Jikaris was in no hurry. Since the clan-gathering festival lasted for months, traders rarely offered their most valuable and exquisite merchandise early on, preferring to wait for larger crowds so that prices could go higher.

Days after the herds were out of sight, the khan would stop at mid-afternoon to set up camp and prepare for a large meal; the next morning, it took them hours to break camp and move out again. Scouts rode ahead to report on the terrain, the weather, and any other clans they sighted.

Saan was walking beside Sen Sherufa when they finally crested a rise of grassy hills and saw a hazy blue expanse that spread infinitely far to the south. The Saedran woman stopped in the middle of recounting one of her favorite tales of the Traveler. The refreshing smell of salt air and the unexpected sea breeze stole the words from her throat.

"It's the southern sea!" Saan blurted.

Asaddan joined them, and Sherufa said in amazement, "You didn't lie, Asaddan, nor even exaggerate. This ocean..." She shook her head. "This entire *continent* exceeds all the boundaries of my imagination."

The big Nunghal looked at the expanse of water as if it were a strange landscape even to him. "You know the Middlesea's boundaries, but here storms come up from the south and batter the coastline. The Nunghal-Su have sturdy ships. Ruad is very proud of them, though his own vessel was wrecked by a storm. I would rather place my faith on dry, solid land."

Puffing, Imir joined them to stare at the sight before them. Since their time in the sand coracle, the former soldan-shah had stopped shaving his scalp and face, and now his whole head was fringed in a fuzz of tightly curled iron-gray hair. Looking out at the water, his expression dawned with wonder. "No Uraban has ever before gazed upon this sea!"

"Well, Sen Sherufa and I saw it first," Saan teased.

Riding behind them, Khan Jikaris topped the hill, drew a deep breath, and let it out as a sigh. His companion Ruad seemed transfixed as he stared at the ocean with immense longing. Saan remembered the same expression on Asaddan's face after he stepped from the sand coracle onto the grasslands of his clan. The khan, though, was far more interested in the hundreds of colorful tents and stalls that filled the meadows and pastures above the beach.

The Nunghal-Ari procession trampled the grasses in the pristine meadow that the early riders had reserved so that the khan and his party could establish their camp there.

The following day, full of excitement to see the stalls, vendors, and representatives of the Nunghal-Su, Saan accompanied Sen Sherufa out to explore. He looked down into the harbor at a hundred strange, thick-hulled ships with stout masts and an unfamiliar arrangement of sails and rigging. He hoped one of the seafaring Nunghals would take him aboard so he could study the design and learn their nautical skills, which he could bring back to Soldan-Shah Omra.

The khan gave Saan's grandfather a sack of coins to spend, and Imir told the young man in a conspiratorial whisper that he intended to buy "something very special" for Sherufa. Jikaris also gave coins to Saan and to the Saedran woman for their own needs.

As the morning warmed, Saan and Sherufa walked among the gathered Nunghals. Clan leaders sat across from each other at low tables as they shared drinks and conversation. He could easily spot the seafaring Nunghal-Su by their distinctive dress, similar to the clothes Ruad wore. Their harsh dialect was difficult to understand, but the two strangers made themselves understood.

Fishermen sold smoked carcasses of a large spiny fish that Saan had never seen before. Nunghal-Su stalls offered shells and coral necklaces, while the nomadic clans sold polished chunks of rose quartz, finely ground crystal lenses for spyglasses, tanned hides and worked leather goods, and barrels of salted and cured buffalo meat.

Sen Sherufa stopped at a mapmaker's stall, intrigued by the charts displayed there. She perused the details of the southern coastline, with arrows marking strong currents; the blank areas of water were decorated with fanciful depictions of sea serpents and storm patterns.

"How accurate is this map?" she asked the mapmaker.

He bristled, as if she had insulted him. "Nunghal-Su navigate with these charts. Our clans have explored every inch of the coastline, as far as we can. Our lives depend upon maps." He had a long mustache that drooped past his chin and a stubble of beard that had been shaved no less than a week before. "Where are you from? Your appearance is strange."

The mapmaker scoffed when they told him about Uraba and the soldanates, how they had crossed the Great Desert and became guests of Khan Jikaris. Facing his disbelief, Sen Sherufa remarked, "You asked us to believe in you. Now believe in us."

With a lifetime on the sea, the mapmaker had only vaguely heard of the Great Desert. He showed Sherufa his charts, asking her to point out its location. Since the Nunghal-Su were concerned only with the coastline and the sea, he had little information about the land's interior, where the nomadic clans herded buffalo. The Saedran woman used her finger to sketch out the general border of the Great Desert, then farther north she traced the soldanates of Uraba and finally the Middlesea.

Saan, however, was intent on the contours of the southern coastline, which he had never before seen. He compared this with what he remembered of Uraban geography from Omra's tactical maps, extended the Nunghal shoreline in his imagination...and made an intuitive leap. He spoke in Uraban, so the mapmaker would not understand him. "Sen Sherufa, see here. As the coastline extends to the west, it curves northward to the limit of Nunghal-Su explorations. By my guess...isn't our southernmost city of Lahjar not far from here?"

Sherufa was automatically skeptical. "No one can sail south beyond Lahjar. The heat and the reefs block all passage."

Saan gave her a wry smile. "Yes, and no one could cross the Great Desert, for that was the edge of the world. Apparently, our information is flawed."

Sherufa asked the mapmaker in his own language, "Why have your ships not traveled farther north, here?"

The Nunghal shook his head. "Reefs. Shoals. Bad currents."

Saan excitedly extended the coastline with his finger. "If the southern sea is indeed the lower half of the continent of Uraba, wouldn't the coast connect all the way around here? To Lahjar?"

Sherufa muttered as her thoughts tried to catch up to her words. "And if this is a true representation of the coast of the southern sea, then we know the shape of the whole continent! Think of what that means."

Saan felt his excitement build, thinking as Omra had taught him. "If my grandfather can form an alliance with the Nunghals, then their navies could sail up this coast, round the cape, and travel north to Lahjar. They could join us in our battles with the Aidenists!"

"That wasn't exactly what I meant." Sherufa's expression showed how deeply preoccupied she was. "It is a Saedran thing." She paid the Nunghal merchant his asking price for the chart, too engrossed in the discovery to haggle.

112   *Corag Reach*

Frozen. Starving. Lost.

Hannes's mind was as numb as his feet, as his hands. His body continued to move without conscious volition, plodding through this forsaken wilderness. The mountains around him were like monstrous jaws ready to grind him into pulp. He did not know how long it had been since his escape from the Gremurr mines.

The endless nights had been black, freezing, and windy; the mockingly clear days were so cold that the air itself felt as if it might shatter. The watery yellow sun shone down without warmth. Even both blankets wrapped around him—now sodden, frozen, and tattered—barely kept him warm.

His toes had burned for a long time, but now they were frozen. Wrapped in spare rags, his fingers were as stiff as wood; he could bend them only when he concentrated, and with a great deal of agony. The cold reawakened his old scars, first a tingling, then a throbbing, then excruciating pain.

Corag Reach should have been a promised land, but Prester Hannes saw it only as a land of broken promises. The slave masters in Gremurr had been correct: Any man of lesser resolve, or with less faith in Ondun, would have perished long ago. He no longer felt any energy or joy from the fact that he was back in Tierra. He was going to die here.

On his journey, he made his way over passes that funneled the harsh winds, then he stumbled down into steep valleys. He forded silvery rushing streams, with water that was indescribably cold even on feet that had seemed too numb to feel anything more. On hardy bushes he found handfuls of berries — it seemed like a miracle, and they tasted delicious, though he suffered stomach cramps for hours afterward. For the past several days, Hannes had eaten nothing but snow and lichens chipped from boulders.

No words had passed his chapped lips for a very long time, but in his mind he uttered prayer after prayer, recited scriptures from the Book of Aiden, begged for some sort of guidance to take him home. He staggered along, anchored by his faith, and propelled forward by his instinct to stay alive.

He sought any way through the heart of the mountains, trying to work his way downhill. If he passed out of the snow line and found the tundra again, and after that the forests, he might discover people in far-flung villages who could help him and feed him. True Aidenists at last.

Finally the snow and scree and endless rivulets of meltwater gave way to patchy grasses, then expansive alpine meadows with a riot of brilliant wildflowers. Stupefied, Hannes gazed at the colors, drawn to them. Ahead, through his tears, he saw cream-colored dots, moving shapes that his weary and disoriented vision finally identified: *sheep!* Dozens of them.

Hannes left the rocky pinnacles behind, stumbling, falling, and sliding over a last patch of snow into the steep meadow. He rolled onto the cushioning flowers and grasses, breathing hard, sobbing. Eventually, he got to his hands and knees and looked up. Like a miracle, he spotted a cottage built from fieldstones. A tiny curl of smoke rose from the chimney.

Hannes lurched to his feet and stared. Surely he was hallucinating! But the cottage remained there, surrounded by languid sheep.

He moved toward the structure, nearly dead, but the cottage did not seem to grow any closer. He heard a dog barking, a strange sound that reminded him of Asha's villa. He fell down again.

The dog began barking around him, but it did not attack. Hannes opened his eyes, lifted his head, and saw a man there, dressed like a shepherd. "May the Compass guide you!" he gasped, barely able to speak the traditional Aidenist blessing.

Like a song of angels in his ears, the man responded, "And the Compass guide you. Where are you from? How did you get here?" The man helped Hannes to his feet and held him as he swayed, weaker than he'd ever imagined he could be. "Who are you?"

"Hannes, Prester Hannes...I escaped...from the Urecari."

The shepherd picked him up as if he were no more than a sack of grain, and placed him over his shoulder. "My name is Criston Vora. My cottage has a warm fire and nourishing food. You look like you could use both."

Hannes had already collapsed and was beyond responding.

113 *Nunghal Clan Gathering*

During the Nunghal gathering, Saan spent many days exploring tents and stalls, playing games with other Nunghal boys, learning about the crafts and traditions of the different clans. He was a sponge, absorbing their dialects, their stories, their bawdy jokes; he was eager to find some way to use the new information to help Soldan-Shah Omra, when he and his companions returned home to Olabar.

Saan was interested in the rounded ships of the Nunghal-Su anchored in a hodgepodge floating metropolis in the natural harbor. Constructed of dark iron-hard wood, these were more than sailing vessels: They were *homes* for the Nunghal families, with decks stacked several levels higher than Saan had ever seen on Uraban vessels. The rigging was an incomprehensible cat's cradle of ropes, and the arrangement of sails formed a mosaic of fabric.

The Nunghal-Su believed that their god had given them the oceans of the world as their domain. They lived on the seas and came ashore only when absolutely necessary; the clan gathering was the longest time the ships remained anchored all year. Now the clustered ships looked like a city of sails and masts.

As he walked along the shore, staring out at the conglomeration of vessels, Saan came upon Ruad. Now that he'd returned to the southern ocean, the shamed Nunghal-Su was vibrant and restored. The gauntness of his face had filled out, erasing the shadows around his eyes. He had unbound his long hair so that it flew in the salty breezes with an exuberance that matched his expression. He stood next to a dinghy he was about to take to his clan ship, which lay at anchor in the deeper water.

"Ah, Saan! Are you not tired of having your feet in the dirt? Come with me — we can dine in my cabin and imagine we are out on the open sea." He shaded his eyes to look out at all the vessels. "I can't wait to set off once more."

Saan couldn't conceal his grin. "Your ships are fascinating . . . though I don't know how you can tell which is which."

"That is like asking a mother how she can recognize her own child." Ruad let out a snort, and Saan helped him push the dinghy into the water. "Our ships are our homes — and, oh, I am so glad to be *home*. Climb aboard." He gestured toward the small boat. "But you'd better be willing to do some of the rowing."

"I'll do all of it, in exchange for your hospitality."

The harbor waters were calm, and Saan pulled at the oars, threading a path through all the anchored ships, going where Ruad directed him. The clusters of ships reminded Saan of the herds of buffalo on the plains. "Where do you *go* with all these ships? How do you keep from running into one another?"

"When you walk among the crowds back there at the clan gathering, do you constantly worry about crashing into other men and women? We are master sailors!"

"Well, I still admire your ability," Saan said.

At the compliment, Ruad appeared crestfallen, however, and his voice fell quiet. "The Nunghal-Su would not say that of me, since I did lose my ship and many of my crew."

Saan frowned. "But you survived."

"Please do not remind me of my crimes. I am glad to be allowed back onboard."

They butted up against the storage barrels floating at the side of Ruad's clan ship at the waterline. Saan swung out of the dinghy, climbed onto the barrels, then scrambled up the rope ladder to reach the main deck, with Ruad close behind.

Saan studied the workings of the ship as Ruad showed him the decks, the storage compartments and complex rigging. Aboard, families hung tapestries and beaded curtains across private cabins. Women fed their children, men tossed sharp daggers at a target painted on a mast, boys scrambled up the rigging and swung from high ropes.

Remembering what he and Sen Sherufa had postulated after looking at the charts of the southern coastline, Saan asked, "What's the greatest distance the Nunghal-Su have sailed? How far have you gone?"

"Far enough, but not so far that we would sail off the edge of the world. Any fool who risks *that* deserves his fate."

"Is there really a precipice, a watery cliff that plunges into nowhere?" Saan had always been skeptical of such tales. "If that's true, why haven't all the seas drained away to nothing by now?"

"It is not for me to explain the intentions of God—but I do not doubt what I have heard. I will never doubt it again."

"But what if, instead of finding the edge of the world, you find the port city of Lahjar, and then the rest of Uraba?" Saan couldn't keep the excitement from his voice. "Would you be willing to make the attempt?"

"I would not." Ruad tersely shook his head. "It is not for us to go so far. People could not survive it."

Saan was disappointed. "Most would not have survived crossing the Great Desert, either—but Asaddan did. And then we did—so it can be done." He imagined how the war with Tierra would change if all these imposing Nunghal-Su vessels sailed up in a great fleet to swarm the Aidenist coastal villages. With this incredible navy *and* firepowder, the enemy would stand no chance.

"Just consider it, Ruad. After you're back at sea, when you feel the call of the far horizon…think about where else you might go."

"The world is a big enough place, and the sea is vaster than my imagination. I don't have to see all of it."

"But *I* would like to," Saan said, gazing out over the crowded ships and harbor to the sea beyond.

114 *Corag Highlands*

After a dozen years of self-imposed isolation in the mountain meadows, Criston Vora barely remembered what it was like to have human company. He had forgotten how to be a good host, but he had not forgotten his humanity. The terrible privation that this skeletal, frostbitten man had endured tugged at his heart. He recalled when he'd been cast adrift on the *Luminara*'s wreckage with Prester Jerard, barely surviving. Criston knew how to help.

First he put the man by the fire, wrapped him in woolen blankets and covered him with a thick fleece. Even so, Hannes shivered uncontrollably, thrashing in internal nightmares and frigid delirium. The man's hands and part of his face bore a waxy sheen of scars that suggested another horrific but old injury. His severely frostbitten skin had large areas covered with purplish patches marked with white spots and blisters.

Criston heated water and added aromatic herbs for a weak tea, then forced the prester to drink it. He prepared a broth with chunks of mutton, carrots, and wild onions, and when his visitor was awake enough to take food, Criston strained out the solid parts and gave him the hearty broth.

The man would likely lose several of his fingers and toes to frostbite, but Criston was no Saedran physician, nor even a village herb-wife. Hannes could not be moved until he regained some of his strength, so Criston cleaned the blisters and wounds as best he could, hoping the poor man would not suffer and die of gangrene before Criston could get him to help.

The dog, now old and limping, sat beside the cot where Hannes rested. For years, good Jerard had helped tend the flocks, but lately his joints and muscles ached too much for vigorous activity, and Criston was glad to let him keep the guest company. Stirring from his cot, Hannes occasionally reached over to stroke the dog's head, though he did not seem to know how to be comfortable around a pet.

"My dog has scars like you do." Criston said when Hannes was awake but still resting. He pointed out the white line along Jerard's left flank from when he'd defended the flock against a wolf. Criston had patched him up, but at times the dog still whimpered in his sleep. "Jerard can't tell me his story, but I saw him get those wounds. You, Prester Hannes, will have to tell me your tale."

Hannes took a long time to gather the strength to explain how he'd been a pilgrim in Ishalem, where Urecari slavers had captured him and taken him to the Gremurr mines. The prester talked of how he escaped into the mountains, but he couldn't remember many details of his grueling trek. "It is with Aiden's blessing that I finally found you. I might have died the next day up there, but Ondun arranged another miracle, and I am here to continue His great work."

As he listened to the story, Criston sensed that his guest kept many secrets, but after what the prester had been through, Criston didn't have any right to press him for further details. Besides, he didn't want Hannes inquiring into *his* reasons for withdrawing from the rest of humanity and living alone. The battered and water-stained volume of Captain Shay's journal sat on a rickety shelf on his wall; he often reread it during the winter nights, but right now he called no attention to the book or the sad history it embodied.

He guided the conversation to a safer subject. "I've never

heard of Urecari mines down there. Even if the mountains of Corag are impassable, that coast is above the Edict Line and therefore belongs to Tierra."

"Urecari lie and cheat," Hannes said. "They do not abide by treaties."

Criston sighed. "The Gremurr mines may as well be on the other side of the world. No one can travel through the mountains."

"I did. On Tierran soil, the Urecari are mining metal to make weapons and arm their soldiers against good Aidenists."

Though he had cut himself off from politics and the world, Criston felt anger bubble up within him. He thought of innocent fishing villages like Windcatch, raiders sweeping in to set fire to houses and kirks, killing people, taking away children . . . and Adrea.

Hardening his resolve, Criston decided to tell the prester his own tale after all, the first time he had spoken of such things since turning his back on the sea. When he was finished, Criston felt exhausted and drained, and cathartic tears slid down his cheeks.

Hannes stared at Criston's fishhook pendant, the now-tarnished but deeply prized emblem that Prester Jerard had given him. He rose from the cot, touched the fishhook and blessed him. "I must go back to Calay," he said in a hoarse voice. "I need to report to the prester-marshall."

"You'll need a doctor sooner than that. I've done all the healing I can here, but caring for your frostbite is beyond my skill."

"Ondun will keep me whole," Hannes said.

Criston made preparations, packing food and fashioning a walking staff for Hannes. Leaving the sheep to tend themselves in the big meadows, they set off at dawn, proceeding at a slow pace. Old Jerard refused to be left behind; his tail wagged with determination though he plodded along with a stiff-legged gait, instead of bounding.

Hannes would let a doctor tend him at the river settlement while they waited for the next riverboat to arrive. When they reached the small town and rickety wharf on the bank where barges stopped once or twice a week, Criston assessed the current flowing to where it would empty into the Oceansea and felt a faint longing to go aboard with Prester Hannes.

He could accompany his guest to Calay, or he could return to Windcatch and reclaim a normal life. Once a year, he still wrote his letter, placed it in a bottle, and made the pilgrimage to the sea. Occasionally, he visited Ciarlo back at his old home. But that was all. There would never be a normal life without Adrea.

"I can't go with you," he said to the prester. "Not yet."

"I understand, my son." Hannes gave him another blessing. "You have your faith and your own mission in life, as I have mine."

People came to the docks to see them. The local prester, both overjoyed and dismayed to see Hannes, told Criston, "I will take care of him and get him a doctor."

After the two men said their awkward farewells, Criston whistled for slow-moving Jerard. He did not want to stay for a warm meal, because being around so many people made him uncomfortable. He and the dog headed back to the calm emptiness of the mountains.

115 *Nunghal Lands*

To signal the end of the annual clan-gathering festival, the anchored Nunghal-Su ships fired off their immense cannons, belching orange blasts and resounding booms into the sky. Standing on the deck of his large vessel in the heart of the cluster, Ruad whistled and waved his arms. Saan's grandfather was so delighted by the explosions that he looked ten years younger.

With careful deliberation, Sen Sherufa had kept an accurate tally of days since their crossing of the Great Desert. Taking her makeshift calendar to Saan and Imir, she pointed to their schedule. "Half a year has passed, and the winds will be turning northward any day. We have to start making our plans very soon. We'll need the khan's help to fix the damaged sand coracle in time. We'll need supplies, too. We've got to find coal or something to burn that will keep the balloon inflated. There's a lot of work to do, Imir."

Though he felt completely at home among the Nunghals, Saan agreed. "We need to get back to Olabar so we can tell my father everything we've learned."

"Firepowder and Nunghal navies will change his plans for war, that is certain," Imir said. "Maybe it'll be enough to make the Aidenists surrender quickly and end this constant conflict." Saan knew his grandfather had never wanted to go to war in the first place.

"I wish you would stay longer among us, but I certainly understand your desire to go home," Asaddan said, crossing his arms over his chest as he gazed at the rocking Nunghal-Su ships in the harbor. He scrubbed Saan's blond hair with his hand. "Maybe you should let this one stay with us. I'll teach him a few more things!"

Saan swatted at him, laughing. "I need to get back to my mother—and Soldan-Shah Omra. How do you expect him to fight a war without me?"

The big Nunghal chuckled. "How, indeed?"

While the departing Nunghal-Ari clans fanned out from the seacoast, Khan Jikaris dispatched workers and supplies to the site of the grounded sand coracle at the edge of the desert, giving his blessing to their return home, so long as they sent more emissaries back. More organized and practical than the lackadaisical khan, Asaddan knew where to get supplies of coal, reeds, and wood, as well as thick, smelly tar to seal and protect the outer surfaces of the basket and the silk balloon sack. He sent a group of young men northward at a fast pace.

By the time Asaddan, Saan, Sherufa, and Imir reached the site in the north, the seasonal winds were already brisk. Their coracle lay battered but undisturbed where they had left it; the silken sack deflated, folded, and anchored with large stones; the splintered wicker basket tied down and sheltered. The young Nunghals Asaddan sent ahead had set up work tents for the large project. Several baskets of coal had already arrived.

Saan worked hard with his Nunghal companions to patch the odd vessel. Though he was not quite thirteen, the clans considered him an adult, and he was pleased with what he had achieved among them. When he returned home, he would convince Omra to let him participate in the real war planning against the Aidenists.

He teased Asaddan. "This trip will be easier than the last. Without you taking up so much room in the coracle basket, we can carry a lot more coal."

The Nunghal flexed his large bicep. "I'll find my way back to see you again—wait and see."

Imir took him at his word. "If you do, I will have a goldsmith make you a new tooth, so your smile can dazzle even the khan."

"Then how would I whistle?" He let out a shrill tone that startled the nearby buffalo.

Sen Sherufa watched the preparations, often testing the wind. Her thick hair blew in disarray until she tied it back. Imir remained close beside her, touching her shoulder from time to time, and she did not object. "This voyage will not be as frightening as the last, since we *know* it can be done. After we get back, we can build an entire fleet of bigger coracles and begin trade across the Great Desert with the Nunghals."

"We should also try to sail ships past Lahjar and around to the southern sea, to see if my theory is right," Saan decided.

"Or maybe I will convince Ruad to make the voyage from this side of the world," Asaddan said. "I would like to join him in that." When Saan stared at him in surprise, he shrugged his broad shoulders. "It can't be any more difficult than walking across the Great Desert!"

With the coracle repaired and the balloon sack inflated, the three Urabans waved goodbye as whooping Nunghals disconnected the ropes. The straining balloon lifted them higher, until they could see the panorama of extensive grasslands, the herds of buffalo, the nomadic riders—and the sea of dunes. Riding brisk air currents, their coracle raced north across the expanse of sand.

Although he would miss the land of the Nunghals, Saan carried a great contentment within him. He had experienced a tremendous, life-changing adventure and had learned about the world, the Nunghal culture, their beliefs, and their simple yet intricate way of life. He had a different perspective now, an exciting breadth of knowledge and imagination. Though the wasteland stretched on and on, Saan knew that the Great Desert was *not* the edge of the world. He couldn't wait to tell Omra and his mother the things he had seen. . . .

Several days later, nearing home, they passed over a desert bandit encampment, different from the oasis they had seen on their outbound journey. Imir scowled down at it. "Always in the past, the bandits have vanished into the sands like desert ghosts, but if we build more sand coracles, our archers can attack their encampments from above—wipe them out like the vermin they are." He drew obvious satisfaction from the idea. "That, at least, will be a decisive war . . . one we can win."

They finally passed the edge of the Great Desert back into Uraba and continued to drift across Missinia, traversing many more leagues before the baskets of fuel gave out. When the sand coracle gradually settled to the ground and Saan and his companions climbed out of the basket onto solid land, he felt quite happy to be home.

By now, his little brother Criston would be almost a year old, and his sisters had probably grown by several inches. By now, the Uraban armies might have defeated the Tierrans once and for all. He couldn't wait to hear the news from Soldan-Shah Omra.

116 *Calay*

Prester Hannes wept when he finally caught sight of Calay from the riverboat. Returning to it now after so many tribulations, he felt that the blessed capital city of Tierra was as sacred as lost Ishalem. Hannes had been trapped in the purgatory of Uraba for thirteen years after the burning of the great city, and before that he had hidden among the Urecari, watching, learning. A spy for God.

Now, reaching Calay was his true reward for long and faithful service, saved from the jaws of hell itself. How could any pilgrim to any shrine feel more blessed than he did right now?

His frostbitten hands and feet were bandaged, and the pain had dulled to the point where he could ignore it. Under the ministrations of the local healer, he had lost only three toes and two fingers; no gangrene had set in, and the stumps were healing nicely. He felt invigorated and whole, ready and able to do much more for the cause of Aiden. But first he had to report to the prester-marshall all that he had done and all he had seen — particularly the extensive Gremurr mines in Tierran territory.

After Hannes disembarked from the riverboat, he walked in a daze along the docks in the Farmers' District. His new clothes fit him poorly, because the rivertown prester had been a broader-shouldered man, but at least they weren't Urecari clothes. At least they weren't a slave's clothes.

No one knew who he was. He wandered through the various districts, drinking in the smells, sounds, and sights. Home. *Safe.*

It was a miracle. When people talked around him, the buzz of conversation sounded alien, yet wonderful—the Tierran language was music to his ears. Tears sprang to his eyes as he saw pennants and wooden business signs that unabashedly displayed the fishhook symbol.

The rivertown prester had given him a new pendant, and Hannes clung to the symbolic fishhook even when he slept, swearing to himself that he would never again be deprived of the outward sign of his faith.

On his way to the Royal District and the city's main kirk, he was pleased to see another small kirk with beautiful Iborian-style architecture, built in the name of King Korastine's second wife, who had died several years before. Hannes felt sad at the reminder of how long he had been gone, how much he had missed. He hadn't even known King Korastine had married again. Little Princess Anjine was fully grown and ready to become queen, and now the king had a young son, as well.

But those were temporal matters, and Prester Hannes was more concerned with spiritual things. He touched the fishhook in the hollow of his throat, whispered a quiet prayer, and headed toward the magnificent towers of the main Aidenist kirk, near the castle.

With reverent gratitude, he passed through the tall, always-open doors into the voluminous interior. Most worshippers came for the traditional dawn service, but even in the afternoon some of the faithful had come to pray, to study the relics and paintings, or to converse quietly with the attending presters.

One man in clean white vestments came forward, smiling a welcome to Hannes. "May the Compass guide you." He hesitated upon seeing Hannes's scarred cheek, his missing eyebrow, but then he recognized the pendant, saw the trappings of office that the village prester had given him.

In a gruff voice, Hannes said, "I need to see Prester-Marshall Baine. For many years now, I have been on a holy mission that he commanded. He must hear my report."

The kirk prester was flustered. "Prester-Marshall...Baine?"

"Tell him it is Hannes. He will remember me well."

"But...surely you mean Prester-Marshall Rudio?"

"Rudio?" Vaguely remembering a prester of that name, Hannes felt a growing dread rise in his chest. "Has something happened to Prester-Marshall Baine?"

In halting words, the prester explained how Baine and a reconstruction crew had been horribly martyred in Ishalem. "But that was a dozen years ago, sir, and the Urecari have committed many more crimes since."

Hannes reeled, entirely unbalanced by the news, his grief and anguish transformed to an even deeper hatred of the Urecari. While he had continued his good works in the name of Ondun across the soldanates, the evil Urecari had been committing even more heinous acts. It seemed the heretics had balanced out every triumph Hannes had made with an atrocity of their own. He lowered his head, and his shoulders convulsed as he struggled to contain his emotions.

The other prester was deeply alarmed by his reaction. "You have been gone a long time, haven't you, sir?"

"An eternity. And I have a terrible story to tell." Feeling a resolve like steel harden within him, he straightened. He had never expected his work to be done. "But now I've returned, and I will do anything necessary to protect, preserve, and strengthen the true faith."

The prester said, "Let me take you to the prester-marshall. He and the king need to hear your tale."

*   *   *

After Prester-Marshall Rudio checked in the church records and verified that Hannes had indeed been sent on a secret mission by Baine, years ago, the old religious leader hurried him to the castle and asked for an immediate audience with King Korastine.

When he stood in the private conference chamber, Hannes was shocked to see how much older the king appeared as he came in limping, rubbing a gouty knee. The weight of the long, simmering war and the death of Ilrida had exhausted him. Now the only true spark in his life was the nearly completed Arkship on which he would soon depart in search of Terravitae.

When Hannes repeated his long tale, Korastine nodded sadly, his eyes tinged with nostalgia. "Prester-Marshall Baine was a good friend and adviser, a true visionary. He changed our attitude toward exploring the world. I credit him with the goal we now have. The Arkship will succeed in finding Holy Joron, mark my words. I—the King of Tierra and descendant of Aiden himself—have his True Compass, which will guide us back to Terravitae."

"Yes, I saw your ship," Hannes said, tears brimming in his eyes. "It reminds me of Aiden's holy Arkship, which I watched burn to ashes in Ishalem."

"May the Compass guide us in our quest for Terravitae," said Prester-Marshall Rudio.

Hannes nodded, but that was not enough. "Now, let me tell you about the mines at Gremurr, how you can reach them . . . and why you must destroy them."

117 *Olabar Palace*

With Soldan-Shah Omra gone so long on his campaign to recapture Ishalem, Istar knew that Cliaparia was still scheming to do them harm. She kept a close watch on her daughters and rarely left little Criston; she also missed Saan terribly, and hoped—*expected*—him to return soon.

When Omra's youngest wife went into labor, the entire mood in the palace changed. An army of doctors and midwives came to attend Naori, making sure that nothing went wrong with the birth. A group of sikaras led by Fyiri burned prayer strips and set ribbons into the wind, offering blessings to Naori and the baby.

Though the young woman thrashed and wailed in pain, the birth was uneventful. The midwives handed her a pink and healthy infant boy—Omra's second son, next in the line of succession. In the meeting square, from the empty platforms where the two giant bronze statues had once stood, criers shouted out the news that the soldan-shah had a new heir.

Safe in her own quarters, Istar felt relieved and satisfied to hear the announcement. Now even if Cliaparia did manage to get pregnant again, she had become irrelevant.

During the last few weeks of Naori's pregnancy, Cliaparia had become the young woman's closest friend and companion, worming her way into Naori's confidence by plying her with obsequious attention. Istar had always been on cordial terms with the third wife, but she let Cliaparia play her transparent games, while she attended her own daughters and little Criston.

Istar waited a suitable time for Naori to rest and recover before going to her chambers to see Omra's other son. Adreala and Istala were taken to their morning classes, where the sikaras taught them how to write and inscribe prayers. Altiara, one of Istar's handmaidens, volunteered to put Criston to bed for a nap before the sunset religious ceremonies began. The young woman had watched over Criston many times before, and Istar kissed the boy's smooth forehead before she left.

Wrapping fine silk scarves and sashes about herself, Istar went to Naori's chambers. She bowed her head respectfully as she entered the third wife's bedroom. The new mother lay in bed, propped up with many pillows, holding the newborn in a blanket as it suckled on her breast. Naori's dark brown eyes sparkled. "Oh, Istar—I knew you would come! See the baby, he's beautiful, and healthy, and perfect."

Cliaparia sat like a guard dog at Naori's side, not bothering to hide her flash of resentment. She poured a cup of lukewarm herbal tea. "Here, Naori, drink this. It will help you regain your strength."

Obviously Cliaparia wanted the young mother to be indebted to her, but Naori was oblivious. "You are so sweet, Cliaparia. Could you please empty my washbasin? The water is dirty, and I'd like to refresh myself." In that instant, Cliaparia's role changed from that of a dear companion to little more than a servant, and she knew it. Istar tried to hide her smile, but did not succeed.

"I think I am going to name him Omra after his father, or maybe Imir. But it hasn't been decided yet," Naori bubbled to Istar, aglow with the happiness of new motherhood, expecting everyone to be as overjoyed as she was. "Would you like to hold him, Istar?"

Taking the baby, Istar looked appreciatively down at the

infant. He was indeed beautiful. "Someday he and my little Criston will play together."

"They will be great friends," Naori vowed and took the baby back. Lingering long enough to see Cliaparia return with the washbasin, Istar bowed again to Naori and took her leave.

As she approached her own quarters, she heard screams.

The usual guard was gone from the corridor. Istar began to run, her sandals slapping on the tiles. A baby was wailing—screaming. Little Criston! She pushed through the beaded curtains so violently that strings tore, scattering colored glass spheres all over the floor. Altiara was frantic, holding her face in her hands in horror. The guard had smashed something on the floor and ground it furiously under his boot heel.

In his crib, Criston lay shrieking, and Istar ran toward him. "What happened!"

In disgust, the guard looked down at the tiles where a hairy multi-legged mess lay in a pool of its own splattered ooze.

"What happened?" Istar rounded on Altiara. "Answer me!" She shook the handmaiden back into reason.

"S-sand spider! In the crib! It bit—"

Istar heard nothing more as she tore away her baby's blankets to see two angry red punctures in his side. Sand spiders were as deadly as they were rare, and their poison had no known antidote. The large desert creatures sometimes came into the city hidden in baskets carried by caravans. Her gaze jerked toward the dead creature. A spider, larger than her splayed hand...the venom in that one bite would have been sufficient to kill ten grown men. Her baby—her precious baby boy...

She held Criston. He was already twitching with convulsions. Angry red splotches covered his pale skin.

"I don't know how it happened, my lady!" Altiara wailed. "I

checked his bedding. I was sure it was safe. I screamed for the guard as soon as I saw..."

Istar did not care about how or why—not now. The spider had been killed, but it was too late. Her little boy didn't have a chance.

Istar could merely hold and rock him, weeping as he convulsed. His pale skin turned bluish black from internal hemorrhaging as the poison spread through his system. She caressed his cheek, told him to hush, to rest. But when his wails finally faded into silence, she took no comfort from his peace.

Her searing cry of grief was as sharp and painful as the bite of a scimitar. Altiara collapsed to the floor, striking her forehead against the tiles and sobbing.

The guard looked deeply shamed. "I could not act more quickly, my lady. I came as soon—"

A harsh, low moan continued to come not just from Istar's throat, but from the depths of her soul, and she didn't think it would ever end. As the commotion drew alarms and curiosity seekers from around the palace, Istar looked through the liquid vision of tears to see shocked people crowding, staring. She refused to let go of the baby, though he was already dead. More guards arrived, led by Kel Rovic himself, much too late to do anything.

Among the onlookers, only one face showed no grief at all. Cliaparia looked smug and not particularly sad. "I see you are no longer the mother of the soldan-shah's heir." With that she left, back straight, head held high.

In that instant, Istar knew. Cliaparia had murdered her son.

118 *Corag Highlands*

Alone in his cottage, Criston could feel winter coming on. For weeks now he had been stockpiling firewood: chopping dead trees, splitting logs, and piling the wood against the side of the stone-walled cottage. He needed enough fuel to keep him and Jerard warm throughout the season.

Each day as he went out to gather wood, old Jerard plodded alongside him, never letting his master out of sight. Inside the cottage, the dog sat dutiful and patient as Criston struck a spark to light the fire; when the blaze was going, the dog stretched out to let the heat warm his bones. His dark fur had become frosted with more and more silver, and when the dog slept, he twitched and stirred, dreaming of chasing fat marmots or fending off wolves.

The trek down to the rivertown with Prester Hannes had exhausted the dog, and after they returned to the high meadow, old Jerard no longer had the energy to run among the sheep. Instead, he lounged all day in the grass in front of the cottage, watching his master do the daily chores.

While he fixed his own dinner, Criston talked to the dog, halfway convinced that Jerard could understand him. The dog's teeth had gone bad, and so Criston cooked meat and cut it into small pieces that Jerard could chew and swallow; Criston didn't mind. Jerard had been his faithful companion for thirteen years.

After they finished their meal, he sat in his large creaking chair with his whittling knife and a block of wood to make another ship model. His life was content, solid, and unremarkable, though sometimes—when he opened his emotional wall by a thin crack—he did miss the sea.

As the fire burned low and full dark fell outside, Jerard stirred from the hearth, shook his head, and looked up with his soulful brown eyes. Criston said, "Good boy," out of habit.

Jerard heaved himself to his four paws and limped over to Criston's chair. He sat on his haunches, tail wagging vaguely. With a plaintive whine, he put his head in Criston's lap. Criston petted him, frowning, sure that something was wrong. Jerard's tail thumped twice on the floor. His lungs expanded as he heaved one long breath and let it out like a sigh.

Then, from one instant to the next, the dog was dead. Quietly and peacefully, his spirit floated away like smoke up the chimney. Criston felt the sudden heaviness as the dog slumped against him.

He could only stare, unblinking. In shock, he petted the dog's head once more, then lay his brow against the warm black fur. He couldn't move. Criston had known this time was coming and, aware of the dog's pain and weariness, had both dreaded it and bitterly prayed for Jerard's release and peace.

But it didn't matter how much he had prepared his heart—it could never be enough. Criston held poor Jerard, and the tears poured from his eyes like a sudden monsoon. Without conscious volition, he slid out of the chair to the floor beside the dog and held him all through the night until the fire went out, sometime before dawn.

He buried Jerard under a towering cairn, tearing rocks from the wall of his cottage and stacking the heavy stones high and deep so that predators could not reach the dog's body. The task took him most of the day. With the partly dismantled cottage in a shambles, Criston slept out in the open that night, wrapped in a blanket next to the cairn.

"You were a good dog, Jerard," he said before he slept. "Faithful and true. I hope Ondun has fields for you to run in and other dogs to play with." Criston stroked one of the smooth stones as though he were petting his friend one last time. "I hope I was as good a companion to you as you were to me."

In the morning, he rose, stiff and sore in the chill of dawn. From inside the cottage he retrieved the few things he thought he might need, a few carvings, Captain Shay's old sea monster journal. On his trek, he would inform the mountain villagers that he had left his sheep and cottage behind; someone from the village could claim and care for the flock. With Jerard gone, that part of his life was over.

He removed the fishhook pendant from his neck, the pendant Prester Jerard had given him so long ago, and draped it lovingly between the stones of the dog's cairn.

Criston had had enough of the mountains, enough of solid ground beneath his feet. Feeling the call again for the first time in years, he set off on foot and left the Corag highlands behind him. At long last, Criston Vora headed back to the sea.

119 *Uraba*

Many Urabans had seen the sand coracle as it flew over the southern edge of Missinia. Riders came out to greet the returning travelers, escorting Saan, Imir, and Sen Sherufa to the city of Arikara, where they were welcomed with excitement and disbelief. Soldan Xivir and his sister Lithio had, with heavy hearts, concluded that they were lost and would never come back from the Great Desert.

Imir was happy to report the location of the desert bandit encampments, and explained how sand coracles could be used to hunt them down. Saan took two separate baths just to get all the grit from his pores and hair. The Nunghal clans traditionally scrubbed themselves in streams and lakes, or swam in the cold ocean; they had never heard of a heated and perfumed bath. Saan enjoyed returning to civilization.

That evening, facing the banquet Xivir's kitchens had prepared for them, Saan realized how much he'd missed the taste of good Uraban food. They savored pies stuffed with minced pigeon, eggs, cinnamon, and walnuts, and he ate an entire bowl of salt-cured olives. He couldn't remember the last time he'd eaten meat other than buffalo or fish.

Lithio had saved a seat at the table for the former soldan-shah, but he chose to sit next to Sen Sherufa. His wife seemed more amused than jealous. She made much of Imir's appearance now that his hair and beard had grown back; just to be contrary, she claimed that she had liked him better bald.

After enjoying the hospitality of the Missinian soldan, the companions were anxious to return to Olabar. Sen Sherufa wanted to be back among her own people, and Saan longed to see his mother and sisters again, but he was most enthusiastic to tell all his adventures to Omra. His father would be proud of the things he had learned and experienced.

"That may have to wait, young man," Xivir answered. "The soldan-shah departed with his armies to recapture the isthmus of Ishalem, once and for all." Hearing this, Saan was crestfallen to have missed such a grand opportunity to fight with the Urecari armies on such an important conquest.

The next day, Xivir provided a caravan to take them overland back to the capital. Swift riders were dispatched to carry the news of their imminent arrival to Olabar, and by the time

Saan and the group reached the capital city, banners had been hung and ribbons fluttered on poles to welcome them.

But Saan noticed a subdued mood, the remnants of black crepe and drooping flags that marked a time of mourning. Olabar was a confused mixture of extreme emotions. Kel Rovik and a group of uniformed guards came to greet them before the palace's main arch. The guard captain saluted formally to Imir, then showed respect to Saan, as Omra always ordered the guards to do.

"Something is wrong," Saan blurted. "What's happened?"

Rovik frowned, hesitant. "It is not my place to—"

"Give us the news," Imir said, sounding once more like the soldan-shah, though he was nearly unrecognizable with his gray hair and beard. "I order you."

"Soldan-Shah Omra has a new son by his third wife, Naori. But—" Rovik drew a deep breath, as though facing a battle. "His other son, the heir, died from the bite of a sand spider."

Saan reeled. His baby brother was dead! "I have to see my mother." He ran past Kel Rovik and the guards into the familiar halls. He found Istar in her quarters, kneeling in her best garments, scrubbing the floor cracks between the tiles with rags, polishing, as if she were once again a slave. She looked up at him with empty eyes and stared, as if he were a ghost or hallucination. Then she got to her feet. "You're back! Saan! Safe and *alive.*"

When she threw her arms around him, he hugged her tightly. "I came back to you, Mother. I promised I would. But..." He didn't know what else to say, how to speak to her.

With a sob, Istar said, "Criston is dead."

Saan could sense that a great darkness lived within her, a heavy shadow that had fallen on her heart. She pressed her face against his shoulder, and her damp tears felt cool as they evaporated on his skin. "I love you, Mother," he said. Her body was racked with shudders. Istar cried and cried, and he tried to soothe her.

Then, oddly, she just *stopped*, as if she had run out of grief, run out of tears. She released her hold on Saan and stood back, straightening her garments, squaring her shoulders, and wiping her face. He was afraid to ask what had caused this abrupt change in her.

"You returned. You came home," his mother said quietly, as if she still couldn't believe it. "But I need to be alone for a while."

She bent down and continued her frenetic cleaning.

When Sen Sherufa returned to her home in the Saedran District of Olabar, she could barely contain her excitement. She still had the Nunghal map that showed the detailed coastline of the southern sea. Ever since looking upon the great unexplored waters and studying the charts in the mapmaker's stall, she had been planning how to disseminate the information to other Saedrans. Such a world-shaking revelation had to be added to the Mappa Mundi. It was the best information they had. The news needed to be shared, but privately.

Aldo na-Curic had given her so much information about the Tierran continent that now she wanted to return the favor—if only she could find a way to deliver a copy of the new map to him.

Alone in her home, with the doors and curtains closed in the vain hope that her neighbors would not interrupt her—not yet—she took out fresh sheets of paper and began to copy the map. Sooner or later, she would have to decide how to describe her exploits to her eager neighbors. She was accustomed to repeating tales of other heroes, but she'd never done anything herself that warranted retelling.

A knock came at her door, the kindly clockmaker who lived across the street, pleased to see she had come home at last. But Sherufa deflected his questions. "I will talk to the entire congregation during the next temple meeting—I promise. But first I need to rest and think."

She spent the night with oil lamps lit as she hunched over her papers, making copies of the Nunghal map and writing a letter. To Aldo na-Curic.

The next day, she went to a clever Saedran engineer two streets away who, following her instructions, fabricated an ingenious double-locked cylinder as intricate as any Saedran navigation device. He engraved the combination and instructions right on the outside shell, using the coded Saedran language that no one else could read, so that only a Saedran would be able to open the cylinder.

The craftsman demonstrated the finished device for her. Satisfied, Sherufa rolled up the map, sealed the ends of the container, and put out the word that she was looking for a man willing to travel swiftly and secretly away from Uraba, up to Calay.

She finally found a wiry-looking man who looked eager and earnest, a man who claimed to have made the journey several times before. He swept off his hat, revealing dark hair, dark eyes, and a smile designed to set her off guard. With his nondescript features, he could pass for either Uraban or Tierran—which was good.

"It is a long and difficult journey, Lady Saedran," he cautioned. "My fee will not be small."

"Your fee will be adequate. I'll pay you up front, but this sealed cylinder contains clear instructions to the recipient that you are to receive an even greater amount when you reach your destination and deliver the cylinder to a Saedran chartsman in Calay, preferably one named Aldo na-Curic."

The man pursed his lips. "And how am I to find him?"

"Go to the Saedran District and ask."

He tapped the cylinder, looking at it curiously. "And what does this contain? Will I be considered a spy?"

"You are not a spy, and the contents do not concern you. It is locked with a cipher you cannot defeat." Realizing that he needed more of an explanation, Sen Sherufa added with a sigh, "It is a Saedran religious matter. It would mean nothing to you, even if you did break open the device."

"As you say, Lady Saedran." The man described how he had guided caravans of pilgrims across the Wahilir mountains to Ishalem. "You can count on me. Yal Dolicar is at your service."

Sen Sherufa entrusted the map into his hands. He packed up the sealed cylinder, took the money she offered, and departed for Tierra.

120 *Ishalem*

Destiny demanded it — Ishalem would be his.

For the first time in history, the holy city that had held Urec's Arkship would belong entirely to the Urecari. The conquest would allow no further intrusion from Aidenists, Saedrans, charlatan merchants, sellers of fake relics, or heretics. Ishalem rightly belonged to the followers of Urec.

Tomorrow, Omra and his armies would take it all back.

As he made his preparations, the full moon shone down upon the ruins of the city. His scouts rode hard under the silver light, skirting the squalid pilgrim settlements that had sprung up in the ruins.

Their long journey had taken the better part of two months. Omra and his mounted troops had ridden across Abilan, through Yuarej, and into Inner Wahilir. With Kel Unwar leading the cavalry, they rode up the Middlesea coast from where they had disembarked at Sioara until they reached Ishalem. Racing across the isthmus, they made contact with the captains of the waiting war galleys anchored down the western coast. Meanwhile, Kel Zarouk's fleet of armed ships had sailed up from Khenara and now lay at anchor out of sight, waiting for the appointed time.

Omra spent the entire night pacing the fireless camp, thinking of the following dawn when the Aidenists would be at their sunrise services. That was when they would be most vulnerable.

His scouts returned, bowing before the soldan-shah. "We found a dozen or so Aidenist encampments, Soldan-Shah. One holds a small group of Tierran soldiers, but they do not seem well armed or well fortified. They are not prepared for our assault."

Omra nodded. The capture of Ishalem would be the first full-scale battle in many years, and afterward neither side could ever go back to the previous level of tensions. Nor did he want to. Although he expected to encounter little resistance, the soldan-shah was determined to make a spectacular mounted assault. Ishalem was an important spiritual victory, and conquering it must be an overwhelming affair, because the glory of Ondun demanded it.

A second group of scouts reported that they had found eleven groups of Urecari pilgrims on the southern and eastern ends of the ruins. Omra frowned. "In the frenzy of battle, they might become unfortunate victims. Have our men move them to safety in the hills. Tell them to rejoice, for when this day is done, we can begin to rebuild Ishalem."

In the blackest hour before dawn, he roused his men from their blankets on the hard ground, telling them to mount their horses. They cinched the saddles tight and drew their sharp scimitars, waiting for the sun to appear. On the opposite side of the isthmus, soldiers from Kel Zarouk's warships would be marching up the coast.

When dawn spilled over the horizon, Omra raised his hand and brought it down in a chopping motion. A blaring horn played an abrupt call to arms. His horsemen charged forward with a thunder of hooves that stirred up the weathered old ash, as though the ground itself had begun to smoke.

On the opposite side of Ishalem, foot soldiers charged into the Aidenist camps. A handful of astonished Tierran guards scrambled for their weapons and shouted a warning, but Omra's army cut them down and rode after the screaming, fleeing pilgrims. The well-coordinated Uraban military assault could have wiped out an entire garrison of Tierran soldiers; instead, it was merely a slaughter of pathetic mendicants, squatters, and pilgrims.

Kel Zarouk's war galleys set sail and raced to the old Ishalem harbors, where several Aidenist ships had already cut their ropes and fled out to sea. Omra's warships pursued them, but managed to trap only two of the many Tierran vessels; the other ships slipped away into the morning fog. Undoubtedly, they would rush back to Calay and inform the king of what had happened here.

But if all had gone according to plan in the Tierran capital, Korastine would have his own tragedy to deal with.

The sun had been up for less than two hours when Omra declared his victory. He was the undisputed conqueror, and

Ishalem had fallen without much of a fight. Before the Aidenists could respond, he would set up a fortress and mount patrols. His war galleys would remain in place to secure his hold on the holy city.

Ishalem would never again fall into enemy hands.

His soldiers rejoiced, riding their mounts up and down familiar streets that were now little more than burn scars among the collapsed remnants of buildings. Scrub grass, weeds, and thorny shrubs had grown in the cracks, leaving an appearance of overgrown bleakness.

The men unfurled their banners and planted the fern symbol of Urec to mark their territory. Some took great joy in thrusting their pennant poles through the dead bodies of Aidenist pilgrims, leaving the colors to flutter defiantly; others pitched their tents and claimed land for themselves, already planning to build homes and become new noblemen in a new city. The Urecari pilgrims, frightened by the carnage they had just witnessed, emerged from their hiding places with trepidation rather than triumph.

Omra, though, stood among the ashes and felt the burning dust sting his eyes. Alone, he ascended the hill in the center of the city, where the ruins of Urec's Arkship had rested. From here, he could survey the shadowed remnants of what had once been the greatest, holiest city in the world.

Instead of grandeur and blessings, this scabbed ghost of Ishalem spoke only of disappointment and loss.

Omra took a deep breath. The air had fallen eerily silent. He rubbed the soot and blood from his hands onto his tunic, feeling troubled. This was victory?

121 *Calay*

When King Korastine retired for the night, he felt a contentment and anticipation that had been absent from his life ever since the death of Ilrida. The Arkship was finished. Within weeks, after supplies were loaded in the hold and the last members of the crew were chosen, she would be ready to set sail.

Kissing his young son good night, Korastine felt both an overwhelming joy and longing. "I will see you in the morning, Tomas." At times, the king was sure he could see Ilrida's spirit moving behind the boy's pale face. Tomas had a quiet, loving innocence, and Korastine hoped the boy wouldn't lose it as he grew older. Tomas threw his arms around his father's neck. "Will I watch you sail away in the big ship soon? Can I go, too?"

"You can watch me, but you have to stay here. Anjine will take care of you. She'll be Tierra's queen, and you will be the little prince. Our land needs you."

He had already let Anjine step into the role as much as possible, knowing that she would make a formidable queen. The Urabans would rue the fact that they had continued their war.

Though it was a warm night, servants had built a fire in his bedroom hearth. The gout in his knee bothered him more and more, especially in damp weather, but he struggled not to let it show, fearing that someone—Anjine, probably—would try to talk him out of taking the Arkship voyage. He had waited years for this, and he wasn't going to let a sore leg deter him.

By candlelight, he turned his attention to the precious relics he kept here in his private rooms. With the upcoming voyage in mind, Korastine looked at the sea-turtle shell with its mysterious carved map that hinted at the wonders of the unknown and all the open sea that the new Arkship would need to cross.

The Saedrans were supplying a talented chartsman for the voyage, a man who would not only interpret the turtle-shell map, but decide how best to take advantage of currents and prevailing winds. Sen Leo had highly recommended Sen Aldo na-Curic. The rest of the Arkship's crew had already been selected, including the captain, a prester, and many competent seamen, as well as Korastine and Destrar Broeck. This would be a voyage unlike any in history.

Considering the loss of the *Luminara*, Korastine had feared he might have trouble obtaining volunteers, but he couldn't have been more wrong. The Arkship's very size promoted great confidence; if such a design had been good enough for Aiden and his crew, it would protect the men of Tierra as well.

Craftsmen in the main Aidenist kirk had meticulously etched verses and prayers into the glittery surface of the ice dragon's horn, and Kjelnar would install the imposing shaft before the ship's departure, to confer magical safeguards onto the vessel.

Next to the turtle shell on the shelf, Korastine looked at the lustrous icon of Holy Joron, the image Ilrida had loved so well. He closed his eyes and longed to be transported to that mysterious land of Terravitae. Would she be waiting there for him? If the Arkship ever did reach its destination, he knew with bittersweet sadness that he would not be returning to Calay. Korastine would stay with Holy Joron and perhaps find peace there. That was what he really wanted.

The ancient Captain's Compass, polished and repaired as best as his instrument makers were able, also sat in his room, its gold polished to a gleam, its crystal face clean and transparent. The needle wavered uncertainly, as though trying to remember its way back home. Korastine would carry Aiden's Compass on board himself and install it next to the magnetic compass.

Lastly, his gaze fell upon the detailed sympathetic model of the Arkship that Sen Leo had so carefully crafted—the twinned counterpart to the actual vessel. To his surprise, he saw a tiny curl of smoke rising from the hold, and fire flickered from the waist hatch. Flames scurried like fiery mice up the ropes of the rigging.

Still in his robe, Korastine burst through the door into the corridor and shouted. "To the Arkship! Fire! *Fire!*" Limping on his sore knee, he hurried down the hallway in bare feet, his nightclothes flapping behind him. "To the docks! The Arkship is on fire!"

He was not the first to see the disaster. Bells from the kirks were already ringing, and he heard an outcry in the streets. Townspeople were rushing down to the docks in Shipbuilders' Bay, carrying anything possible to help fight the fire. Korastine had a horrific memory of that terrible last night in Ishalem.

As soon as he saw the enormous vessel engulfed in flames, the shrouds a fiery spiderweb with curls of greasy black smoke winding up into the night air, Korastine knew it was too late. And he realized that this was no ordinary, accidental fire.

Some young men were fleeing the docks, fighting through the crowds away from the vessel. He recognized many of the youthful workers who had volunteered to build the Arkship and couldn't understand what they were doing or why they ran in the opposite direction.

Then he saw what had been painted in bold red on the Arkship's hull: *the unfurling fern of Urec.*

Pitch and whale oil had been poured across the decks and into the Arkship's hold, then ignited by thrown torches so that the fire quickly spread. Water crews hauled up buckets from the bay to splash water on the flames, but the pitch and oil made the fire inextinguishable. Several clear-thinking men rushed to adjacent ships in Shipbuilders' Bay to keep the fire from spreading across the docks.

When some of the fleeing young Arkship workers were caught and confronted, they struggled, spitting curses in the Uraban language. Realizing they couldn't escape, they took up knives and plunged them into their own chests or throats. Others, cornered at the ends of piers, dove into the water and swam away, either drowning or simply vanishing.

Bleary-eyed, his long hair tousled and his beard sticking out in wild directions, the shipwright Kjelnar stalked up to Korastine, also in his nightclothes. The Iborian man gaped at the burning Arkship and the flurry of men trying to douse it with a bucket brigade. Nothing could stop the flames.

"It seems I won't be captain after all," Kjelnar said.

Standing together in shared awe and misery, the two men wept as they watched their hopes go up in smoke.

122 *Olabar*

Istar could have asked Saan for help, or she could have demanded assistance from Kel Rovik and the palace guards who were sympathetic to her. But she decided that vengeance was a private matter to be savored, or at least endured, alone. She knew the answers, but she did not know the details...yet.

Without Omra, she had suffered through the funeral for baby Criston, accompanied by Saan, her two daughters, old Imir, and a roomful of functionaries. Even Naori attended, carrying her infant boy, who was now the only surviving son of the soldan-shah. Istar knew the sweet young woman meant no insult to her.

Cliaparia also came, dutifully dressed in mourning colors; the smoke-gray veil across her face covered a triumphant smile, but her eyes still twinkled.

Istar was deaf to the murmured expressions of sympathy. Omra wasn't here. He didn't know. When he did return, she feared he would blame her for the death of the baby, and Istar didn't know if she could bear that.

As the only way to keep her sanity, she hardened her heart, try-ing to convince herself—even whispering the words aloud as she lay in the darkness of an empty night—that Saan was her only true son, that little Criston was a child born of a marriage she had never wanted, to a man she still did not allow herself to love. But that was a lie. Criston had been her baby, her flesh and blood, and she had loved the child as much as it was possible for a mother to love.

And he had been murdered.

The day after the funeral, without announcing herself, Istar slipped into the private room of Altiara, the handmaiden respon-sible for watching her baby on that fateful night. The other hand-maidens saw Istar, but did not intervene. She was, after all, the wife of the soldan-shah.

Altiara was not in her room, busy with her daily chores. Istar ransacked the young woman's possessions, searched in her cabi-nets, under her bed, on shelves and in corners. Hidden beneath a pile of folded silks, she discovered a small cage of fine brass wire ... the sort of cage that sellers of exotic creatures would have used to hold a captive spider—a sand spider. Istar crushed the delicate cage in her grip and dropped the ruined mass.

She stalked out of the handmaiden's chambers and encoun-tered a serving woman in the hall. "Where is Altiara? I must see her. Now."

One look at Istar's fearsome countenance spurred an instant reply. "She is up in the Sunset Tower, my lady, unpacking garments for the autumn festival." The young servant continued to talk, but Istar was already moving. She ascended the winding stair to the open parapet, where once, she remembered, Omra had brought her to watch the blazing orange sunset. Istar had no room for fond memories now.

Altiara was working by herself, her face gaunt, her eyes shadowed with grief... or perhaps guilt? The handmaiden had removed piled silks from large cedar chests and sorted them on the clean tile floor. Breezes from the open balcony stirred the fabric, bringing a chill to the air.

Altiara looked up as Istar entered. "My lady!" She rose to her feet and bowed her head.

Istar slid forward like a striking cobra and grabbed all of Altiara's necklaces with hands that had grown strong with determination. "I found the cage. I know what you did to my son." Altiara's knees gave out, and only Istar's iron-hard grasp yanked her back up. "The name. Who ordered this?" Istar shook her once, hard. "*Now!*"

"She...she threatened me!"

"And you did not think to warn me?"

"Cliaparia would have had me killed. She told me I would be rewarded. But I...I can't—"

Istar neither wanted nor needed to hear more. Amazed at her own strength, she picked up the trembling handmaiden and carried her to the open balcony. Altiara screamed and struggled, but Istar looked at her with eyes that were already dead. "Cliaparia is not the one you should have feared."

As though she were discarding a soiled garment, Istar simply tossed the young woman off the balcony, not hearing the long, thin scream—or when it was cut short on the flagstones below.

Istar felt like a machine, a machine of stone and hate. For years, the war between Uraba and Tierra had dominated the events of the world. Now she fought her own war within the palace.

She moved down into the grand hall, listening to the faint cries and commotion outside in the courtyard as someone discovered the handmaiden's body. Kel Rovik and his guards rushed outside, but Istar turned in the other direction.

Utterly calm, she asked several slaves where she might find Cliaparia, until one announced, "The First Wife has gone to the bazaar at the harbor docks. She wanted to find a gift for the soldan-shah for when he returns from Ishalem."

Istar took no escort, told no one where she was going, not even Saan. Leaving the palace, she walked the streets of Olabar, followed the winding lanes and alleys. She passed stalls of vendors and weavers, potion-sellers and candle-makers. The savory smells of roasting meat skewers did not entice her. A stray cat brushed against her legs, but she ignored it and walked on.

Finally, she saw Cliaparia out on one of the wooden piers, where fishermen hung their nets for mending...nets with leaden weights, spherical glass floats, and long lines with many rows of sharp fishhooks.

A bevy of chattering handmaidens surrounded Cliaparia, carrying satchels filled with items she had already bought. Now Cliaparia stopped to watch an old man who sat atop a wooden stool. With arthritic yet still-nimble fingers, he crafted intricate sculptures of knots and strings—just like her brother, Ciarlo, had made.

Ciarlo...She thought of her beloved Criston...and her murdered son who had the same precious name. Her revenge was a building wave, curling, cresting, and ready to crash down.

The handmaidens noticed Istar first. Cliaparia looked up to see her walking without any escort or guards. With a sneer on her face and an insult on her lips, Cliaparia sniffed. "If it isn't the grieving mother. Are you sure your other children are safe?"

Istar lashed out with her dagger, stabbing downward into the hateful woman's left breast. "Murderer." She yanked out the blade, then rammed it home again in the side of Cliaparia's neck. "You killed the soldan-shah's heir." She stabbed again. "You killed *my son!*"

The handmaidens screamed. Cliaparia looked astonished, gasping wetly as Istar pulled the blade free again. Cliaparia flailed her pale hands against the bright crimson blood fountaining from her wounds. Feebly, she tried to fend off further attack, but Istar merely shoved the dying woman into the nets, where the sharp fishhooks bit into her skin, her clothes. She hung like an unsatisfactory catch, wriggling desperately.

There were more screams now. The old man with his knotted sculptures knocked over his stool as he staggered backward. Men came running, but the gathering crowd drew back in horror as Cliaparia opened and closed her mouth. The stains of red grew larger and larger.

No one interfered with Istar. She focused only on Cliaparia. "Now *I* am First Wife of the soldan-shah." Then, with her blade she severed the cords that held up the drying net.

Cliaparia fell to the dock boards in a bloody heap, tangled in the net, caught on the fishhooks. In disgust and white-hot anger, Istar shoved the dying woman off the edge of the dock. Cliaparia splashed into the water and quickly sank.

123 *Calay*

By the next morning the fire in the Arkship had burned out, but the air remained heavy with ash and shattered hopes. Anjine stood next to her little brother, so angry that she could not speak. All the work, all the dreams, all the hopes for finding Terravitae... all the desperate anticipation that had kept her father functioning since the death of Ilrida. Anjine's eyes were red, not just from the thick smoke that hung like a pall in the air.

Tomas was crying, even though he didn't understand. His confused emotions whiplashed back and forth. "Did the big ship burn? Why did the big ship burn?"

But she had no answers for his questions, not yet. She just stood, squeezing his shoulder so hard he flinched. "Hush, now."

"We should have installed the ice dragon's horn," Korastine said. "It would have protected the ship." He stood with the Saedran scholar Sen Leo na-Hadra; if anything, the Saedran looked more devastated than her father did.

"Men will always find ways to destroy other things," Sen Leo said. "Nothing can provide sure protection...even the horn of an ice dragon."

Wearing his naval uniform, Mateo walked up to present himself to Anjine. While he was back in Calay between patrols, Anjine had contacted Comdar Delnas and requested that Mateo be made captain of his own ship. Now, though, she considered transferring him from the navy into the royal guard, so he could be close. She needed his protection.

Now that the Arkship was destroyed, Anjine wanted to make

Mateo promise that he would apprehend the Urecari who had done such a monstrous thing. But she couldn't let herself show weakness in public, or show any personal feelings. She stood straight and drew deep breaths. Mateo would know what to do, regardless.

He looked at the king but seemed to decide that Korastine was not yet ready to hear the details; instead, he spoke directly to Anjine. "There were dozens of the saboteurs, Princess. At least ten killed themselves, but we captured six alive."

"They were fanatics. Anyone who could do such a thing is a mindless, spiteful monster." Anjine clung to her anger as if it were Sapier's fishhook.

"They were coordinated as well," Mateo continued. "All of them young men, the oldest no more than eighteen. Three of them refused to speak at all, though their guilt was quite plain. The others broke under extreme torture." His expression did not flinch, as if he thought nothing of the necessary pain he had inflicted. Her heart ached to see how much he had changed, and to consider what must have happened to change him so.

Neither she nor Mateo were innocent children. They had been when Ishalem burned, but now Anjine was different, too. She made military decisions, ordered men into combat. Some of those men had never returned. They were all casualties of war.

Feeling a new and frightful resolve, Anjine said, "You did your job, Captain. They are animals. You cannot show them common human mercies."

He gave a cursory nod, and a dark expression clouded his face, showing only a hint of the dangerous storm he held inside. Still, Mateo kept his report terse and professional. "There's more, Princess Anjine. Some were young men who had already signed on as cabin boys for the Arkship's voyage."

"They would have sailed on the ship?"

"They had many plans within plans…and this may not be their only attack. One prisoner revealed that the Urabans have captured many Tierran children over the years, indoctrinated them in the religion of Urec, and turned them loose here as spies and infiltrators. Calay could be rife with them…and they look just like us, so we would never know."

Anjine felt nauseated. "Handle it, Mateo. Stay here and take over the royal guard. There is no better man to root out evil."

Mateo's expression softened as he gazed at her. He touched her arm, and suddenly he looked very young again. He whispered, "I'm sorry, Tolli. I wish I could have done more." Then he became formal once more. "I serve at Your Majesty's command," he said, his gaze encompassing both Anjine and her father. But Anjine understood that, for the first time, he was addressing her as a queen.

"Thank you," she whispered, and he bowed, then set off to rally the royal guards.

The hulk of the Arkship lay like a beached sea beast, burned all the way to the waterline. The hold had flooded, and the ship had sunk to the shallow bottom of Shipbuilders' Bay. Almost nothing could be salvaged from it.

"This is a crippling blow, a heart-wrenching loss." Korastine raised his head wearily, yet his expression was oddly confident. "But it is not a blow that will defeat us." He looked at his daughter, then at Sen Leo. Although the grief was still plain in his tone, he sounded surprisingly optimistic. "Our Arkship has burned, and the *Luminara* was lost, but that doesn't mean Terravitae is lost. The land still waits for us. We just have to find a way to travel there."

"And we still have the ice dragon's horn," Kjelnar said.

"And Aiden's Compass," the king added.

Anjine was encouraged by her father's renewed hope. No

matter what Korastine said, though, she wondered if he had the strength for another such effort. His staunch bravery had been shaken in a fundamental way by the barbaric Urabans.

Therefore, she would shoulder the necessary burden. She would be the strength of Tierra. "Yes, Father. I vow that we will discover Terravitae. We will find Holy Joron and will reconnect with Ondun's original people. This, I swear."

The men muttered in agreement, but Anjine did not tell them the new purpose that made her so determined: If they could succeed in finding Terravitae and forming an alliance with Holy Joron, then the people in that holy land would help her armies vanquish the evil Urecari.

124 *Calay, Saedran District*

A man disembarked from a boat in the Merchants' District and began to ask around Calay, even in the uproar of the city after the burning of the Arkship. "I am looking for a Saedran chartsman named Aldo na-Curic." The traveler pretended that he could not give any answers, yet he dropped enough hints to intrigue his listeners. "I have something for him — a special gift I brought from the far corners of the world." He lowered his voice. "He will want to have it, believe me."

Since Aldo was a chartsman for hire, he was easily found. Many of the ship captains knew of him, and they directed the stranger to the Saedran District, where he stopped in at various shops, talked to an apothecary and a woman who made intricate wind chimes. Finally someone pointed him to the house of the painter Biento and his wife, Yura, where Aldo still lived.

Before Aldo heard the persistent knocking, he had been feeling sick and stunned about the loss of the great vessel on which he would have served as chartsman. Now it would be years before he'd have such an opportunity again — if ever.

Even though his thoughts were preoccupied, when he opened the door he recognized Yal Dolicar immediately. Thirteen years had passed since this man had cheated him, but with his perfect memory as a Saedran chartsman Aldo never forgot a face. He froze.

The man's smile was warm, his greeting exuberant — and he did not recognize Aldo at all, nor did he notice anything amiss. Aldo was no longer a wide-eyed and gullible young man who had just passed his test. Instead, he'd traveled from one continent to another, seen many things he had only dreamed of before. He was considered a Sen among his people.

Yal Dolicar was leaner and older, too, and his dark, curly hair hung longer, but he was the same. No doubt about it. He carried an aura of earnestness and sincerity, which he had cultivated well over the years. This time, though, Aldo was not fooled. "I am Aldo." He made no move to let the visitor inside his home. "And you are Yal Dolicar. What is it you want?"

The other man was startled. "You know my name?" Then he gave a foolish-looking, embarrassed grin. "Ah! You must have heard me asking around Calay for you."

"No. We have met before." Aldo was pleased to keep Dolicar off guard. "What is it you want of me? I have much work to do." He didn't go into further detail about how the man had taken advantage of him, duped him with a counterfeit map, made Aldo excited about possibilities that were, in fact, a lie.

Recovering with a proud flourish, accustomed to pressing ahead in spite of his listeners' suspicions, Dolicar produced an intriguing metal cylinder from within his tunic. "I have traveled from the soldanates of Uraba and survived many perils to bring this to you. I accepted this dangerous mission from a Saedran woman named Sen Sherufa na-Oa—and here I am."

Aldo blinked. Sen Sherufa! How could Dolicar know her name, and Aldo's connection to her, unless there was some kernel of truth to what this man said?

He reached out for the cylinder, and Yal Dolicar pulled it back. "A certain financial arrangement was made. I received a partial payment for expenses before I departed from Olabar, and Sen Sherufa promised me an additional one hundred silver pieces upon delivery of this item."

"One hundred silver pieces—did she, now?" Aldo was no longer the gullible man Dolicar had once duped. "Then let me see what I am paying for."

Grudgingly, the man handed him the cylinder. Aldo read the engraved markings and deciphered the instructions on how to work the locking mechanism along with its carefully set combination. The inscription in Saedran characters convinced him the message was real. He smirked. "Forgive me, Yal Dolicar, but this says I am to pay you *fifty* silver pieces, not one hundred."

"That's not true!" Dolicar protested, but without much conviction.

Aldo pointed to the incomprehensible letters, and he could tell by Dolicar's face that he would not further argue the point. "Wait here." He left Dolicar standing on the threshold. When it looked as if he might presume to step inside, Aldo closed the door in his face. The man wouldn't leave without his money.

Aldo's family kept some of their own funds in the house, and he withdrew the appropriate number of coins, put the rest back, and rearranged the books and furniture, so that an observant man like Dolicar would not guess where the money was hidden. He opened the door, and Dolicar held out his hand, patient and content. Aldo counted out the coins. "There—forty silver pieces."

"We agreed that I am to receive fifty!" Dolicar sounded annoyed.

"Yes, fifty silver pieces—but I have deducted ten silvers for the false map you sold me when I was a young man."

Dolicar blinked, drew a quick breath and recovered himself. "I sold you a map? I am sure you are mistaken."

"I'm sure I am not. You made a fool out of me then, but you also taught me a lesson."

"Ah, I vaguely remember it now." He ran a finger along his lips. "So that map was false? I assure you, the man who gave it to me was quite believable."

"You said you drew it yourself."

"Then perhaps the lesson I taught you was worth ten silver pieces?" He sounded unreasonably hopeful.

"No."

Dolicar shrugged. "All right then, forty silver pieces, damn you. You've taught me a lesson, too—never deal with Saedrans."

Aldo took Sherufa's sealed cylinder, and the man walked away in a huff. Once he was alone, Aldo followed the instructions and worked the container's clever mechanism. He noticed numerous tiny scratch marks around the side and the seal, which suggested that Yal Dolicar must have tried to foil the locks himself.

Aldo opened the cylinder and reached inside, his pulse pounding. He drew out a few pages of tightly rolled parchment and unfurled them to reveal a map showing the coastline of a strange land, as well as a letter that Sen Sherufa had written him.

She described her journey across the Great Desert, the discovery of the new land to the south, and the unexpected coastline and another whole sea! Aldo stared, taken aback. It was too fantastic to be true. The continent of Uraba was far larger than anyone had ever guessed.

He and Sherufa had already redefined their perception of the world and greatly expanded the Mappa Mundi, but this discovery went beyond anything he had ever dreamed. Now that the Arkship had been destroyed, he would not be going on his long-awaited voyage of discovery . . . at least not soon.

But this sketch changed everything. Aldo rolled the map, reinserted it into the cylinder, and sealed the end. Then he ran to the Saedran temple to see Sen Leo.

125 *Olabar*

Not caring that she was covered with blood, Istar turned on the dock to face all the frightened fishermen, merchants, customers, and the horrified handmaidens who had accompanied Cliaparia. She felt cold, impenetrable, and utterly justified in her actions.

She looked down at her hands, saw the red wetness coating her blade and her fingers. Almost casually she tossed the knife into the water, where it sank near the net-wrapped body of the treacherous woman.

Istar had killed more than her baby's murderer—she had killed the anger and grief within her. She had purged herself of vengeance, hatred, all emotion whatsoever, like a torch that had flared brightly in a wind gust, then flickered and died. The woman she truly was, a woman named Adrea, had perished long ago in a raid on Windcatch. The best part of her had not survived that day.

All the subsequent years in Uraba had a strange dreamlike quality. She had made hard choices to protect Saan, but he was a strong young man who could fend for himself and make his own decisions. He had a life, thanks to her, though it was not the life she would have chosen for him. From now on, Istar did not, in fact, feel she had any stake in what might happen to him.

Leaving the horrified audience and the bloody stain in the water beside the pilings, she walked back off the pier to be enfolded in the winding streets of the bazaar. She realized how ruthless she had become, and it made her feel hollow.

Far behind her, one of the handmaidens screamed again. Istar turned a corner and walked deeper into the labyrinth.

Over the years, she had learned from Omra; he had taught her to accept the requirements of survival without regard for her passions or her heart's voice. She had learned how to protect herself and her family... except that she had failed baby Criston. She had just discovered that she could commit murder without hesitation and without remorse, when necessary. Both Altiara and Cliaparia were dead at her hands, within the space of hours.

That would have been inconceivable to the bright-eyed young woman named Adrea, who had waved goodbye to her brave young sailor in Calay.

Hushed voices followed her through the marketplace, rumors spreading with the speed of a furious squall. Her golden-brown hair was unkempt. Crimson stains covered her clothes. She wandered like a lost woman, seeing little, as she headed in the vague direction of the Olabar palace. People shrank back into doorways as she passed. Merchants ducked into the shadows beneath their awnings.

Istar stopped next to a purveyor of exotic items to get her

bearings, to think. The man looked at her nervously but did not speak, did not offer his wares. On the table beneath his purple silk awning, he displayed odd trinkets, mystical pieces of twisted driftwood, coral-encrusted artifacts retrieved from sunken ships, all manner of flotsam and jetsam tossed up by the vagaries of the sea.

Her eyes were drawn by one particular item—a rolled-up, water-stained letter inside a chipped and dirty glass bottle. Something tugged at her—the handwriting was in the Tierran language, words that had become unfamiliar to her for so long. She reached out to touch it. The mostly dried blood on her fingers left a faint red smudge on the side of the bottle. She removed the cork, pulled the brittle papers out and unrolled them.

Stammering but falling back into his old habits, the merchant said, "It is a letter found floating in the sea. But it hasn't been translated, since nobody can read the Aidenist scrawl."

Many of the words had faded with time and the elements, but she could read what it said. She saw a strand of golden hair clinging to one of the pages.

She knew the hand that had written it.

Swept away, her mind floated in even greater disbelief. She was stunned. She drank in the longing thoughts that Criston had written to her—*to her!* Her long-lost dear sweet Criston. According to the date, the letter had been written only three years earlier. Three years! He still remembered her.

She picked up the letter, holding it, reading the lines over and over again. *Criston!* The ice in her heart shattered and melted. The hollowness in her chest was filled by a sudden crashing tide of emotion.

As abruptly as she had lost everything, surrendered everything, Istar—*Adrea*—realized how much she had truly lost, how much had been *taken* from her. She clutched the papers to her breast and closed her eyes as tears trickled out from beneath her eyclids, tcars of both sadness and joy. Tears of longing. Tears of hope.

126 *Calay*

When he arrived back in the capital city, Criston Vora felt as if he had emerged newborn and infinitely changed from a long sleep within a chrysalis. He made his way to King Korastine's castle, carrying only his satchel with a few belongings. He had trimmed his beard and hair and washed himself, but it was the expression on his face that captivated the eyes of those who saw him, like a lodestone's hold on a floating needle.

He squared his shoulders and stood unhurried and unconcerned as he presented himself to the guards at the gate. "I seek an audience with King Korastine. My name is Criston Vora, and I sent a letter to the king years ago. I am the last and only survivor of the *Luminara* expedition. And I have a tale to tell him. I think he would like to hear it."

Wandering through Calay, he had seen the burned wreck of the Arkship and learned of the king's continued dreams of exploration. Criston considered it a sign. So the dream did not die with the *Luminara*.

He was led into the castle's throne room, where the weary-looking king sat on his blockish throne beside Princess Anjine in a gilded chair that had been raised to the same height on the platform. On her lap sprawled a mottled cat, whose golden eyes watched the activity in the room.

Criston formally bent his knee and bowed his head. People

from the castle rushed into the chamber, chattering about who the mysterious stranger claimed to be.

"Majesty, a dozen years ago, I set sail with Captain Andon Shay aboard the *Luminara,* but our ship was destroyed by the Leviathan." An astonished reaction rippled throughout the room, but Korastine merely watched him. "The crew was lost, but I was eventually rescued by Soeland whalers. I made it back to my village of Windcatch, only to find that Urecari raiders had wrecked my life at home, killed my friends. My wife was gone, either taken or killed."

Anjine spoke up. "Where have you been all this time? We knew from our ship model that the *Luminara* had been destroyed, and we received a letter—"

"That was my letter, a long time ago." Criston hung his head. "I could not bear to come to you in person, until now." He didn't elaborate.

"We have all been scarred in many ways." Korastine called for food and wine, then shouted, "Send for Sen Leo na-Hadra. He will want to hear this as well. We read your letter, but didn't know how much to believe."

"Believe all of it." He reached into his pack and removed the battered, leather-bound book of Captain Shay's sea-serpent sketches.

Criston had known he would need to recount his story of the voyage, the sea serpents, the island of skeletons and their never-ending war, the Leviathan. He would have to tell about being cast adrift with Prester Jerard, then being pulled along by the black sea serpent. He had rehearsed his words many times, and now he was prepared to lay them out like a supplicant offering a confession. There would be time, and there would be many questions.

While he waited, servants set up a table for the food. Curiosity-seekers gathered in the doorways to listen. Criston slung his pack off his shoulder and opened it to withdraw his detailed hand-carved models of new ship designs. He presented the models to the king.

"I know of your Arkship project, Majesty. I come not only to offer you my story, but my services as well. I have already been to the edge of the world. If that is where you need to go again, then I want to be part of the expedition."

Glossary

ABILAN one of the soldanates of Uraba.

ADREA wife of Criston Vora.

ADREALA first daughter of Adrea by Omra.

AIDEN one of the two brothers who sailed from Terravitae to discover the world. The descendants of his crew populated Tierra.

AIDEN'S LIGHTHOUSE a tall lighthouse on the western side of Ishalem.

AIDENIST follower of the Book of Aiden.

ALAMONT one of the five reaches of Tierra, rich agricultural land led by Destrar Shenro.

ALDO NA-CURIC young Saedran, chosen as a chartsman.

ALTIARA one of Istar's handmaidens in the Olabar court.

ANDOUK soldan of Yuarej, father of Cliaparia.

ANJINE the daughter of King Korastine.

ARKSHIP ancient vessel wrecked in Ishalem, believed to be the original vessel belonging either to Aiden or Urec.

ARIKARA capital city of Missinia.

ASHA second wife of Soldan-Shah Imir, a lover of animals.

ASADDAN Nunghal refugee who crossed the Great Desert to Missinia.

ATTAR soldan of Outer Wahilir, cousin of Soldan Huttan.

BAINE prester-marshall of the Aidenist church; he called for further exploration of the world.

BARTHO father of Prester Hannes.

BIENTO NA-CURIC Saedran painter, Aldo's father.

BOOK OF AIDEN Aidenist holy book.

BORA'S BASTION capital city of Alamont Reach.

BORNAN, EREO father of Mateo, a captain in the royal guard who died saving the king.

BORNAN, MATEO ward of King Korastine, raised in the castle after his father was killed in the line of duty.

BROECK destrar of Iboria Reach.

BURILO the son of the Missinia soldan, Xivir, Omra's cousin.

CALAVIK capital city of Iboria Reach.

CALAY capital city of Tierra.

CAPTAIN'S COMPASS a compass that always points home.

CHARTSMAN a Saedran navigator possessing perfect memory.

CIARLO brother of Adrea, lame in one leg. He mends fishnets, and is studying to become a prester.

CINDON Criston Vora's small boat, named after his father.

CITHARA daughter of Cliaparia and Omra.

CLIAPARIA Omra's second wife.

COMDAR leader of Tierran army and navy.

CORAG one of the five reaches of Tierra, a mountainous region led by Destrar Siescu.

CUAR Uraban unit of currency.

DELNAS, COMDAR leader of the Tierran military.

DESTRAR the leader of one of the five Tierran reaches.

DIREC NA-TAYA Saedran candlemaker in Ishalem.

DOLICAR, YAL a confidence man willing to take on any job.

DOLPHIN'S WAKE merchant ship.

EDICT LINE the boundary agreed to by the leaders of Tierra and Uraba, dividing the world in half.

ERIETTA one of the five reaches of Tierra, mainly rangeland, led by Destrar Unsul.

ERIMA ur-sikara from Lahjar, successor to Lukai.

EYE OF UREC symbol painted on the sails of Uraban ships.

FARPORT capital city of Soeland Reach.

FASHIA the wife of Urec.

FENNAN prester in the village of Windcatch.

FILLOK brother of the soldan of Outer Wahilir, killed in an ill-advised raid against a Tierran trading ship.

FISHHOOK Tierran trading ship captained by Andon Shay.

FRANCOSI new captain of the *Dolphin's Wake*.

FYIRI young sikara.

GILADEN Uraban ambassador who brokered the Edict.

GOLDEN FERN fern with mythic properties, supposedly planted by Urec before he became the Traveler. Anyone who finds the fern is destined for greatness.

GREAT DESERT arid wasteland in the south of Uraba.

GREMURR secret Uraban mines on the northern coast of the Middlesea, in Tierran territory.

HANNES prester assigned to live among the Urecari to observe their culture.

HUTTAN soldan of Inner Wahilir, cousin of Soldan Attar.

IBORIA one of the five reaches of Tierra, the region to the far north, led by Destrar Broeck.

ILNA NA-CURIC younger sister of Aldo.

ILRIDA daughter of Destrar Broeck, second wife of King Korastine.

IMIR the soldan-shah of the Urabans, father of Omra.

INNER WAHILIR one of the soldanates of Uraba.

ISHALEM the holy city, site of the wrecked Arkship, considered the center of both the Aidenist and Urecari religions.

ISTALA second daughter of Adrea by Omra.

ISTAR young wife of Zarif Omra.

JERARD old prester serving aboard the *Luminara*.

JIKARIS khan of the Nunghal-Ari.

JORON the third son of Ondun, who remained behind in Terravitae when Aiden and Urec sailed away.

KEL rank of captain in the soldan-shah's army.

KELPLILIES flowers on the migratory seaweed that drifts into the Windcatch harbor.

KEMM one of Anjine's handmaidens.

KHENARA port city on the Oceansea coast of Uraba.

KIRACLE Korastine's father, previous king of Tierra.

KIRK Aidenist church.

KJELNAR Iborian shipwright.

KORASTINE the king of Tierra, father of Anjine.

LAHJAR port city on Oceansea coast of Uraba, the farthest settlement south.

LANDING DAY Aidenist festival commemorating the landing of Aiden's Arkship.

LEO NA-HADRA, SEN old Saedran scholar, adviser of King Korastine, teacher of Aldo na-Curic.

LIORAN, SEN chartsman aboard the *Dolphin's Wake*.

LEVIATHAN terrible sea monster, possibly legendary.

LITHIO first wife of Soldan-Shah Imir, mother of Omra.

LOOM, THE a constellation.

LUKAI ur-sikara of the Urecari church.

LUMINARA magnificent exploration vessel dispatched from Tierra to discover the world.

MAYVAR influential noble from Alamont, father of Queen Sena.

MIDDLESEA vast sea to the east of Ishalem.

MIROS nephew of an ancient rebellious destrar of Corag.

MISSINIA one of the soldanates of Uraba.

NAORI third wife of Soldan-Shah Omra.

NIKOL NA-FENDA, SEN Saedran chartsman on the *Luminara*.

NUNGHAL a race inhabiting the Uraban continent to the south of the Great Desert. They are composed of two branches, the nomadic Nunghal-Ari and the seafaring Nunghal-Su.

NUNGHAL-ARI nomadic branch of the Nunghals.

NUNGHAL-SU seafaring branch of the Nunghals.

OCEANSEA vast sea to the west of Ishalem.

OENAR former soldan-shah of Uraba, great-grandfather of Imir, the subject of a large bronze statue.

OLABAR capital city of Uraba.

OLACU rebellious Corag destrar in ancient feud.

OLBA turbanlike head covering, usually white, worn by Urecari men.

ONDUN the creator of the world, father of three sons: Aiden, Urec, and Joron.

ONDUN'S LIGHTNING ship on which Aldo served as chartsman.

ORICO cook aboard the *Luminara*.

OSMUC captain of the *Dolphin's Wake*.

OUROUSSA port city on Oceansea coast of Uraba.

OUTER WAHILIR one of the soldanates of Uraba.

PELITON capital city of Erietta Reach.

PILGRIMS' PATH processional path up the hill to the Arkship in Ishalem.

PRESTER an Aidenist priest.

PRESTER-MARSHALL leader of the Aidenist church.

RAATHGIR name of the Iborian ice dragon.

RAGNAL Iborian treecutter.

RAVEN'S HEAD mountain peak in Corag.

RAVEN small patrol ship on which Mateo served as first mate.

RA'VIR Tierran children raised by Urecari to become spies and saboteurs, named after an opportunistic bird that lays its eggs in other birds' nests.

REEFSPUR Tierran coastal fishing village.

RENNERT, JAN captain of *Ondun's Lightning*.

ROVIK the kel of the soldan-shah's palace guards.

RUAD an outcast of the Nunghal-Su.

RUDIO old, conservative prester-marshall, successor to Bainc.

SAAN son of Criston and Adrea.

SAEDRANS "Ondun's Stepchildren," independent people not descended from either Aiden or Urec. Saedrans serve as chartsmen, engineers, doctors, apothecaries, and other scientific professions.

SAND DERVISHES desert demons that lure travelers into the sand.

SAPIER grandson of Aiden, founder of Aidenist church. In a legend, he caught a sea serpent with a fishhook and rode it to safe waters.

SAZAR leader of a clan of rivermen; he calls himself the "river destrar."

SEN term of respect and accomplishment for Saedrans.

SENA first wife of King Korastine, mother of Anjine; died of pneumonia.

SENTINEL mountain peak in Corag.

SHAY, CAPTAIN ANDON captain of the *Luminara*.

SHENRO destrar of Alamont Reach.

SHERUFA NA-OA, SEN Saedran scholar in Olabar.

SHIP'S PROW stone carving outside of Stoneholm.

SIESCU destrar of Corag Reach.

SIKARA priestess in the Urecari church.

SIOARA a port on the Middlesea, capital of Inner Wahilir.

SMOLLA one of Anjine's handmaidens.

SOELAND one of the five reaches of Tierra, a group of islands led by Destrar Tavishel.

SOLDAN leader of one of the regions of Uraba.

SOLDAN-SHAH the soldan of soldans, leader of all Uraba.

STONEHOLM capital city of Corag Reach.

SUNSET TOWER westernmost tower in the Olabar palace.

TAVISHEL destrar of Soeland Reach.

TEACHER mysterious hooded figure in charge of Omra's *ra'vir* program.

TENÉR port city on Oceansea coast of Uraba.

TERRAVITAE the original land where Ondun created his people, from which Aiden and Urec departed on their voyage.

THUNDER CRAG mountain peak in Corag.

TIERRA the northern continent, composed of five reaches; its population follows the Aidenist religion.

TRAVELER wandering old man who leaves tales of his travels, rumored to be either Aiden or Urec.

TRAWNA captain of the Tierran patrol ship *Raven*.

TYCHO kitten given to Anjine by Mateo.

UISHEL young woman from Soeland, Mateo's first love.

UNSUL destrar of Erietta Reach.

UNWAR kel in the Uraban military, captain of the horse soldiers.

URABA the southern continent, composed of five reaches; its population follows the Urecari religion.

UREC one of the two brothers who sailed from Terravitae to discover the world. The descendants of his crew populated Uraba.

UREC'S LIGHTHOUSE a tall lighthouse on the eastern side of Ishalem.

UREC'S LOG Urecari holy book.

URECARI follower of Urec's Log.

UR-SIKARA lead sikara of the Urecari church.

VILLIKI third wife of Soldan-Shah Imir, mother of Tukar.

VORA, CINDON father of Criston, a fisherman lost at sea.

VORA, CRISTON sailor, fisherman, who volunteered to join the *Luminara* expedition. Criston is married to Adrea.

VORA, TELHA mother of Criston.

WEN NA-CURIC younger brother of Aldo.

WILKA wife of Destrar Broeck, lost in a snowstorm.

WILLIN first mate on the *Luminara*.

WINDCATCH small Tierran fishing village on the Oceansea coast, home of Criston and Adrea.

XARIES a Uraban board game similar to chess.

XIVIR soldan of Missinia.

YARADIN ancient Tierran king who faced a rebellion during his reign.

YUAREJ one of the soldanates of Uraba.

YURA NA-CURIC Aldo's mother.

ZADAR work master in the Gremurr mines.

ZARIF Uraban title of prince.

ZAROUK kel in the Uraban military, veteran who served under Soldan-Shah Imir.

Author's Note

Are You Listening?

From the time I first began to write my fantastical novels and stories, I have been heavily influenced by the music I listen to. In high school and college, my imagination was inspired by the progressive rock of Rush, Kansas, Pink Floyd, Styx, the Alan Parsons Project—their songs provided (and continue to provide) the seeds for many works of fiction. Today, with the modern resurgence of progressive rock, I have followed the work of Dream Theater, Lana Lane, Rocket Scientists, Tool, Coheed and Cambria, Lacuna Coil, Powerman 5000, A Perfect Circle, and many others.

In my mind, there has always been a great cross-fertilization between fantastic fiction and music. Many progressive rock songs are directly inspired by science fiction or fantasy, and vice versa. It has long been a dream of mine to marry the two, to create a tandem project of a fantasy novel and rock CD, words and music developed together. As I began work on Terra Incognita, the opportunity arose. I got to know Shawn Gordon, who owns the label ProgRock Records and is a fan of my Saga of Seven Suns. When I suggested the idea of a joint novel/CD to him, he was as excited as I was. We could take one story line of *The Edge of the World,* adapt it, and write a CD around it at the same time as I wrote the draft of the book. Shawn put me in touch with the prolific and talented composer and keyboardist Erik Norlander—I had already enjoyed his solo albums, his collaborations with his wife, Lana Lane, and his band, Rocket Scientists. Erik was also a fan of my writing and he eagerly agreed to write the music for the Terra Incognita CD, while my wife, Rebecca Moesta, and I would write the lyrics.

Los Angeles bassist/producer Kurt Barabas, founding member of Under the Sun, also joined our team in the early stages. Rebecca and I took a short vacation to Carlsbad Caverns and Roswell, New Mexico, during which we mapped out the twelve tracks for the CD. As a result, the six of us — Rebecca and I, Shawn Gordon, Erik Norlander, Lana Lane, and Kurt Barabas — decided to call ourselves "Roswell Six."

As Erik wrote music for the lyrics Rebecca and I submitted, Lana sang the demo tracks and we all listened and tweaked. As the "Queen of Symphonic Rock," Lana was perfect to sing the female vocals as the character Adrea, and Michael Sadler from the band Saga would sing the male lead as Criston Vora. James LaBrie, lead singer for Dream Theater, signed aboard as Omra (with such enthusiasm that he even read the full 700-page manuscript to get into character). The vocals for Captain Andon Shay, the last character, were provided by John Payne from the band Asia Featuring John Payne. David Ragsdale, the violinist from Kansas, also joined the project, as well as Gary Wehrkamp from Shadow Gallery on electric guitars (Gary had already corresponded with me, a fan of my novels), Chris Quirarte from Prymary on drums, Chris Brown from Ghost Circus on guitars, and Mike Alvarez on cello.

The resulting CD — *Terra Incognita: Beyond the Horizon* by Roswell Six — is truly a dream come true for me. It expands and enhances the novel, so I hope you will all give it a listen, just as I hope that fans of the music will check out the book. www .wordfire.com.

Acknowledgments

Fred Ogden generously read the manuscript with an eye to weeding out any egregious nautical mistakes. Patrick Simmons created the wonderful maps, helping to shape the world of Terra Incognita and bring it to life. Lee Gibbons produced an exceptional cover, which captures precisely the feel I wanted to convey in the book. I would also like to thank Stephen Dedman for taking us to the fabulous Shipwreck Museum in Freemantle, West Australia, which provided great story detail for this novel.

Darren Nash tackled the editorial duties; he was closely involved in this project from proposal, to the 100-page chapter outline, through several drafts of the manuscript. Tim Holman, Alex Lencicki, and Jennifer Flax at Orbit Books gave Terra Incognita their full support and have pulled many strings to help get attention for the novel. Mary Thomson typed the stream of chapters as fast as I could dictate them, and also added her own expertise on the most esoteric details. My ever-helpful cadre of test readers—Deb Ray, Diane Jones, Louis Moesta, and of course my wife, Rebecca Moesta—went through several iterations of the manuscript, giving me plenty of insight and suggestions.

For musical inspiration and their general enthusiasm, I'd like to thank my fellow members of Roswell Six—Shawn Gordon, Erik Norlander, Kurt Barabas, and Lana Lane—who took the lyrics written by Rebecca Moesta and me and produced an incredible rock CD, *Terra Incognita: Beyond the Horizon*. Erik wrote the wonderful music. Special applause also to the performers on the CD, James LaBrie, Michael Sadler, John Payne, Gary Wehrkamp, Chris Quirarte, Chris Brown, Mike Alvarez, and David Ragsdale.

extras

orbit

meet the author

Steven L. Sears

KEVIN J. ANDERSON has written forty-six national and international bestsellers and has over twenty million books in print worldwide in thirty languages. He has been nominated for the Nebula Award, the Bram Stoker Award, and the SFX Readers' Choice Award. He is best known for his highly popular *Dune* novels, written with Brian Herbert, his numerous *Star Wars* and *X-Files* novels, and his original science fiction epic, The Saga of the Seven Seas. Find out more about Kevin Anderson at www.wordfire.com.

interview

You're a very prolific author, primarily known for writing big science fiction epics, such as the Saga of Seven Suns, the Dune *novels with Brian Herbert, and even* Star Wars. *How does it feel to be writing fantasy instead of SF?*

My mind works in terms of stories rather than genres. I have indeed done historical fantasy before — *Captain Nemo,* and *The Martian War* — and even wrote a traditional quest fantasy, the *Gamearth* Trilogy, early in my career, but readers do tend to think of me as an SF guy.

However, I don't see Terra Incognita as being fundamentally different from the Saga of Seven Suns — it's got a sprawling scope with many story lines, exotic lands (instead of planets), sailing ships instead of starships, sea serpents instead of aliens, a hint of magic instead of exotic technology, continents and religions clashing rather than planets and galactic empires. But although the "stage dressing" is different, in a world that looks like our Age of Discovery rather than a far-future interstellar society, the characters and politics and dramas that make a grand story are the same.

How is Terra Incognita different from other fantasies on the market?

For one thing, you won't find bearded wizards with pyrotechnic spells or dragons or elves or dwarves. You won't find any enchanted swords or a monolithic evil force that threatens to destroy all Good in the world. Though my novels take place in a world of my own imagining, Terra Incognita is more mainstream than outright fantasy, with only a hint of magic. Yes, I have mysterious unexplored lands and amazing legends that may or may not be true, but at its core, these books are about sailing ships and brave explorers, along with a terrible religious war like our Crusades. And while I may have a sea monster or two, they are natural creatures, not magical monsters.

So, more of a millennial, religious-based grand conflict than a traditional fantasy quest?

Some parts of *The Edge of the World* are very dark and tragic, as well as very passionate. I'm dealing with clashes of civilizations, intolerance, and fanaticism—as well as genuine faith. The story is certainly something that occurs all too often in real history: a series of stupid actions on both sides that have grave consequences, ratcheting up the violence and hatred beyond any possibility of a peaceful resolution.

But the story also parallels our Age of Discovery, a time of hope and wonder, when people had a sense that there were marvelous things Out There just waiting to be found if only a sea captain sailed far enough and survived enough perils.

As I did thoroughly in the Seven Suns novels, I turn the spotlight on all sides of the conflict and really get into the heads of people representing diametrically opposed points of view. There are three major religions in the Terra Incognita universe, and I have explored the attitudes of characters ranging from the everyday man on the street to the most powerful leaders.

It sounds unique. What was your inspiration for the series?

These books have lived in my imagination for more than fifteen years, when I first stumbled upon the European legend of Prester John, who ruled a mythical Christian kingdom on a distant, unexplored area of the map. The quest to find Prester John (and to seek an alliance with him against the invading Moorish armies) provided the real impetus for Portugal's Prince Henry the Navigator to launch some of history's greatest voyages of discovery in the fifteenth century.

Now, after completing a series of successful epic projects—ranging from the colorful universes of *Star Wars, Dune,* and my own Saga of Seven Suns—I finally have the opportunity to write the story that has been whispering in my ear for so long. *The Edge of the World* sets the idea of Prester John in a fantasy universe where sea serpents are real, where a little bit of magic works, where the unexplored areas on the map are larger than the known areas.

And though this is a fantasy series, it's got a direct connection to rock music. Tell us about that.

I've always been inspired by the music I listen to, the lyrics of Rush, Kansas, Styx, Pink Floyd, Dream Theater, Lana Lane, Rocket Scientists, Shadow Gallery, and many other progressive rock artists. There's a clear link between the readers of SF/F and the fans of that kind of music.

For *The Edge of the World,* we put together a unique synthesis—a new rock CD, where my wife and I wrote the lyrics based on a story line in the novel, while accomplished keyboardist-composer Erik Norlander (Rocket Scientists) wrote the music, and Shawn Gordon produced the CD for his label ProgRock Records. Some of my favorite vocalists and musicians performed on the album: Lana Lane provided the female vocals for the character of Adrea; Michael Sadler (formerly of Saga) sang the part of Criston Vora; James LaBrie (Dream Theater) sang Omra; John Payne (Asia Featuring John Payne) sang Captain Shay. Kurt Barabas (Under the Sun), one of the founding members of our group, played bass, Gary Wehrkamp (Shadow Gallery) played guitar, David Ragsdale (Kansas) played violins, Chris Quirarte (Prymary) laid down the drum tracks, Chris Brown (Ghost Circus) provided both acoustic and electric guitar, and Mike Alvarez played cello. Under the band name Roswell Six the CD is *Terra Incognita: Beyond the Horizon* and it works in perfect synergy with the novel.

Now that you have finished the seven volumes in the Saga of Seven Suns, will you ever return to that universe?

I planned Seven Suns from start to finish as seven volumes, with a very clear story arc that genuinely ended. I wanted to do something practically unheard of in the genre: write a big epic series where I reliably turned in every volume on time, year after year, and finished the story where it ended, rather than dragging it on and on. I did that, and I'm very pleased with the result.

After spending seven years of my life in that universe, I am thrilled to dive into something completely different but just as fascinating, the fantasy world of Terra Incognita, which I plan as a trilogy. That's what I need to focus on right now. Once I finish those books, however, my "science fiction batteries" will have recharged and I'm thinking of returning to the Seven Suns universe. It's a big landscape with plenty of opportunities for other stories; however, I would do an independent story with some new characters and a few familiar ones, set a decade or two later.

Right now, though, I'm sailing off in the Terra Incognita books, already writing book two. Bring on the sea monsters!

introducing

If you enjoyed
THE EDGE OF THE WORLD,
look out for

THE MAP OF ALL THINGS

Book Two of the Terra Incognita Trilogy

by Kevin J. Anderson

The great wall across Ishalem would be completed soon, blocking off the isthmus from the Aidenist enemy. With such a mammoth barrier in place, Soldan-Shah Omra knew the Holy City would at last be safe — safe in Urecari hands.

From the high hill in the center of Ishalem, where once had rested the ancient wreck of a huge wooden Arkship, Urec's ship, Omra watched the flurry of construction workers. The sweating, muscular men — some of them slaves taken from Tierran villages — used log rollers and slick lubricating mud to pull blocks into place and extend the wall across the strip of land, seven miles long, stone after stone after stone.

Omra thought of it as "God's Barricade." Once the wall cut

off Tierra, the other half of the world would wither and die like a branch broken from a tree . . . as they deserved.

Soldiers patrolled north of the boundary line to guard against Aidenist forays, as the evil men had done several times previously. As the wall neared completion after five years, their enemies grew increasingly desperate—and the soldan-shah felt increasingly secure.

Kel Unwar, one of the commanders who had swept through the squalid pilgrim settlements on the site of Ishalem, guided the immense construction project. Though a military leader, Unwar was more gifted as an engineer, commanding work teams through impossible tasks rather than guiding armies through impossible odds. When Omra had first challenged him to build the wall, Unwar had stared off into the distance, thoughts turning in his mind, his brow furrowed. "It is a task such as no man has ever attempted, Soldan-Shah. Such an undertaking . . . it will be magnificent!"

But Omra's efforts did not stop there. It was his goal to restore the true glory of Ishalem. Eighteen years earlier, the city had been poised on an uneasy peace, sacred to both Aidenists and Urecari, before a careless spark had unleashed the fires of war. Now, from all around him, in all the districts of the blank canvas of the city, he could hear the sounds of construction, the clink of hammers, the hauling of ropes, the grunting and calls of hardworking men. It was a joyful noise, a satisfying racket.

Perhaps, from whatever far-distant world where He now lived, Ondun would hear and turn His gaze back toward this world and see that the people He had left behind were once again worthy. . . .

The thudding of hooves interrupted Omra's reverie. Astride a fine dapple-gray stallion rode Vishkar, the new soldan of Outer

Wahilir, ascending what had once been the Pilgrim's Path, where supplicants climbed up to the wreck of Urec's ship. With a steady gait, the stallion carried Vishkar to the top of the hill.

Vishkar was twenty years Omra's senior, with a wide, squarish face and barrel chest. The quirk of his smile always brought a brief chill to Omra — the man looked so much like his daughter Istar, Omra's first wife, his first true love, who had died in childbirth so long ago.

Vishkar slid off the saddle, bowed, then extracted a long cylinder from his saddlebag. "A fine afternoon, Soldan-Shah — and it will be even finer once I show you these plans." He unrolled the paper, holding it flat, but looking around for a place to display the drawing; finally, he used his horse's flank as a makeshift table. The stallion grazed unconcernedly. "My Saedran has outdone himself, Sire. Sen Bira na-Lanis has created the most magnificent design! The western church will be far more impressive than the eastern one." Vishkar always tried to coax details about his competitor's plans for the other side of the city, but Omra would not say.

"Soldan Huttan has often told me the same thing, but he doesn't use a Saedran architect. Wouldn't it be better to have a true follower of Urec design the Church of Urec, rather than a Saedran?"

Instead of looking abashed, Vishkar shook his head. "No, Soldan-Shah. It is best to use the most talented architect, no matter what belief he holds."

During his planned rebuilding of Ishalem, Omra had issued a challenge to the soldans of neighboring Outer and Inner Wahilir. In the city's glory days, a tall Aidenist kirk had dominated the western side, while the main Urecari church towered over the eastern district. Both structures had been leveled in the great fire, and now the soldan-shah had commanded that the two churches be rebuilt—only this time, *both* would be raised to the glory of Urec, both would sport the unfurling fern symbol. The new Ishalem would have no place for the Aidenist fishhook.

Several years ago, Attar—the soldan of Outer Wahilir—along with his wives, his sons, and anyone even remotely in line for the seat of power, had been poisoned by a heinous Aidenist assassin, and the death had left a hole in the ruling families. For his replacement, Soldan-Shah Omra shirked tradition by choosing a man he felt was totally reliable as well as loyal to him. As the father of his first wife, Vishkar was a man Omra respected, a wealthy and stable Olabar merchant whose ships plied the Middlesea. Long ago, by choosing a merchant's daughter as his first wife, Omra had incensed many entrenched noble families, but had earned the appreciation from merchants and business-men. Now, as soldan-shah, he remembered that, and the man ruled the entire rich soldanate with its major coastal cities, its shipyards, and its trading ports.

Omra had instructed each of the two soldans, Vishkar and Huttan, to rebuild one of the city's two grand churches. Though stodgy old Huttan had complained, Vishkar accepted the task with relish and vowed to prove himself.

Now, spreading out the parchment on the grazing stallion's flank, the soldan pointed to the drawing's turrets and minarets, the large vaulted worship chamber with a spiraling walkway that resembled the unfurling fern. Sparkling windows would admit a flood of light. Sikara priestesses would call prayers from the highest balconies or burn prayer ribbons and notes in bra-ziers there.

"It does, indeed, look magnificent, Vishkar." Omra could see that this was far more ambitious than what Soldan Huttan planned.

The stallion's head jerked up, ears pricked. Someone was coming. Omra saw a thin man running up the Pilgrim's Path as if a host of demons were on his heels. He was covered with dust, dirt, and powder, and he carried a rolled object in his hand. Guards ran behind him — not in pursuit, but in shared excitement.

Omra turned to face the newcomer. Panting and gasping, the man reached the hilltop, bent over, and coughed. He rested his weight on his knees, barely managing to keep from vomiting after the exertion.

Vishkar blinked in surprise. "Sen Bira? I hardly recognized you!" He turned to the soldan-shah. "Sire, this is my Saedran architect. He has been excavating the ruins of the old Aidenist kirk."

"My apologies, Soldan-Shah — I needed to see you right away." Sen Bira shook dust out of his tangled hair, tried in vain to neaten his appearance. He gulped a breath of air. "I . . . I should have taken a horse."

The guards came up quickly beside the Saedran, embarrassed that he had outrun them. "Soldan-Shah!" said the captain, "This man has made a discovery —"

"He was about to explain himself," Omra said, and nodded at the man once more. "Go on — my curiosity is piqued."

With an effort, Sen Bira na-Lanis composed himself. "We broke through the floor and catacomb levels today, Soldan-Shah. The Aidenist kirk burned to the ground in the great fire, but underground we found a bricked-up vault that has been sealed for uncounted centuries." He raised the rolled cylinder. It was an ancient letter container, a tube of varnished and preserved leather.

Vishkar snatched the aged container and, without opening it, passed it to Omra.

Sen Bira looked at them both squarely. "It's the Map, Sire—the original Map."

Frowning, Omra opened the case and carefully withdrew a well-preserved sheet of parchment, unrolling it with painstaking care. He saw glorious illuminated text and illustrations, the chart of a land he had never seen before; incredibly intricate details showed islands and reefs along a strange coastline, along with fanciful illustrations of sea serpents and tentacled things. The writing was so ornate and archaic that Omra had trouble deciphering the letters.

"It's the *Map*," Sen Bira repeated. He pointed a dirty finger close to the coastline but took care not to touch the parchment. "See here, it says TERRAVITAE."

Dumbstruck, Omra straightened, looked at Vishkar, then back at the Saedran. "Are you saying this is *Urec's* original Map? The one given to him by Ondun Himself before the two brothers sailed away?"

"I believe so, Soldan-Shah," the Saedran said quietly. "Sealed in a catacomb, it has been there, undisturbed, for an impossible amount of time."

"But Urec lost his map," Vishkar argued. "We know all the stories. That's why Urec could never find his way back home."

"Others say the Aidenists took it," Omra said flatly.

Sen Bira's eyes traveled over the unbelievable treasure. "The legends are so old, who can say what is true and what is not? Many tales change over the years."

extras

"The truth doesn't change," Vishkar said.

Omra marveled at the map as possibilities blossomed in his mind. He was breathing quickly, and his pulse raced. "If this is indeed Urec's original Map, then why was it hidden beneath an *Aidenist* kirk?"

VISIT THE ORBIT BLOG AT

www.orbitbooks.net

FEATURING

BREAKING NEWS
FORTHCOMING RELEASES
LINKS TO AUTHOR SITES
EXCLUSIVE INTERVIEWS
EARLY EXTRACTS

AND COMMENTARY FROM OUR EDITORS

WITH REGULAR UPDATES FROM OUR TEAM,
ORBITBOOKS.NET IS YOUR SOURCE
FOR ALL THINGS ORBITAL.

WHILE YOU'RE THERE, JOIN OUR EMAIL LIST
TO RECEIVE INFORMATION ON SPECIAL OFFERS,
GIVEAWAYS, AND MORE.

imagine. explore. engage.